THE HOUSE ON KALALUA

Davies McGinnis

ISBN: 1532822146
ISBN 13: 9781532822148
Library of Congress Control Number: 2016906664
CreateSpace Independent Publishing Platform
North Charleston, South Carolina

I felt the gentle spring rain on my wrinkled old face. I felt the bark of the tree, against which I was pinned, open to let the life-giving moisture percolate deep down to its soul, and as life flowed into the tree, so life ebbed out of me.

My father, Louis Thierry D'Emeraude, died in 1932, when I was sixteen years old. Rudy died in 1974, when I was fifty-eight years old. They had been my Spymasters, and I learned all the tricks of my trade from them and Lev Tashvin, Roza and Kusco, now all long gone. Ah well, I know all the answers to all the mysteries now. I know who drove my dear old Thunderbird over the edge of the slope to crush me against the sycamore, and for all the reasons those in power had to kill me, I was killed in the end for a very unimportant personal jealousy. Had my killer realized who I had been; how important I had been in the grand scheme of things? I don't think so.

Now I know all the secrets of existence, of being: that good and evil are rhythms eternally linked as part of the same multi-rhythmic composition of opposites: this way, that way, back from four dimensions to the glorious expanse of ten, eleven, twenty-six and on and on in what is the Cosmic consciousness: the opposite of the intangible nothing from whence it came, to fill the void with…a more tangible something.

CHAPTER ONE

1994

D on't be fooled by a name: the broad street, that led out of town to the forest, lake and snow-capped mountain ridge beyond, bore no resemblance to the exotic island resort. Kalalua was a strange misnomer for a street in a town in the hinterland of the American Pacific Northwest. The Chatsle House looked just as out of time and place as the name of the street on which it was situated. The big old German-style hunting lodge lay on its vast forested estate that took up the far northern reaches of Kalalua. The colored lights strung in the branches of the mighty evergreens, that lined the long curving driveway, had been put up back in the 1940's, and were still in place and functioning fifty years later. These oddities were only some of the many enigmatic features of the place.

The land rover came to a stop on the flat crest of the driveway across from the kitchen-entrance. From there, the drive sloped down again to the garage at the edge of the forest behind the house. We got out and strolled around to the front. I mounted the wide flagstone steps, and despite the cold biting air of an early afternoon in fall, the hot summer's night Kitty Occley had been murdered came flooding back in vivid detail. The thirty or so years between then and the present had done little to dim the memory. The cold wind scattered the brown sear leaves across the terrace, and the frantic scuttling and scratching sound was as of skeletal fingers tearing at the fabric of the present to reveal a past truth concealed beneath.

Mike McNiall owned the place now. He'd bought the estate on Mrs. Chatsle's death. He'd done it on some strange impulse born out of nostalgia for those carefree days of our youth spent at the lake, and with the notion that it would be a fitting tribute of sorts to his elder brother, Fletch, and the other boys who had sacrificed everything in the abattoir that had been Vietnam.

I am not sure how the Chatsle House had come to represent those days in our minds, but it had. We of that generation could not pass the place without recalling those times. Our old haunts – the fun places we less wealthily endowed frequented, like Harve's Pool Hall and the diner - seemed too frivolous, too familiar after Vietnam. The wild times we had known in those places, untrammeled by notions of duty, honor and sacrifice, were like specters now, invoking feelings of survivors' guilt. The Chatsle House with its air of mystery, closed-off, apart, and already cloaked in a shroud of evil gone unpunished, seemed more appropriate as a focal point for our memories. The place reflected the decadence of those who created wars to line their coffers and our coffins, but apart from all that, the house also seemed sad, as if it yearned to rekindle some of the warmth, the gaiety and love it must have known before everything went so horribly wrong.

Andy Chatsle had been an integral part of the fun-loving wealthy set who had dominated the lake in the summertime, and yet he also had stood apart from them in some indefinable way. Most people attributed this to his French mother. She certainly had kept her distance from the tennis and sailing club devotees - those rich women with insatiable appetites for fund-raising and monitoring the socially acceptable mores and morals; mores and morals they themselves flaunted and desecrated every evening in the shadowy recesses of post-cocktail hours. We, on the other hand, were of the booze and pool hall crowd. We cleaned the houses, mowed the lawns and repaired the cars and boats of the cocktail set, and Kitty Occley had been one of us.

Mike may have bought the Chatsle place, but he couldn't bring himself to live in it. He hadn't even cleared out their things. The rooms were still furnished like a 1940's luxury penthouse apartment movie set; long creamy leather couches set around elegant glass coffee tables, big open white-streaked-with-grey marble fireplace, with ormolu clock and fancy ornaments on the mantel, long sleek oak furniture, oriental vases, oriental prints on the oak-paneled walls, a black, shiny baby-grand piano in a recess under the wide oak staircase, fine cream linen drapes on large windows that looked out on the great expanse of lawn at the front, and the drive and forest at the sides.

The beautifully carved oak front door opened right into the living room, with its polished wooden floor covered by a smoky grey carpet. The door at the other end of the room opened into the kitchen, which was rather dreary, despite all the shining stainless steel. The large trees outside the long side windows and the covered porch at that kitchen side of the house kept out the sun. There were two narrow doors on the right hand side as one entered the kitchen from the living room. One was a walk-in pantry, the other led down some stone steps to a vast basement, illuminated by a single swinging light-bulb that cast moving shadows over the thick stone walls. It smelled musty down there, although it was quite clean and dry. There was a huge freezer, now empty, a workbench and, on the wall, a board on which hung all the tools one could possibly need. There were gardening tools, flowerpots, trowels and forks on the side ledges, and two big wooden block tables on which were jars and crates. The shelves were lined with jars of preserved fruits and vegetables. It almost made the Chatsles seem like a normal family, but they hadn't been. Their life had been a social whirl. Biff Chatsle had spent most of his time away on business, and Mrs. Chatsle and Andy often had joined him. When they were home, there had been wild parties, the talk of the society pages in Seattle and San Francisco. When Andy was very young, too young to travel with easily, Mrs. Chatsle had a live-in maid, an African American lady, named...now what was her name? Well, in any case, when Andy was a child, Mrs. Chatsle and this maid and Andy were the only real family the house had known.

On the right of the wide oak staircase were doors that led to the downstairs master bedroom, a small bathroom and Biff Chatsle's study. Upstairs there were three large bedrooms, each with its own bathroom. A small staircase on the upstairs landing led up to the attic that ran the whole length of the house. One of the bedrooms had been Mrs. Chatsle's study. It was a cozy room, with a small fireplace, deep cushioned couch and chair, a tapestry rocking chair and, in front of the large window under the eaves, was a desk with a leather swivel chair. The walls were lined with bookcases overflowing with leather bound books, glossy art books, even the occasional paperback. I scanned their titles. Many were written in foreign languages. French, Spanish and German, I could recognize and read, but there were many others, some in oriental script, that I could not understand. Mrs. Chatsle had been an avid reader with eclectic taste.

"She wrote as well, Sal," said Mike. "Her diaries, years of them, are up in the attic. I'd sure appreciate it if you'd go through them for me, and sort out her other papers as well, especially those dealing with the Missing in Action groups."

The Chatsle family had fascinated me when I was a child. They still did.

"I can hardly wait to get my hands on those diaries."

"I hope you'll feel the same way after you've begun," laughed Mike. "There are hundreds of papers and notebooks. They look like pretty dry reading to me. The FBI cleaned out Biff's study when he died in that car accident. Old man Phelps, who was the caretaker here in those days, told my dad that three or four big old black vans had arrived at the house, and men went through the place, taking away stacks of papers and files. Mrs. Chatsle's lawyers did the same when she died. They told me I could dispose of anything left behind as I saw fit, so it can't be important stuff. I was kinda sorry about that. I am as intrigued by the family as you are, Sal. Well, if you can find anything to peak your interest, have at it. Write a novel about them or something."

"Just what was on my mind, Mike. There's got to be a great story in this house."

There was Andy's old room, which would suit Sean. Harvard, Stanford and Yale pennants were on the walls still. Andy's cashmere sweaters and suits were in the closet. Mike said that Sean was welcome to use them, but I didn't like the idea at all.

"Fine, then I'll give them to the Goodwill. Boy, will we have a better-dressed lot roaming around the streets!"

"They are very expensive clothes," I replied, fingering a fine sports jacket.

"Old Andy was the only guy I knew who wore pink," said Rob, a look of distaste on his face. "Can't say I fancy that color myself."

I poked his arm. "You are so set in your ways, Rob. The boys are too. There is nothing wrong with a man wearing pink. I like it. Andy used to look good in these sweaters."

Rob and Mike exchanged amused glances.

"Sal here was quite keen on old Andy when she was a kid, weren't you, Sal? Had quite a crush on him, she did." Rob nudged me, a smirk on his face.

"I was just fascinated by him. We all were. You two were as well, as I recall."

"No we weren't. He was such a mystery, and after Kitty's murder, and poor Kev insisting that he'd seen Andy on the ridge that day, pink sweater and all, well... it made for some interest didn't it?" Rob said in an offhand sort of way.

Mike went on to the last bedroom. It came as quite a shock. It was done out with a young girl in mind. Mike watched my response closely, nodding his head the while, as if he too had been mystified by it.

"What do you think?"

"They didn't have any young girls in the family, did they?"

"Not that I am aware of."

There was a small four-poster bed trimmed in white and lavender lace. The drapes were likewise lavender and white lace. The furniture was white, and the small fireplace was painted white also. There was a pretty armchair and a window seat and a small rocking chair, white book shelves full of girls' books, all the usual classics, Jane Austen, the Bronte sisters, George Eliot, Winnie the Pooh stories, and some books by French authors, Balzac, Proust, as well as Stendahl, Dumas and more modern ones like Simone de Beauvoir, Sartre and Camus.

"Maybe Mrs. C. liked to use this room – return to her childhood days in France?" Mike continued thoughtfully.

"Why would she have two rooms? She has some of these books in her study too."

"Maybe she wanted a daughter," offered Rob. "Or maybe she had a niece coming to live with her, something like that I bet."

We sauntered around in silence. Mike took us into the huge attic and pulled on the light string. The long raftered space lit up, and was bright and airy, despite the closed shutters. There were large canvases wrapped in sacking placed against the walls, expensive antique bric-a-brac, rolls of oriental silks and satin fabrics. They were stacked, waiting to be collected by packers from some of the art galleries and museums in Seattle, and from even as far away as

San Francisco. There were two big wooden trunks. One was full of old clothes, and the other was filled with what was left of Mrs. Chatsle's papers and diaries.

"These are the ones I want you to collate for me, Sal."

"But some are written in some Oriental script, Mike. I can't read those. I can read the ones in French…"

"Well that's a start at least. Maybe you can get one of those young Vietnamese girls you tutor in English to look them over for you; see if they can identify the language."

We pulled the string to turn off the light bulb as we left the attic, and Mike closed the door behind us.

"Aren't you scared someone will rob the place, Mike?" Rob asked as we went back down the stairs and out into the gathering gloom of early evening.

"No. I've locked it up pretty securely. It's an eerie old place at night. Deer roam the estate, even saw a mountain lion on the ridge, but there is a team of security guards paid for out of the Chatsle coffers to keep an eye on it while it is unoccupied."

"Thank God for that! There were some pretty expensive objets d'art up in that attic," said Rob with a sniff.

"That's why I'd be so grateful if you and Sal took it over until your house is completed. You could keep a loving eye on it, feed the deer, keep the lawn trimmed, do the odd repair here and there."

Rob rubbed his soft dark brown beard thoughtfully.

"I don't know, Mike. I mean it's real generous of you and all to let us stay here free of charge, but quite frankly the place gives me the creeps."

"It needs a family," I interjected. "I know you guys will laugh at me…" They were already, as they pretended to blow their hands to keep them warm, and studiously avoided looking at me. I continued, "I sense the sorrow here that comes from solitude and neglect. The house needs to be full of people again, especially young people like Sean, Tali, Brad and Gary. They will make the old place live again."

Mike put his arm around my shoulders.

"I was hoping you'd feel that way, Sal. If truth be told, I also feel sorry for the old place. Deb will not live here. She likes our light, bright, Danish Modern too much. This dated stuff makes her depressed. I'm not sure what I'll do with the place down the road; turn it into a luxury condo park maybe, and keep the old lodge as the office and recreational center, but for now, I'd love for you and Rob to give it some family time again."

We walked back to the car. Rob noticed that the garage was occupied.

"Oh yes," said Mike, somewhat hesitantly. "That's Mrs. Chatsle's blue Thunderbird, the car that killed her by pinning her against this sycamore here. Do you see this deep notch out of the bark?" Mike patted the stout, scarred trunk of the huge sycamore that stood across and down the slope some from the kitchen entrance to the house. The house itself was on the flat top of the sloping driveway.

"How on earth did the car do that?" exclaimed Rob, examining the distance from the flat crest down to the tree.

"She was unloading groceries. She must have left the brake off. In any case, the car rolled down and pinned her against the tree. She was in her late seventies and frail. It would have killed her outright."

"But it's flat here near the kitchen door," Rob replied.

"Well maybe she parked on the edge of the rise." Mike and Rob raised their heads to look back at the tree off to the side of the rising slope. "Must have dragged her some," Mike added, rubbing his chin thoughtfully.

"My God, yes!" gasped Rob, walking down to the tree. "Also," he added,

"Why would she park on the edge? She'd have farther to carry the groceries. Surely she'd have parked here." Rob retraced his steps to the flat pavement right outside the kitchen door. He looked back at us for confirmation. We nodded in agreement. "Strange," muttered Rob. "Very strange!"

"Yes, well that's the Chatsles for you," said Mike. "Their lives were shrouded in mystery, and their activities were always a little on the dubious side." There was a loud crack above our heads. We nearly jumped out of our skins! "Who? What the Hell?!" exclaimed Mike.

"It's that shutter on the attic window," I said, stepping back to point up to the attic eaves. The shutter slammed open and shut again in an icy blast of wind.

"What is that doing flapping about?" said Mike angrily. "All the shutters were closed, weren't they?" Rob and I nodded. We had used the electric light to see in the attic. There hadn't been drafts in the house. I remembered Mike pulling the string to turn on the light when we entered the attic, and pulling it to turn off the light when we left. It had plunged everything back into complete darkness. We looked at one another in silence for several seconds.

"It was an extra strong blast of wind," offered Rob. "Those latches are old...but then again, I'd noticed that the house was securely locked up, windows and all. There was no sign of weather damage in any of the rooms."

"Damn right!" exclaimed Mike. "It's locked up tighter than a drum."

"It seems to be latched firmly now," I said, indicating that it was tightly secured, and resisting other strong wind gusts.

We walked around to the front of the house again. The screen door was closed, but the front door behind it was slightly ajar.

"Well there's the reason right there," said Mike, a measure of relief evident in his voice. "The wind went up through the house and blew the shutter open from the inside." That reassurance held until we stood at the foot of the stairs to the attic and examined the tightly sealed door before us. We exchanged glances and laughed nervously. "I've had enough of this," said Mike firmly. "Ghosts or no ghosts, are you going to take the place?" Rob smiled at me, but his eyes begged me to turn down the offer. I looked around. The whole house seemed to be holding its breath in anticipation of my answer. The rooms looked so inviting. Everything was exquisitely expensive and elegant, but inviting nevertheless. I suddenly had doubts about how it would stand up to my rambunctious family.

"Mike, you know how…well… active our kids can be; teenage get-togethers, slumber parties, not to mention old Bubba running in and out with his muddy paws and over-exuberant tail swatting everything within reach, his hair, his drool everywhere…Are you sure you want us here?"

Mike laughed. "Of course; it's just what the place needs, and your old house, Sal, was immaculate. I know this place will be in caring, loving hands."

"Well, if you're sure then, we'll take up your generous offer," I replied with a self-satisfied smile. Mike looked at Rob for corroboration. Rob nodded, but added, as we locked the front door and stood once again on the wide flagstone terrace looking over the lawn to the huge trees that lined the driveway,

"It's Sal who will be spending most of her time alone here. There will be the odd weekend when I'll be away on business, and when the kids are off on sports trips… you will be alone here then, Sal. Can you handle that?"

I clapped my gloved hands together enthusiastically, and with a gung ho bravado I felt only a momentary qualm about, I replied,

"I think I shall love it. I do have Bubba after all. We'll take long walks around the grounds and through the forest. Bubs will love it. There are the deer and other wildlife too…it's wonderful here. The house is warm and cozy. Bubba, Bugsy and I will share that splendid fireplace on those nights you will be gone."

Rob started off down the steps.

"Yes, well, I think I'd put my faith in Bugsy if I were you. Old Bubs is an inveterate coward." He turned to smile up at us. His wonderful kind brown eyes crinkled at the corners. Mike and I laughed.

"He is not a coward," I protested. "Bubs is my hero." I watched Mike and Rob exchange knowing glances.

"I'd go with the rabbit," added Mike. They chuckled some more. Well Bugsy was a formidable buck rabbit.

As we drove around the bend in the driveway, I turned for one last look at the house that soon would be our temporary home. The fire glow of a dying autumn sun lit up the old place. In that golden rosy light that penetrated the long, low sweeping branches of the giant evergreens to illuminate the lawn, a doe and her fawn grazed peacefully.

"Look at that, Rob," I whispered, pulling at his jacket sleeve.

"Beautiful," he replied, smiling softly.

"It is a special place. It makes me feel warm inside. I think we'll love it here so much, we won't want to leave." Yes, I thought to myself, as we drove out through the main gates, and Mike nodded to the caretaker, I shall hate having to leave here.

CHAPTER TWO

K evin Occley was standing at the traffic lights on the corner of Kalalua as Mike McNiall drove out through the gates of the Chatsle Estate. He had the Bremers in the backseat of his shining new Land Rover: a nice couple – the Bremers. It hadn't seemed so long ago that they'd all been pesky kids hanging around Henson's old garage and boat repair shed up at the lake. Mike was Fletch's tow-haired kid brother, and Rob Bremer was his pal, dark haired, friendly-faced kid. Sal Bremer was Sal McDonnell then – pretty little gal, straight blonde hair, blue eyes, tallish, long-legged, like a fine little filly. Her half-brother, John McDonnell, was related to the rich Kemps on his mother's side, and he'd been a close pal of Andy Chatsle. The two of them, John and Andy, the Chatsles and Kemps as a whole, had more intellectual tastes than the rest of those wealthy kids.

The lights changed, and Kevin strolled across the wide avenue to report in at the caretaker's hut.

"See Mike leave?" old man Potter said, jerking this thumb after the Land Rover as it disappeared over the hill into town. Kevin nodded as he filled in his timesheet. "Must be nice to have so much money," the old fellow continued, picking up his backpack, and making ready to leave for the night. "You okay?" he added, taking one last look around to make sure he'd got everything. Kevin smiled and nodded. "Okay then, well I'm off to my dinner and Monday Night Football. Have a good one." The old man walked down the drive, closed the big gates behind him, and, turning up his tattered old jacket collar against the cold wind, he strolled off into the twilight.

Kevin poured himself a cup of hot coffee from the pot on the little brazier in the hut. He sat in the chair, placed his legs up on the desk and stretched. He nursed the hot cup in his hands, which were red with cold, and twisted his thin lips into a quiet smile. He had a longish, thin face, which was quite attractive, light brown hair, which one could call fair, and no sign of grey, even though he was in his fifties. He was slight of build, lean, not too tall, about average height, just under six feet. He had kind grey eyes. His was a face that inspired trust. He looked as if he knew what he was about. His eyes held a smile, but one could tell on closer examination that he'd had a hard life.

Kevin put down his cup and rubbed his tired eyes. So here he was – a guard on the Chatsle estate. What a turn up for the books! God, how those Chatsles had messed up his life! He dragged his legs off the desk and stood up. He stretched again, and gazed up through the trees at the house, illuminated by the pale ghostly-cold light of an early October moon. He stepped outside the hut, his hands in his trouser pockets. The air smelled of dead leaves, not yet turned to mulch. There was the faint hint of deer musk borne on the wind. It brought back memories of lying in wait on frosty mornings, well before sun-up – the ground hard beneath his well-padded body, little puffs of warm breath before his eyes, and a stag drinking warily from the river. The stag would raise its magnificent head to meet the first golden rays of the sun that had begun to creep up over the ridge, and.... No, Kev never wanted to kill again. Vietnam had put an end to all that. Life, all life was precious to him now. It had been before, and he'd always regretted killing an animal, but now he saw it for the brutal act it was. Man the hunter, be damned! Kev never would hold a gun in his hands again. He detested the goddamned things.

Kev felt cold through to his soul. He shivered, and after reaching back inside the hut for his parka, he started off up the driveway to check on the house. His footsteps crunched over the gravel. He saw the flashlights way off in the trees. The security guards were checking out the forest. The puffs of warm air in front of their lights came from their dogs.

The house was in total darkness – no light left on inside. Mike had pulled the drapes across the windows before they had locked up. Kev quickly scaled the drainpipe to an attic window under the eaves. He moved out onto the ledge, balancing precariously. The shutter opened, nearly knocking him off balance.

"Careful," he hissed. A silvery laugh, light as air, answered from inside the attic. Kevin edged his way around the shutter, swung his legs over the sill, and landed softly on the attic floor. He didn't greet anyone, for there was no one to greet. She'd gone, shutting the attic door behind her. He made his way to the trunk full of Mrs. Chatsle's diaries, and pulled out the one he had been working on for over a week now. He put it in his jacket pocket, and climbed back out of the window, eased along the ledge and down the pipe. Once on the ground, he crossed to the driveway just in time to shout out to the security patrol. They were heading his way through the trees.

"Everything okay Kev?"

"Sure; tight as a bank safe." The men and dogs gathered in the light of the flashlights. The dogs whined excitedly, knowing it was chow time. The men, laughing and talking merrily, headed back down the drive to the guard hut.

Kev watched the men and dogs go off through the trees again. They'd had their coffee break and sandwiches. The dogs had been fed and watered. Now they would walk the perimeter and hole up in the hut up on the ridge. Kev was alone at last. He peered out towards the main gate – all looked well – no nosey stragglers peering into the grounds, no noisy teenagers driving around – hardly anyone about, it was so cold. The wind shook the traffic lights that hung over the Kalalua intersection. Kev settled by the brazier, coffee cup replenished and in hand. The enticing aroma of hazelnut filled the confined space. Kev sighed contentedly, put his legs back up on the desk, pulled the red leather diary out of his jacket pocket, and after admiring for the umpteenth time the silky paper that smelled of jasmine and the fine delicate oriental script that covered each page, he began to read. Up at the house, the shutter on the attic window gently, quietly, was pulled to and latched again, and all was still.

Kev had fallen asleep. Mrs. Chatsle's diary was more of a continuous monologue; no dates, just the year covered by that journal, and the mention now and again of a day of the week, a month of the year. She hadn't stuck to the year of the journal either, but had described events earlier in her past. It was so disjointed that Kev often felt as if he were reading her dreams and musings. The book lay open on his lap. It was written in Chinese, which Kev could read. The year was 1964: the year his beloved sister, Kit, had been murdered - 1964 – the worst year of Kev's life. It had been a glorious summer out at the lake. He'd turned twenty-two that June, and Kitty had been all of nineteen.

⚔ ⚔

Summer, 1964:
"If we're living the dream, what've we got to be scared about? We're the people ain't we? We decide what we want, don't we? Well, Hell,

what're those fat cats in DC getting het up about? Just so long as they keep up the illusion that we're living in the best country in the world, they can forget sharing their wealth. Hell, when I make it big, I won't share either." Manny Mack chewed on his gum for a few seconds, deep in thought.

"Wait for it," Kev said quietly to himself. "And here it comes."

"Now if I'm hurting real bad, then I'll get nasty and want those freeloaders in DC to start sharing out what they've got stashed away offa our hard earned taxes," Manny concluded with a flourish.

"Thus speaks the great philosopher and political expert of Henson's Garage & Boat Repair," Kev muttered to himself as he hammered another nail in the planking on the Caventry boat, but wait – Manny had not finished. He continued his political treatise, a thin homemade cigarette dangling off his bottom lip.

"I'll repair the fancy boats and cars of these rich little college boys hamming it up out there on the lake, just so long as they pay me and tip me big time. If they start cheating on that, well then I might get to feel like all those poor, hard-done-by stiffs in them other countries. I might decide to dance in time with 'ol Khrushchev there, but only to see what it gets me – Manny Mack," he concluded, with a resounding thump on his meager chest. They all held their breath, hoping against hope that he had finished this time, but no such luck. "Me and mine –I'll do what pays off for me and mine, just like those rich palookas do. If it ain't a crime against the Constitution for them to own me and rip off the likes of us poor, hard working bozos, then it ain't no crime if I wanna own a piece of 'em."

"Steppin' in time with 'ol Khrushchev may get you in trouble with J. Edgar and his federales," laughed Kitty. She smiled flirtatiously, and smoothing down her summer dress and yanking up on the bodice straps to better enhance her assets, she swayed seductively down the dusty lane to the marina. Manny smiled dreamily as he watched her go. No other girl came close to Kit in the looks department, nor in personality neither he thought to himself. He gave a wistful sigh, knowing that a long skinny streak of dirty water like himself, with a shock of bright orange hair that clashed with his honker, which was the size and color of a large red chili pepper, didn't stand a chance with her.

"Kit's alright," said Pete Mingus, flicking his stub in the grass. "But she's pure trouble on three inch heels sometimes. The kid needs to watch out who she bats them baby blues at. Those rich guys are a vicious lot if taken for a ride, and no one rides them like 'ol Kit there."

"Any of 'em touch her and they've got me and Kev to answer to – right, Kev?" Manny bent down to holler back to Kev, who was working under a boat ramp in the deep, dark recesses of the shed.

"Yeah, yeah, but who'll do the time? Certainly, not 'em," Pete jerked an oily thumb over the lake to a group of young men, who were laughing uproariously at the attempts of one of their number to balance on a water ski while knocking back a beer. Their noisy carefree larking about showed their dominance over the lake. If Pete, Manny or Kev and their gang had carried on like that, just harmless fooling around, the cops would have been called in no time. Manny chewed on his cigarette stub while reflecting on how unfair the system was. Didn't he work just as hard as they did? It was a different kind of work to be sure, hard, dirty, physical labor, but why should that be less respectable, less socially acceptable than working with the old noggin' as those rich kids did? Why some of 'em didn't even work hard at that! They just sat on their fancy duffs and lived offa good 'ol Dad. They didn't have to worry. They knew they'd get their mitts on the family business one day.

"'Tain't fair at all," Manny muttered, more or less to himself. The others were lost in their own thoughts as they watched "Fortune's Favorites" cavort about in the water.

"Hey, c'mon, let's get to it," Kev shouted out of the depths of the dark, musty, oily garage. "We've got Caventry's boat to finish by five. Get your butts in gear." Grumbling about their fate, they ambled back to work, rubbing their hands on oily grease cloths and overalls. Kev paused a moment after the others had gone back to work on the ramps, to peer through the rotting planks of the shed at the "Fun and Frolicsome" taking their ease. As he was turning away, his eye caught a flicker of pink and white moving through the trees. He smiled slowly - Kit up to her mischief again. She could sure tease those guys. He felt a twinge of anxiety, and looked over at the rowdy bunch. They were laughing and yelling at Kit, waving her over. Nah, she was okay. She knew how to work 'em. Then why didn't he like it? Kit deserved her fun, and, hey, she might get a rich husband out of it. He knew those guys' folks, and they'd fight tooth and claw to prevent lovely, but definitely unconnected, Kit Occley from sharing any of their wealth. Only those who could contribute more to the family treasure chest need apply, but it hadn't been like that a generation ago.

The Occley, Mingus and Mack men had fought alongside the Caventrys, Kemps, Birklys and Wingos in the Pacific Theater of the last war. They had gone to school together before that, and they'd all been right old pals, but not now. The Occleys, Macks and Minguses had been content to take any old job on their return from the war, whereas the Caventrys, Kemps, Birklys and Wingos had used the GI Bill to go to college to learn how to make the system work for them.

Collie Kemp had been a little 'ol greengrocer – now look at those supermarkets, one in every town and city of the Northwest, a multimillion dollar concern – and all due to his son, Fred Kemp, whose business acumen had been acquired in business school after the war. Same with Wint Wingo, who'd left his father's shoe shop to go to law school, and Curt Caventry, who didn't follow in his dad's footsteps to become a train driver, but who went in for banking instead. Joe Birkly, no dirt farmer he, like his dad – no, he went to medical school, and so on, and so on. Kev slapped his oily rag against his thigh. He tightened his lips on a bolt he had in his mouth, and set about screwing nut and bolt into the hull of Curt Caventry's boat. Not my old man though, he thought, no, not him. He drank his life away. That had suited him just fine; dead of liver failure at thirty-six, leaving the wife and two little kids to fend for themselves. Luck of the draw, Kev guessed. Mom was still waiting tables at the diner, and likely to do so to her dying day, but not Kit – no, that wasn't for Kit. She had plans. Kev smiled to himself – not our Kit. Well, good luck to her. A gal had to do what a gal had to do to get by. A rich fella might fall for her. It was more likely than a rich gal, Claire Caventry, for example, falling for him, even if their old dads had gone to school and to the war together. Just a generation removed, and yet now light-years apart.

There was a loud outburst of laughter from across the lake. He heard Kit's sexy laugh. She had a sharp wit that always hit home, and judging by the laughter, some poor mug had been on the receiving end of it. Kev smiled again as he resumed his work. "Go get 'em, gal. The World's your oyster", he muttered to himself.

The World proved to be no such thing for Kitty Occley. Earth was to be but a brief sojourn for the beautiful winsome Kit. Her body, badly beaten, as if to obliterate all traces of her beauty, her very existence, battered as if in intense anger, but not with any sexual rage, for she had not been raped, was found four nights later by Dub Mason in the woods that lined a sandy pebbly track. Dub had happened upon the tragically poignant sight while stumbling back in a drunken stupor to his shack on the edge of a dingy backwater of the lake.

Kit had a date that night according to her mother and brother, but with whom, they didn't know. Kevin Occley said that for the past three days or so Kitty had been hanging out with the rich kids at the lake. On the night of the murder, he, Manny Mack, Pete and Phil Mingus had been at the local hangout, Harve's, playing pool all evening. It had been a hot sticky night. The bugs had been out in droves. Colm Mack, Rob Bremer and Mike McNiall had been watching them play, and teasing that little pest Maisie Flahertie and her gal pals. Colm had noticed that Rusty Kemp had gone by with a carload of guys and gals. They'd gone up the lane at top speed, going in the direction of the lake, and spreading great clouds of sand and gravel into the air in their wake.

"They was all laughin' and screamin', radio blaring away. College kids, most of 'em." Colm hadn't noticed if Kitty Occley had been with them or not. "I'm sure I would'of," Colm said. "Kit kinda stood out in a crowd, with that bright yella hair and all. You'd notice if Kit was around."

The DA asked if he had noticed the time. Well, he'd checked his watch right after they'd gone by, just to see if he'd needed to head home, and...hey, yeah, Kev had called out to him to ask him the time. It had been around eleven thirty.

Everyone had been interrogated. All had alibis. The rich crowd provided alibis for one another, as did the poor crowd for one another. No one was unaccounted for. Ken Birkly had turned up later at Rusty Kemp's house, but he had been with Claire Caventry in his car, and they had stopped to...

"Well, you know – smooch around a little..."

Kit hadn't been with them all evening, or so they testified to a man (and woman). She'd been with them that afternoon:

"She'd been a lot of laughs. She'd always been fun, witty, flirty – you know. No?...Well – no, not loose, no proof of that," they stammered. "No, no one of their number had had...well – intimate relations with her. No, never that – just harmless flirtations, that was all. Kit was – well – you know – a guy had to be careful, didn't he? Didn't want to get trapped into marriage; had a name to make for oneself after all. Money had to be protected. Well – yes – just because of her background, one had to assume, didn't one, that Kit was on the make with them, otherwise, why didn't she hang around with her own crowd? Yes, Sir, we realize that to assume makes an ass out of u and me – old joke, Sir – very funny. Well, yes, we guess Kit would have made a very attractive wife. She was quite a catch with those looks of hers, and she was bright too – but, but, but – well, not to put too fine a point on it – yes, it's true that she didn't have any money, working people, you know, no connections. We don't know, Sir, are they always after our money, our social prestige? We guess so. We think so, but we may be wrong. Yes, Sir, we realize we are snobs, but there you have it, don't you? They want what we've got. They envy us." - And so on and so on; all the rich guys' testimonies ran along these lines. Yes, there you had it, neatly defined. There were those who had money and those who hadn't.

They had liked Kit. Well, the guys had anyway. They had been right decent to her all told. She hadn't had anything on any of them, so why not ask her crowd?

Now the formula switched from that employed by those who had a surfeit of self-esteem and financial chauvinism to that used by the have-nots, with their own brand of cocky self-vindication. The gist of the latters' testimonies was that no one had been hurt or spurned by Kit:

"Why we'd bin kids together. We was real proud of her. Sure we're ordinary Joes, but every once in a while, out of such simple stock comes a real gem, a perfect rose, and that had bin Kit. She'd had more grace and beauty, and brains too, than all those rich gals put together – more class too. Yes, Kit had class – born with it – it wasn't like the class those rich gals bought. It was genuine class, and Kit had bin born with it. Yeah, they'd all wanted to be her fella, but she was like one of the guys to them – had bin one of the gang ever since she'd bin a littl'un. Cute? Yeah, so cute." Tears came to eyes. Big louts, suddenly searching for handkerchiefs – all except one – the one who should have been crying his heart out – her big brother, Kev. Kev had been tight-lipped, white with rage. He'd break down in time, but not there and then, not during his testimony.

Ah, the tricks of fate! Kev had left Harve's at ten thirty that evening to say goodbye to his pal, Seb Gretavia. Seb never stayed in one place too long. He was always on the move, taking up whatever job became available. When he'd earned enough, he'd disappear for a while, off on another adventure. This time, some Mexican fruit pickers had convinced him to go with them to California to pick fruit. Kev had returned to Harve's by eleven fifteen or thereabouts – at least several minutes before he'd asked Colm Mack for the time.

It came out that Kev had a big quarrel with Kit before she'd left for her date that evening. He'd been red with rage, according to old Bud Thurow, who had been in the diner when Kev had...

"Bashed his way through the door, yellin at his Ma. He'd wanted to know who Kit had gone out with. His Ma wouldna tell him, if'n he didna calm down. Then she pulled him to her and whispered in his ear. Kev went kinda crazy."

Old Bud had given lie to Patti's and Kev's testimonies that they hadn't known who Kit's date had been. "Sure didna cotton to him at all," Bud concluded, a self important toothless smile on his saggy old face. Bud was such a permanent fixture in the diner that people tended to give him about as much attention as they gave to the dead flies stuck in the overhead lights. "Said, he'd kill him, and I think he wan too happy with Kit neither," Bud added, nodding his head excitedly, full of the significance and importance of his testimony. One could see the mind of the DA, Wint Wingo, working a mile a minute.

"Who was this man with whom the deceased had a date?" Wint fixed old Bud with a steely eye and educated brogue.

"Dee, who?" Bud asked, unimpressed. Wint raised his eyes to the heavens.

"Kitty Occley," he elucidated.

"Well, darn well say so, Wint. Why you've known old Kit all of her life. We all have – ever since she was a bright young'un." Bud teared up some, and even Wint looked sad and apologetic for a moment.

"I'm sorry, Bud. Who was Kit's date?"

"Dunno," replied Bud, blowing his nose loudly in his tattered old handkerchief. "Didna catch his name."

"Andy Chatsle," confessed Patti and Kev; both now charged with perjury.

Andrew Louis Chatsle – son of Biff Chatsle, one of the wealthiest old boys around - why Wild Biff Chatsle threw the most lavish, outrageous parties. He had ridden his white horse up the flagstone steps right on into the house at one party last summer. Kev realized the enormity of his folly in accusing someone like Andy Chatsle, when he'd seen the absolute and utter incredulity register on Wint Wingo's face. Wint had asked if he knew the family well. Kev had not.

"I fix their cars sometimes. They are generous. They called me and Kit, and my mom by our first names, but I always called Mr... Chatsle, Mr... Chatsle and Mrs.... Chatsle, Mrs....Chatsle." Kev had drifted into a murmur. He knew that he sounded ridiculous. "She's French," he'd added, coughing to clear his throat – his voice had gone dry with fear and uncertainty. Kev never had liked being the center of attention. "Her name is Colette, or something like that."

"You mean Mrs. Chatsle's name?" said Wint, with a superior drawl.

"Her name is Celeste." Honestly, what one had to endure with these hicks!

"Okay, Celeste then. Have it your way," replied Kev. "If you know her, why ask me?"

The DA knew Biff Chatsle very well. They were bosom buddies of like ilk. Celeste, Wint knew less well. He would have known her a whole lot better if she hadn't axed his advances with such a firm unequivocal rejection. He could have brought charges against her of bodily harm, but he couldn't risk his very lucrative friendship with

Biff. He had put up with the very embarrassing discomfort for a few weeks, telling his sexually voracious wife, Diana, that he'd been hit by a thundering serve off Kerr Toddy's squash racket – a safe explanation as Kerr had left to spend three years on an engineering project up the Mekong in Vietnam. Hopefully Diana would forget all about the inconvenience it had caused her by the time Kerr got back. If truth be known, Diana had not been inconvenienced in any way. She'd had Curt Caventry to console her.

"It couldn't have been Andrew," drawled Wint as he closed in for the kill. "Andrew is in France, and has been there all summer."

"No kiddin'!" exclaimed Kev, genuinely surprised. "But Mom said it was him." Kev had looked over at his mother, who red-eyed with tears, hanky pressed to her nose, had shaken her head in disbelief.

"I thought it was him, Kev," she shouted. "Honest I did, cos he and Kit loved each other." Kev looked stunned.

Wint smirked at him. "Yanking your chain, no doubt; I gather Kit liked to tease you about the rich guys with whom she flirted." Kev could have decked him, but Kit had been fanciful and a tease.

"No doubt," Kev mumbled, but he was sure that he'd seen Andy earlier that day, the day Kit had been murdered.

Kev had been driving up on the ridge. He liked to drive up there. He had finished repairing a tractor for Old Man Birkly, Ken's grandpa. It was a shame that Joe and Ken didn't do more for the old guy. They certainly could afford to help him out. Kev had decided to take his lunch up on the ridge. He'd had an hour to spare before he had to go back to the garage. He also wanted to test the repairs he'd made to the truck's suspension, wanted to see how it would hold up over the rough terrain. He'd seen, or he thought he'd seen, Andy hiking a trail on a lower slope. He'd been quite a way off, but Kev had his binoculars with him.

"Yep," he'd told the DA. "Always have 'em with me, in case I spot a bear or mountain lion." There had been a lot of trees in the way, but then who else had such blond hair as Andy? Who else moved with such an easy grace? Andy was a distinctive figure. "Had a sort of relaxed, stylish sort of walk, even when hiking, and even his outdoor clothes were kinda stylish. Wasn't him, you say? Ah well, I guess you're right." But Kev hadn't been convinced. He knew he'd seen Andy on that slope.

Kev was arrested, and in deep trouble there for a while. It looked bad for him. No one could trace Seb Gretavia. He'd vanished into thin air somewhere along the Oregon coast. Kev's white-faced anger turned to white-faced fear.

"He's desperate. We gotta do somethin'," urged Manny Mack. "He didn' whack Kit. God, he loved her. He'd have protected her, no matter what. Her life meant more to him than his own. Ah c'mon, he hated Chatsle, but he wouldna killed Kit over him – no way. Let's get a petition going that says so." Manny Mack collapsed in the throes of a frustrated sense of justice – and then, at the last minute, after the jury had returned a verdict of guilty, and before Kev was to be shipped off to the penitentiary, who should turn up in New York City, and hear from his old auntie that they'd been trying to find him, but old Seb himself. He had decided to give up on the idea of fruit picking, and had gone to work on the boats on the Mississippi instead. When he'd finished with that, he'd decided to try his luck in Chicago, and from there he'd gone to New York.

The DA tried to pin the murder on them both:

"Seb being black and all, it would have been downright convenient if he'd done it," said Manny Mack, with a sneer. "That would've suited those rich fellas just fine." But Seb had traveled with four others that night; two had been white men, for the honest testimony of the two Mexicans questioned had not been given any credence. The white men, however, when they'd been traced, had been believed when they had vouched for Seb and Kev, saying that they'd remembered Kev had chatted with them before they'd set off. It had just gone eleven o'clock when they'd left. They remembered the time, because the fruit truck always left at eleven o'clock exactly. Some checking proved that this had been so, because it always was so. Slim Hackney took pride in the punctuality of his fruit trucks setting off south to California, but when he had been questioned before, he apparently hadn't given such close attention to the men who traveled on the trucks, for he hadn't been able to vouch for the Mexicans, let alone Kev and Seb. The two white guys he remembered vaguely.

"Thank God, there was whites on that truck," said Manny Mack. "And thank God they were believed!"

If Kev had been at the fruit truck stop at eleven, then he hadn't had time to meet up with Kit and kill her. There had been only five or ten minutes tops between his leaving Seb and the men and his return to Harve's. Seb and friends vouched for Kev's having been with them from the time he had left Harve's to their setting off. Kev had been saved in the nick of time.

"Saved in the nick, before going off to the nick, as the Limeys say," laughed Manny Mack, with nervous relief at such a close call.

Kev didn't laugh. He didn't feel like laughing ever again. He knew he'd seen Andy Chatsle that afternoon. Who else wore pink sweaters, for crying out loud?

Kev woke up, and jumped to his feet, nearly stumbling over backwards as his legs were stiff from being up on the desk. God, what time was it? He looked up at the big round clock on the wall – two thirty. The security guards would be making their circuit through the woods near the house in about twenty minutes. He'd have to high tail it to get the diary back before that. That was it on the ridge for those guys. They'd return to the hut with him now for the rest of the shift. Kev ran up the drive. He shimmied up the drainpipe, and tottered out along the ledge. The shutter had been opened already – thank God! He scrambled in and replaced the diary and locked the trunk. He shimmied back down the pipe and was getting his breath back when the guys emerged from the trees. They greeted him warmly. He told them everything seemed okay from his end. How about their night? It had been uneventful all around. The dogs whined and whimpered in the cold as they all strolled back to the hut. Kev, his hands plunged deep into the pockets of his parka, thought to himself that he was getting too old for this, but he had to read those diaries, as rambling as they were. One of Mrs. Chatsle's rambles might give a clue to their involvement in Kit's murder. God he had loved his kid sister! She'd been a wonderful girl.

Up at the house, the shutter was firmly latched again, but not before a slender dark shadow, just a tad lighter than the darkness of the attic behind it, had stood by the open window and watched the tree-tops sway against a cold night sky, in which a pale moon sailed like a ghostly pirate ship of old. On the ridge, a lone cougar turned and slunk away into the trees, and in its garage, the blue Thunderbird's headlights caught the moonlight in their inscrutable depths.

CHAPTER THREE

Mike, true to his word, involved me in the collation of Mrs. Chatsle's papers. The Missing in Action groups had agreed to take all her correspondence and copies of the talks she had given nationwide and in Vietnam during and after the war. She had given numerous testimonies before Senate Committees. She hadn't just hoped and prayed that Andy was alive; she'd believed it with all her heart.

The first day I went up to the attic to begin work on her diaries, I felt like an intruder. It was so still and quiet up there. I couldn't stand the claustrophobia that came from having an electric light on during the day, so I threw open the shutters to let in the bright crisp fall sunshine. I took a few diaries over to the window, and stood there, looking out from under the overhanging eaves over the tree tops that stretched all the way to the pale blue of the far horizon, translucent in the sun's white glow. The air smelled fresh, a hint of apple mixed with the smoke of a wood-burning stove. I looked down at the blue Thunderbird waiting on the flat crest of the driveway. I used it now, much to Rob's annoyance. He regarded the car much as he would a psychotic killer, but I liked it. It was a great car, and I felt perfectly safe driving it…and parking it; although I always made sure that the brake was on, and I unloaded my groceries up at the kitchen door, all the time keeping a wary eye on the car. I felt silly and a little like I was betraying the trust I so defiantly championed in the Thunderbird. We all now referred to it as the Bluebird – a more reassuring name, suggesting happiness and good fortune.

I settled in an old armchair I'd found in the back corner of the attic, and had moved to the window, but the eagerness with which I'd begun soon diminished. In her French, English and German diaries, Mrs. Chatsle had recorded only the minutiae of everyday existence: their appointments, guest lists for dinner, dates for going to other people's for dinner or parties, dates when Biff, herself or Andy were away, dates when they were to return, birthdays, anniversaries, and in the earlier diaries, dates of Andy's school and sports events. On some days, she'd recorded intriguing initials, almost like code, but she'd left no hint as to how to interpret them. I was bitterly disappointed. It had been easy to scan all the diaries with only trivial accounts written on each page. I eyed the ones written in oriental script. In these, every single page was crammed full of characters. Now these may also have been appointments, oriental script being more ornate and taking up more space, but I doubted it. The characters were delicate, tiny, so fine, and the papers so silky soft, fragile and scented with jasmine. I convinced myself that my novel, plus an insight into the mysterious goings-on in the Chatsle house, lay in these oriental diaries. I'd have to get My-An, the Vietnamese girl I tutored in English, to have a look at them.

Like all Asian students, My-An was busy with her studies. Her music, helping her mother, grandmother and great-grandmother learn English, as well as helping them in their florist shop, took up all of her free time. My kids were hard workers, but not like My-An, who never seemed to have time for herself. When I asked her if she had any family left in Vietnam, she replied that the only family she had left consisted of the three older women and a cousin in Seattle; all their other relatives had been killed in the war; fighting for South Vietnam along with our boys against the communists from the North.

My-An was only twelve years old, and she had been born in Marseilles, well after the Vietnam War was over. Naturally she spoke French, but her grandmother insisted that they speak only Vietnamese at home, so My-An was fluent in both languages. She told me that her mother, grandmother and great-grandmother, along with her cousin, who had been nineteen years old at the time, had left Ho Chi Minh City, Saigon, as I will always call it, in the late seventies. They had escaped at night, part of the tragic exodus of Boat People. My-An said that they had told her that it had been a terrifying experience, but they hadn't gone into details. They had been taken in by the Indonesians initially, and from there they had gone on to France. My-An had been born and raised in Marseilles – well, until she had reached the age of ten. Her French father had died, and the women had decided to join her cousin, who had come to America after she'd completed her studies in journalism at the Sorbonne. This cousin now worked as a freelance journalist in Seattle. My-An was very proud of her, and boasted that her cousin could speak six languages fluently. My-An was interested in languages too, and hoped to become a translator at the UN.

I put the diaries away. I had hoped that Mrs. Chatsle might have mentioned her friendship with my half-brother John's mother, Connie Kemp, my father's first wife. John and Andy had played together as small children, before Connie had taken John to live in San Diego. John had been about nine or ten by then, but he visited the Chatsles when he came back to us every summer, and he and

Andy kept up a correspondence right up until Andy went missing in Vietnam.

"No such luck," I muttered to myself, as I fastened the shutters. It had clouded up outside, and a soft chilling drizzle had begun to fall. I left the attic, closing the heavy door behind me, and I wandered aimlessly about the house, thinking of how I'd parlay what I had known about the Chatsles, with what I could glean out of what remained of them in the house, into a novel. I lit a fire in the large fireplace, and it blazed away, lending a cozy air to the elegant, spacious living room. I stood at the huge picture window. The lawn was shrouded in a pale green tinted moist haze. The house was warm and quiet, except for the ticking of the grandfather clock in the entrance way. I turned and went back up the wide oak stairs. Sean had taken up residence in Andy's old room; Tali was in, what we called, the young girl's room. Gary now lived in Seattle, where he did underwater repairs on ships. Brad had his own apartment in town, and he was football coach and counselor at Sean and Tali's high school. Sean was in his senior year, and Tali was in her junior year. I looked at their baby photographs that I had hung on the wall at the top of the stairs. I'd had Brad and Gary close together, about a year and a half apart in age. I'd been nineteen when I'd had Brad and just twenty-one when I'd had Gary. Sean and Tali were also a year and a half apart in age, but I'd had them later in my twenties. Sean had been born about five years after the first two boys. Now Sean was eighteen and my baby girl was about to turn seventeen. Brad, Gary and Tali were blonde and blue-eyed like me, but Sean was dark like Rob. He looked just like Rob had at his age.

Rob and I had married right after graduating from high school. My parents had helped out so that I could continue my studies in languages at the local university. Rob had gone to technical college in Seattle with Mike McNiall, and Mike had hired Rob as his chief draftsman, when he'd taken over his father's construction company. They'd been hugely successful, with contracts to build luxury hotels, office blocks and government buildings in many overseas countries, especially developing countries, in addition to their building contracts here nationwide.

Mike was extremely wealthy and generous with his money. He had lost his elder brother, Fletch, in Vietnam, and so, like Mrs. Chatsle, he had taken a special interest in helping those who still had loved ones missing in action in Southeast Asia. He took an interest in helping the Vietnamese refugees who came to these shores too, and he lobbied in Washington to resume trading relations with Vietnam. Mike didn't hold any grudges, and after making several trips to Vietnam, he discovered that the Vietnamese were a very forgiving people, and that they had a lot for which to forgive us.

I went into Tali's room. She loved it. In perusing the books on the bookshelves, she'd discovered a delightful novel, "Le Grand Meaulnes", written by a young Frenchman, Alain Fournier. He had written only this book before he'd been killed in action in the First World War. Naturally, Tali, who was an incurable romantic, was deeply moved by the poignancy of this, and this book and this ill-fated young man had become the focus of her fantasies and her poems.

I bent down to examine some of Tali's sketches that lay spread out on the carpet by the fireplace. A gust of wind blew the rain against the window and startled me. I heard the attic door slam shut. I thought that I had closed it. It suddenly seemed as if the shadows cast by that rainy afternoon deepened, and the air in the house became colder. I shivered and decided to light the fire in Tali's room, so that it would be warm and cozy when she got in from school. I admit that I felt a little scared. I could feel my skin turning to goose bumps. The air became even colder. Downstairs seemed a long way away. I thought that this was pure nonsense, and busied myself with lighting the fire, and then tidying up Tali's sketches. I noticed that one drawing, still in her sketch pad, was entitled "The Beautiful Boy". There was also a short poem attached to the page:

"He comes to me in my dreams
His soft blond hair hanging in his amethyst eyes
He bends over me, lovingly, caressingly,
Begging me to awaken.
I open my eyes…
SCREAMS strangle me –
Those eyes, those wonderful eyes
Have become black with hate.
His beautiful flesh shrinks to whitened bone."

I felt my own flesh crawl. Tali had a sense of the dramatic, but I found this disturbing. No doubt, she had Alain Fournier in mind, but it was Andy Chatsle who had formed in my mind as I read the poem, and it was Andy Chatsle's face that stared up at me out of Tali's sketch pad.

I nearly jumped out of my skin when I heard the front door crash open, and I felt intense relief on hearing Tali and her friends run up the stairs; their excited chatter instantly shattering the cold gloom. The house seemed warm and glowing in mellow welcoming firelight again. I went to greet the girls, giving a passing glance up the shadowed stairs to the attic. The shadows seemed to hover momentarily, and then they dissolved in a sudden burst of sunshine that broke through the heavy layers of grey, misty, rain-soaked air outside, just before the sun dropped behind the trees on the far ridge.

Rob and I had taken the downstairs master bedroom, and in bed that night I showed him the initials I had found on one page of the diary for 1964, a year Mrs. Chatsle had recorded everything in oriental script. 1964 had been the year of Kitty's murder. Kitty had died in the August of that year. The page with the interesting initials had been dated in August and read: "KO c A t B t c PO".

"What do you think they refer to?" I asked Rob. He was reading a thriller, and annoyed at the interruption, especially when the letters made no sense to him. He lowered his glasses and looked at me over the rims.

"Good Lord, Sal! They could mean anything." Rob went back to reading. I stared at the letters.

"KO could be Kitty or Kevin Occley?"

"Or not," growled Rob.

"A could be Andy and B, Biff?" - I looked over at Rob and got no response. "It's in English, so c could be see?"

"Right, like we spell see with a c in English," retorted Rob as he snuggled further down in the blankets.

"KO to see A, or it could be KO c something, saw something and B was to see PO, don't you think?" I looked at Rob, a satisfied smile on my face. He slammed his book shut, reached over and turned off the light.

"Goodnight!" he snarled, but I sat in the darkness, the smile still playing on my lips. Who could PO be? Then it hit me – of course, PO could be Patti Occley, Kitty's and Kevin's mother, who worked in Harve's Diner. Now that left B. If it wasn't Biff, then who or where or what was B? I re-read the initials: KO (Kitty or Kevin Occley) saw Andy at B to see PO (Patti Occley). Wait –what if it read, Kitty or Kevin saw Andy and told Biff to see Patti Occley.... but what about? I turned to look at Rob, but his only response was a loud snore. Rob was right; this was making no sense, and was giving me a splitting headache. I sighed and snuggled down in the bed. Rob grunted happily as I cosied up to his broad back.

"Goodnight, love," he murmured drowsily. I lent over and gave him a swift kiss. He smiled contentedly, and rolled over to cuddle me in his arms.

⊱ ⊰

Amazing that out of a jumble of admittedly appropriate initials, Sal Bremer had managed to work it out. I liked this Sal Bremer, who loved the house, the car, her children, husband, animals, all aspects of life, as they should be loved, but, as good as it looked now, there was going to be a tough battle ahead as good and evil circled, intertwined.

CHAPTER FOUR

K ev Occley slumped in the armchair and stared gloomily out of
    the window of his downtown apartment at the rain-drenched
evening. The street lamps created puddles of shimmering orange
light on the sidewalk. The cold wet night air outside seemed enticing compared with the heavy smell of fish left over in the cramped
room after Kev's dinner. Kev chewed on a thumbnail. Now that the
Bremers had moved into the Chatsle house, he could no longer sneak
into the attic at night to get the diaries. The Bremers looked after
the estate, and there no longer was a need for security guards and a
night watchman at the gate - not that Kev needed to read anymore.
He'd read the relevant entries concerning the year of Kitty's murder,
and the preceding and following years; 1963 through 1965. There
had been nothing of interest. There had been, in fact, no mention
of Kitty at all, not even in Andy's childhood years. Kev thought over
those years, and how that evening Kit had danced off to meet her
mystery lover might have fitted in with her childhood fantasies.

⛫⛫

1964:
Kev had arrived home after work to find Kit prancing and pirouetting in front of the closet door mirror.

"Gotta date?" he'd asked, smiling in appreciation of her beauty and grace.

"And you'll never guess with whom," she'd teased.

"Oh, let's see; one of those chinless wonders of the la-di-dah set," he'd quipped, while washing the black grease off his hands at the kitchen sink. She'd come into the kitchen and given him a secret smile, her eyes sparkling.

"Not at all chinless - he's way over their heads." She'd turned on her heel and had gone back into the small bedroom to gaze once more into the mirror. Her expression had become serious and pensive. "He's incredible," she'd almost whispered as if to herself. She'd been lost in thought for a moment. "He's beautiful," she'd added. Kev had been watching her the while, leaning against the bedroom doorjamb, as he'd dried his hands. He'd raised his eyebrows questioningly at the term beautiful being applied to a man. His questioning look soon had turned to one of concern. Kit had looked worried. Her carefree, happy mood had evaporated. She had looked sad and troubled.

"Don't go if you're not sure," he'd said, getting bad vibes. He and Kit had been that close. They'd had to watch out for each other all their lives. They could sense each other's forebodings.

"Oh, I'm going," she'd replied, coming out of her reverie. "I have dreamed of this all my life. It's meant to be. I understand him better than anyone. I know how to ease his pain. I've known how to help him ever since that day I found him crying his eyes out on the banks of that old backwater pond near Dub Mason's shack. I felt his anguish with all my heart. I love him Kev. I have loved him ever since that day." Kit had that fey side to her that annoyed Kev, because it separated them. He hadn't any patience for those 'out there' notions. He'd always thought that this secret love of Kit's had been imaginary – a sort of Prince Charming to her Cinderella. He'd never paid serious attention to this make-believe world of hers, but it had been part of her magic, and had contrasted so sharply with her usual common sense and no nonsense pithy wit. Kit had been a beautiful, beguiling enigma.

"You mean that this guy you've gone on about ever since you were five years old is real?!" Kev had exclaimed. Kit had turned from the mirror to which her gaze had been fixed, as if she were trying to peer through the glass to a wonderland beyond. Her eyes were still glazed, but she had forced herself back to the here and now. She had approached Kev, and had taken his face in her hands.

"Of course he is real, Kev."

"Who is he?" Kev had asked, but she'd smiled softly, secretively, and turned away to reach for her white fluffy jacket. Kev had grabbed her arm.

"What do you mean by his pain, Kit? Is he some kind of nut?"

"No, of course not," she'd laughed. "He's wonderful, and he says that I am the only woman capable of rescuing him. I am the only woman ever to have reached him, to have penetrated his inner being, his soul."

It had seemed that she'd floated on air as she'd gone out of the door.

"Kit!" he'd yelled. "Come back here! Who the hell is this guy?" he had muttered angrily as he'd tossed the hand towel aside, and had made to follow her, but when he had reached the sandy lane to the highway, Kit had disappeared from view, and only clouds of dust and grit hung in the air. Someone in a car had to have been waiting for her, and they had driven off right away. Kev, still muttering angrily to himself, had stormed off to the diner to see if his mother knew who this guy was.

He remembered that on his way there, he'd thought over that day, long ago, when Kit, then five years old, had come wandering back from the pond to find him. He'd been busy trying to get his lasso over the post box way down at the end of the lane. He'd been eight then. He'd noticed that Kit had been crying.

"What's up now?" he'd asked impatiently. Little sisters could be a right pain, although as little sisters went, Kit was a terrific little kid.

"I met a sad little prince," she'd said, a sad old look on her face. "He's so pretty, yellow hair and all, not curly like mine, but soft and silky like Reb's mane." Reb had been the palomino on the Birkly Farm. Kit had liked to sneak onto their land to visit him, take him apples.

"Don't be stupid!" Kev had snapped. "Boys ain't pretty. They are handsome or good-looking. Pretty is sissy stuff."

Kit had raised her little hand to shield her eyes from the sun as she'd squinted up at him.

"Well, he's pretty. He's got beautiful blue eyes and all."

"Well, why's he bawling fit to bust like a gal?"

"He told me his Mama had dressed him up real nice. He likes his ma. She tells him all these stories about Vetnum, a magical place. Like China, he says.

He don't like his pa. His pa looked at him in his nice get-up, and he got angry, and said that he looked like a girl. His pa said that his ma was trying to change him into a girl, and that had frightened him, and he'd run away to the pond. I gave him my hanky..."

"Kit!" Kev had roared. "What did Ma tell you? Never loan out your hanky or your comb to other folks. You'll get germs and lice and stuff – might have to cut off all your golden curls," he'd added smugly. Kit had stared at him in steady appraisal.

"I'd have to cut off my curls cos I loaned him my hanky?" she'd replied, rubbing her hand across her tiny snub nose. She'd screwed up her face, skeptically. Kev had been about to correct himself, but he couldn't be bothered. Instead, he'd said, adopting an ominous tone,

"Maybe." He'd watched Kit's response to that. Sometimes she'd bow to his superior knowledge. Sometimes she'd look like she was mulling it over and coming to the opposite point of view – like she had done then. "In any case," he'd added. "Shouldna be talking to strange kids."

"Kids're alright," she'd shot back defiantly. "It's growed ups, you shouldna talk to."

Kev had strode off, and she'd followed in his wake, still lost in her thoughts about this boy.

"He's a prince, you know," she'd added as they had strode through the tall grass home.

"Yah, right!" Kev had thought to himself.

"He's real too."

"Go on."

"Yes, he is then."

"Okay, what's his name?"

"Can't tell you. It's a secret, he said." That clinched it for Kev. The boy prince was one of Kit's make-believe friends. They had been fairy folk, magical princes and princesses, right out of the fairy tales Ma had read to them every night when they had been very young.

Most Saturday afternoons after that one, Kit would tell him she was going off to meet her prince at the pond.

"Yeh, yeh," he'd scoffed. "Bet he's a big old bullfrog. You keep kissing him, Kit, hoping he'll turn into a prince, and you'll get warts all over your face," he'd shouted after her. She'd turned, and skipping backwards for a few steps, through a gnat-filled sunbeam that had lit up her hair like gold, she'd shouted back,

"We don kiss. That's sissy stuff. He don like that. He don ever let his ma kiss him anymore. He don like her now, cos she was dressing him like a girl. He wants to be big and strong like his pa, the King."

"That a fact?" Kev had laughed. "You'd better not like kissin' neither, or I'll tell Ma, and she'll paddle your butt."

"Course I don like kissin," She'd tossed her curls in girlish defiance, turned and skipped off to meet her prince.

The years had sped by, and Kev had other playmates and demands on his Saturday afternoons. Kit had pursued her own distractions. He'd wondered just how long she'd been meeting this freak, as he'd stormed off to the diner.

The diner had been empty of customers, except for Old Bud, who had been sitting alone farther down the bar, but Kev had given him no mind.

"Ma," he'd hollered. "Who's this fella Kit's been seeing all these years? I don like it. I don like it one bit. Damn, I thought she'd made him up." Patti had been drying some dishes.

"Oh, calm down, Kev. It's nothing. She's infatuated with him, that's all – always has bin. Nothin' can come of it. They're just good pals; kinda sweet really, even if a bit far-fetched. I mean they're so different. I jus don know how they've kept up that sweet littl' ol' companionship all these years. He seems to need to confide in Kit, which is understandable. That ma of his is so cool, so above it all. His pa is a nice fella. I've always liked him – easy going, not like her."

"Ma, who the hell are you talking about?"

Patti had glanced at old Bud, and pulled Kev nearer. He had been angry and had resisted. He had wanted answers out loud. Patti had pursed her lips, and had tapped her foot angrily while she'd waited for him to give in and let her whisper in his ear.

"No!" he'd exclaimed, when he had yielded and she'd whispered in his ear, her breath smelling of peppermints. "You're kidding me! No, no, no, not him! He's strange! You know what I mean." Kev had spread out his hand, and tilted it back and for, sign language for, of dubious sexual orientation.

"He's not!" Patti had shouted in her turn. "He's definitely not. You're just saying that cos he dresses nicely, and he's gone to university, and likes all those arty things. If a fella isn't dressed in greasy

41

overalls, or doing physical labor, all you guys think he's..." She glanced over at Bud, who had been watching them through those glass bottle bottom eyeglasses of his. "Well you know...strange," she'd hissed in Kev's ear. Kev had glared at her.

"How come you're so sure he ain't?" he'd asked, suspicions mounting. "Ma, I swear, if he's used our Kit jus for his own fun and games, I'll kill him, and I'll give Kit something to think about too."

Patti had shaken her head in denial. "No, no, nothing like that - they're just very close."

Kev had smashed his fist down on the counter. "Ma, what world do you live in? Honest to God, I got my job cut out for me with you and Kit. You both act like you were born yesterday – no lights on upstairs. What is the matter with you? Wasn't Dad enough? Didn't you learn anything from him?"

Patti had put down her towel, and had looked steadily at him, tears filling her pinky blue eyes.

"This ain't like that, Kev. You don't understand. Just trust her will you? Kit's got a good head on her shoulders, and even though she's got a soft spot for this fella, it's becos he needs her. He don't brag about her to the other guys. It's bin a secret – their secret."

Kev had stared at her in disbelief. "Sure of that are you? Kept it a secret, did he? I bet he did. Why? Is he ashamed of our Kit? Is he ashamed of this...oh so lovely friendship, that he has to keep it secret from his rich pals? Sure he needs her, but she's just not quite good enough to own up to, is she? Keep it secret, my ass!" Kev had turned and stormed back out of the diner, and gone to Harve's to get his thoughts straight and his temper cooled by playing a few games of pool. He'd sort them out later; that damned Andy Chatsle and his sissy pink sweaters! Well, he wasn't going to use Kit, and hurt her. By God, he wasn't! What kind of mixed-up bastard, was he?

Kev had calmed down, playing pool in the dark, cigarette smoke-filled air of the pool hall, his pals all around. Kev had come to realize that, what had hurt him the most, was that Kit had this secret she'd kept from him all these years. He'd been her hero, her protector and confidante. They had helped each other through thick and thin. They'd told each other all their deepest longings and dreams, feelings and worries, and yet old Kit had held out over this, which had torn at his heart and hurt him to his very core.

⇥ ⇤

"Kit, Oh Kit," he'd felt like sobbing out then, and did so now, while recalling all this. Instead, he'd played pool that long ago fateful night with deadly precision and a cold unerring accuracy.

After he'd been acquitted, Kev couldn't settle to anything. He still had hurt, deep in his soul. As far as the system was concerned, Kitty Occley's murder had gone unsolved, unpunished. Kev knew that the whole thing just stank.

"They've gotten away with another one," he'd told old Seb, who had nodded his head in sad resignation. Patti had agreed, when Kev had told her that he needed to go off with Scb for a while.

"Do you good to get away from here," she'd said. She'd made her peace with the place years ago. It had been, and still was, all she'd ever expected from life. She'd never expected much. Seb and Kev had loaded up their packs and set off:

"Those rich guys could swear night was day, and get away with it. They all stick together in one jammy old mess. It's them against us. They always think we're after their stuff. Hey, I don want their stuff. I wan my own – earned by my own sweat and tears. They were given riches, and they used their wits to earn more, and that's fine by me. I jus' got ma wits, and maybe, jus maybe, I'll get some kind of wonderful down the road. I ain't got champagne tastes. Jus like a nice little old home to call ma own, maybe have somethin' to help my kids along, if'n I get any, but I tell you, it's their par'noid reality against that old common sense of us. It's their reality, ain't it?" old Seb had mused as they'd sauntered along that long dusty highway to future horizons.

Two years later, Kev and Seb found themselves in yet another paranoid reality of the rich and powerful – 'Nam.

CHAPTER FIVE

Rob and I had Mike and Deb over for dinner just before Halloween. Rob had told Mike all about the strange goings-on in the house: a light in the basement that kept coming back on after we were sure we'd switched it off; opening and closing shutters in the attic, Tali's drawing of Andy Chatsle, when she never had seen a photograph of him, and had no idea what he'd looked like; although we'd kept Tali in the dark about this, so as not to frighten her. She had a rich enough imagination as it was. Rob was worried about her safety, but he also could not give credence to Andy's ghost haunting the place. The house gave him the creeps, but he refused to speculate as to why it did. Mike, of course, wanted to know it all. He seemed pleased whenever these unaccountable things happened.

"Puts the price of the property up, does it, Mike?" Rob, in rather a mean spirit, asked.

Mike laughed. "I see you have a low opinion of my motives as always, Rob, but no. I just want to find some connection with those years. I guess I still miss Fletch. Any indication that there is a life after death makes me feel good somehow. I want to know old Fletch is happy wherever he is. If the Chatsles are the only ones who come through that veil between this world and the next, well so be it; at least it gives me some hope, some consolation. You don't believe that they could do any real harm, do you?"

Rob glowered at Mike. "It's the Chatsles for God's sake, of course they can do some real harm. Didn't they always? Just ask poor old Kev."

"I'm beginning to feel uncomfortable with all this," Deb said, picking up her martini and moving over to the couch by the fire. "I don't come from around here, remember. I've no idea what you're talking about, but I don't like it."

I sat down beside her. "It's just the old days, Deb. People have woven all kinds of stories about them. You watch, the Chatsle house will become the stuff of legends and tall tales in a hundred years or so, and you will be credited as one of its owners – rather exciting, don't you think; if you step out of the here and now and take the long view?"

"I'm never going to live here, Sal – never," Deb replied firmly.

Mike rested his arm along the elegant mantle-piece, his Jack Daniels in hand. Rob crouched in front of the fire with a poker to stoke up the flames. We watched as the log crackled and the flames flared up. Rob stood up, put the poker back on its holder, retrieved his bourbon-on-the-rocks from the coffee table, and sat in the large comfy armchair at the fireside.

"I know all about the Kitty Occley murder, and that Kev was found guilty and then acquitted thanks to some fellow called Seb, who seems to be a legend around here already," said Deb. "But just how many of the old gang were killed in 'Nam?"

"A lot of boys from around here were killed in Vietnam. We knew most of them: some only by name, reputation; some we had known in school, but they hadn't been close friends, or even friends, just people whose lives had co-existed with ours at some time in our young lives," I replied. "Some we'd only heard of, because they were related to folks who lived here. Out of our gang, well, Fletch, but he was part of the rich set really, only Mike slummed it with us, but Fletch was a great guy. He wasn't snobby like the others. He was great to us kids. He'd walk off after talking to us, and there on the ground where he had stood would be some shiny dimes, enough for each one of us." I paused and smiled sadly into my martini. Rob and Mike did the same. Deb watched us, then took a sip of her drink.

"Fletch was good to me," said Rob. "I kinda hero-worshipped him like Mike did." The two men smiled wistfully at each other.

"Fletch was a big old blond bear of a guy, just like Mike," I said. "Had the same sparkling blue eyes, same slow, shy smile like Mike's; but for the four years separating them, you'd have sworn they were identical twins."

"Yes, I've seen the photos," said Deb, taking another sip of her martini, "But like Tali, I've never seen a photo of the Chatsles. I'd especially like to see what Andy looked like. Mike said there were no family photos here."

"True," I replied.

"I figure that the CIA boys took them, and Mrs. Chatsle's lawyers," said Mike. "After all, they didn't think that we'd want them."

Deb sat upright. "God, here we are talking about what happened thirty years ago. I hate it. It's this damn house; it makes you think of those times."

I could tell that this outburst had not pleased Rob and Mike. They held onto those memories, as if letting them go was some kind of betrayal to those who had died. I was just as guilty of this as they were, so I took it upon myself to explain to Deb why this was so:

"Our families have shared tragic losses in Vietnam, Deb. Fletch was killed there, and out of our set there was Colm Mack, Manny's younger brother, and Pete Mingus, Rob's cousin, Mitch, and my cousin, Todd, and Tony Arviso. Rollie Parks committed suicide a few years after his return from the war. Cooper Held drank himself to death after he got back, and Andy Chatsle and Seb Stan Gretavia were missing in action. Everyone still fully expects Seb to turn up any day, but so far he hasn't.

Fletch and Andy were the only victims from the rich set on the lake, well, and Tank Birkly, Ken's brother. Tank had been a pilot. He'd bombed many villages, dropped napalm on the poor civilians, and his mind hasn't been right since his return. He's gone through about four divorces, and can't settle to a job. He's taken to drugs also, and sometimes he goes crazy, drives around the lakeside firing off his old rifle. After these episodes, he disappears for a while. Rumor has it that Ken pays for him to go to one of those fancy drug treatment centers somewhere in the Californian desert.

Good old Manny Mack lost it there for a while too, after Colm was killed on a special mission. He took to drink, ended up on skid row in Seattle. Kev and Phil Mingus tracked him down, and dried him out themselves, with some help from Alcoholics Anonymous and Father Petrie, who is as good a town priest as one can find anywhere. He was one of the boys, and he'd been in Vietnam. He helped Manny Mack get over his breakdown, but Manny couldn't take living here any longer, and he went off to work in a garage in a neighboring town. Kev Occley, Father Petrie and Phil Mingus visit him often, and so far Manny has held it together. Mike and Rob called in on him a few times too, over the years, but Rob said that they reminded him too much of Colm, as Colm had been of Rob's and Mike's age. Manny would remember teaching them all how to play pool and how to bowl. It would upset him all over again, and he'd breakdown in tears, so Mike and Rob stopped going.

Colm had been killed while on a special mission into Laos, or so rumor had it. Kev had been on that mission, as had Tony Arviso, and the mission had been led by none other than Andy Chatsle. Andy had gone missing on that mission, and so had Seb, although

Seb had been doing advanced recon in another area, and had not been with them when they had been attacked. Only Kev and two other young soldiers, also with special forces, returned alive, but not unscathed; all three of them had been badly wounded. The medics marveled how they had made it back to the pick up point, the LZ, in the state they'd been in. One of the youngsters died later of his wounds. Kev had been at death's door, but he'd made it. There was some talk that Andy had made them take chances, and hadn't listened to Kev, who had much more experience in jungle warfare and secret missions behind enemy lines than had Andy, Kev having done three tours of duty in Vietnam with Delta forces. Andy'd been on his first mission. He was an intelligence officer in charge of this top-secret recon into Laos, where our forces had no business being. Andy had very little direct experience of jungle warfare up to that time.

Kev and the other young soldier, who survived, had been questioned relentlessly by military intelligence. Kev's previous accusations against Andy, as regards Kitty's murder, had been brought to their attention by Mrs. Chatsle, but Kev had been cleared of any implication in Andy's disappearance. Unpopular officers, who took risks with the lives of their men, had been "fragged", blown up with a casual grenade toss, but that had not been the case here, or so the young soldier claimed. They hadn't liked Andy. He had risked their lives unnecessarily, but Kev had looked after them. Kev had been a good guy; he'd known his stuff, never had taken unnecessary risks, and they had trusted his judgment. Kev had argued with Andy sure, but he'd done what Andy had wanted, and it had got most of the mission force killed. The young soldier and his friend, the other one who survived to get back to base, but later died of his wounds, had made it, only because Kev had dragged them along with him, despite his own severe injuries. They'd all been ambushed and cut down by machine gun fire. Andy had disappeared around a bend in the trail. There had been an explosion, and they'd never seen him again. They'd been too preoccupied trying to save themselves to look for Andy. The jungle had been alive with North Vietnamese troops. Kev had dragged them through the underbrush for miles to get to the pick up point. There was no way they could have stuck around to try and find Andy's body.

In fact, Andy's body never has been found. The military verdict was that Kev and the young soldier had nothing to do with Andy's death, and had not been derelict in their duty in trying to save him. The young soldier had testified that Kev had tried to get around that bend many times to reach Andy, while they'd been under intense fire, until he'd had to give up, and get himself and the two young men out of there.

Mrs. Chatsle had not been satisfied with the verdict. She had interrogated Kev on his return. She'd tracked down the young soldier, and offered him a fortune, if he would confess to Kev's implication in Andy's disappearance, but the young man had resisted temptation. He would not have been alive if it hadn't been for Kev, and he wouldn't have been in such a physical mess and all his buddies dead, if Andy hadn't been so goddamn gung ho and ruthless with their lives. Mrs. Chatsle had to cease and desist. Kev had been amazingly tolerant considering, and he'd later helped her with her MIA work. They even had become close in the last few years, although people attributed Kev's willingness to help in tracking down Andy to the fact that he'd want Andy to be alive as much as Mrs. Chatsle, but for a very different reason – to prove that Andy had killed Kitty."

"Kev Occley is a good guy," said Deb. "I took my car over for him to repair the other day. He's quiet, reserved, doesn't talk much, but you get the gut feeling that he's an honest, hard-working type – salt of the earth sort - good-looking too. He doesn't look like he's fifty. He looks like a pop star – no – he looks like that actor that died. Oh what was his name?"

"James Dean?" I offered.

"Yes, that's the one."

"Sal, thinks he's like Kevin Bacon. He has the same first name anyway," laughed Rob.

"Has Kev ever been married?" Deb asked.

Rob looked at Mike, a teasing smirk on his face. "Watch out, Mike, all the girls like old Kev."

"I'm not worried," said Mike, moving to sit next to his wife, and putting a proprietary arm around her slender shoulders. "I trust Deb, and even though Deb is gorgeous and a temptation to any man, as is Sal too, I also trust Kev."

Rob and I nodded in agreement. Deb gave Mike a quick affectionate kiss on the cheek. He stroked her dark red hair.

"The only gal I remember Kev showing an interest in was Claire Caventry."

"No, really?!" exclaimed Deb. "But she is such a bitch." We all nodded in agreement.

"She is a looker though, tall, leggy, kinda classy looking. She was a stunner in those days, when we were teenagers. Fletch told me that she used to tease old Ken by saying she fancied Kev. It drove Ken wild, Kev just being a garage mechanic, his mother, a waitress in the diner, and here was Ken, son of a wealthy doctor, clever himself, going off to med school in San Francisco. Oh it drove Ken mad. They were always arguing those two, Ken and Claire, and I gather they still do, even though they've been married years now."

"It is not a happy marriage," said Deb, her gossip face on. "She has had several affairs, but I don't think that Ken has, at least, not that I've heard of."

"No, it's sad. Ken adores her, worships the ground she walks on," replied Mike sadly. "Claire Caventry is trouble these days, and a senator to boot."

"How could Kev have liked her?" asked Deb in surprise.

"I don't think he'd liked any of that lot, and certainly not since Kitty's murder, but Claire had been more friendly than the rest of them once, when we'd been young. She'd been kinda nice, not so affected and toffee-nosed as she is now. She had hung around the garage a few times, talking to Kev, and he'd said that he thought she was attractive and nice, that's all. Nothing ever could have come of it, and Kev realized that. He knew Claire was just curious about working class boys, like rich girls get sometimes."

Deb objected to this. "I am a rich girl, and I resent that comment. I don't mind what work a man does; if I fancy him that's all that matters."

"But you married a rich man," said Rob, a sly smile on his face. Deb looked at him, anger evident on her small, pert face.

"I'd have married Mike, even if he'd been poor," she snapped.

"That's true," laughed Mike. "When we first met, I was digging out a drainage ditch with my men. I wanted to do some physical activity. I was feeling stodgy, out of condition, so I plunged on in, against the Ditch Diggers' Union, I know, but the guys didn't object. Up comes this cute little red head, lovely fawn-like brown eyes, to ask us the way to some street or other, and I lose my heart to her right there and then. I asked her to have a coffee with me, and things went on from there."

"And when I accepted the invitation to get a coffee with Mike, I thought he was the most attractive guy I'd ever seen, and I didn't care what he did for a living. I didn't usually go off with men like that, in fact, I was stuck up, but I couldn't resist Mike."

"Lucky for you he turned out to be the boss, the owner of the whole construction outfit," said Rob, unable to resist a dig at Deb's expense. She gave him a pointed look.

"You are impossible, Rob Bremer. I'll never be anything but a poor self-involved little rich gal from San Francisco to you, will I?"

"I'm sorry, Deb. If truth be known, you've improved a lot from those early days of our friendship. You have to admit, you were a bit much then."

Deb had not been easy to take to. She'd missed San Francisco, her job there, her friends, the wonderful things to do in that beautiful city, the restaurants, the theater, the lovely parks and walks by the sea, the shops, but after a few years, she'd settled down. After a few visits back to her family and friends in San Francisco, she'd found them a little artificial, not involved with the problems and needs of those less fortunate, a little out of touch with what was really important in life, and she'd found love and warm, unquestioning acceptance here with us, even if Rob did tease her relentlessly. Our kids adored her, and the feeling was mutual. Mike and Deb had not had children of their own. They'd got married in their late thirties. Deb had suffered several dangerous miscarriages, and had gone to full term with one baby, but had suffered pre-eclampsia, and lost the child, and very nearly her own life. Mike had been distraught at the thought of losing Deb, and so they had given up on the idea. It was a pity, for they would have made great parents. We all were in our mid-forties now, and the four of us, Mike and Deb, Rob and I, had taken several wonderful exotic holidays together, gone through a few painful family losses and illnesses together, and come out of it all as firm and loyal friends.

Mike and Deb left about one in the morning. Rob helped me clear away the empty glasses. I was filling the dish washer, while Rob went to check that the door to the basement was locked. He never liked to leave it open at night.

"Sal," he shouted back at me. "Did you go down the basement after I went down for the bottle of wine to have with dinner?" I wiped my hands on a dishcloth, and joined him on the basement steps.

"No. I haven't been down the basement all day." Tali was spending the weekend at a friend's house, and Sean and Brad were off on a football trip. Gary, of course, was in Seattle. "Did Mike go down there?"

Rob shook his head. "No, Mike stayed up here feeding Bubba some of the roast, while I went down for the wine. I remember turning off this darn light bulb, but look, Sal, it's on again. Sean and I have taken it apart, put in a new bulb, checked the wiring, switch, everything, and they are all normal, but here it is on again. I just don't get it."

"Pull it off now, and we'll check it first thing tomorrow morning, when we take Bubs for a walk."

Eight o'clock the next morning, the light was on, burning brightly.

"Damn house gives me the creeps," snarled Rob, as Bubs pushed past him, knocking the door back against the kitchen wall in his eagerness to set off through the woods. "See, even Bubs wants out."

"And he'll want back in just as eagerly when he's hungry, cold and ready to take a nap by the fire," I laughed. I determined my response to all these strange goings-on by how the animals reacted. Bugsy and Bubba seemed fine with the house. They were never restless or upset when indoors, and if the house didn't frighten them, then I wasn't going to be scared either.

Yes, well, unknown to Sal, Bubs and Bugsy have made a friend. There were, shall we say, presences acknowledged by animals as harmless and welcome, while there were others… Ah well, let's just say, there were others not so welcome, not so harmless. Bubs and Bugsy will be aware of them when they make an unwelcome, but unavoidable, appearance.

CHAPTER SIX

K ev arrived home from a day's hard work at the garage, and thought to himself, that he really should clean up the place one of these evenings. Ma was too tired to do it. She worked hard enough as it was, cleaning that greasy spoon of a diner. He hadn't known Kelly long enough to impose on her good nature, which he already had done by cancelling several dates, not turning up for others. Kelly was a sweet lady, and good looking too, in a natural, down-home sort of way. She must have the hots for him, for she'd tolerated his treatment of her and hung in there. He liked her a lot, but he had a mission that he had to put above all other considerations. Oh there were times when he'd thought that Vietnam had addled his brain, but it had been addled well before that. He'd been Kit's protector when they'd been kids, and he had failed her when it had mattered most. He had to make it up to her for that.

Kev ate his microwave TV dinner, sitting in the dark, watching the cat, Tin Pan, hunt in the alley behind his apartment block. He drifted off into the past again, only this time, he thought over all that he had learned about Mrs. Chatsle's life. He thought back to that winter's afternoon, when, having finished going over the MIA papers with her, she had asked him to make them a vodka martini a piece, and they'd sat on either side of a roaring fire, the heat from which, along with the martinis, had made Kev very sleepy. Mrs. Chatsle had gazed into the flames, and in a quiet, hypnotic, beautiful voice, she'd told him all about her childhood, or had she? Kev had fallen asleep, and when he had awakened, Mrs. Chatsle had gone to bed, leaving a note asking him to lock up the house before he left. Had he dreamt it all?

1915:

French Indochina: Saigon:

Louis Thierry D'Emeraude had been handsome in his youth. A life spent in the pursuit of knowledge, and a thirst for new exciting experiences had led him to follow a career in France's colonial civil service, which had led, in turn, to the French colonies of Indochina.

D'Emeraude gazed at his reflection in the rust-spotted mirror over the stained sink. Twenty years in that fetid paradise had destroyed his looks. He beheld his sagging features, yellowed by disease and addiction. Even his sagging eyes, with their swollen lids, were yellow. He held his puffy, heavily veined hands out in front of him for inspection, and even they were yellow; the nails and fingers were stained brown from the nicotine, as brown as the sink. He shook his head and examined his teeth, those that were left, and even they were as yellow as aged ivory. He had no one to blame but himself. He had given himself up willingly enough to all the temptations and vices of the god-forsaken place. He'd been overlooked for numerous promotions, which, with his keen intellect and his rapport with the locals, should have been his, but for his damned disgusting need for that infernal stuff. He'd had to be content with the position of surveyor and diarist for the engineering expeditions up the Delta and beyond, all the way to the Khone Falls. He knew that river like the back of his hand. All the fortunes and ills of his life had been bestowed on him by that river – the mighty, duplicitous and intoxicatingly exciting Mekong.

D'Emeraude lived in a small house in Saigon, near the river. The house had a red tiled roof, over which bougainvillea grew in wild profusion. The other houses were clustered together, and reached out into the water, but D'Emeraude's stood a little apart and farther up the slope from the river bank. It was a hovel. There wasn't any other way to describe it, but it was a hovel with a certain adventurer's charm about it:

The lower level that opened out onto a grey muddy slope down to the river functioned as a bathroom. There was a rusty bath tub in it, a toilet of the roughest sort, a rust-stained sink and mirror, and high on the outer wall, there was a long narrow window made up as a mosaic of different colored pieces of glass, so that the bathroom had a rainbow-hued gloom that added to the jaundiced hue of D'Emeraude's features.

A narrow flight of rickety stairs led to the upper level, which again was really only one room, but D'Emeraude had used a bamboo lattice screen to divide it into a small study and even smaller bedroom. A large roll-top desk, with drawers and pigeon-holes bulging with papers, took up most of the study. Narrow bookcases lined the walls, their shelves overburdened with books and papers that also spilled out onto the floor. A scarred and torn old leather couch took pride of place in front of the screen. The couch looked as if it might have been comfortable at one time, but it long since had taken on a rancid sheen and the impression of D'Emeraude's form. Stained glass doors opened out onto a narrow balcony, on which D'Emeraude had placed an old wrought iron chair, so that he could sit out there at night, while he smoked a cigar and sipped on an aperitif, and watched the hustle and bustle of life in the alleys that led down to the river. Alongside the balcony was the bamboo-shuttered window of the bedroom section. This contained a narrow camp bed and a small table, on which was a white cracked wash basin and pitcher. A bamboo pole strung along one wall held D'Emeraude's three suits, all somewhat shabby and stained; a creased white suit for the office, a creased khaki suit for expeditions and grey baggy trousers and black moth-eaten velvet jacket for social functions. Fortunately, Tamarind trees, jasmine and other heavily scented plants and bushes surrounded the house, and these helped to mask the sour human odors of the place.

D'Emeraude lived alone, finding female companionship, when needed, in the local brothels. He loved to spend the tropical evenings reading the works of great minds. He sought this mental stimulation as eagerly as he sought the opiates to which he was addicted. He had four old friends, also the nuts and bolts of empire, only, like D'Emeraude, they were closet heretics. They did not believe in the supremacy of the European. They did not hold with the self-appointed right of Europeans to possess other countries, other peoples, and turn them into slaves, second-class citizens in their own land; all to serve some delusions of grandeur on the part of the colonizing powers. These men, Dr. Pantin, Father Colbert, Professor Deschamps and Raoul Langlois, would gather in D'Emeraude's cramped study four to five nights a week, when D'Emeraude was home, and not off up the Mekong, to thrash out finer points of logic, history, literature and politics; all the impedimenta of civilized man. They had been passionate young men once, eager to embrace the lifestyles and ideas of societies different from their own. They had not been willing exponents of the European way, but had launched themselves enthusiastically into all the exotic pursuits of the East. Their sexual appetites had become dulled with age, and their lust for other, less physically demanding, seductions had taken their place, and of these, the most redeeming were their love of intellectual discussion and their pursuit of armchair adventures of the mind. Thus would D'Emeraude have lived out his days, had not life had more up its sleeve for him.

In April of 1915, D'Emeraude was sent to Thu Dau Mot to settle some local labor dispute on a French owned rubber plantation. The French overseer was a brute of a man, with whom D'Emeraude had had some previous run-ins. The Vietnamese, who worked on the plantation, had a hard life, especially as the overseer, one Stepanek, was a slave driver, who regarded them merely as livestock of empire,

An informer had told Stepanek, that the local village elder had been consorting with nationalist brigands – giving them shelter and food; letting them indoctrinate his peasants with nationalist dogma, urging them to rise up against their French oppressors. Stepanek had taken a gang of his thugs to the village elder's hut with the intention of giving him a thrashing before calling the police to take him away to the island prison of Poulo Condore. The village elder had mustered his people too, and Stepanek, for once, had found himself in a very serious stand-off – his men with their guns and cudgels, being surrounded by peasants, whose numbers had been swollen with nationalist rebels, all bearing pointed sticks and machetes.

D'Emeraude had been sent for by his anxious supervisor, who had received a frantic call from one of Stepanek's men. The owner of the plantation was, of course, absent – taking his ease in his villa in the South of France. Should the colonial civil service lackeys not be able to protect his holdings in his, more or less, permanent absence, however, said plantation owner would bring the wrath of the government in Paris down on all their heads. D'Emeraude had been sent to forestall such a catastrophe.

D'Emeraude arrived after a long and tedious journey, to find Stepanek and his men beaten and tied up in a work shed, while the village elder and his men, whose ranks since had been depleted of political insurgents, held sway. The old man was a foul-mouthed, skinny wretch, who demanded his rights. He had acquired all the appropriate jargon from his nationalist puppeteers – this was his country – the foreigners had no right to bleed it of its resources – no right to treat the Vietnamese as slaves within their own land. D'Emeraude listened patiently, nodded sympathetically, but what could the old man hope to change, given the reality of his situation at this point in time? Way down the road, maybe – if the Vietnamese united in their efforts, well then, possibly, a change could be effected, but now…the French ruled his country with an iron fist.

The old man squatted on the earthen floor of his hut and rocked back and forth, holding his head in his hands. Saliva dripped out of his toothless mouth as the intensity of his emotions prevented the act of swallowing – his throat was full of rage and protest at the injustices, the colossal unfairness of life.

Stepanek was freed, and he charged towards them, bullwhip in hand, swearing that he was going to flay the rotten useless swine to the bone. D'Emeraude caught his arm, and wrenching it back, caused Stepanek to drop the whip. Stepanek spat at him, and threatened D'Emeraude with a similar fate to that of the peasants if he cared for them that much. D'Emeraude laughed and turned his back on Stepanek, who immediately bent to retrieve his whip, but D'Emeraude trod down on Stepanek's hand, causing him to scream out in pain. D'Emeraude hauled him to his feet and gave him a punch to the jaw that knocked Stepanek out cold. The other French guards growled and took a hesitant step towards D'Emeraude, but he was an official from Saigon after all. They had to be careful.

"Take him away," D'Emeraude ordered in a quiet, calm voice. "I will see that he is replaced. I shall inform the Baron that Stepanek is not running his plantation efficiently. The profits from this place are down. It is not producing enough rubber to meet the demand. The Baron will be more than eager to see this fool replaced. Take him now – go!" The men scrambled to heave Stepanek to his feet, and then they hauled him off.

The peasants, their village elder included, were silenced by this unexpected turn of events, and they regarded D'Emeraude with expressions of extreme wariness. He told them to take the rest of the day off, but that he expected them to work all the harder from then on. He would see that they would get a fair overseer, who would allow them to hold meetings every Sunday.

"If rubber production increases, I'll see that the Baron appoints Vietnamese overseers, and I shall act as arbitrator between you and the French Consul in Saigon. Your grievances will be addressed. It is in France's interest to build up your economy. Yes, for France's benefit, it is true, but also for yours. France is interested in your independence – colonies are too expensive to maintain these days, but France has need of your manpower to help win this war in Europe. She also has need of the rubber. If France wins, then your independence will be assured. The men in Europe – the soldiers fighting in the war – fight to end empire. They will herald in the dawn of a new age for the ordinary working peoples all over the world. With socialism will come independence for all nations now under the imperialists' heel." D'Emeraude paused. He hoped he had sounded convincing. It was what he hoped for and believed in with all his heart.

The peasants had followed his diatribe silently. Their sullen faces had shown no reaction whatsoever. D'Emeraude had spoken in Vietnamese, not French. It should have had more appeal. If there were, and there most probably were, nationalist spies in their ranks, then this should have appealed to them. He could see them running off to Saigon as quickly as they could, to get their influential contacts in the government to appoint one of their number as overseer. There was a long awkward silence, broken eventually by the village elder. He got up off his haunches, and smiling broadly, revealing his toothless gums again, he clapped D'Emeraude on the back, and started yelling orders to the others to prepare a feast in D'Emeraude's honor. D'Emeraude must spend the night with them. This was a test of his sincerity in supporting them. Was D'Emeraude their man, or would he beat a hasty retreat to the cool luxury of the plantation mansion?

D'Emeraude dismissed his police escort to the house, but he stayed in the peasant village. D'Emeraude's speech of earlier that evening may have come from the heart, but he knew that, whether France won or lost the war in Europe, the French would have need of all the income their colonies could muster to recoup their losses in money and manpower. No, independence for Indochina was a long way off, and why did he get the feeling that, despite the old village elder's enthusiasm for what he, D'Emeraude, had said, and his warm gratitude for D'Emeraude's sympathetic stand, neither he nor any of them had fallen for his promises? They had accepted the speech for what it really was – a conciliatory nostrum to deal with the present trouble – nothing more, and amazingly, they had yielded to this for now.

The evening's meager festivities had been fun. Opium pipes had been much in evidence, and the intoxicating fumes had helped to make the mosquitoes seem less relentless, and the smells of human and animal waste less stomach-churning. The effects of the opiate mingled with the overpowering scents of the surrounding jungle to addle further the mind and senses. The strident cacophony of sounds that filled the night, which was made darker and more opaque by the density of the forest canopy overhead, both dulled and pierced D'Emeraude's brain. The dancing flames of the fire illuminated the small native faces that surrounded him; their small black eyes watching him intently.

D'Emeraude thought that the village elder was a dissolute old bastard, and yet he held a grudging admiration for his courage in making a stand against Stepanek and his thugs. Somewhere in his brain, under the drug-induced fug, his mind was functioning still, and he knew that to have made that stand, the old man must have very strong support from the nationalist guerrillas in the forests. He may even be one of their leaders. D'Emeraude could well find himself held hostage before the night was out, and he knew that the government in Saigon would not pay a franc for his release, nor concede to even the smallest, most insignificant of demands. D'Emeraude was entirely expendable.

The old man and his equally toothless old wife drew nearer to D'Emeraude. D'Emeraude smiled sleepily, aware that this could be it for him, but no – the wife began to tell him that she had come from a very wealthy family in Hué. Unfortunately, one of her sisters had fallen in love with a French colonel stationed there in the old imperial city. This colonel had been very honorable, and had married her sister, when the girl had found herself to be pregnant with his child. The old man spat and belched in disgust at this.

"My wife's stupid relatives had been pleased by this," he said with a sneer. "What foolish people they are! Didn't they realize that the child of such a mixed breeding would never be accepted, not by us, and not by the French? There will be no place for half-breeds in Vietnam's battle for independence."

"The French will accept them," D'Emeraude said, not without a hint of pride in his voice. "There are many people of mixed heritage in France. They will be able to go there." D'Emeraude paused to take a puff on his pipe. He closed his rheumy eyes in bliss. The old couple shared a sly smile.

"That is not the end of the story," the old man said. D'Emeraude nodded lazily at him and smiled. His eyelids were heavy, and his voice slurred, when he told the old man to continue with his tale. "This couple had a daughter. They loved her very much. Her French father taught her many things that girls usually do not learn. He made her very learned – a scholar. My wife's sister's relatives were expelled from court in Hué for corrupt practices. This was the beginning of their bad karma for having relations with the foreigners." The old man spat at his wife, and she huddled over in shame. "Disgusting, filthy family!" and he made as if to hit his wife, but she bowed lower and missed the swipe. D'Emeraude felt like bursting out laughing, but he bit his quivering lips, and tried to focus on the old man's face. D'Emeraude knew that he was being subjected to some artful theater, but to what purpose? "They were the lackeys of the French and their Vietnamese puppets," continued the old man, kicking his wife, and she squealed and huddled away from him in terror. D'Emeraude enjoyed their theatrics.

"What happened to her – to the daughter of this mixed couple?" he asked, but now guessing at the outcome.

"My wife's family fled into the jungle to join the nationalists in the mountains of the North. My wife's sister and her French husband had to move to a garrison in the Red River province. There had been a lot of fighting there between the Nationalists, helped by Chinese bandits, and the French. The garrison was attacked, and my wife's sister and her husband were killed. Their daughter had been left in Hué with friends. She was twelve years old. These rotten French friends, may they die in their own dung, went back to France, and left the girl in a missionary orphanage here, but the nosey stinking priest looked up her family connections, and found that she had relatives here in the South." The old man lost his temper grandly at this point in his tale, berating his wife, hitting her with a stick, and calling her all kinds of derogatory names. The wife wailed, and the rest of their family joined in, until D'Emeraude couldn't stand it any longer.

"Alright, alright," he shouted, staggering to his feet, and pulling them apart, while fending off the others, who beat on his back with their hard, tiny fists. "So the priest tracked you down here, and gave you the girl to look after."

"Yes, may his soul rot in his hell," screamed the old man. "We barely have enough to feed our own children and ourselves, and he sends us one more, and what a one! She is a witch, I tell you. She torments us day and night." The old man covered his face with his hands, but D'Emeraude caught the sharp glint of cunning in his eyes, as he peered through his fingers to see the effect of all this on D'Emeraude. D'Emeraude had smiled with equal cunning, and the old man saw that the jig was up. "What could we do?" he continued, calmer now, adopting a more tragic mien. "She had to be our slave. She eats what scraps are left after the animals. We tried to sell her on the city streets and the highway, but she is a wild thing. She fights like a cornered cat. She refuses to speak our language, and will only speak French. She bites us, claws at us – to tell the truth, we are terrified of her. She could be of use to us through all the languages she speaks, and she can read and write. She could be most helpful, but she refuses to work for us. She is a useless half and half person, belonging nowhere, unless, as you say, France will own to her. We tried to give her to that pig of a French overseer. He likes young girls, but she nearly killed him, and she was beaten and put in jail, but even they would not keep her for long."

"Twelve, you say?" D'Emeraude was beginning to feel sorry for the girl ending up in this hellish place after her privileged upbringing.

"No, not now," screamed the old man. "We have suffered the wild thing for six years. She is eighteen now, and still wild." D'Emeraude's pity definitely was aroused. Six years of this kind of treatment would make any civilized person wild.

He wondered if the girl were sane after all this brutal, inhuman treatment. The wife screamed for her daughters to bring out the girl. The men gazed into the fire, the sticks crackled and sparks shot up into the black night sky. There was a scuffle. The old man yelled curses in the direction of a dilapidated pig sty. Eventually, the old wife and her two daughters dragged from out of that pig sty a pile of rags and matted hair, and pushed it into the firelight. The old man grabbed the hair and yanked the face into view. D'Emeraude gasped, and stood up. The girl was filthy and smelled of pigs, her face was muddy, but her eyes were diamond bright. She stared at him with fierce determination and...curiosity. Yes, she was intensely, hopefully, curious, as to whether he could be her salvation. She was sane after all. She was also beautiful. Her coloring, her hair, her eyes, reflected her Vietnamese heritage, but her fine straight nose, her sharply pointed jaw line, high classical cheekbones, her height – she was tall and thin, but straight, proud in her bearing – these betrayed her French heritage.

"What is your name?" D'Emeraude asked her in French. Before she could answer, he told her his name and his position in the colonial government, and that he had no intention of harming her. Her eyes narrowed in distrust. He switched to English, guessing that her father may have included that language in her schooling. He told her he would send her to France to complete her education. He lived in a slum in Saigon, but he had a house with servants in Marseilles. From there, she could go to Paris to study, or Toulon. Many wealthy Vietnamese and youngsters of mixed heritage, whose parents were well-off, went to Paris to complete their education, or to Toulon. Her father must have discussed this possibility with her.

"If you have the aptitude that is," added D'Emeraude craftily. He knew she'd respond to this challenge.

"Of course, I do," she snapped back in English. "I speak Vietnamese, Chinese, English, German and French. I know Latin and Greek. I have learned mathematics and the sciences. My father got me the very best tutors. I was to study medicine in Paris. Now look at me!"

D'Emeraude felt overwhelming pity for her.

"Maybe I can help salvage that dream," he said kindly. She shook off those holding her, and stood proud and tall.

"My name is Marie-Claire Aspinall," she said.

"Her mother name her Minh," screamed the old woman. "That her Vietnamese name – Minh – ha! – no right for her – she better named after the pigs."

"My name is Marie-Claire Aspinall," the girl said firmly.

"And Marie-Claire Aspinall, you shall be," said D'Emeraude, offering her his hand. She accepted it quite readily.

"Hey, you wait. You cannot take her. She is our slave. You pay big time for her," the old man screamed, grabbing at D'Emeraude's sleeve. D'Emeraude shook him off.

"How much?" he snarled. He paid the old couple an exorbitant sum of money, and had the wits to have them sign a contract he hastily drew up, stating that he was the girl's guardian. The next morning, they went into the nearby town and had French and Vietnamese lawyers make it a legal and above-board guardianship.

Stepanek and the overseers laughed at him.

"You won't get a moment's peace of mind. She will kill you while you sleep. Better keep a loaded revolver under your pillow."

With these warnings echoing behind them, D'Emeraude and Marie-Claire rode off on horseback through the jungle, their police escort in their wake. They arrived at the local train station, where they boarded the train back to Saigon.

It was four a.m. Kev had awakened with a splitting headache. He decided he'd try to sleep on until around nine or so, and then, for the first time in his life, he'd call in sick. He never had taken a holiday, but he felt deep in his bones that this stuff he'd recalled Mrs. Chatsle telling him, or that he had dreamed of twice now, was important. He must find a way of getting at those earlier diaries that he had ignored before, thinking them of little relevance.

Mrs. Chatsle had accepted his help in her MIA work rather reluctantly at first, but she had come to discuss more things with him as the years went by. Their relationship had been strictly a business one. She had given the orders, but she had come to rely more and more on his knowledge of the military aspects of Andy's time in Vietnam. She had told him that her mother had been half Vietnamese and half French, but she had seemed to want to keep discussion of the Vietnamese part down to the bare minimum. She'd acted like it was of no relevance in her crusade to find Andy, but Kev had strong vibes to the contrary. There was a lot here that needed explaining. Mrs. Chatsle had led a mysterious and complicated life, full of intrigue and spies. They had been involved in that complex web woven by the wealthy and powerful that extends its sticky, nasty, insidious influence all over the world. Was it at all possible that Kit had stumbled inadvertently and fatally into this mesh in some way that had threatened their evil machinations?

Henson had reacted as if Kev were mortally ill to call in sick. He wanted to get a doctor, paramedics, all kinds of emergency help. Kev laughed and told him that he just had a hangover, and possibly a touch of the flu. Henson told him to take as long as he liked to get over it. He owed Kev time off in any case, and he was relieved that Kev was taking some at last.

Kev made some fried eggs and toast, replenished his coffee mug, and settled down at the kitchen table to write down his recollections. Tin Pan, his long skinny orange cat, had slunk in through the open kitchen window, and now sat on the table at Kev's elbow, washing himself. A gust of cold, wet air blew in, and Kev got up to close the window. Old Tin Pan would sleep on his cushion by the heater vent for the rest of the day in any case. Tin Pan jumped down off the table, after licking up the left-over egg stains from Kev's plate, and he pounded around on his cushion, purring loudly, until he got it just right, then he settled for a long nap. Kev smiled. The old cat had been worth all the trouble of rescuing him from that bunch of rotten kids bent on clubbing him to death. Kev had waded in and picked up the terrified bundle of bloodied orange fur, and taken him to the Vet – Kelly Flynn - who had worked for days to save the cat's life. Tin Pan had made it, and Kev had met the new love interest in his life. That woman never had given up on

Tin Pan. That was a woman worth having on your side. Kev smiled. He knew that Kelly, in her early forties, was in no rush. She'd wait for him. She was that steady type, who knew whom she wanted, and he thanked his lucky stars that the man she wanted was him. Kev got up from the table, and settled in the armchair near Tin Pan, who was snoring away, whiskers all atwitch.

"Smell a rat, old fella? Well so do I," and taking a sip of coffee, Kev wrote on.

CHAPTER SEVEN

I gave classes at the local Youth Center for those newly arrived immigrants who needed to learn English. We had a large community of Asians in our town, drawn by Mike's construction company, and by the many technological and research laboratories and computer industries in the area. The Korean, Japanese and Vietnamese immigrants needed help with their English, whereas the Indians, Pakistanis and the Chinese from Hong Kong and Taiwan, usually spoke better English than most Americans.

One evening after class, I showed My-An one of the diaries, and asked her if she recognized the language. It was written in the letters of our alphabet, but phonetically it sounded like Chinese. She said at once that it was Vietnamese. I asked her if she'd like to earn some extra pocket money by helping me translate Mrs. Chatsle's diaries. It would be good practice for her in translating from Vietnamese into English. She'd pick up English idioms in no time. A guarded look came into her eyes. She told me that she was very busy, and that she didn't think she'd have the time to devote to such a lengthy enterprise. I was surprised. Nothing had seemed

too much for her before. She had asked me only last week if I had
any extra chores I wanted doing, so why the sudden reluctance?

"I thought that you wanted extra work," I said. She shook her
head sadly, but offered no further excuse.

At our next class, My-An had a change of heart, and she happily offered to translate the diaries for me, if she could take them
home to do them. She promised me that she'd keep them safe. I
told her that I could not let her have them. They belonged to the
Chatsle estate, and I was working on them for Mike. He would not
like them to be removed from the safety of the house, but I'd check
with him about it nevertheless. He may be even more keen to have
them translated, and so he'd let her work on them at home, but
when I phoned him later that evening, Mike adamantly refused to
let them out of my sight.

"No, Sal. She has to work on them at the house. The diaries
shouldn't be taken off to goodness knows where, by goodness
knows whom, like that. I know that they've been scanned for anything of importance, but I'm not so sure the CIA got everything.
They may have missed something."

"Such as, Mike?"

"Well, something about Kitty Occley's murder, or something
about Andy and Seb, or even something about why there is a girl's
bedroom in the house?"

I was skeptical about these reasons Mike had given, but I told
My-An at our next class that the diaries had to stay at the house,
and she understood. She said that she was very sorry, but she would
be unable to work with me on them in that case, as she just didn't
have the time to come all the way out to the house.

On the following Monday morning, however, I was disturbed
from my housework by Bubba's barking. I was surprised to see a little old Vietnamese lady coming up the driveway. I went out on the
front lawn to greet her. As she drew nearer, I could see that she was
My-An's grandmother. I had seen her once before at their florist

shop. She had been watering the plants in the background, while I'd chatted with My-An and her mother, Chao. We exchanged bows and greetings.

"If it pleases you, I will translate for you," she said. I was somewhat surprised at this. I'd thought that her English was not good enough. My-An had said that she was helping her mother, grandmother and great-grandmother to learn English, but this lady seemed quite proficient already.

"Is your English good enough?" I asked, feeling very arrogant for so doing. She nodded her small, neat, grey-haired head. She didn't smile. She looked a little sad. I was beginning to feel that I was asking them to do something that caused them much pain, and that certainly was an imposition in some way. I found myself apologizing. The old lady merely bowed her head, and replied that it was no imposition. If they appeared reluctant or reserved, it was because they were afraid that they would let me down in some way, after I had been so kind to them. They did not want to seem ungrateful, and to make mistakes in the translation would be the height of ingratitude. They wanted to help me, and so they wanted to do good work. My-An was way too busy to concentrate fully on the work, and so was My-An's mother, but she had some free time to give the diaries the attention, and hopefully the expertise, I needed. I smiled and joked that my teaching must be a lot better than I'd imagined, for she spoke English very well, so My-An, my pupil, must have taught her well. This apparently was not the right thing to say, for she suddenly had a guarded look, just as My-An had when I'd asked her to translate Mrs. Chatsle's diaries. I quickly reassured her that any help she could give me would be welcome, and she should not worry about being word-perfect; the gist would do just fine.

I made her a cup of green tea – she preferred this to coffee – and I left her sitting in the kitchen – also where she preferred to work. She admired the leather binding, texture and scent of the pages of the two diaries I had brought down to work on. She told me that only one of the diaries was written in Vietnamese; the other, the one in oriental script, was written in Mandarin Chinese, but not to worry, as she could read that as well. She asked me who had written them, and I told her that the late lady of the house, a Mrs. Chatsle had kept these diaries over the years. She nodded, put on her spectacles, and asked if I needed a written or oral translation.

"Just tell me what is written there, and I'll take notes if it is interesting," I replied. She nodded again and scanned the page in silence. Then, lowering her glasses to peer over them at me, she asked what I wanted to know about this person. I was a little taken aback at this. What business was it of hers what I wanted to know? All she had to do was tell me what Mrs. Chatsle had written. She could tell that I was annoyed by her question, but she still sat there, waiting patiently and persistently for my reply. Much to my annoyance, I found myself telling her all about my fascination with the Chatsle family, and Mrs. Chatsle in particular. I loved her house. I could feel her presence. Her personality was in everything, except the preserves. I just could not see her making preserves somehow. The old lady actually cracked a smile at this. I went on to praise Mrs. Chatsle's creativeness, her talents, her appreciation for the fine and intellectual aspects of life. I laughed at my imaginings, and said that she must think me crazy. She didn't smile at this, but nodded.

"No," she said, much to my relief, for I thought that she agreed with me that I was crazy. "This I understand. You care about her. I think that this is a good thing." So I had won her approval, and it mattered to me that I had. She read on quietly. I got up and put the breakfast dishes in the dishwasher. I fed Bubba and Bugsy, all the time watching her out of the corner of my eye. Finally, she looked up at me. I put down the animals' water bowls and sat with her at the kitchen table. She told me a marvelous tale of Mrs. Chatsle's exotic and rather sad childhood. She told me how Mrs. Chatsle's parents had met, and how her father had rescued her mother from an awful existence, and had taken her back to Saigon with him:

━◄+ +►━

Saigon: 1915 – 1916:

Needless to say, the lives of D'Emeraude and his four old friends: Dr. Pantin, Father Colbert, Professor Marius Deschamps and Raoul Langlois, changed irrevocably with the girl's arrival in their midst. The old house was transformed before their eyes. D'Emeraude could not afford new furniture, so the girl worked night and day refurbishing his old things. She scrubbed every inch of the place. She worked on the couch until it regained most of its former splendor and comfort. She painted the mildewed peeling walls white. She polished the desk until it glowed. She organized D'Emeraude's papers into neat files and stored them in labeled boxes on the shelves. She dusted and tidied all his books and surveying instruments. She put his maps and charts in neatly rolled bundles, and his many photographs of the Mekong expeditions, she framed and put on the newly painted walls. She made the frames herself. She aired, washed and re-stuffed his old mattress, but refused D'Emeraud's kind offer of it for her use. She insisted on sleeping on a new bed mat that could be cleaned easily every day.

Fresh flowers festooned the place. The girl had shaped up the men's shoddy old lives. She indulged them in their smoking and drinking habits, airing out the room the next morning, until it was fresh and bright and ready for the next evening's assault. She sat on her haunches at night brushing her now clean and shiny, silky, black hair, while she listened to the men discuss problems in philosophy, science and politics. Pantin taught her the basic rudiments of medicine. She helped out in his clinics and surgery. Deschamps taught her history and anthropology, Colbert taught her the Classics, and Langlois taught her higher mathematics. D'Emeraude introduced her to their socialist politics. They did not teach her in any formal way, but taught her to see connections, trends and influences, to recognize where interdisciplinary efforts overlapped. She was smart - a quick study.

"She is better than opium," chuckled Deschamps. "I do not know when I have felt so rejuvenated, so alive. She has brought my studies alive for me again, and she has made them as exciting as I found them in my youth."

The girl listened, asked pertinent questions, wrote brilliant essays that showed great aptitude, but she revealed very little of how she felt, or what she was thinking on a more personal level.

D'Emeraude's looks improved remarkably. He washed and shaved, and took years off his appearance. He was forty years old, and he had looked more like sixty before the girl had come into his life. His dull hair took on its former blond color. His eyes brightened to silver green once more. His bent, rail-thin form, which had a tensile strength, now became more muscular and straight. His sagging jowls became bare to the bone again, revealing a firm square jaw line. He had a straight nose, pronounced cheek bones, and his teeth took on a whiter sheen due to regular brushing with tree bark. He was a handsome man, even more so than he had been in his youth, for his face had developed the attractive cragginess of maturity. His four friends had watched these transformations, and they had speculated on how the relationship between D'Emeraude and the girl might change over time, maybe from a fatherly concern on D'Emeraude's part, to something entirely more romantic. He had been a confirmed bachelor like the others; only Deschamps was married. Madame Deschamps, Estelle, was a warm and understanding woman, who tolerated her husband's evenings away from home in the company of his friends. The Deschamps had three sons, all of whom were grown up and studying back in France.

D'Emeraude had got rid of his old camp bed and mattress, and had taken to using a simple mat, such as the girl used. It was cleaner, and made for a better night's sleep; free from the bites of bed bugs and lice, and it was cooler. D'Emeraude slept on his mat in the study, leaving the bedroom for the girl's use. Each took great care to ensure the privacy of the other. The only new acquisition that the girl had insisted upon was a new mirror in the bathroom. She had filled in the toilet hole with soil and lime, and had planted flowers in it. She had gone to the market and got several bamboo poles, which she used to build a short jetty over the fast-flowing river. She then built a shed over the jetty, and this became their new toilet. The river waters bore away all the waste, and the place smelled fresher, the perfume from flowers pervading every nook and cranny.

One evening in December of 1915, D'Emeraude arrived home to the usual sweet and savory smell of dinner being prepared, but instead of the light from the small, smoky paraffin lamp, the house was illuminated by many candles. D'Emeraude paused on the rickety stairs, and then climbing more slowly, he peered up into the room. The girl sat there on the straw matted floor, the food neatly and prettily arranged around her, flowers placed between each dish. She had a large red hibiscus in her hair, and her white ao dai was spotlessly clean and freshly scented. The candlelight made her jet hair shine.

"It is my birthday," she said, smiling shyly.

"My dear child," D'Emeraude replied. He forced himself to use the word child. Lately he had begun to think of her as anything but a child.

"I am not a child." She interrupted him. "I am a woman of nineteen, and I have a request to make of you."

D'Emeraude raised his eyebrows in surprise. "Anything within my power..." he began, but she got up, and moved with a swift grace to his side. She placed a long elegant finger against his lips, and she whispered breathlessly,

"I want to be your wife."

Colbert, the priest, conducted the marriage service a week later. They did not have a honeymoon, but returned instead to the old house, and wined and dined the four men and Madame Deschamps. When their modest gifts had been opened and admired, their guests left, rather shyly, self-consciously, no one quite having come to terms with this new state of affairs, even if they had speculated on such an outcome. The newly weds were undeterred. They were in a world of their own. D'Emeraude never had known such bliss, such good fortune. The girl was gentle, and despite the fact that he had had many lovers, and she never had had one before, she was the more confident and expert at the art of lovemaking of the two that night. He felt re-born, rejuvenated and innocent. She made him feel clean and good, as if fate had granted him a new youth, a fresh start that this time involved love. Marie-Claire, a virgin on her wedding night, proved herself to be as skillful in the art of lovemaking as she was in everything else. D'Emeraude even began to speculate on the existence of a beneficent god, but he couldn't think what he had done to deserve such a wonderful, beautiful, clever, young wife.

Two months later – in February - Marie-Claire told him that she was pregnant. She had fainted while helping Pantin in his surgery, and he had examined her and told her the good news.

"Dr. Pantin believes that the child will be born in September or October, she said quietly, her eyes lowered. D'Emeraude embraced her, his eyes full of tears of happiness. Once she saw his pleasure at the news, she was relieved, and hugged him with joy.

"Do not worry," she said. "This baby will cost you nothing. I can look after all its needs." D'Emeraude assured her that, as penny-pinching as he was wont to be, the baby and she would lack for nothing. They were his world, but what about her plans to go to medical school in Paris? She shook her head. "I am learning all I need here with Dr. Pantin, and when we have time and money, I can get my nursing qualifications here in Saigon."

D'Emeraude took her face in his hands. "You will go to medical school in France. You will be wasted in this place."

Marie-Claire had surprised the men with her lack of sympathy for her mother's people. She had detested her Vietnamese heritage, and had wanted to be considered French. Just as the village elder had said, she refused to speak Vietnamese, even after her arrival in Saigon. She seemed to have worshiped her French father. She told D'Emeraude that she had trusted him at first sight, because he resembled her father in his coloring. Her father too had been blond, and his eyes had been green also, but she had been cursed with her mother's Vietnamese coloring. D'Emeraude told her that she had been most fortunate, for her mother must have been a beautiful woman.

Over the months, the men had tried to tell her about the myths and history of the Vietnamese; how brave and resilient they were, and how resourceful and cunning. Why, they even had defeated both the Chinese and the Mongols, who had vastly outnumbered them in manpower. The wily and tenacious Vietnamese had seen them off and out of their beloved country, but finally, it had been her trips with Dr Pantin into the depths of the forests of the Delta that had won her over to the side of her mother's people. She helped Pantin treat them, deliver their babies, perform surgery on them, heal their often horrendous injuries, and she'd come to admire their fortitude under harsh conditions, and she'd come to see also how brutal, unfair and exploitative were their French overlords.

The change in her had been taking place slowly, but after she, D'Emeraude, Pantin and Colbert had been called out one night to help some nationalist guerillas, shot while they'd been trying to blow up an isolated police garrison in the swamps of the Delta, she went over completely to the Vietnamese point of view, and insisted on speaking only Vietnamese. She had witnessed extreme barbarism on the part of the French that night. They had shot women and children in their attacks of reprisal on the villages around the garrison. It had shocked her and repelled her, so much so, that it severed forever her ties to France.

This change in Marie-Claire came as an immense relief to D'Emeraude and his friends, for they had been working on behalf of the local guerrillas for some time, unbeknownst of course to their bosses in the French colonial service. They hid insurgents on the run. Pantin made frequent trips into the jungles and mountains to treat their wounds. They gathered together enough money to ship those wanted by the French authorities in Saigon to France, and they were aided in this by a dissolute old French sea captain, Yves Desforges. Once in France, the nationalists could work with those struggling to change French opinion at home. Most of these anti-colonial groups received backing from the socialist parties in France.

D'Emeraude, Pantin, Langlois, Colbert, the Deschamps and Captain Desforges belonged to an ancient organization that believed in the destruction of the secrets concocted by the wealthy and powerful throughout the world to keep wars and social upheavals going. Generation after generation, turmoil was the order of human life, and thus people were kept trapped by the practical issues of survival and the ideological, emotional blackmail of patriotism. They could not get on with the more functional and adaptive thoughts of ever changing their unfair and unjust governmental systems. These systems were always run by the wealthy and powerful for their own benefit, and not that of the people, who paid for it all with their taxes, taken from their hard-earned wages.

This ancient group of secret destroyers could not prevent wars, and they did not assassinate or gain power and wealth for themselves, but they betrayed those whose power was getting out of hand by using totally independent whistle-blowers, who, while being fed information by this secret society, were not aware of its existence. It had called itself, The Society of The Red Dragon, and had been formed at the dawn of human civilization. They upheld no particular belief, doctrine or dogma, religious or political. They served ordinary life, and the right to live it in fair, secure, peaceful, supportive societies, that helped the people get ahead with no strings attached. A society should be a good thing, and not a coercive, repressive entity that made living even harder, more banal and time consuming. It should afford all people time for creativity and personal enlightenment and advancement of all its peoples, not just the rich.

Initiation into the organization was a mystery to all its members. It seemed to them that it had happened without their being aware of it, and it was beyond their conscious recall afterwards, but it was the most important thing that had ever happened to them, and they took enormous pride and pleasure in the nature of their assignments, which were honorable. Sometimes betrayal was essential in saving innocent lives. To betray an ideology, or even a nation, is nothing compared with betraying one's sense of common decency towards all life.

D'Emeraude and his friends, like all members of the society, wore the ring of the entwined red and white dragons, made of gold from the hills of a far off ancient place, where the sacred mountain was located: The Mountain at the Dawn of Time. Very wise men and women had met on this mountain eons ago to form their society to protect ordinary peoples the world over from the selfish machinations of those in power. D'Emeraude wanted Marie-Claire to join them in their work, but it was not up to him to determine whether she did join or not.

One night, close to the end of her pregnancy, they lay in each other's arms. Marie-Claire talked about her work with Pantin, and how she wanted to become a doctor to help the poor in the outlying jungle villages. She hated helping Pantin in his other clinics, where he treated the wealthy, selfish, arrogant Europeans.

"They act as if they are entitled to the best medical treatment available, and act as if such treatment is wasted on the poor native people. The poor, on the other hand, are so grateful for any help we can give them," the girl said, sighing, and leaning her head on his shoulder. D'Emeraude took the opportunity to hint at the work of this organization to which he and his friends belonged. The girl struggled up to kneel in front of him. "You know?" she said excitedly. "You know of the Red Dragons? I am so glad, so relieved, but I guessed that you must be one, all of you must belong, otherwise, why else would I have been given into your care? Why else would you all have helped me to continue my education? My Papa was a Red Dragon. I don't know how I became one, but I did." She scrambled on her knees over to a cardboard box in which she kept her private things, and she withdrew a very small jewelry case. She took it to D'Emeraude, who had raised himself on one arm to gaze after her in amazement. She opened the box to reveal the ring of entwined dragons. D'Emeraude looked at it in disbelief. Then he got up, went to his desk, unlocked a small drawer, and brought out a small velvet case, which held his dragon ring. On seeing the ring, the girl went into peels of musical laughter. D"Emeraude had never felt so happy, so magical, so complete in every way.

Later, in the early hours before the dawn of the new day, October 5, 1916, Marie-Claire went into labor. D'Emeraude ran along the streets by the river to get Pantin. He prayed as he ran that all would go smoothly. He could not live without the girl. She was a part of him now. He wished that he had not got her pregnant. Pregnancy could be dangerous, especially in this climate. He could not lose her, and even if mother and child lived, he'd have to share Marie-Claire with the infant. Their lives would never be as blissful again as they had been this last year – just the two of them, and those evenings spent in intellectual exchanges with his old friends, when Marie-Claire had surprised them all with her brilliant, agile mind – all gone. Now an infant's constant crying would disturb their days and nights. Why, oh why, had he been so shortsighted?

Pantin had gone back to the house with D'Emeraude, and after several agonizing hours of hard labor, Marie-Claire had given birth to a daughter with a mop of jet black hair and silvery green eyes. D'Emeraude had stood and watched them from the doorway. Mother and child only had eyes for each other.

"And her name?" he'd asked, to gain some of her attention.

"Dominique," she'd replied, not taking her eyes off her daughter. "Dominique, after my father. His name was Dominic Aspinall, and my mother's name was Loan."

"Will she be named Dominique Loan?" asked D'Emeraude. The girl turned to him for the first time since she'd held her daughter in her arms, and smiled softly.

"Do you want to name her after someone?"

"My mother," replied D'Emeraude, remembering that gentle woman's love for him, and how, unable to deal with her absence there, he had not returned to his home in Marseilles since her death. "Her name was Sophie – Sophia."

"Welcome my tiny ugly one," whispered the girl. D'Emeraude smiled at her use of the old Vietnamese custom of saying that their babies were ugly, so that the gods would not be jealous and take them away. "Welcome, Dominique Loan Sophia."

"D'Emeraude," for the girl had omitted this, and D'Emeraude suddenly felt worried. "Dominique Loan Sophia D'Emeraude," he added, but the girl ignored him, and was lost once again in her love for her daughter.

D'Emeraude's worries proved to be unfounded. He was pleasantly surprised to find that his daughter was a gem of a child. She had a happy, undemanding disposition, even when she was ill, or her needs were not met. If she were thwarted in some way, she would change her plan of action, or merely wait until her needs could be seen to. She really was the perfect child, and D'Emeraude came to adore her. This was just as well, for the blissful early years of his marriage were coming to an end.

The family had spent wonderful times together during the child's first five years of life. Marie-Claire and Mino had accompanied D'Emeraude on his expeditions up the Mekong. All three had stood and marveled at the beauty of the ancient temple city of Angkor Wat, and they had pressed farther into the jungles of Cambodia to discover even more temple cities, all overgrown with exotic jungle vines and flowers, and inhabited by gloriously colored birds, reptiles and insects, as well as by crowds of raucous monkeys. D'Emeraude had known a father's joy and fulfillment on seeing his daughter fall in love with these wild and beautiful places. She was not timid. She loved all the sights and sounds, even the roar of the waterfalls and cataracts that had put fear into many a man. D'Emeraude told her how important the flood cycles of the river were to the region. The life cycles of the fish, that were the main source of protein for the peoples of the lake city of Phnom Penh, depended on the flood cycles of the Mekong. The existence of humans, animals and plants in the region depended on this exquisitely sensitive balance that had evolved between them and the mighty Mckong.

The D'Emeraudes traveled as far as Ventiane, the capital of Laos. They passed through the huge red cliff gorges that were heavily forested, and the dense jungle stretched to the far mountains on the horizon. They visited the crowded waterfront villages along the wider expanses of the river, and the child watched the village children play with avid curiosity and longing, but they tended to make fun of her. The mothers laughed at Marie-Claire for marrying a foreigner, for now her child had strange eyes. When she had been an infant, Mino had been delighted by the laughter of the children, and had smiled happily in response, but as she grew older, she realized that they did not like her, and that she was different from them in some way. There was something wrong with the way she looked. Mino avoided other children and showered her affection on animals instead, and animals returned that affection. They gave her their unconditional acceptance and love. This annoyed Marie-Claire, who wanted her daughter to understand the plight of the people. She wanted her to show compassion for her own species, but the child was reticent about doing this. She did not want to visit the sick and poor with her mother, rather she wanted to be with her father, and explore with him the wonders of the jungle, with its rich diversity of life and its wild, intoxicating beauty.

There was no doubt that the child adored, above all else, her young, beautiful and exciting mother, and she was miserable if she displeased her mother in any way, but the older she became, the more her mother found fault with her. She found fault with her lessons. She stormed out of the house if the child made the simplest of mistakes. She ranted on at the child if she found her wasting her time, as Marie-Claire put it, with animals, or if the child were alone, playing quietly by herself. She should go out and help others, otherwise of what use was she? When Mino pointed out to her mother that people did not like her to be with them, whether they were Vietnamese or French, her mother flew into a rage, and told her it was because she was an ugly child, full of self-pity, and a coward to boot.

D'Emeraude had been just as stunned as the child by this change in her mother towards her, but as Marie-Claire had avoided him of late, and had found fault with everything he did too, there was little he could do to help, but love the little girl, and tell her often how beautiful and clever she was.

"Your mother is scared the gods will take you from her. That is why she tells you that you are ugly and stupid, so the gods will not be jealous of her for having such a wonderful child," he'd whispered in her ear, while she had wept silently into her pillow, and the child had believed him, and thrown her arms around his neck and kissed him. She would greet her mother with loving joy on her mother's return home from her medical trips to far-flung villages. These absences grew longer and more frequent, until, after Marie-Claire had been gone for several weeks, D'Emeraude realized that she wasn't coming home again, and told the child her mother had gone off to live with those who needed her help more than they did. He made the mother out to be a saint, and this is what saints did. They put others before their own loved ones, because they knew that their loved ones were in no need of their help. The child had listened quietly and nodded. "Your mother will be proud of you for making this sacrifice," D'Emeraude said. "She knows she can rely on you to be strong. That is why she tested you, found fault with you, so that you would be strong when the time came for her to leave you. She must do her work helping others who cannot help themselves as you and I can." The child did not cry. She would make her wonderful, saintly mother proud of her.

Pantin had told D'Emeraude the heart-breaking news that his beautiful young wife had left him for a handsome young revolutionary. They had met when Marie-Claire had visited a guerilla stronghold in the mountains. Admiration quickly had turned to love, and Marie-Claire had abandoned her husband and child to go off with this man to fight for Vietnam's freedom and independence from France. She was also pregnant with his child.

The old Frenchmen, along with Madame Deschamps, who had taken over the mothering of the child, decided that Mino would be much better off in France. She could pass for a full-blooded French girl. Only her silky black hair betrayed her Vietnamese blood, and even that lightened in the sun to a sort of mid brown.

"Her soul will remain here," sighed D'Emeraude, whose own heart, mind and soul had been captivated by Indochina and its peoples. He dreaded the thought of exposing Mino to the cold, drab bleakness of Europe, but she might be well accepted there, so it would be for the best if they set sail for France. It had been years since he'd been home in any case. Roza and Kusco had been looking after his villa in Marseilles, and Marseilles had given him his sense of adventure as a child. It was an exciting, vibrant port city, where Mino would be exposed to a cosmopolitan lifestyle. Why all the peoples of the world came through Marseilles at one time or another. Yes, Marseilles was a wonderful place to bring up the child.

D'Emeraude looked out of the window at the girl, who was playing with a small kitten on the muddy slope down to the river. She was a skinny child, but healthy and tanned. Her golden skin emphasized even more her light silvery green eyes. She raised her head, and saw him watching her. She waved a small grubby hand in greeting. Her loving, innocent smile broke the man's heart.

Preparations were made for their departure. The kitten, Violet, would accompany them. The day before they were to leave on 'The Spirit of France', Captain Yves Desforges's ship, Madame Deschamps took the child, now almost six years old, for one last trip to the market to buy her a brush and comb set. Madame Deschamps was occupied in haggling over the price of a very attractive mother-of-pearl set, when the child gasped, and letting go of the lady's hand, she ran off as fast as she could, quickly disappearing from view in the crowds. Madame Deschamps screamed and gave chase, urging all around her to help her stop the child. The stall vendors were much amused at her predicament, and only laughed at her. The poor lady was frantic. The child never had done anything like this before. She was such a considerate child. As she hurried along, Madame Deschamps knew in her heart that something had made the child run off, and that something could only have been an animal in distress, or, dread of dreads, she had seen her mother. If she had seen her mother, and the look on the child's face as she'd run away, indicated that she had, then Madame Deschamps regretted it bitterly. Her old heart felt as if it were breaking as she hurriedly pushed her way through the throng of shoppers and vendors, praying the while that it had not been so, that the child had not seen that uncaring woman.

Madame Deschamps was about to follow the crowd across the square of the Rue Catinat, when she noticed a small figure standing all forlorn at the top of the road that led down to the peasants' huts, clustered along the river bank. There was a look of bewilderment and pain on the small pointed face. She looked up as Madame Deschamps walked slowly and breathlessly up to her, mopping the perspiration from her round, red face.

"I am sorry," the child said. Madame Deschamps put a plump arm around her painfully thin shoulders.

"It is nothing my little one."

"I saw my mother." She looked down the lane. The old lady nodded sympathetically, but said nothing. "She is still beautiful and young." The child began to sob uncontrollably. "Why did she run away from me? She could have talked to me, hugged me," the child gasped, trying to get her breath, her whole heart breaking. "I would not have asked her to give up her brave work. I would have been a good girl, like she wanted, and gone off with her to help the people. I was so naughty before, not caring, but I'm different now. I see I have to help others less fortunate than I am. I want to work with her." The child sobbed. Madame Deschamps held her close.

"My little one, it would be too dangerous for you. Your mother is protecting you, but she has to do this good work, and she couldn't care for you as well. That would make her worry about you."

There was a long period of silence, as the child dried her tears, and lifted her face to look at the old lady. Madame Deschamps was taken aback by the expression of sad acceptance in one so young.

"Madame, my mother had a baby. She has a beautiful Vietnamese baby with her. That child, she has not abandoned. That child, she has kept with her. Then why couldn't she have kept me also?"

Madame Deschamps had to think quickly. "That is not her child, but one of the poor peasant's children. Your mother has brought it to the hospital. Perhaps it is sick?" Madame Deschamps waited, praying for her to accept this explanation. The girl turned, and taking the lady's hand, suggested that they go home. As they walked along, Madame Deschamps tense with worry about her, the little girl said softly,

"She was nursing the baby, Madame. My mother told me that women can only nurse babies after they have given birth to them. She could no longer nurse me, after I turned one. She told me so. She must just have had that baby to be able to nurse it like that." Madame Deschamps gazed off down the road. It was amazing what this little one knew, and the good old lady's heart broke, and she wept, and the child held her close, her little arms unable to encompass the good woman's girth. They stood like that, as the gentle breeze stirred the red dust around them up into the tropical blue-white sky, and the orange-red petals fell on them from the surrounding tamarind trees.

"Do not tell Papa," the child whispered. "It will hurt him so."

On a cold, grey day, when the Mistral blew sand and dust in an eye-blistering whirlwind that blotted out the warmth and vibrant colors of the Mediterranean coastline, a man in a shabby white suit, panama hat clutched to his long graying blond hair, walked down the gangplank of a rusty old ship. He was followed by a small girl in a flowered smock. On her feet, she wore heavy rubber sandals, and in her thin tanned arms, she held a young, grey and black striped cat. They were met by a large gypsy woman and a small, strange, little old fellow, with big sad eyes and wispy hair. The D'Emeraude's had arrived back in La Belle France.

⊷+ +⊶

My heart nearly broke. The old lady closed the diary and sat looking down at her clasped hands in her lap for a few moments. She seemed to be composing herself.

"This book ends with their return to Marseilles," she said quietly. I placed a hand on her thin shoulder.

"What a sad story!" I said. "Would you like some more tea? I know I need something to help me get over it." She refused the tea. I said that I hoped that I had not tired her. She shook her head.

"No, not at all. Those times were hard on my people. The French were often harsh. All we ever wanted was to be free to run our own country. You Americans understand this surely? This is a very tragic story. Vietnamese mothers are very loving usually. You must not think badly of us, because of what this mother did. The times were such, that one had to make choices, and this woman chose her Vietnamese people over her French family. This kind of problem arises in mixed marriages, and maybe that is why we try to avoid them, but even so, in my old country, even within all Vietnamese families, of mixed blood or pure, brother ended up fighting brother, children took up opposite sides to their parents. The war there was also a civil war, and you Americans also know how cruel and tragic such wars can be."

I nodded. "This was hard on you. I will understand if you do not want to continue with the work."

"No," she said firmly. "I want to do this. I am interested in this woman's life now."

I laughed. "Yes, it's catching." She looked at me in alarm. "No - not like an illness," I added quickly. "Mrs. Chatsle is an enigma, a fascinating person. She is mysterious, and one wants to know more about her, almost against one's better judgment, or even one's volition. Do you know what I mean?"

"Oh, yes," she said sadly. "I most certainly do."

"I had no idea that she was Vietnamese," I continued. She gave me a sharp look.

"She was not," she replied firmly. "She was only one quarter Vietnamese. Only her grandmother was full-blood Vietnamese.

This lady's father and grandfather were French. She was raised in France, and she was French; nothing Vietnamese about her at all."

I was taken aback at the vehemence with which she insisted that Mrs. Chatsle had not been Vietnamese. Not only was she translating the woman's life story, but she was also her judge and interpreter on a more psychological level as well.

The diary written in Chinese was an account of Mrs. Chatsle's childhood in Marseilles. She was brought up by an amazing cast of characters. Her father was eccentric enough, but there was an old gypsy woman named Roza, who ran a brothel near the Villa D'Emeraude, and a strange little old sailor named Kusco, who kept nosey neighbors and school officials at bay, by claiming to be a pederast. Then there had been the dashing, mysterious Rudy Von Silvren, a man who had lost his face in the First World War, and who was the spy master of the Red Dragon Society of spies, an organization that worked to maintain a balance of power in the world: even Mrs. Nguyen had to laugh at this.

"She was a writer?" she asked. "Then these must be her stories."

"Oh no! Do you think?" I squealed. I had not thought of that possibility. No wonder the CIA had left these behind, as being of no account. This spy ring was a creation of Mrs. Chatsle's imagination. I had to admit to feeling bitterly disappointed. She must have written these ideas in Vietnamese and Chinese to prevent them from being stolen. How was I ever going to be able to tell fact from fiction in her life?

Mrs. Nguyen, still chuckling away to herself, refused to stay to lunch. She said that she had to get back to help her daughter in the shop. She did take up my offer of a ride home. Rob had left the jeep on the crest of the drive deliberately. I think his purpose was that I use it while he was away with Mike on business in Seattle. The Bluebird had been parked behind the jeep, and I'd have had to maneuver some to get it clear, so I yielded to Rob's paranoia and took the jeep instead. Mrs. Nguyen stood and stared at the

Bluebird for a few moments, while I locked up. I wondered if she had heard how Mrs. Chatsle had died. The old lady turned to look at me, and I was sure that I saw tears glisten in her eyes. In any case, she seemed relieved when we took the jeep.

She didn't say much on the way. She let me prattle on about my kids. The Nguyen florist shop, named 'Tranquil Fragrances', was tiny, with a plant nursery in the back. It had become the flower shop of choice for special occasions, so they must be doing very well. The three women and My-An lived in a small apartment above the shop.

Mrs. Nguyen turned and bowed her head in farewell after she got out of the jeep. She went into the shop, and I drove off, but only as far as a wide driveway, where I turned to go back the way I had come. I happened to glance over at the shop window as I drove by, and I caught Mrs. Nguyen, her daughter, Chao, and My-An huddled together behind some tall ferns. They were talking excitedly, nervously, while watching my every move. I also noticed, in that brief glance, that the great-grandmother was standing behind the blinds of the small upstairs window, watching me through a raised slat.

Ah, it is true after all, that fact is stranger than fiction, but at this point in time, it is better that we conceal fact as fiction. She was chuckling to herself, until she saw the Thunderbird. The tears were a nice, if somewhat confusing, touch. Had she sensed my ethereal presence in the house? It would not have been beyond her abilities to have done so – right up her alley in fact. Be careful, Sal Bremer, and keep your wits about you. I don't open and close windows, neither do I turn lights on and off. I certainly am not a cold dark shadow in the alcove to the attic stairs.

CHAPTER EIGHT

The afternoon light was fading. Kev leaned over to turn on the lamp. Tin Pan stirred and stretched, flexing his shivs. Kev looked down at the cat.

"You think the woman made it all up?" he muttered. The cat looked up at him as if he understood, and had shared the story with Kev through some weird feline telepathy. Kev shrugged and got up. "Guess it's real," he added. Mrs. Chatsle had told him that cold, grey winter's afternoon that her name was really Dominique. Kev had found it hard to relate the sweet child called Mino in her story to the hard, opinionated Celeste Chatsle, and the fact that she had referred to herself in the third person in her narrative had further divorced the woman from the child she had been, making it easier for Kev to feel sympathy for the little girl.

Whatever her name had been, and no matter how vindictive she had become in later life, Kev had to admit that Mrs. Chatsle had been pretty decent to him after he'd been cleared by the military court of any wrong doing in Andy's disappearance, and that young soldier had told her repeatedly how Kev had tried to get to

Andy while under heavy fire. Yes, that had changed her attitude towards him. She must have realized then, that given their history, Kev would be as keen as she was to find Andy, and to keep him alive. They had pooled their resources and efforts after that, and he'd come to like her, even, grudgingly, to admire her. No clues as to Kitty's murder still, but Kev was finding himself caught up in Mrs. Chatsle's life nevertheless.

Tin Pan followed Kev into the kitchen. Kev pulled down the blinds, poured himself some coffee and opened a tin of food for the cat. Old Tin Pan ate heartily. Kev reached behind the blinds to slip open the window in case Tin Pan wanted to go out after his dinner. The air felt good; cold, fresh and brisk, and laden with moisture. It was overcast, but not raining. That dull, leaden, grey sky would soon turn to black. The street lights were on already.

The phone rang out shrilly. Kev hated that sudden jarring effect it had on the senses. Tin Pan did too, for he leapt onto the sink and disappeared out into the dusk. Kev calmed himself and picked up the receiver.

"Kev, you alright?" It was Kelly. Kev smiled at the sound of her voice with its Canadian burr.

"Sure, why?"

"I ran into Henson, and he said that you were off sick today, and that had never happened before in all the years you've worked for him. You should have called me. I'd have got you medicines, lunch, whatever. Do you need anything – anything at all? The company of a lovely lady for example?" she added hopefully. Kev took several seconds to think this over. He hadn't quite come out of Mrs. Chatsle's world yet. He'd known the lure of the east: the exotic, erotic freedoms wrapped up in an aura of fading decadent colonial splendor; the hectic pace of a nation on the cusp of change, and a people who couldn't wait any longer to be free of all foreign shackles. He'd known the fear of not belonging there – an unwanted presence to be exploited, but never accepted, and yet he'd admired them as a people. If you worked with them, then they could be the most grateful and kindest people on earth. They just wanted to run their own country their way. What was so wrong with that? Americans hadn't been too keen on being dictated to by a foreign power, so why should they think any other people would be? Kev remembered the young girls in their virginal white ao dais, so graceful, so lovely...

"Kev are you still there?" Kelly's voice was shrill with impatience.

"I'm sorry, Kel, I've only just woken up. I'm still a bit groggy. Sure, come on over. I'd love your company."

"Sure? You took your time in deciding."

"I'm sure. Come on over."

"I'll be there in half an hour. I'll pick up something for dinner, and for Tin Pan. See ya."

Ah well, he needed a break in any case, but he really wanted to get lost in that world again. How did one join that Society of The Red Dragon? It sounded good to him, at least in theory. Kev wandered back into the living room. No, he'd had enough of that kind of life: spies, intrigue, secrets, watching one's back all the time. He went to sit in his armchair, taking a quick look around to see just how untidy the place was. It wasn't spic n' span, but it was passable in the dark. He gave a brief laugh as he sat down and reached for his notes that he'd left on the lamp table, but he felt only air, the notes had gone. Kev jumped up and went into the kitchen, the small bathroom – no notes anywhere. He'd felt a draft of cold air on his neck while he'd been talking to Kelly on the kitchen phone. The door to the apartment was unlocked. Someone could have slipped in unnoticed and taken the notes. It must have been the girl. Ah well, she'd let him into the Chatsle attic to see the diaries, maybe she wanted to look at what Mrs. Chatsle had told him in person. It must all have been in those earlier diaries though, so why would she take his notes? They would be no way near as accurate as the diaries. He went into the bedroom to put on some cologne before Kelly arrived, and there on his pillow was a note written in Vietnamese. It was a warning that to remember too much of the past was not good for one's future. Kev felt a shiver run down his spine. Well that's all he remembered of Mrs. Chatsle's story. That was all she had told him. He'd need the diaries to continue with her story, and that seemed nigh on impossible now that the Bremers lived in the house. The girl had not left this note; he knew this now, so it was likely that she hadn't taken his notes. Who the hell had, and who was trying to threaten him off? He felt that he was being manipulated by two factions: the girl represented those who wanted the mystery uncovered, and now there was someone, or some group, who wanted the mystery to stay as just that – a mystery.

Kev had been pleasantly surprised when the girl had left a trail of notes for him to follow when he'd been night watchman on the Chatsle estate, notes that had led him to the diaries in the attic. He never had seen the girl, just her slender shadow disappearing out of a door, and her silvery laugh as she'd run away into the darkness of the house. She had warned him never to follow her, and he hadn't, but why, he couldn't say. He had so desperately wanted her to be an intangible entity, a spirit – Kit – yes, he'd wanted her to be Kit, and he hadn't chased her, because he hadn't wanted to find out that she wasn't Kit returned from the dead. It had been an impossible dream, but for a few weeks he had lived it and known the greatest joy he'd known since Kit's murder had wiped all joy from his life. Yes, maybe Vietnam had addled his brain. The threatening note, however, snapped him back into reality. Now here was something very tangible, and his training with Delta Forces had made him respond to threats with a cold calculating calm that controlled any feelings of fear, and replaced them with a deadly determination to remove the cause of those fears. He placed the note in his wallet.

At last, here was the long awaited proof that something very rotten lay behind Kit's murder, and the Chatsle Family and their shady dealings in high places were at the core of it all. Kev was so relieved to know this for sure at last, that he even smiled as he heard Kelly's light steps running up the outside stairs.

CHAPTER NINE

It was Halloween, and the old house glowed in its harvest colors of russet, orange and pale gold. Tali intended to have her annual party and séance, despite Rob's and Sean's protests. In fact, Rob and Sean had announced their intention of going out with the boys, leaving Tali and her girlfriends to their "girlie frolics and amusements", that Sean was certain would end in hysterical calls to their boyfriends to come and rescue them – all a come-on, of course. Tali heard him out with a look of much tried patience on her face, as she tapped her nails the while on the top of the kitchen table. I had the role of chaperon, but I'd perform my duties by sitting in our downstairs master bedroom reading my book, the door firmly closed. Tali and her friends were rather serious young ladies with quite mature and sophisticated tastes, so they wouldn't require constant supervision.

Tali had spent the day decorating the room with candles, the fragrances of which – apples, cinnamon, pumpkin spice and wood berry – had filled the air, when they had been lit at sundown. She had succeeded in preventing Sean and Rob from decking

out the flagstone terrace and steps with ghostly demonic appari-
tions, which she'd considered too gauche and infantile for words.
Instead, bales of hay, stacks of perfectly shaped bright orange
pumpkins, other multi-colored gourds and garlands of dried fall
flowers decorated the terrace and steps, and made the old place
look beautiful, warm and welcoming.

Rob and Sean left in the truck, and passed on the driveway, on
their way out, three carloads of young ladies arriving. There were
exclamations of admiration and awe as the girls mounted the wide
flagstone steps to the carved oak door, where Tali, resplendent in
a flowing gown of pale peach, waited to greet them. The peach
color set off to perfection Tali's creamy complexion, soft blue eyes
and mid-brown hair, streaked with blonde highlights. After taking
their coats, I left them to it, and retired to my room to read. Mrs.
Nguyen had been too busy to translate, because they'd had such a
rush of customers wanting garlands and gourds for Halloween, but
she'd sent me a book on the history of Vietnam, which was proving
fascinating reading, and that was the book in which I intended to
become immersed.

The evening passed quietly enough. There was only the hum of
quiet conversation, the occasional peal of laughter, a voice raised
for emphasis or in protest. At eleven o'clock, I put on my parka and
woolen cap and gloves to take Bubba for a stroll before bedtime.
Bugsy was fast asleep already, nose all atwitch. We avoided the girls
in the living room, and slipped out through the side kitchen door.

A gusty wind had arisen that tossed the fairy lights strung
through the trees that lined the driveway. They looked festive. Tali
had asked Rob to switch them on for the party. To think that they
still worked after all these years! Bubba snorted and sniffed around
the undergrowth, his tail up and wagging. I stuck my hands deep
into my pockets and looked back at the house. It did look marvelous, and I felt very happy for it. It should glow with company, be
decked out festively as of old, and I took a few moments to imagine

how we'd decorate it at Christmas, although a good covering of snow most probably would provide the necessary seasonal ambiance. The old house would look wonderful in the snow.

The downstairs windows glowed with candlelight, and I noticed that the light was on in the cellar again. I could see its faint glow through the tiny side window. Ah well, we were used to that strangely persistent little light by now. I whistled for Bubba, and he ran up to me, his tongue lolling happily. In the distance, I heard the faint rumble of thunder. The gusts of wind had become stronger and colder. Big old clouds hid the Halloween moon, and as we turned back, a smattering of rain started to fall.

I went around to the front of the house to collect the more delicate garlands and put them in the large storage shed near the cellar steps. I grabbed some burlap bags and fastened them over the bales of hay and the pumpkins – heavy work that went unnoticed by the young ladies, warm and dry inside. I put the lock on the shed door, and was about to go into the kitchen, when my eye was caught by a light moving across the attic window under the eaves. Shadows of the tossing trees cast by intermittent moonlight, danced over the upper part of the house, but this glow was of a hand held lamp or candle. I strode angrily across the terrace. If those girls were fooling around among those expensive antiques after I'd expressly forbidden Tali to take her friends up to the attic, I'd ground her for a month. I tore off my cap and gloves, and with a flushed face, wet with rain, I barged into the living room, bound and determined that heads would roll, only to be greeted by the peaceful scene of all the young girls strewn in various relaxed, comfortable poses over the rugs and couches, while Tali read them a ghost story she had written.

"Mom, you're soaked! Oh God, no! Keep Bubba out of here!" The girls leapt to their feet, squealing as they fended off Bubba's excited greeting – his wet, muddy tail thwacking everyone in reach. I grabbed Bubs by his collar and put him back in the kitchen and closed the door. The smell of wet, muddy dog hung in the air.

"Tali, did you go up into the attic just now?" I gasped, brushing wet hair from my eyes. They all insisted that they hadn't left the living room all evening, except for necessary trips to the downstairs powder room. They hugged one another in gleeful terror, and insisted on following me up to the attic to check on the source of the mysterious light. I made them stop at the top of the stairs, while I mounted the steps up to the attic door. I glanced back at their young, eagerly expectant, somewhat scared faces illuminated by candlelight, and I opened the door, which groaned as if on cue. The girls gasped and hugged one another. I reached for the string and pulled on the electric light. There were moans of protest and complaints, mainly from Tali, that I had destroyed the supernatural atmosphere, but I held my ground. I turned to survey the attic, and found myself plunged into darkness as a bolt of lightning, accompanied by a jarring thud of thunder, fused the lights.

There were screams of real terror now from the girls huddled together at the top of the main staircase, and needless to say, I was a quivering mass of nerves myself. I took several deep breaths to calm down. Tali approached me with a lit candle. The attic was in total darkness, with the shutters tightly closed and locked. There was no candle, no lamp in evidence in the room. Suddenly, the overhead light flickered some, and then came back on. I stared at the firmly closed shutters, and no light could have shone through them to the outside. One had to have been open for me to have seen the light within. Tali followed my gaze, and then winking, she gently nudged me.

"Good one, Mom. They're terrified – well done!" She turned, and returning to the others, who were now a little pale and unsure, she suggested that it was the perfect time for a séance. There were several muffled protests, but Tali pooh-poohed them with the assurance that came from having been in on my trick, or so she so blithely thought. The others looked to me for reassurance, and I didn't feel up to being able to give them any. Tali gave me a conspiratorial wink, which the girls caught, and they began to suspect that they'd been set-up. The superegos among them did not want to appear to have been fooled, so they hustled the more timid ones back to the living room for the séance, assuring them it was all poppycock in any case. I tried to get Tali to talk to me in the kitchen, but she refused to catch my eye, and when I asked her outright, she jokingly waved me away back to my room, no doubt thinking that my reluctance to go on with the séance was part of the act. I didn't return to my room, but I sat on the stairs to follow the proceedings. Some of the girls were relieved by my presence there in the shadows, but the more suspicious ones suspected a trick, and they kept an eye on me as Tali began to invoke the spirits from beyond.

To my great relief nothing happened, but then, just as Tali was on the point of giving up, a piercing scream rent the air, and Amy Jackson sprang up with a look of terror on her freckled face as she pointed open-mouthed at the window. A small speck of light was moving around in all directions. There was some reddish smoke, and out of it appeared a demonic face, white with black eyes, lips and nose. The mouth itself was blood red, and then it hit me, and amid all the screaming and Bubba's excited barking, I began to laugh. Tali, noticing this, rushed to the door and yanked it open. Boys, some in vampire masks, others in white skull masks, and all wearing black capes, leered in on her, uttering blood-curdling groans. Tali was furious, and lashed out at them. The other girls caught on, and a general free-for-all ensued. The angry shrieks turned to ones of delight, as slaps and thumps gave way to tickles, hugs and kisses.

Sean and Rob appeared in the doorway, broad smiles on their faces. They had planned this all along, and had driven off to collect the girls' boyfriends, and had dressed them up as assorted Draculas. Then they all had returned, and had crept up on the house in the pouring rain. It must have looked to the casual observer as if an army of ninjas were about to attack us. It had been great fun, and even Bubba had been allowed to leap about barking with joy and relief that he hadn't been called upon to protect us, but for the rest of the evening, while we partied on, Bubba kept looking at the front door and growling to himself. I just happened to glance over at him, when I was bringing in some more hamburgers from the kitchen, and he was standing, looking up the main staircase, his hackles slightly raised, his tail low and almost threatening, but not quite. I went over and looked up the stairs with him. All was in darkness, except for a flickering shadow on the attic steps. Bubba barked up at me, and I gave him a burger, and he happily wolfed it down. He tried for more burgers that evening by acting out the part of good watchdog at the foot of the stairs, until he accepted the fact that we'd tumbled to his ruse, and then he gave up.

After everyone had left, and we'd more or less tidied up and calmed down Bubba, Rob and I got ready for bed.

"Nice touch with the light in the attic," I said as I got into bed. Rob leaned out of the bathroom, his mouth full of toothpaste,

"Say what?" he gurgled. Consoling myself with the thought that he'd never confess to it anyway, I snuggled down under the comforter, a smile of relief on my face.

It has begun in earnest, for they are gathering. The animals sense something is wrong, but my presence reassures them for now. Did that stupid séance lure them here? Of course not! They are very much of this earthly existence.

CHAPTER TEN

K ev and Tin Pan spent the weekend before Halloween at
Kelly's log cabin on the outskirts of town. There were romantic evenings in front of a blazing log fire, long walks through
rain-drenched evergreen forests, and so naturally the relationship
heated up some. Kev finally gave in to this.

Kelly was petite, slender and delicate in appearance, yet she
could handle big old farm horses, belligerent cows and large, angry dogs just as easily as she could treat a bird or hamster. He
liked her warm honey blonde hair, her soft brown eyes; oh, yes,
she was quite a lovely and capable little lady. She'd had two live-in
relationships that hadn't worked out: the first had been a lawyer,
and he'd gone off with a lady colleague of his. He hadn't been the
outdoorsy sort at all. Then there'd been an engineer, who loved
the great outdoors, as did Kelly. They had liked all the same kinds
of things, but they'd both had impossible schedules that had kept
them apart. Naturally, he'd expected her to give up her practice,
but Kelly had worked too hard and long to get where she was, and

she loved her patients too much to give up on them. Kev admired this the most about her.

"I'm around all the time," he said. "I admire what you do, and I could help you out on occasion, if you needed me to." She snuggled up to him.

"You're quite a guy, you know that?" Kev sat up in bed, a worried look on his face. Kelly looked perplexed, and she wondered what she had said to upset him now. "I'm not clingy, Kev."

"It's not that," Kev replied, turning to stroke her hair. "I thank my lucky stars that you put up with me, I really do, but I've got a past, Kel." He told her the whole story. It had taken several long walks, many intimate huddles by the fire, during which there had been time-out for - well - more pressing demands, until finally he'd told her it all. Kelly had asked pertinent questions along the way that had helped Kev sort out a few tangles in his thinking, but other than that, Kelly had refrained from giving any kind of opinion.

"Can I help you in any way?" she said. Kev could have married her on the spot, but he only shook his head.

"The answers are in those diaries, or stories, or whatever you want to call them. I think that childhood of hers in Vietnam is the key to what happened later. It started way back there, and I'm not entirely convinced that Society of Red Dragons is a figment of her vivid imagination at all."

"A woman helped you get the diaries?" Kelly said, a hint of jealousy evident in her tone and manner. Kev smiled.

"Yes, but I've never seen her. I've only heard her laugh. It's eerie, believe me. Don't worry, Kel, I like my women earthy and real." That had ended that for the rest of the night. They'd made passionate love by firelight, and the tall evergreens outside had swayed in the rain-drenched gusts, sending scurrying shadows over the little log cabin. There had been four cats and three dogs in that cabin, but only Tin Pan had stirred from his cozy niche by the fire to jump on the sill and edge behind the wooden blinds to look out into the stormy night.

Tin Pan's enlarged pupils had taken in movement – a figure had moved stealthily back down the track. The cat had watched intently, his fur raised slightly. The retreating figure had turned for one last look back at the cabin, and the cat had snarled and hissed in alarm, his hackles raised, fur at maximum extension, and he'd leapt down to hide under the quilt that covered the lovers, lost in their love-making. It had taken old Tin Pan several moments to still his beating heart, and even then he'd lain awake, listening, pondering in his feline way on what he'd learned in his other lives, not always as a cat, just what those evil ones planned to do next. It was why he was here after all, to protect Kev.

On Monday morning – Halloween – Kev and Tin Pan returned to Kev's apartment to find a large folder waiting on the kitchen bar. Much to Kev's surprise, it contained notes taken from a diary labeled 1932. Was this how he was to go on now, working from notes taken by his mystery visitor? However had she managed to get access to the diaries with the Bremers in the house, and what about those who did not want him to pursue the matter any further?

Kev arrived home that night, after work, eager to start reading. He and Tin Pan had their dinner, and they settled by the heater, but peace and quiet were to elude them. First, Patti came around to collect his dirty laundry, and to tell him that she was going to the movies with Madge Mingus and Gloria Mack, and that he'd get his things back on Wednesday night. Then Kelly called, and they talked lover's idle talk of reassurances for two hours or so. She wanted him and Tin Pan to move in with her. Kev was reluctant to do so, as he wanted his evenings free to read the notes on the diaries, should they keep coming, and to do his other MIA work. Kelly worked long hard hours during the day, and liked her evenings free for rest and relaxation, and Kev figured prominently in Kelly's ideas of what constituted rest and relaxation. He'd have no time for reading and analyzing the notes on Mrs. Chatsle's diaries. Kelly promised that she'd curl up beside him, and read some of the stuff with him, or watch TV. Kev knew that it would be a lost cause, and he'd find himself joining her to watch TV, or she'd tempt him into other activities. Kelly was angry when he put her off yet again.

"Just how long is this going to take, Kev?" He answered that he had no idea, but to mollify her, he promised they'd spend every evening together for the rest of the week. Kelly settled for that, finally, and he could get down to reading the notes.

⟞⟝ ⟞⟝

Marseilles: 1932:

The night before my father died, the Mistral blew dust, sand, grit and Rudy Von Silvren into our lives. I was sitting in the dark, looking out of my bedroom window. The wind was ferocious, tearing at the trees and scrub bushes, tossing great whirlwinds of dust, sand and gravel into the air. The old villa moaned and groaned under the Mistral's relentless onslaught. The shutters to my window hung on by one rusty hinge apiece, and they blew back and forth, but they held. I sat in the darkness with my old cat, Violet, beside me. I was sixteen years old, and I was so advanced in my studies, that I was to go to the Sorbonne the following autumn to pursue a degree in political science and oriental studies.

Violet and I saw him struggle against the wind's fury as he stumbled along the dirt track to the villa – La Villa D'Emeraude – set among rocks and boulders, scrub brush and windswept trees on a cliff overlooking the Mediterranean Sea. He clambered over the pile of rocks that once had been our garden wall, and I heard him curse as he caught his foot on an upturned flagstone on the path to our front door. He yanked hard on the bell rope, and its harsh clanging echoed right up to the creaking rafters that barely supported the blistering, peeling ceilings. The branches of the mimosa trees battered the already broken red tiles of the roof, sending even more of them crashing down to shatter on the hard mud of the neglected vegetable garden. I moved quickly to my door, and pressing my ear against it, I listened.

I heard him greet Roza in the cavernous drafty hallway, and then he ran lightly up the wide staircase to my father's study. I returned to my bed, snuggled under the sheets and waited. Violet looked from me to the door, her pert little ears alert, her beautiful eyes large and dark. She gave an anxious, questioning mew. I waited a long time, until my eyelids became too heavy to keep open.

I was a quicksilver tomboy – a law unto myself. Roza and Kusco had given me the freedom to learn what worked and what didn't in life. They were Red Dragons, and Roza had been custodian of the villa during the long years of my father's absence. She could tell the future from what she knew about the human heart, and this she claimed was not difficult, as humans showed very little diversity in their natures: we were made up of only a small range of emotions, and we had very limited imaginations that could handle only a very human-oriented range of possibilities. There hadn't been anyone since the ancient ones who could transmute and psyche-shift among an infinite variety of possibilities, and they had lived centuries before recorded history. They belonged to the world of myth and legend, but they once had been real enough. Man had removed himself from the natural world, and had lost many talents and abilities by so doing. Yes, humans had lost the magic of the symmetries of existences, that now only the other animals still retained, but at least humans had kept some vague notions of other abilities out there, and aptly had named them – supernatural.

Kusco looked like the silent movie star, Buster Keaton, or so Rudy claimed. He wore a black and white striped sailor's shirt with a red bandana tied around his scrawny neck, and he wore black, wide-legged matelot trousers. He was a small, agile man, with large sad eyes and wispy brown hair. He wore espadrilles that added an inch to his height, and he ran a dingy café on the waterfront with the aid of a huge grey and pink macaw named Ferdinand, whose vocabulary was as salty and raunchy as the café's customers. The café was aptly named 'The Dirty Parrot'. It was the meeting point for all the political dissidents who arrived on French soil to plot revolution in their own countries. Kusco provided these freedom fighters with identity papers, and brought them to the villa, where Roza and my father prepared them for life in France, by getting them jobs as laborers, students, artisans, photographers' assistants, kitchen workers and so on. My father introduced them to the communist groups, or socialist groups, depending on their degree of fanaticism for the cause of working peoples the world over. Many opted for communism, as the communists gave more effective support in their struggles for independence, but at a price, for with them, dogma always took precedence over independence and freedom, but then that was pretty much the case with all human ideologies.

Roza ran a brothel, which made her a social pariah among the more morally hypocritical citizens of the city, and Kusco fostered a totally fabricated reputation of being a pederast. This kept nosey neighbors and their obnoxious children away from us. I played only with the orphaned wharf rats and children of the thieves and brigands, who operated in the more dubious parts of town. My teachers had brought social workers to our home, but we managed to chase them off. I was a brilliant student, and I was more than able to defend myself, so they finally ceased bothering us, and I led a happy, carefree childhood – without a beautiful, exciting, clever young mother, for whom I had been an ugly French child. Roza and her girls had taken her place, and they made much of me. They praised my intelligence, my dominance over the local boys in my gang, and they even told me that I was stunningly beautiful, with my long silver green eyes and silky jet black hair, cut short like a boy's. My father described me as having a gamine beauty, and this pleased me. I acquired my attitude to the opposite sex from Roza's prostitutes, and they gave me a worldly wisdom beyond my years.

Roza shook me awake. She stood over me, the light from her wavering candle making her already large and sinister features even more alarming. She was ugly, but she was kind, and she tolerated all my tantrums and wayward ways, and I loved her and Kusco. I scrambled out of bed and followed Roza to my father's study. Our shadows – hers, large and imposing – mine, tall and thin – had flickered over the cracked walls of the twisting corridors. The smells of rain soaked dust, mildew, honeysuckle, jacaranda, lilac and night-scented jasmine, intermingled with those of Roza's cooking – bouillabaisse, fish and onions, musty apples, oranges and lemons, all these odors were borne on the cold drafts that blew through every window, every nook and cranny. We opened the ornately carved oak door to my father's inner sanctum, and were greeted by the sweet heavy scent of opium and cognac. Present too, were the sickening odors of illness and decay.

My father sat hunched over in his throne-like chair by the fire. Rudy stood, legs apart, as if he were on the deck of a ship at sea, his hands clasped behind his back; his back turned to the fire – a masterful pose. The firelight bounced off his pearlized white mask of a face, badly scarred, and as distorted as a work by Picasso. His obsidian black eyes gleamed and glittered. His long jet-black hair was tied in a ponytail at the nape of his broad neck.

My father looked like an old battle-worn lion – his golden mane tattered, discolored with grey. He was only in his late fifties, but he looked ancient. He wore his long fur-lined, faded wine and gold robe, and he looked like a Tartar, his long, bony, yellow-stained fingers encrusted with rings – one of which was the entwined dragons. We helped him to his feet, and with Roza leading the way, Kusco, Rudy and I managed to get him downstairs to the kitchen.

We ate by candlelight, the Mistral howling and protesting outside the shaking shutters. In the wee small hours of the new day,
while it was still night outside, Rudy eventually got to the point of
his visit – I was to be initiated into the society of spies. I was to spy
for them within the intellectual circles of Paris. There were fascist groups and communist groups. I was to join the latter and spy
on the former. I was to be on the look-out for fascist plots to get
France to side with Hitler's Reich, and I was to keep an eye on the
Stalinists within the communist camp, and report on their plots
against the more moderate socialist elements within the party. My
Dragon contact would be the old Georgian Cossack associate of
Rudy's, Lev Tashvin. We would meet as needed, and all I had to do,
if I needed him, was to leave a plain red card in a postage pigeon
hole, labeled Gustav Mickelhausen, in the offices of the Hotel de
Ville. Lev would meet me the next day at a small café – Chatte
Rouge – in a back alley of Montparnasse, at noon.

My father hated the whole idea, and made Rudy promise that
he'd guard me with his life, if necessary, and that he'd never use
me as sexual bait to get his information. Rudy had to promise on
the sacred text of the Dragons, but I knew it was an unrealistic
demand on my father's part. Rudy was unscrupulous enough not
to take an oath seriously, even such a powerful one, and I had fun
at his expense by being difficult. I took great enjoyment in baiting
the grand spymaster, and it gave my father the desperate reassurance he needed that I could look out for my own safety, and that
I was not easily led. Roza and Kusco were well aware that I was as
unscrupulous and ruthless as Rudy, and just as immoral.

Having tormented Rudy to the point of his losing all patience
with me, I flaunted off into the peach and blue-grey haze of a calmer dawn, to ride Dreyfus flat-out across the wet, windswept beach.
After we'd satisfied our need to break free, I reined in Dreyfus,
and patted his long, black, sand flecked mane – we were both covered in specks of wet sand – and we raised our heads to face the

rising sun in the east. As its sea salt apricot rays lit up our faces, my heart felt a sudden lurch, as if it spat out something, and I felt the kiss of a soft whispery breeze on my cheek. Dreyfus screamed, tossing his wet mane, while his dark eyes followed something into the sky, and then he whinnied again, softly, as he did when my father brought him apples. I suddenly felt that old familiar cold panic of abandonment. Rudy was approaching us along the cliff path, his long coat flying out behind him, and I knew my father had died with the dawn, as he'd always said he would – in the dawn after a Mistral, for the colors reminded him of a monsoon dawn in that far off place where we'd both left our hearts ten years before.

Kev awoke the next morning wishing he was wealthy enough to stay home and read all day long, but alas he wasn't. He was so immersed in Mrs. Chatsle's early life that he didn't want to come back to the daily drudgery of his existence. At least repairing cars gave him a chance to think over what he'd read. He suppressed the nagging notion that Mrs. Chatsle had been writing pure fiction, and even if she had been, it may have been a way for her to reveal certain truths about her life that would escape the attention of other interested, but decidedly more ruthless parties, and Kev had evidence aplenty that these existed.

CHAPTER ELEVEN

K ev had dinner with Kelly at some new Italian restaurant in town, called Luigi's. The food had been pretty good, and he'd brought a doggie bag back for old Tin Pan, who liked pasta and the occasional shrimp. Kev was feeling full, and he took some Alka Seltzer. He'd never get any work done at this rate. He had eaten too much, got too romantic and was now too sleepy to stay up reading. He lay there watching Tin Pan lick his chops that were redolent of garlic and marinara sauce. Kev could still taste the garlic bread, and the Chianti had given him a heavy head. The only way he'd finish the notes he'd found on his return to the apartment that night would be if they contained real eye-opening revelations. Kev started on the first page:

⇥⬩ ⬩⇤

Paris: Spring, 1936:
It is early Spring, and it is snowing. I am in Paris, studying at the Sorbonne. I have joined the communist intellectuals of the Left

Bank, but I have not joined the communist party yet. Rudy does not want me to, and I am relieved, for I detest political dogma, dogma of all kinds, and I do not wish to join anything. I sit on my cot bed in the cramped cell-like room, smoking a cigarette and gazing through my small window of yellowed glass over the rooftops of the city. The sky, the heavy clouds, the snow covered streets and roofs appear as if bathed in a golden haze. It all looks so heavenly, but looks are deceptive.

"Alphonse Lambert – that is the name of your target. He is a fascist, but he has approached us under the guise of being an ardent Stalinist. Ehrenberg passed him onto us, claiming that he is a card-carrying member of the party, but this is not so. Claudine tells us, he is a protégé of Brasillach's, and that he studied at Maurras's feet, that old arch-royalist! We want you to take him under your wing – see what he is after."

I got to my feet and lit a cigarette. My companion – a young man named Gilles – propped himself up on an elbow, and admired my naked form, which was slender – no fat anywhere – almost boy-like. I was superb in the art of lovemaking, and I was intelligent too, what more could a Frenchman ask?

"Well?" he pressed. I exhaled a long stream of smoke through my thin, finely formed nostrils.

"When does all this happen?" I asked, not at all interested.

"He is with us now, and he'll be at La Coupole tonight with Drabert and Clement."

"Do they know that he is a spy?"

Gilles nodded. "We all do."

"Risky, don't you think, to spread it around like that?"

"Dominique, you know we are all committed to the cause."

I turned to look at him. I could tell that he found all this caution tedious. He got out of bed, and strode in all his masculine glory to the toilet behind the screen in the corner. I smiled to myself as I heard the urine splash long and loud into the bowl. Gilles coughed as all men do, as if they want to clear all their orifices at one go. He poured the bucket of water down the toilet to flush it. He washed his hands and reached for a cigarette, narrowing his eyes sexily as he held it firmly between his thin lips and lit it. His soft light brown hair fell over his forehead. He inhaled, savoring the effects, and then he slowly exhaled, knowing that he looked sexy, which in turn made him feel sexy. He glanced at me, as I leaned against the sloping wall of the window alcove, watching him impassively. Gilles looked for his trousers. He was all business now, full of his own importance, and showing me, a mere woman, a sex toy, that the fun and games were over. He needn't have worried. I would do the job efficiently and effectively, and without the attendant egotism of a male. I had no messy emotions, and Gilles knew this. I bet that he often wondered whether I loved him, for to his male way of thinking I could not possibly love so well if I didn't love him, but then again he was French, and Frenchmen know that women can deceive in that regard, so Gilles would wonder, but not really care one way or another. I wasn't like the other girls, in that I didn't carry the deceit as far as to be clinging and pouting. I never asked when I'd see him again, and I never looked for him or put myself in his way, going to places I knew he'd be, at times I knew he'd be there, and I never asked him how he felt about me. He glanced over at me as he buttoned his shirt, his cigarette clamped between his thin lips. I gazed out of the window, wishing to have time to myself. I sensed his thoughts as he did up his shoelaces, one foot at a time up on my rickety old white wicker chair. He'd told me that I wasn't beautiful, but that I had a fascinating face, at which he never tired of looking. He took the cigarette out of his mouth and walked the two steps it took to be near me. He gently turned my face to his, and smiling softly, he looked into my eyes. I smiled, thinking that if he wanted to see tears, he was going to be disappointed.

"Alright?" he asked. I nodded. He knew that I'd have to sleep with Alphonse Lambert and become his girl, but he didn't mention it, and neither did I. What would be the point of such indulgence? These were desperate times after all. We both had a job to do. Gilles kissed me lightly, lingeringly, on the lips, and then he put on his jacket as he went out of the door, turning at the last moment to give me a boyish grin and a wink, then he was gone. I smoked my cigarette as I listened to him clatter down the narrow staircase. I opened the window to lean out and watch him walk up the alleyway with that jaunty energetic stride of his. He whistled the Internationale. He didn't look up, and I closed the window softly.

God, it was cold! I slipped into my baggy olive green corduroy trousers and pulled my fluffy old grey sweater over my head. I placed my pillow on the alcove window ledge, and leaning against it, I peered out at the snow tumbling from a grey-white sky. Rudy had kept his promise to my father, in that he had not asked me to sleep with anyone to gain information. I had acted on my own initiative in that regard. The fascists were frightening. The Communists were either ruthless street bullies, or impatient, ineffectual intellectuals. I didn't agree with Rudy that Stalin was in the pay of the capitalists. The new revolutionary regime in Russia had to be ruthless in establishing itself, to ward off all its enemies. Kirov and Trotsky had been too open to negotiation with the western democracies. The wily capitalists would have torn them apart. Stalin was the man to frighten the west, and to force the new order on a confused people faced with a totally different way of living and thinking. The irony lay in the fact that the communist regime under Stalin was just as oppressive as the Tsarist one it had replaced, but it had kept the capitalists at bay, and inspired the downtrodden working classes throughout the world.

Rudy saw this working class revolution in Russia, run by murderers and ruthless men, as ultimately doomed to failure, and he held firmly to the belief that this would be exactly the sort of communist leadership that the capitalists would want to see, would even pay to support and encourage. A tolerant working class leader, full of compassion and good ideas that would advance the workers and ease the lot of the poor and oppressed, would be the last thing the western capitalist oligarchies would want, especially under the precarious social and economic conditions of a depression worldwide. The capitalist states could not give these disenfranchised victims recourse to a caring, compassionate new classless society based on equality - a state that would drain the wealth of those rich capitalists and aristocratic classes by making them pay their fair share of taxes. No – a socialist state had to fail, had to be seen to be undesirable, even frightening and alarming. Stalin was their man, and he did the job beautifully, but I still did not believe that he was in the pay of the west, as did Rudy. Stalin would never take such risks, opening himself up to blackmail if he didn't do as the capitalists wanted – no, he'd never give anyone that kind of control over him. I also didn't think that the western capitalists were that clever in psychological warfare, to use a leader to provide them with propaganda they could use to make communism and socialism seem so evil and oppressive. The situation was nowhere near as contrived and complicated as Rudy liked to make out. I believed that we fell into such situations without much thought at all. Humans were not good at seeing the ramifications of their present actions way down the road. The long-term view and the big picture were difficult for the less than clever men who ran our governments. The complex present gave them enough to wrangle with, without worrying about the complexities of an unknown future outcome of their present actions.

I snuggled into my pillow and took some long puffs on my cigarette. The setting sun had managed to penetrate the dark snow clouds in a burst of glory that filled the tiny apartment with a golden haze. I raised my face to its dying rays, and that brought back memories of that long ago time that, over the years, I had tried so unsuccessfully to bury in the far recesses of my mind – memories of an exotic, heavenly scented place, memories of the loving embraces and reassurances of a beautiful young mother, who had spent the hot, mellow, golden sunsets with me, teaching me, laughing with me, singing soul-caressing lullabies. I closed my eyes and sank back into a blessed innocence.

Kev found himself in that strangely sexual, hypnotic state of falling in love with the young woman, Dominique D'Emeraude. He had been aroused by her almost mystical sensuality. He had been even more excited by her ideas. She had advocated some heady stuff, and hinted at a less than honorable agenda followed by the western democracies. Well heck, he knew, all the people knew, that the wealthy get richer, and will do anything to perpetuate that status quo, and people who help them achieve this get rich and powerful support for so doing. To consolidate their hold on power, government leaders the world over suck up to their wealthy backers, and stick it to their people. A leader, who won't do this, doesn't last long. Kev began to feel an edgy precariousness to all this, but he had to continue. This was just the kind of stuff with which Kit may have become involved, inadvertently, and it may have got her killed.

The next morning, Kev took all the notes he already had and locked them in his safe deposit box at the bank.

CHAPTER TWELVE

Mrs. Nguyen had read the diary for 1932 to me, and we'd sat in silence, sipping our green tea.

"She was a communist then?" I began tentatively. Mrs. Nguyen pursed her thin lips, and shifted herself on the hard kitchen chair. She had refused to move to a more comfortable chair, and she had held herself stiffly while she had translated. "Would you like to sit in the living room?" I pressed. She shook her head. She seemed to be deep in thought. I sighed, and was about to get up to rinse out my teacup.

"It is of no consequence," she said suddenly. I sat back down, only to start to rise again, thinking she had decided to go into the living room. "I mean that it is of no consequence if she were a communist or not," she added. I sat down again.

"It would be of incredible significance here, if she had been a communist," I replied. "Her husband supplied materials for the military. There were rumors that he worked for the CIA; that was why he was away a great deal. He traveled all over the world with his work."

Mrs. Nguyen looked at me as if she were wondering what to say next.

"I mean that it is of no consequence who or what this Dominique D'Emeraude is or was. She is a figment of the woman's imagination. We are reading works of fiction."

"Do you really believe that?" I asked, a look of skepticism on my face. She nodded enthusiastically, and smiled broadly, showing her worn down, brown teeth.

"She traveled with her husband. She must have learned much, seen much, and she would have had time to make up stories while her husband did his work. These diaries dated way back are not any older looking or more worn by time than these more recent ones. I think that she bought these lovely notebooks on her trips to Asia, and she pretended that each was a different year in the life of this girl."

"You don't understand. There was a murder here in 1964. It concerned a young girl, who may have been involved with Andy Chatsle in some way. The folks around here think that Kitty Occley, she was the girl, found out something, and the Chatsles had to silence her."

Mrs. Nguyen gave me a long hard look.

"I think that is silly local supposition. When a girl is killed, there are many reasons, especially where love between the poor and the rich are concerned. I have heard this story of Kitty Occley. Many still talk of it here. These Chatsles could have been innocent, and were in no way connected to the murder."

"Do you know how Mrs. Chatsle died?"

"She was killed by that blue car there." Mrs. Nguyen pointed to the Thunderbird on the driveway, and she hung her head. I told her that it was under very strange circumstances. The car was an excellent car, and it had been parked on the flat driveway. Someone must have released the brake and pushed it, dragging Mrs. Chatsle along with it to the edge of the slope, for the whole tragic thing to have happened. Mrs. Nguyen kept her head down, but shook it from side to side.

"No, no," she muttered. "Your imagination is too active."

I got up and decided to let it go at that. I asked her if she wanted to continue with the diary for 1936. She spent several moments just staring at the book, her long, thin, bony hand gently caressing its cover.

"I do not want to do this one, "she said finally. I was stunned. She looked up at me. "I am tired. I do not feel well." I felt awful, thinking that I had been too pushy. I had worn her out.

"I am so sorry Mrs. Nguyen. Your English is so good that I forget just how taxing this translation must be for you. Please let me take you home. We can do this another day, when you are feeling better."

She raised her hand. "No, please. I will send my granddaughter to do this diary for you. She will come after school." I protested, saying that My-An would be too tired and too busy with her schoolwork. We could wait. She got her things together, and we walked outside. I don't know if I wanted to test her, but some devilment made me go to the Thunderbird. I opened the passenger door for her to get in. She stood on the kitchen step, and shook her head. Her face was pale and she looked terrified. I relented. She was ill after all, and elderly. How cruel and thoughtless of me to tease her this way. I got the jeep instead. We did not talk all the way into town. She did not turn and bow when she left me, but hurried into the florist shop. I parked the jeep and followed her. She had disappeared into the back room. Her daughter, Chao, greeted me, a look of concern on her face.

"I just wanted to make sure Mrs. Nguyen is alright," I said. "She seems to be ill."

Chao was nervous and concerned too, so I offered to drive them both to the hospital, but Mrs. Nguyen reappeared, looking much better. She explained that she had drunk too much tea, and needed a bathroom, but had been too shy to use ours, so she had needed to get home quickly. She apologized, and we all laughed. I asked her one more time if she was sure that she didn't need to go to hospital for a check-up, and she assured me that she didn't. She did look much better. I thanked her again for her help with the translations, and then I left. I got into the jeep, and before driving off, I glanced up at the apartment window, and sure enough, the slat in the blinds fell back into place suddenly.

I was alone with Bubs and Bugsy that evening. Rob was working until very late, and Tali and Sean had practice until late after school, and then they were going to a friend's party. I ate my dinner in front of the fire in the living room. Suddenly Bubs ran to the front door, barking his head off. Bugsy hopped under the couch. I grabbed a poker. We never had visitors after dark, who hadn't called ahead to say that they were coming. I peered out from behind the heavy drapes, and there, standing in the lights of the terrace, was a very cold and scared My-An. I grabbed Bubs by the collar and let her in, scolding her the while for coming out alone in the dark, and walking up the long, scary driveway by herself. She admitted that she'd been terrified. I took her parka, and sat her by the fire, while I got her a cup of hot chocolate.

"Honestly, My-An, I never expected you to come out tonight to do the translation. I told your mother and grandmother that it wasn't urgent. It could wait. I will pay you big time for doing this."

She shook her head. "No payment is necessary. You are very generous to us as it is, very kind, but I would like to do this as soon as possible, so that I can get back to my own studies."

I nodded, and went into the kitchen to retrieve the diary for 1936. I flipped through the silken, scented pages, as I walked back into the living room and the warmth of the roaring fire.

"Your grandmother thinks that it is all fiction, that Mrs. Chatsle was writing a novel." My-An smiled nervously and nodded in agreement. She didn't respond with any chitchat, but immediately got down to perusing the pages. She read silently to herself, and then, haltingly, began to translate each page:

⇒⋕ ⋕⇐

Paris: Autumn, 1936:

The most amazing and unthinkable thing has happened – Roza phoned me today, all the way from home (Marseilles). My God, I wish I had been there when they'd arrived! Roza and Kusco must have been shocked to their very core - two youngsters appearing like that, out of the night, fresh off Desforges's ship that had arrived from Saigon, and Roza and Kusco most probably thought that they were the usual political exiles looking for a helping hand, but they weren't. Well the boy was. He had come to France to escape arrest by the authorities in Saigon, but the girl had another agenda entirely. Roza wheezed with excitement as she told me her news. She could barely contain herself as she lowered the boom.

"Ah my beloved one, you will never guess who this child is. She stood shivering in the dark, and told Kusco and me that she was looking for Louis Thierry D'Emeraude. We told her the sad news that he had died. She took a few seconds to adjust to this, and then she raised her eyes to ours and asked after you, Dominique D'Emeraude. We told her that you were a student in Paris, and no longer involved with helping Vietnamese political exiles. We asked her how she knew of you, and then she told us...My God, Dominique, she said that she is your sister!"

Roza waited, guessing that I needed time to digest this stunning piece of information. Actually, I froze. I saw in my mind's eye, my mother running away from me through the crowds in the market square. She clutched the baby to her chest. She ignored my cries, begging her to take me too. The baby – I tried to focus my memory on the baby. It had looked like any other normal Vietnamese baby – from what I could make out. It had a shock of black baby hair, and the eyes had been slanted and black, but I had not been sure about this. I may have seen it that way, because in my self pity, I believed my mother had left me, because of my mixed up looks, and she now had the child she wanted – a Vietnamese baby that looked the part.

"Mino, Mino, are you still there?" Roza's voice brought me back to the present startling situation.

"What is her name, and how old is she?"

"She says that her name is Lien, and that she is fourteen years old."

"Does she look Vietnamese?" – a long pause – Roza was trying to figure out my state of mind. She knew all about my sorrow. She had listened to my nightly sobs, my adolescent rants at my father about my looks, and how I, too, had wanted to look Vietnamese, so that my mother would not have left me. How I must have hurt him when I'd reached that uncaring, selfish age! Roza took the plunge:

"She looks Vietnamese. Her eyes and hair are black."

"Well, the age is right. I don't know if my mother had a girl or a boy. Did my father know?"

"Yes, Pantin told him before you left Saigon that Marie-Claire had a daughter."

"Must be her then. Who is the other youngster?"

"A young boy of eighteen - his father has sent him to Paris to study engineering, and to get him out of Saigon, where he is wanted by the police for his nationalist activities. The father works for the French colonial government, and he strongly objects to his son's fight to free Vietnam from colonial rule. The father did not know of Captain Desforges's connection to the Indochinese nationalist groups here. He had to book his son on the earliest ship out of Saigon to avoid his arrest, and Desforges' boat had been it. The young boy could hardly contain his excitement when Desforges told him he could continue his fight in Paris.

The girl's passage had been agreed to by Desforges long before the boy turned up in need of help. Pantin had been contacted by Marie-Claire. She and her husband had to escape to the North, and their life there would be extremely dangerous and primitive. They had taught the girl themselves, but Marie-Claire told Pantin that she had reached the stage in her studies where she would need professional teaching, and so she should go to school in France and train to become a doctor, then she could return to help them in their fight for independence. Pantin brought the girl back to Saigon, and shipped her out with Desforges. Naturally, when they found that they were fighting for the same cause, the youngsters became firm friends. The boy had heard of Lien's parents' bravery in attacking French garrisons and strongholds. They were his heroes, so naturally he was thrilled to be sharing the same fate as their daughter. It looks to me as if the girl hero-worships this boy. She follows his every move with childlike infatuation. She is of that tender age when young girls have such infatuations for older boys, and this youth is quite handsome, quite the looker. He is very smart too. I think that your little sister is going through the pangs of first love, Mino. What shall Kusco and I do with them? He is to attend university in Paris, but what shall I do with her? She will want to go to Paris with him. Can you find her a good school there? I know that she cannot live with you. The boy has lodgings arranged for him already by his father."

The Spanish Civil War had broken out that summer, and I was to go to fight on the Republican side with Rudy and Lev, and the fascist spy, Alphonse Lambert would be with us. We wanted to see who his contacts were in Spain, and then we'd kill him. I had been successful in seducing Alphonse enough that he believed that I'd betray my leftist friends to follow him, that I'd become a fascist. His arrogant belief that women who give their bodies also give their mind and spirit over to their lovers was such that I had easily convinced him to reveal his secret mission to me. We were lovers. I had no room in my apartment for a child, and one from Indochina. My motives would be immediately suspect, and it might show him that I still harbored communist leanings, as the communists and other socialist parties also supported the Indochinese fight for independence. I thought for a moment about this. Alphonse may like it. It would show that the communists still trusted us, and it might provide him and his extreme Right-Wing friends with information about who in the government was working to break up France's empire; not that I'd ever let him get within a hundred miles of such information. I'd kill him first. There was still the fact that we were lovers, and couldn't share the apartment with a young girl. No, it was impossible.

Roza called again the following day. They had arrived at a solution. Lien would travel to Paris with the boy. He'd contacted his relatives, who lived on the outskirts of the city, and they had agreed to take Lien. They lived near a good school, and she could go there and board with them. Roza and Kusco had sufficient money in the funds my father had left them to help Indochinese students get board, schooling and work while in France. Roza added that Lien still wished to meet with me. She had a letter for me from our mother. My mind and heart exploded into a trillion pieces. I had to take several moments to get myself together. My mother had written to me. I would read her words, hold a letter she had written, touched with those long elegant fingers. She had thought of me at the time she had written the letter at least. It was possible that this long awaited missal would explain all at last, and tell me that she'd always loved me, and had been torn apart at having to leave me behind, because my green eyes would have betrayed our tie to the hated French. Oh God, if she loved me, grieved at giving me up, then my whole life would be devoted to her cause. Maybe she had loved me more than this Vietnamese daughter, and maybe she had told me so in the letter. I had to get hold of that letter at all costs. It would mean my salvation, my rebirth, even if it meant that I had to see a half sister I loathed and envied with all my heart.

On a cold, rainy October afternoon, so dark and dreary that the lights of the station café and magazine stalls were switched on way ahead of dusk, we three stood on the platform in the clouds of steam that belched forth from the huge black behemoth that had brought them to Paris from the sunny south. We looked at one another in silence. I studied the young girl's face, looking for traces of the mother whose image had filled my dreams every night before I'd fallen asleep. She studied me just as closely, looking for what I didn't know, possibly a trace of the Vietnamese heritage I supposedly shared with her. Had I detected a gleam of relief in her eyes; relief that I was an aberration after all, and that she had been the chosen one? Had our mother told her so, and now she saw it with her own eyes, and was basking in self-satisfaction? I felt tears of anger swell in my throat, and I quickly turned to the boy. He bowed his head in greeting. He also looked a little stunned at my appearance. Had he expected me to look Vietnamese? He took my breath away for a second too, for he was extremely handsome; tall, slender athletic build, black hair swept off his forehead, kind black eyes, finely chiseled aristocratic bone structure. His manners and his French were impeccable, but I spoke to him in Vietnamese.

"What is your name?" I asked with a deliberate sneer.

"Khien."

"He is a hero," the girl interrupted, angry at the superior tone I had adopted towards him. "Like me, he wants a free, independent Vietnam. We want the French out." - Well, that put her cards on the table!

"My, my," I replied coldly. "You have cut your teeth on nationalist propaganda and dogma to be sure. Are you capable of thinking for yourself, or do your parents tell you what to think?" That, I hoped, put my cards on the table. There must have been some kind of big sister reflex, whether I acknowledged her as my sister or not, for I further emphasized my contempt for her outburst by flicking my finger against her forehead. She recoiled in amazement at the familiarity and physicality of such a gesture. Well, she had to get used to having a big sister. I pre-empted her. I was our mother's first born, and entitled to respect from a younger sibling. I showed her that I understood this. She had not thought of me as an elder sister until then, as was evident from the look of surprise on her face, that was followed by a look that bore traces of amusement, pleased amusement, as if she were happy to have been treated like a younger sister. "Do I have any more rude younger brothers and sisters?" I asked, hoping that I did, for that would not make her special in our mother's affections, while I was still our mother's only half-breed child, and her firstborn. She looked amazed at this too. She hadn't expected me to be like this. She'd expected a French girl, with French values, who never had known, or wanted to know, her Vietnamese relations. Unfortunately, she shook her head. She was my mother's only other child. Good, then I could keep on hating her.

The boy, Khien, explained that his relatives had given him their address. He could take a taxi there, and maybe I'd send Lien on later to his other uncle's house. I could go along too, to satisfy myself that she was in good hands. The girl shot me a sour look. It was evident that she wanted to go with the boy right there and then. They both watched me in silence for a few moments. The boy, I thought, was eager to discharge his caretaking duties and be on his way. He was eighteen, after all, and Lien was only fourteen, and bookish-looking with it. She did not look anything like the mother I'd remembered. I'd noticed, being experienced in such things, that the boy had looked at me quite differently. He'd blushed every time I'd looked his way, and what is more my sister had noticed it too, and was angered by it. Well, well, let me see - had I got the love and attention of someone she loved, most probably yearned for with all her adolescent heart? What if he abandoned his friendship with her, because she wasn't the right age and didn't have the right looks, for me, who was almost the right age, and had the right looks, well at least those that attracted him? What a turn up for the books that would be! It was a revenge beautifully and skillfully crafted by Fate.

"That is alright," I said. "She can go with you. You can drop her off at your uncle's. Here is your taxi fare." I handed them some money, but he refused to take it.

"The lady in Marseilles gave us more money than we will need. I have sufficient to get myself to my relatives' home and Lien to my other relatives' house. Do not trouble yourself." He seemed angry with me now, and this pleased the girl.

"Look, my apartment isn't far from here," I said, having a sudden change of heart. I hadn't finished playing with them yet. "Come and have some bouillabaisse with me, and then I'll send you on your way." It was a safe invitation as Alphonse was away on business. He'd gone to Berlin, unbeknownst to our communist friends, or so he thought. He was to get his instructions from his SS masters for our planned trip to Spain. I'd gathered that he was to try and set up a trap for an important German anti-Nazi, making it look like this man was supplying arms to the Republican side, when the Nazis had opted to support Franco's Nationalists. Rudy, Lev and I were to foil this plot, and also get rid of some nasty Stalinists on our side – Stalinists who would accompany Rudy to France, preparatory to their trip across the Spanish border. Stalin wanted them to kill Rudy on this trip, but we would kill them instead, and Rudy would let Stalin know that they had died in the Spanish war, and that he was returning to Germany, not Russia, to set up his communist underground there to fight the Nazis. Let Stalin deal with the rampant paranoia that switch in events would create in his evil mind – a Rudy Von Silvren on the loose and beyond control would be enough to give anyone rampant paranoia.

We stood in the downpour and I hailed a taxi. I looked at their sad, forlorn faces as we sped through the busy Parisian streets. People were making their way home through the relentless rain and chill gloom of an October evening. The lights of the many shops cast an orange glow on the wet pavements. Their faces peered out of the rain drenched car window - even the rain was dirty, and ran in dirty rivulets down the glass. What an introduction to the beautiful city of lights!

My apartment was just as dreary, even though I kept it neat and clean. One could still smell the toilet, despite all the disinfectant I had poured down it. The windows let in the cold, damp air. The youngsters looked exceedingly depressed to say the least. I made them take off their soaking raincoats, with which no doubt, Roza had supplied them. We had silky black hair that clung now in oily strands to our wet faces. We had that in common at least.

I prattled on about the Sorbonne, my studies, the wonders of Paris, while I fixed them a meal. They listened quietly, and every so often exchanged dismal looks of dejected acceptance, that here they were, and here they'd have to stay for the time being. Had I turned out to be the sister they had expected? The girl had not seemed to have harbored any hopes that I might be friendly, but if the boy had a more optimistic outlook on her behalf, then he'd been proved wrong. You could see this in his face. He was worried about her, but he whispered reassurances to her that his family would be kind. She'd smiled weakly and nodded her head. She was playing the 'little girl lost and in need of a brave boy's protection' routine like an expert. I'd seen the calculating glint in her eyes, and I sensed that she was quite resourceful in looking after herself, and in getting what she wanted.

When we had eaten, I went downstairs to hail a taxi to take them to their respective addresses. Just before they got into the waiting taxi, I asked the girl if she had a letter for me. She gasped, and said that of course she had. She dug into the pocket of her wet raincoat and pulled out a large dampish envelope. There was no writing on it. She pressed it into my hand and followed the boy into the car. They drove off. I wondered briefly if I'd see them again, but I could hardly contain my emotions about the letter I held in my hands. My mother had communicated with me after all these years. How had she felt as she'd written it? Had she cried, tears coursing down her face, tears of abject misery and regret?

It's not worth writing about here. Suffice it to say that it is not worth mentioning, let alone recording here, for it revealed a lack of acknowledgement of my own identity, the lack of any kind of interest, let alone that of a mother for a child she had abandoned. She hadn't addressed the letter to me. She hadn't written my name at all. She'd asked only that I look after my sister.

━━◅╫ ╫▻━━

My-An stammered in confusion. "That is all," she said, meekly, hanging her head as if in shame.

"My God!" I exclaimed. "Poor Dominique! Her mother's abandonment of her was complete. Oh, poor child!" I thought to myself that this might have explained a lot about Mrs. Chatsle's cold, distant personality, but she had been a loving mother to her son. There had been no doubt that Andy had meant the world to her.

My-An offered no comment. She pulled on her parka, and refused any more cookies and hot chocolate. She needed to go she said, so I drove her home.

On my way back to the house, I prayed that Rob had returned. I never had returned alone to the empty house at night. Bubs and Bugsy were in the jeep with me. For some reason, when I'd taken My-An home, I'd taken the animals along. My-An had looked surprised when I had carried Bugsy into the jeep after putting in Bubs. She had expected Bubs, as I never went anywhere without him, but the rabbit too? She had looked at me as if I were crazy.

As I drove back up the driveway, I noticed that there were no lights on in the house. My heart froze. I knew I'd left the lights on. I had put the guard around the fireplace, and I had left all the downstairs lights on on purpose. The house was plunged in total darkness. I don't know if Bubba picked up on the fear I felt, but he started to growl, a low threatening growl, and his hackles were raised. There was no way I was going into that house. I stopped the car just before we got to the slope that went up to the flat top of the crest. I stopped right next to the old sycamore against which Mrs. Chatsle had died. Bubba's growls had deepened, and his ears were laid back, his fangs bared. I had never seen him like this before.

The blue Thunderbird was parked on the flat surface in front of the kitchen entrance, but it wasn't parked facing the garage on the other side of the slope, as I'd left it. It had been turned around to face the driveway toward the main gate. It faced us. There was no moonlight. The car stood there in perfect darkness, which made its presence more ominous. I turned the key in the ignition of the jeep, but there was no sound. The engine was silent. All was silent, except for the faint sound, through the closed windows, of the tall trees swaying in the wind, and Bubba's throaty growls. I felt the hair rise on the back of my neck and goose bumps form all over. It was freezing cold. I couldn't take much more of it. I would just have to move or freeze. I threw an old car rug over Bugsy, and pulled him close to me. I tried to get Bubs to calm down and huddle with us, but he wouldn't. Then his growls turned to angry frightened barks, and he became restless, jumping all over us in his eagerness to attack something or someone outside. I pushed at him, and peered out into the night. I couldn't see a thing. Then I noticed that the Thunderbird was moving ever so slowly towards the edge of the slope. My heart seemed to stop beating as I watched, open-mouthed, my throat too dry to scream, the car's slow, yet persistent progress that put it on a collision course with us. I quickly unlocked the door, and carrying Bugsy, I struggled out of my seat belt and got out of the jeep. Bubba was out already. He'd pushed his way over us when I'd opened the door. He bounded up the slope to the Thunderbird, but he faced the house, barking the whole time. I yelled for him to come back, but he wouldn't heed me. He had the good sense to stay to the side of the Thunderbird, and I carried Bugsy off the driveway and out of reach of the car, should it plunge down the slope. Suddenly Bubba stopped barking, and with his ears alert, he stared back towards the main gate. I also turned to look in that direction, and there were headlights approaching. Rob's truck pulled into view through the swaying branches of the evergreens. Never had I been so glad to see him in all my life.

When we were safely ensconced in the warm living room, with all the lights on, and glasses of wine in hand, Rob tried to convince me that we needed to find other accommodations until they had finished building our new home. He was bound and determined to get rid of the Thunderbird, but I wouldn't hear of it. Bubba had calmed down, and was dozing in front of the fire.

"There may have been coyotes hanging around the house. Bubba hates coyotes. You know that. Looking back on it all, it seems the most likely explanation for his behavior. Bubba only ever barks at coyotes. He'd never run off after them. He isn't stupid, and he stayed with me and Bugsy. He'd only gone as far away from us as the top of the slope, and he wasn't afraid of the car at all."

"How do you account for the car moving of its own accord?" Rob asked in a voice gruff with emotion. I had given him such a fright, standing there, clutching Bugsy to me, tears running down my face, shaking fit to bust with absolute terror.

"I don't know, Rob. How do you account for the jeep stalling like that at the same time? Is the jeep possessed too? Do we own killer vehicles?" Rob was not to be teased out of this.

"The jeep started fine for me," he said. "It's possible, that in your panic you may have stalled it in some way. Tali kept doing that when she was learning how to drive, just because she was nervous."

"I think I may have exaggerated the movement of the Bluebird too, Rob. It was so dark, it seemed as if the car moved, but you know that when we looked at it, it was still close to the kitchen door, and only slightly forward on the flat. I can't recall if it had been facing the garage or the main gate before I'd taken My-An home. I may have got it wrong." Rob couldn't remember either, which way the car had been parked. Sean and Tali also couldn't remember. Sean thought it had faced the main gate, whereas Tali thought it had faced the garage, because she remembered me parking it that way when I'd come home from shopping the day before. I'd remembered that too, which was why I'd been terrified to see it facing the other way around, but unbeknownst to me, Sean had moved it to get his own car by, and he couldn't remember how he'd parked it. The lights had gone out in the house, because the fuse had blown, so that explained why the house had been dark.

"Goddamn fuse box is ancient," snarled Rob.

The next morning, after everyone had left, I took my coffee outside and checked out the car. It was a beautiful car, so streamlined and strong. I felt safe when out driving in it. I placed my hand on its shining hood.

"I defended you last night. I know you were facing the garage, but somehow you were turned around. I think you were meant to save Bubba, Bugsy and me from whatever danger was in the house. I, like Bubba, had sensed a real danger emanating from the house that night, but whoever or whatever had been there had evaporated, its evil gone by the time we'd all tumbled in and groped around for flashlights. The house had been at peace since, but a sadness had remained. Well I for one was not going to give up on the place or the car. I was going to solve this thing, and banish the evil forever.

I had hidden in my grief. That letter had hurt my very soul to hear my anguish all over again, even though I am passed caring for all that pertained to that earthly life, except for these last few transgressions that need to be

addressed. I had sought release by returning to the cosmic consciousness, and by so doing, I had left the house unprotected. Sal Bremer had been in extreme danger, but fortunately I had been convinced, yet again, that here I must stay to see it through, and the dog had helped, and just in time my helpers had been able to use the car to terrify Sal and keep her away from the house. She had sensed this. Thank goodness Fate had brought this woman to the old house at this oh so crucial time!

CHAPTER THIRTEEN

Kelly Flynn was in love, and all was well with the world. She had found the perfect guy at last. It had taken her until her early forties to find him, but she'd found him. She had not wanted children, so there wasn't any pressure there to hurry up on things. She'd let this relationship follow its own sweet course, which she hoped would extend right on through to the end of her life or Kev's, whichever came first. She wanted to spend every second with Kev, but she had come to realize that he was serious about tracking down his sister's killer, and until she could prove to him that by now, thirty years down the road, maybe his efforts were all in vain, she'd have to back off some, and let him do what he felt he had to, no matter how pointless she thought it all was.

Kev on the other hand was beginning to regret his commitment to this relationship with Kelly. It had been stupid of him. He sensed that he was on the verge of cracking something big, and it would not be without its dangers. Kelly would be a point of weakness in his armor if these people behind Kit's death should prove to be as ruthless as he believed they were.

Kelly had agreed to their getting together on weekends and Wednesday nights, four nights out of the week. Kev wondered if he hadn't been too generous there. He only had three nights free to follow where these notes led him.

He had found the notes taken from the 1936 diary in his locked lunchbox. How had she managed that, whoever she was? He had read them over dinner, with Tin Pan snoring by his side. Kev's notes, however, had included the last paragraph that My-An had decided not to translate for Sal Bremer.

Dominique D'Emeraude had written a concluding paragraph after reading her mother's letter, which had been cruel in its lack of any kind of feeling for the loving and gentle little daughter she had abandoned.

⊶ ⊷

"That night a heart-rending scream, that sent shivers down the spines of the Parisians within earshot, rent the cold wet night air, and the Cosmos coiled in on itself in pain, anguish and torment. If what follows in my life's story shocks you, it was that night I read my mother's letter that started it all. I would punish her by having nothing more to do with my half sister, Lien. She'd get by. Oh, I'd like to have tormented her, to have made her life a living hell, but I knew that Roza and Kusco would lose all respect for me, and the memory of my father's ability to forgive my mother provided me with a more measured perspective, even if I did not exactly possess his capacity to forgive. No, I could not forgive."

⊶ ⊷

Kev sat there, his mouth dry with fear. What had poor Kit stumbled across out there at Dub Mason's dingy backwater all those years ago? A prince she had said, who needed her - a soul in anguish, whom she could help. That would have appealed to Kit. Had Kit mistaken a tale of horror for a fairytale? Kev couldn't stand it. He felt shivers run up and down his spine. The sun had risen already, and he'd be starting another day without having slept, but it was a new day for him, one that offered hope that this obsession was finally going to pay off. He got up.

"Come on Tin Pan, I need to get the taste of this out of my mouth. Want some eggs and bacon?" The cat had stretched, flexed his shivs and followed Kev into the kitchen. Kev felt both excited and scared, wanting both to back away from it all and to plunge on in. He was on the point of avenging Kit's murder, of bringing her killer to a justice that was long overdue, of finally being her knight in shining armor, the big brother she'd expected to right all wrongs done her, to save her from all harm... here Kev broke down and sobbed his heart out.

A pair of rough, tough, muddy boots appeared at the side of the truck under which Kev was lying, repairing a hole in the exhaust.

"Kev, it's Rob Bremer. I need to talk to you for a moment." Kev slid out, his face covered in grease, and he lay there, peering up at Rob, who stood with the bright sun behind him, making it hard for Kev to see his face, but he sensed that Rob was upset about something. Kev scrambled to his feet, and wiped his hands on an oily grease cloth.

"What can I do for you, Rob?"

Rob grimaced - obviously what he had to say did not come easily.

"You're going to think I'm mad, Kev, but I gotta ask you about that darn Blue..." Rob corrected himself, looking even more embarrassed. "Thunderbird of the Chatsles. Did you do the repairs on it for Mrs. Chatsle?"

Kev sighed, and kicked a stone around with the tip of his shoe.

"Why are you asking, Rob? The police asked me if I'd worked on her car when she was killed, and I told them that I hadn't been anywhere near it. I was their prime suspect. Seems like I'm the prime suspect when anyone dies under mysterious circumstances around here."

Rob looked awful. "God, Kev, I never would think that you killed her. No, it's not that. You're going to think I'm mad, but it's that darn car." Rob went on to tell Kev all the weird things that the car had done. "Could it move of its own accord like that?" he asked finally. "That's all I want to know."

Kev shook his head and smiled. "Well it could, if the brake was left off on a slope. There were some cars recalled some years ago, because they jumped a gear if the car was left with the engine still turning over. A car with a powerful engine like the Thunderbird could slip gears if parked with the engine still on, I suppose."

"In reverse gear too?" asked Rob.

"Sure. It's possible. I remember Mrs. Chatsle buying the car, but she didn't bring it to me to fix, and that was surprising, because I always had fixed their cars. I'm guessing that there never had been anything wrong with it, or I'm sure she'd have got me to repair it, or check it over. She hadn't had it very long as I recall. Want me to check it out for you?"

Rob nodded. "If you wouldn't mind, Kev."

"Not at all. You can bring it in tomorrow."

Kev asked Rob to get some coffee with him, and so they went over to the diner. On their way across the track, full of large muddy puddles, which they had to negotiate, Rob told Kev that he and Sean had left the motor running with the car on the flat at the edge of the slope, and the car had not moved out of neutral. They had pushed it and jumped on it while it was in park, and got no response. Kev shook his head, not knowing what else to suggest, but he'd look it over in any case, and repeat the tests.

"Hey boys, what'll you have?" shouted Patti, as they entered the over heated diner that reeked of burning hamburger grease and strong coffee. The smoke filled air stung their eyes and burned their throats.

"Two coffees, please Ma," Kev shouted back. He and Rob settled in a window booth. Kev gave a smile, tinged with some irony, at the now empty booth at the end of the bar. Old Bud Thurow had died long ago, and gone to that great greasy diner in the sky, or had he been reincarnated as one of those flies up in the overhead light? The two men made some desultory remarks about the weather until their coffee came. Patti stopped to ask after Sal and the family, and then she was called away to tend to some impatient customers at the bar. She kept a curious eye on the two men the while. Their conversation seemed to have taken a more serious and thoughtful turn. They spoke in hushed voices, their heads bent close together over the greasy tabletop. They clutched their coffee mugs in their hands, but they didn't drink. Patti was dying to join in, but a noisy group of lumberjacks had stormed in out of a sudden sun shower, and they were hungry and thirsty. Patti tried to keep an eye on Kev and Rob Bremer, while she poured coffee and saw to the food orders. What the devil was Kev telling Rob to make Rob turn pale and worried like that? What did Rob say that made Kev shake his head so angrily? Patti desperately needed to know what was going on between them. Thirty years had gone by for chrissake, yet why did she feel deep in her bones that they were discussing Kit's murder and Kit's relationship to the Chatsles. Patti knew that Kev never had given up his search for Kit's killer, but in the last few years he'd kept tight-lipped about it. He used to share everything with her. Well, it had been her fault. She had screamed at him one day that she was fed up with it all. She wanted to move on; enjoy life again. She was sick of all this stuff and nonsense about conspiracies, ghosts... but what Patti really had felt had been terror. Patti had been scared out her wits at what Kev might discover.

"Well, that's it, Rob, all of it. I'm sorry I trespassed in the house. I should have told Mike, but I hadn't known about the diaries before. Mrs. Chatsle hadn't told me about them. We'd just worked on her MIA stuff. She'd sort of hinted at writing journals over the years, and believe me, my ears pricked up at that. I knew that if they existed, then I wanted to read them, had to get my hands on them. Then she died and I started getting these notes, like a damn paper chase, that led me to the attic. I'm sorry. I know I should have told Mike about it all, but I just had to read those diaries for 1964, and the years before and after. I had to find out what Mrs. Chatsle had written about Kit's involvement with Andy. There was nothing, nothing at all, not even a mention of the murder and the trial – nothing."

"Goddamn it, Kev! It was tantamount to breaking and entering for chrissake! Have you been up there since we moved in, because I could kill you for frightening us with all the weird goings on?"

Kev shook his head in denial. "No, definitely not, Rob. I wouldn't do anything like that – trespass on your privacy. No, as I told you, someone leaves notes for me, notes on what's in the diaries. I have no idea who it is." Kev paused unsure of whether to tell Rob about the threatening note he'd received. He decided to take the plunge. "I was threatened. It's got to be by someone other than the person who leaves the notes, because these people, whoever they are, don't want me to find out what's in those diaries."

Rob paled visibly. "Do you think that Sal is in danger too, because last night was scary – I mean definitely scary, not just harmless little happenings. I sensed real danger when we went into that dark house. Bubba felt it too, and Sal too, I think, although she loves that place and won't admit to it. I'm terrified for her and the kids. I tell you, Kev, I'm going back there and moving us all out tonight."

"Wait, Rob. I don't think Sal is in any danger. I don't think that there's an evil ghost lurking in the house at all – a good spirit maybe. I told you that I didn't want to find out who the girl was who was leaving me the notes, because I wanted to believe that it was Kit. Crazy - I know."

Rob gave a harsh laugh. "Mike feels that way too. I think he seriously hopes that if there are ghosts there, then maybe Fletch will come through too."

"Let's get Mike in on this. I know he'll most probably prosecute me for trespassing, but I think he needs to know all this. Can we all get together at the house tonight? Sal and I have been wasting our time going over the same ground. If you and Sal are up to it, we can get through those diaries in half the time. I think the threat was aimed at me, and me alone."

"What makes you so sure of that, Kev? Last night was definitely a threat made towards us. We have to live in the damn place."

"Don't think I'm crazy, Rob, but I get the feeling that you're protected. There is some being in that house that protects you. I don't know if it's Kit or Mrs. C. herself, but I think that you are actually safer where you are."

Rob was skeptical, afraid to risk his family. All this talk about ghosts from men who should know better was sending icy shivers down his spine.

"Alright, come over tonight after dinner. I'll make sure that Mike is there, although I can't guarantee that he won't want your butt in a sling over those diaries."

Kev smiled with relief. He and Rob stood and shook hands. Then Rob left, pulling up the collar of his parka against the torrential rain outside, rain that fell in bright sunshine! Kev waved at Patti, and was about to leave too, but Patti called to him over the heads of the rowdy men at the bar.

"What gives, Kev? What's with Rob Bremer? He looked mighty upset."

The lumberjacks immediately in front of Patti turned to see what Kev would say.

"Nah, it was just to do with his car. It's got real problems. I had to tell him how much the repairs would be, that's all." The men grunted in sympathy with Rob, and returned to their food, and Kev, whistling a merry tune, left. Patti stood, coffee jug in hand, and watched him run through the shimmering rain to the garage. Her eyes narrowed. They hadn't been talking about no damn car repairs. Of that she was sure.

CHAPTER FOURTEEN

I spent a very interesting morning with Mrs. Nguyen. I gave her diaries from 1937-1945 to translate, and she informed me that there was nothing in them that would shed any light on Kitty Occley's murder. I was stunned at such presumption on her part, and I asked her how she could possibly know that. She looked me straight in the eye, and in a rather cool and assertive tone she told me to be content that what she said was the truth, but if I wanted to know what had happened to Dominique D'Emeraude during the war, she could give me a quick synopsis. I insisted that she use Dominique's own words to tell me what had happened to her. So, assuming an air of petulant condescension, she began to translate from the diaries of the war years:

Somewhere in the Pyrenees, 1937:
Do not be surprised that I skip over my time in Spain. We did what we were sent to do. I seduced the poor German boy, and he

fell in love with me. I didn't have to make him do that. It had not been part of the plan. Lev and I had informed him that Alphonse was out to trap him and his father, one of Germany's important armaments manufacturers, into exposing their anti-Nazi feelings by helping arm the Republican side. Lev and I told him to be cautious, as the Nazis had infiltrated the Republican forces, Alphonse being a prime example, and supposedly myself, but I, of course, was really on the side of the Republic. I had told the boy that Lev and I were little Sancho Panzas cleaning up the messes the dreamers made, protecting those with good intentions, and sabotaging those with bad. In the latter group, we included the Stalinists on the Republican side. Stalin had managed to sow dissension in the ranks of the Left, making defeat inevitable, while the Fascists forces held firm – well, more than those of the Left in any case, giving Franco and his Nationalists certain victory.

Rudy, of course, had managed to miss most of the action. He'd been away on his own little private missions to England, and God only knows what he'd hatched there, but it had to do with setting up a communist anti-Nazi resistance within Germany, and within the ranks of the SS no less! It was Rudy's way of thumbing his nose at Stalin, and neatly avoiding a return to Russia – well for the present.

To sum up, Spain was bloody and horrible, but maybe we should be relieved that Franco won, for if the Republican side had won, the Stalinist element may well have forced them to support Germany when Stalin made the peace pact with Hitler, and France would have been surrounded.

America, 1940:
When war finally did break out, I was in Washington D.C. Rudy had sent me there, as a representative of a sort of nascent French Resistance, to liaise with the Americans. No one had known then that France would fall so soon, or had they? The Dragons had made plans for such an eventuality at least. Rudy had said that

France was full of warring factions. The conservatives, the old ruling classes, the monarchists, etcetera, would most probably side with the fascists. They liked dominating people and telling them what to do, and they hated the communists, but even more so, they hated and feared the more moderate socialists, for here was a possibly attractive voice of reason. They also did not trust the British and their prodigal offspring - America, the ungrateful brat, that France had helped rebel against its controlling parent.

I enjoyed life in America. It was fun, but then I was treated well. I was wined and dined, and I lived in a luxurious townhouse in a wealthy suburb of DC. I enjoyed the company of wealthy businessmen. They were light-hearted and adventurous; self-made millionaires, some of them; others had inherited their wealth, and had come from the old ruling families of colonial days, descendents of the rich founding fathers of the nation. I enjoyed them all. I had numerous fun affairs in Washington, and I'd told Rudy that I no longer wanted to be a Dragon. I had decided to take sides with the capitalists. Rudy had smiled that slow knowing smile of his, and accepted this. We Dragons were free to pick our own sides.

I thought that DC was wonderful fun, until I went to Manhattan. I fell in love with New York. It was free of the political overtones and machinations of DC. It was the capital of corporate America, that was for sure, but it seemed that the working classes decided what was in fashion as far as recreation was concerned, and the wealthy went along, loving the sense of slumming it. The Big Bands were in full swing, and it was all kids together in lovely classless fun. I loved the swing clubs, especially a real dive, a cellar club in an old brownstone building on the lower East Side. The club had the strange name of 'Swinging Moonlight of The Stardust Cat.' Rudy and Lev had taken me there on one of their flying visits to the States to liaise with those who were trying to form an intelligence organization. Emil Franz was advising the Americans. I never had met such a kind and wise man as Dr. Franz. He'd fled the Nazi

Reich in 1933, and had formed a network of exiled Germans, who, in turn, were helping other refugees, who were arriving everyday from war-torn Europe, to find homes and work in America.

The Stardust Cat was owned by Sid Shapiro, a friend of Dr. Franz. The FBI kept a close eye on them and the refugees they helped, to make sure that the communists weren't using these refugee organizations to infiltrate the U.S. They knew that Rudy and Lev were posing as communists to infiltrate the communist underground within Germany, and that they really worked for British Intelligence. British Intelligence had set up a German to spy for them within the SS. His code name was Simon. Now what the British and the Americans didn't know was that Rudy, Lev, Simon and I had our own secret agenda of spying on them all to keep them honest, an almost impossible task!

It hadn't taken me long to smell a rat within the corporate, capitalist paradise that was America, and I had gone running back to the Dragons as quickly as I possibly could, as Rudy and Lev had known I would, once I had worked things out for myself.

I had discovered that some Americans were more concerned with destroying communism, and they tended to lump socialism in with it, than in destroying the true evil of fascism.

"My dear child," Rudy had said, in a somewhat patronizing tone. "When Europe was struggling with its social revolutions, when its working classes were trying to get organized, where do you think the rich, who escaped the guillotine, fled to consolidate their resources and their revenge? In America, some of these exiles formed a worldwide network of the rich and powerful, and it has added new members constantly over the years, for once a leader of the people gets powerful, he also gets rich, and if he is corrupt enough and wants to maintain his position of privilege and his wealth, he'll join this network. They'll make sure that the ordinary people never rise up against them again. They have flooded the literary market with books that make the aristocrats, killed by the guillotine, look like hapless victims. Oh films and books have provided excellent publicity for their cause, just as they have aroused sympathy for themselves with the killing of the Tsar and his family. The working class revolutionaries are made to look like brutal murderers of innocents. No one cares about the poor people cut down by the Tsar's guards in the peaceful protest march of 1905. Mind you, it was stupid of the Bolsheviks and the French revolutionaries to resort to such barbaric revenge. Now sympathy has been created in the people for the wealthy classes, that oh so innocently exploited and brutalized them! In any case, even ordinary people rarely feel sympathy for the down and outs, but they readily feel sorry for the rich."

Rudy was right in a way. I was about to have first hand experience with this worldwide network of the more corrupt rich, and it was to taint the rest of my life with its evil.

In 1941, I met and dated a man who was one of the first agents of the newly formed Office of Strategic Services, OSS. His name was Biff Chatsle, and he came from the Pacific Northwest. His father had made a fortune in lumber, and Biff was ostensibly a supplier of wood and other materials to the military, as well as being a secret agent for the American government and for Emil Franz.

Biff had fallen for me in a big way, and as I now worked for Dr. Franz and for the OSS too, he felt safe in confiding in me. He told me that he had been set up to watch some very wealthy and influential businessmen who supplied the military with some of its weapons. There was an organization called Zurt Enterprises, a strange, yet seemingly innocuous group on the surface, but it had spies in all aspects of government, religion, banking and business concerns, as well as military, media and intelligence institutions. I smiled to myself in thinking that they would be countered by Dragons, who also had spies in all these agencies. Biff didn't know this of course.

"These bad guys have been involved in forming the OSS, but certain parties have been aware of this, hence my role of pretending to be part of this Zurt Enterprise thing, to spy for the good guys in the OSS - good guys like Dr. Franz and his secret group, who work directly with the President and no-one else. FDR has been aware of this evil group for some time. They confound all attempts at making peace, and they would much prefer America to support the Nazis than the British. There are wealthy people in Britain and France, who also feel this way. They much prefer the Nazis to the communists and socialists, who would have them share their wealth."

"But they have infiltrated the communists too, or so you said – all governments, religions are in their control."

"Yes. They are like an invasive cancer at every level in all societies' institutions of power."

I knew this. They were the reason the Red Dragon society had been formed eons ago to try to combat this greedy, selfish control and abuse by some among the extremely wealthy and powerful.

I thanked Biff for trusting me with this information. Biff said that he had been led to trust me by the endorsements I had received from such great guys as Dr. Franz and Max Von Alt, aka Simon. Biff nicknamed me Cici, because that was what I always seemed to be saying when asked to do something, which I also always qualified by finding loopholes in their plans or arguments,

"Si si, but…"

I told Rudy I wanted out. I wanted to return to France to fight for real freedom for the people, but Rudy said that I could be in an amazingly fortuitous position as far as the Dragons were concerned. I'd stumbled on the mother lode, the source of evil, and it was essential that I gain access to it, to expose it, by helping Biff. Why, oh why, did it have to be me?!

I stayed on with the OSS, and kept dating Biff, but the time came when the Americans wanted me to pay the piper. I was to return to Occupied France to spy on the communist elements within the French Resistance, so off I went, somewhat reluctantly, but also with a huge sense of relief.

France: Paris, Haute-Savoie and Marseilles, 1941-1944:
I was sent into France with an OSS colleague, a doctor friend of Emil Franz, by the name of Ben Robie. He was a great fellow, who was very much in love with a German girl. He had to leave her in Hamburg when war broke out, and he had been devastated to do so, but he already was involved in intelligence work for the U.S. military. He had asked for permission, and gained it, to fly for the RAF before America had entered the war in 1941, but now he fought for his own side.

When we arrived in France, we were not impressed by the resistance efforts in Paris or elsewhere. The Right, for the most part, supported Vichy and Petain. The Left were disorganized and confused, especially the communists, as Stalin had sided with the fascists at first, which had thrown off their resistance efforts, and now that Hitler had turned on Stalin, they were struggling to get a more effective resistance movement going. The men sent from Britain by General De Gaulle's Free French forces were not terribly effective, and were often betrayed to the Germans before they could even get going. The French fishermen of Brittany, the wonderful Bretons, had been the first to oppose the invading German forces. They still lived up to their proud Celtic heritage.

By 1942 the communist resistance finally began to be effective. It was the best organized. The Jews within the communist resistance were brave and relentless in attacking the Germans and Vichy, for Vichy readily had adopted their German overlords' rampant anti-Semitism. Resistance efforts throughout France were beginning to become more effective by 1943. There were horrible, brutal reprisals taken by the Germans and the Milice of the Vichy regime after each act of resistance.

I had decided, on my own accord, to leave the resistance network in Paris, where male egos held sway, and made my way up into the Haute Savoie mountains between France and Switzerland. The Maquis, primarily a peasant resistance movement, had begun up in the mountains, and I wanted to join them.

We conducted guerilla warfare, and our units were constantly on the move to avoid detection. We lived in shacks up in the mountains, and winters were extremely hard on us. We had to rely on local villages for food and medicines. This often led to vicious reprisals by the Milice and the Germans on the poor brave people who helped us, but these wonderful people did it any way.

I had notified my American contacts about my intention of joining the Maquis, and there was little they could do about it. They had wanted me to stay in Paris to keep on monitoring the, by now, very popular communists. Ben had joined me in the Haute Savoie, along with one of the Free French agents, who was the most effective fighter and organizer we'd ever had. His name was Raf Devos, and he was also a close friend of Emil Franz, and a Dragon, but only I knew that.

We had been with the Maquis about six weeks, when we were told to arrange a landing site for a special agent, an American, due to fly in from Britain. We waited in the woods that surrounded a high alpine meadow. We could hear the plane approaching in the overcast winter sky. Then all of a sudden anti-aircraft batteries opened up. How had the Germans known? The conditions were not suitable for flying, especially in our mountainous terrain. We thought the Germans would have relaxed their surveillance on such a night, but they hadn't.

The aircraft was hit and on fire. It crash-landed in the meadow. We darted out from the trees, and ran for all we were worth to the burning wreckage. We knew that the Germans would be on their way to the site soon. One man lay on the frozen ground. He was unconscious, and he'd broken his leg, but he was alive, and not too badly singed. The pilot and navigator of the plane were dead when we pulled their bodies out of the flames. One of our men struggled back to the safety of the trees with the injured man draped over his shoulders. The rest of us lay in the trees to provide cover for their escape. We had to give them time to disappear up into the icy crags.

We fought a gun battle with the German troops for the remainder of the night, but we managed to escape one by one back into the ravines and caves of the region before dawn broke. Three days later, I made it up to the main hideout, and found that the American was none other than Biff Chatsle. He was rather the worse for wear. It was freezing in that hut, and we had little by way of supplies and medicines. Biff was conscious, but in great pain, and he had a very high fever. It was decided that we'd have to take him to one of our supporters in the nearest village. There was a doctor there too, who supported our fight. We made the trip down the mountain at night. Two men carried the makeshift stretcher, while four of us went ahead to reconnoiter.

On our way down, it started to snow heavily. The winds came up, and soon we were struggling through a blizzard in complete white out. Fortunately, our village contacts had thought that we'd have to come down from the hut in this weather, or be stuck up there, and with the amount of snow forecast, there was the possibility that if we didn't come down, we would be stuck up there with no supplies until the spring thaw. We never would have survived. They had come out to look for us. We noticed waving lanterns as we came down to the tree line. We cried with relief and joy at seeing them, and we followed those wonderful brave farmers back to the village and safety.

It had taken several hours for us to thaw our frozen bones. The doctor tended to Biff. They kept him hidden in the potato cellar under the kitchen floor of a farmhouse. We had to find shelter wherever we could. I went to the doctor's house, where, for the rest of the winter, I played the part of his wife's cousin from Lyons. The necessary identity papers were drawn up in some haste, for the Germans made house checks regularly in the regions known to harbor the Maquis.

I visited Biff every day, and his leg healed rapidly and well. He could speak excellent French, so had struck up a great rapport with his host family. I had turned twenty-six that autumn. Biff had his thirtieth birthday in the potato cellar on Christmas Day, 1942. I maintained the pretence of being in love with him, and by the end of January, 1943, I was pregnant with his child.

I only felt a tenuous connection to the OSS by now, but the Americans saw their association with me as more binding, and they had sent Biff to check up on me. I'd told him that I wanted to see who was escaping France by way of the Alps into Switzerland, and I wanted to check on the Maquis. They were real heroes. They were the Robin Hoods of the people. I had been curious to see how many of them were communist. This seemed to satisfy Biff, and this is what he'd radioed to the OSS in London. When he could walk again, we'd escaped back into the mountains with the advent of glorious spring weather. Biff seemed to have mollified the Americans on my behalf, and by now, being two months pregnant, I needed to do that, so that I could return to America with Biff at the end of the war, and become an American citizen.

The Germans and the Milice were relentless in tracking us down. Many Maquisards and their local supporters were massacred. Biff and I fled to the south, just one step ahead of the Milice. We dared not stop, and took what rest we could out in the woods, sleeping in the underbrush during torrential spring downpours. We walked on and on, soaked to the skin, freezing and hungry. Biff would leave me out in the woods, while he went to farmhouses in search of food. I was two months pregnant, and thin as a rail. I was sick and weak, but we pressed on day after relentless day, until we finally reached the outskirts of Marseilles. There I collapsed.

Biff went on to the Villa D'Emeraude and got Kusco. Kusco made trips to outlying areas, selling fresh fish, and he, with Biff hidden under the fish and ice, came back for me. I had lain hidden under the scrub brush in Biff's absence. I had watched in terror as trucks full of German soldiers had driven by. It had been a miracle that they hadn't spotted me, hidden there under the scant covering. A snake had slithered on by. It had been a poisonous asp, but I had been quite used to these as a child, and as I hadn't shown any fear, the snake had gone on its way. I had taken its presence as a good sign. We had looked deep into each other's eyes, that snake and I, and there had been complete understanding – a meeting of our souls. Snakes are not evil. They pay a terrible price for reminding us of our weakness and vulnerability, and it is this very human paranoia that is the root of all evil.

Kusco and I were so happy to be reunited, tears ran down our cheeks, and we clung together. It had been ten years since I had left home – ten long years. When I reached the Villa D'Emeraude, Roza and I clung together too. I smelled of fish, but she didn't mind. She had been more of a mother to me than my own had over all these years. I could tell by the look on his face that Biff did not know what to make of these remnants of my family. Roza and Kusco were a little more exotic than Biff was used to.

It came as no surprise that Roza, Kusco and the girls, who worked in Roza's brothel, as well as old Dr. Fleury, were all active members of the resistance in Marseilles. I was so proud of them, and very pleased when they said that they were proud of me. That came as something of a relief, as Roza and Kusco had been bitterly disappointed by the way I had treated my sister.

When we were alone together in that wonderful, smelly, dilapidated old kitchen, where I had found comfort for my loneliness and sadness as a child, Roza told me that my sister, then twenty years old, was doing her medical studies in Paris, and the boy, Khien, had graduated from engineering college. They were engaged to be married, and as soon as Viet Nam was liberated from Japanese occupation, they planned to return, and to work with the Nationalists to convince the French to give them their independence. Roosevelt had hinted strongly that all colonies should be granted independence from colonial rule after the war was over. This had given them hope, that now all the provinces of Viet Nam could be reunited as a free country under its own government.

I thought to myself that France would never give in to this, American views notwithstanding. It was obvious that there were going to be more and more wars after this one was over. It may just be that America was the place for me. I could work for the OSS with Biff, to help my mother's country gain independence from the French, no doubt, from a political standpoint that differed from that of my mother and her Vietnamese husband, or was he still just her lover?

I had met up with Rudy and Lev briefly in 1942, just after I had joined the Maquis. Rudy had sent Lev to smuggle me into Germany, to Hamburg, to help them rescue an important scientist and his family from the clutches of the SS. We had managed to get the doctor and his family to the States, and I had been back in the mountains of the Haute-Savoie by the beginning of December, just in time to rescue Biff.

Biff and I could not hide out in Marseilles for long, and by the beginning of June we were on our way back to join the hard-pressed Maquis forces along the mountain borders between France and Switzerland. The Milice were most vicious, assassinating people daily. The Resistance also attacked the Milice, which meant even more reprisals.

Our son, Andrew Louis Chatsle, the most beautiful baby I had ever seen, and named after Biff's father and my father, had been born on October 31 Halloween, 1943, in a shepherd's hut up in the French Alps. He had long amethyst colored eyes, but his pale golden hair was like that of his French grandfather and great grandfather, and apart from the exotic slant of his eyes, he gave no evidence of having a Vietnamese heritage.

After his birth, we had to move down to winter in a nearby village. It had become apparent, as more and more of our contacts went into hiding, or were arrested and shot, that we had to go to Marseilles to hide out. Biff could work with the Maquis in the south, along with Kusco and Roza, so, traveling along a path less frequented, we managed to get home safely. When we had hit checkpoints, Biff had cut across the woodland, and I had just walked on through with Andy. I had papers for us both, but even with an infant in my arms and documentation showing that I wasn't Jewish or communist, I had been subjected to a thorough interrogation. I had my knife concealed among Andy's blankets, and fortunately it wasn't discovered.

I had seen Jewish mothers with small children being pulled out of the crowds and dragged off to detention centers to await deportation to the camps in Germany. Now that I was a mother, I felt extremely protective of infants, and under the cover of night, I stole back into the town, and using my son as cover, I approached Germans, or Vichy lackeys, I found alone, and slashed their throats. Dangerous, I know, but mothers are supposed to be deadly in the defense of their young. I fought back for the poor mothers who could not. I left sufficient clues on my victims to indicate that they had been working either with the Maquis or the Black Marketeers, and that a Nazi fanatic had taken his, or her, deluded revenge on them. This way I managed to prevent any reprisals. I had taken a risk, but, surprisingly, it had paid off, and I had reduced the number of those evil idiots at the same time. Dragons do not assassinate, but they fight in wars, and kill to defend all innocent life. It's just that Rudy, Lev and I have a wide definition of what constitutes 'defence'.

Our time at the Villa D'Emeraude passed quietly enough. Roza found an old pram, and I took Andy for outings along the cliff path, seeing in my mind's eye, Rudy striding along there the day my father had died. I re-lived the thrill of riding Dreyfus flat out along the wet sands. Dreyfus had long gone, so had sweet Violet, but I still missed them.

One night, when Biff was out on a mission, Kusco and Roza asked me if I had told him about the Dragon Society. I laughed.

"Biff is a good man, but no, he is not Dragon material."

"Where do your allegiances lie, Mino?" asked Roza, her deep dark Gypsy eyes looking right into my soul.

"I think you know," I laughed. She smiled too.

"So you have come to the Dragons of your own free will at last?"

I pulled my ring, the one of the entwined dragons, from my pocket. Roza gasped, but I assured her that I had retrieved it from a safe hiding place, and did not usually carry it around in such a cavalier fashion. She took it in her large meaty hands, and gazed at it. The golden eyes of the red dragon seemed to glow.

"I do not see your son following in our footsteps. I sense that he will be like his father, good, but not a Dragon. I see, through the mists of potentiality, a female figure approaching. It is possible you will have a daughter, and she will be a Dragon."

I snatched the ring back. "That's rubbish; of course my son will be a Dragon. I shall raise him to be one. His father will have very little influence on him if I have my way."

Roza shook her head sadly. "This Biff, he will be unhappy with you, and you will be unhappy with him, not for some years, but there will be conflict over your son."

"Yes, well I've just told you there will be," I replied, somewhat arrogantly. Roza and Kusco exchanged worried glances.

"Your daughter will not be Biff's child," Roza said, a deep sadness in her eyes. Kusco shook his head. Roza continued. "I looked at the tarot yesterday, and I saw a repetition in your life. You will repeat your mother's evil."

I stood up, the hair rising on my neck. I felt goose bumps all over. The drafts in the old house made the candles flicker, and these, in turn, created shadows that darted about the walls and rafters.

"That is impossible, Roza, you know she is the last person I would emulate, and I would never, never, do you hear me, desert a daughter of mine, or a son for that matter." The air was static with tension, with cosmic waves swirling around me from past, present and future. I never had felt so strange, so light, so insubstantial. The quantum indecisiveness collapsed into reality, when the tangible noise of the truck returning over the sandy track to the house broke the spell. I came to my senses, and left Roza and Kusco to greet Biff, while I went off to hide my ring.

Biff, Andy and I traveled back into the Maritime Alps after news reached us of the D-Day landings. The Resistance stepped up its acts of sabotage, and the Germans retaliated even more viciously than before.

De Gaulle and his liberating forces entered Paris in August, and the war was over for Biff and me. We received permission from the United States Army to be married by an American army chaplain in Paris. Biff was to return to Washington to be briefed for a mission into North Viet Nam, where he was to liaise with the local Vietnamese and Chinese guerilla forces fighting the Japanese. I was to stay in Paris until the military had completed the paperwork necessary for Andy and me to go to the United States; then I was to go to Washington to be briefed for the same mission as Biff. We had been selected for this mission, because I could speak several dialects of Chinese and Vietnamese. Andy would go with us, and I felt a strange satisfaction deep inside, that things had turned out this way, that my son would have some experience in his early years of living in the East. I couldn't believe, that after twenty three years away, I would be going back to my spiritual home of Viet Nam.

America, 1944 -1945:

Andy and I arrived on American shores three days after his first birthday, November 3rd, 1944. Biff greeted us all smiles and hugs. I watched him run towards us as we emerged from the door of the airplane that had been sent to New York to bring us to DC. What did I know about this man really? He was very attractive, tall, with a lean athletic build, his French Canadian heritage evident in his long, thin, craggy face, the way his mid-brown hair was shaped to his long head. His hair was straight and fine – strange how men with such fine hair rarely go bald – and the hair was shaved close to his head, military style; the hair left just a tad longer on the top than on the sides. His nut-brown eyes crinkled into deep lines when he smiled. He had a broad smile that wreathed his face in deep, craggy vertical grooves. He had a rugged American handsomeness. He radiated physical fitness and a carefree confidence. I loved him then, I think. The sky above was blue, the few clouds were white and fluffy, the buildings of the naval airfield blinded us with their whiteness and brightness, and the lawns were a vibrant green. I thought to myself that I couldn't just be anywhere in the world. There is a certain feeling to being in America. You want to join in that lovely devil may care attitude, that wonderful sense of being secure and happy. You want so desperately to enjoy being in that movie-land atmosphere.

We underwent our training in DC, and I arranged to have my name changed. I wanted a whole new identity, a new American identity. Biff had nicknamed me Cici. I didn't mind Cici as a nickname, but I insisted that my new name be something more respectable, like Celeste, for example. Biff loved it, and thought it appropriate as my initials would be C.C., just like my nickname; and so Dominique D'Emeraude, the strange exotic looking French girl, became the brand new American, Celeste Chatsle. It was yet another name change for me, for Rudy and Lev had called me

Nika, feeling it to be stronger than my baby nickname of Mino. They still persisted in calling me Nika.

We were given six weeks holiday after we'd completed our training and briefing for our mission into the Yunnan province of China. Biff took us home to the Pacific Northwest, and on the way, he showed me some of the glorious scenery of the West Coast. We had flown to Los Angeles, which was even brighter and whiter, with even bluer skies and, of course, the blue of the Pacific. Now I really felt as if I were in a Hollywood movie.

Biff bought a station wagon car, as he called it. It had wooden framed sides, and to me it seemed huge. I remember telling Biff that the three of us could live in the car quite comfortably. He had laughed at my naivety.

I loved those few days the three of us spent driving up the Pacific coast to Washington State. The scenery was breathtaking: the sky was blue, even in March, when the weather was often cold and blustery in France. The vast mountain ranges along the northern Californian, Oregon and Washington coastlines were still covered in snow. We drove through evergreen forests, where the trees towered up to heights I never had seen before. The Redwoods were amazing, the sequoias and firs, all breathtakingly beautiful in what was left of winter's snow. The smell of pine, cedar, juniper, on the crisp air of early spring, made me heady with the freedom of it all – the freedom of all that untouched, natural beauty, the freedom of those vast blue skies overhead, illuminated by, what seemed to be a much younger, brighter sun. We stopped to admire the pounding waves on the wide beaches of Oregon, and the rock formations that went way out into the ocean, stirred some childhood memories of the China Sea. I loved the twisting wind-blown cypress trees that clung to the cliffs. They reminded me a little of the cliff top eyrie of the Villa D'Emeraude. I stood under the sweeping branches of a cedar tree, and shielding my eyes from the glare of an early afternoon sun, I gazed out over the pounding waves of a deep blue-green ocean, the air redolent of pine, and tried to see in my mind's eye to its far horizons, that would no doubt be shrouded in heavy sea mists of apricot and gold, where my fate awaited me.

We left the coastal mountains behind us, and headed inland through lovely forests full of wildlife: deer, elk, bears, mountain lions, bobcats, wolves, coyotes, amazing woodland birds and early spring flowers. There were acres and acres of huge ferns that carpeted the forest floor. I thought the woodlands would never end, but we rounded a bend in the highway, and suddenly before us lay vast plains of farmland and orchards. The aroma of apples replaced the aromas of the evergreen forest.

We were tanned a golden brown. We were so happy together. Andy was an amazing little fellow, staggering around at a year and half, and very proud of his few perfect little teeth. We were free to laugh and enjoy life again. Biff and I made love while Andy slept a deep, peaceful sleep, and we were free from terror, from hunger, from the sound of falling bombs, gunfire, from the smell of phosphorus, sulfur, blood and rotting flesh. We drank in the intoxicating odors of freedom from fear. We were the most perfect family on earth, and when we arrived at the Chatsle House on Kalalua, I thought it was the most perfect home, and I fell in love with it at first sight.

It wasn't the house that destroyed our fairytale existence. It was Biff's undercover work, and the act he had to put on to be one of these Zurt Enterprise guys. He had to play the part of a rich, right wing man. Our friends were of like ilk. He had to assume a somewhat scurrilous reputation to please them, and he'd had to pretend to an affair and fathering an illegitimate child, to cover for one of these men who had fathered the child in an affair that would have ruined his connections to a rich Seattle family that Zurt Enterprises wanted to bring into their sphere of influence. The whole thing stank, and we were right in the middle of it. I had played the harlot, mixed with scoundrels and killers before, to ultimately destroy them, but none had been as devious and insidiously evil as these men and women with whom we now mixed daily. The danger they posed to us and to Andy, should Biff be discovered, kept us walking on a tightrope of fear and anxiety.

What kept us sane was the house on Kalalua. We loved it. There was something there in that wonderful old house that hinted at some older, more balanced and nurturing natural force.

━┥ ┝━

Mrs. Nguyen removed her spectacles and sat primly at the kitchen table, her eyes focused on her clasped hands in her lap.

"How did you know what was in this diary?"

"I have seen it before," she replied, not looking up. Just then the tension between us was broken by the shrill ringing of the telephone. Feeling very much like a school ma'm challenging a student suspected of cheating, I got up to answer it. I kept a wary, accusatory eye on Mrs. Nguyen as I did so. It was Rob, and he was in an awful state, so much so that I changed from school m'am to concerned wife in a second. Rob ranted on about Kevin Occley breaking into the house to get at the diaries before we moved in, and that now someone gave him notes on what was written in the diaries, and that other more dangerous parties were threatening Kev if he read the diaries. It was all so garbled and confused.

"He's coming over tonight after dinner," Rob continued. "He wants Mike to be there too. He wants to work with you in translating the diaries. He feels you've both been duplicating your efforts, when what you need to do is join up. He is afraid too, Sal. The whole thing is rotten. Someone out there doesn't want those diaries read. I want us out of it, now. I mean it, Sal."

After Rob had rung off, I turned around to look at Mrs. Nguyen. She was watching me intently, and she didn't lower her eyes, but looked at me as if she were aware of what was going on.

"You know what it's all about don't you? Apart from myself, Rob and Mike, only you have had access to what is in the diaries, so only you could have made notes on them for Kevin Occley. Why would you do that? What are you all up to?"

Mrs. Nguyen sighed. "Kevin Occley is coming here tonight to talk to you and your husband and Mr. McNiall?" She was a cool one. I had accused her of betraying our trust, but she had remained unflappable, and she had made no move to deny it. "If you will allow," she continued, "My family would like to come here tonight too, and then we shall explain our part in this story to you all."

"Mrs. Chatsle wasn't writing a novel was she? I take it that her real name was Dominique D'Emeraude?"

"No, sadly, it is not a novel. It is true enough. I knew her when she worked with her husband in Viet Nam. I was part of the Vietnamese Resistance forces fighting the Japanese who occupied our country during the Second World War. Later, I returned to the South to help throw out the French, who wanted to retain their hold over us."

"And later?" I asked. "What about later? Were you fighting on our side with the South Vietnamese, or were you part of the Viet Cong?"

"We Vietnamese do not like the term Viet Cong. It is a demeaning term for those who were fighting bravely for their nation's freedom from foreign control. We were nationalist freedom fighters, honorable, brave people. Many of us were not communist at all, and resented being told what to do by the arrogant communists of the North."

"So you were one of these freedom fighters? You fought against our American boys?"

"Did I resist American presence in my homeland? Did I oppose American imperialism? Did my people struggle to maintain a sane balance, to keep the issue focused on our freedom, when all the big world powers around us used us as a battleground to prove which of their own stupid, vainglorious ideologies was the most worthy? Did my people suffer and die, their lives and livelihoods torn apart, our forests and animals massacred and poisoned, to make the western democracies feel safer and the communists look strong? Go to Hell, the lot of you. America's, Russia's and China's arrogance and paranoia are evil, and you all deserve to be consigned to Hell for all the suffering you have caused. Don't look at me like that, and accuse me of killing American boys. Your lousy government killed your boys – killed their own sons, and in the process devastated my country and my people."

I wasn't going to exchange excuses with her. I decided to take the high road and end this now.

"I am sorry Mrs. Nguyen. I take it that you fought for your country's freedom. In your place, I should most probably have done the same. If you did give Kevin Occley those notes, then you must be helping him find his sister's murderer, but who would be threatening him?"

"Mrs. Bremer, it is a long story, and may I suggest that tonight you let Mrs. Chatsle tell it. You and Mr. Occley have reached a crucial part of her story – her time in China and my country. If you will be so kind as to let my family share this story with you tonight, we may be able to help you. I do not know who is threatening Mr. Occley, or why, but Mrs. Chatsle left these diaries with us when we arrived here from France. She did not trust certain parties within your secret service and government. When she was killed, the diaries were with us, so they were not among the papers she had left for these people to take. They took away nothing of importance, believe me. We returned the diaries to the house after they had left, and we watched over them. Mrs. Chatsle had wanted Kevin Occley to know of them, and we ...well somehow, we felt that it was alright for good people such as you and your family and Mr. McNiall to know of them too. Do not ask how we know this. It is beyond explanation. The evil people have kept an eye on the place.

They know that Kevin Occley has uncovered something of importance, but they don't know what, and they don't know about our
involvement or yours, but they are beginning to panic. The night
that you returned home to a dark house, after dropping off My-An,
you were in extreme danger, but you were protected. Those people
were in the house, suspecting that the diaries were here, but we
were watching the house. We had seen them watch My-An walk up
the drive alone. She had known she was being watched, and you
had sensed her fear when you let her in to translate for you. The
men had watched you leave. Fortunately, you had kept your blinds
and drapes drawn, so they had not seen My-An translate for you,
but by now, they have guessed that is what she is doing. While My-
An translated, we used our secret entryway, and removed the rest
of the diaries from the attic. My-An secreted the one she had been
reading on her person before she left with you, then returned it
later that night, after you and your husband were safely back in
control of the house.

It is time we joined forces. I think that you are a special woman.
You are connected with good people, influential people, and you
know that I am right, don't you? You tensed when I said the name,
Ben Robie. He is part of your family – your brother's father-in-law,
isn't that so? Dr. Robie is a good person also."

My goodness, she was well informed!

"Ben Robie. He is my half-brother's father-in-law, and his wife
is a German from Hamburg, but she is also Welsh and very proud
of it. She was part of the anti-Nazi resistance in Germany during
the war. She was taken prisoner towards the end of the war, and
tortured horribly, but she is an amazing person, and has overcome
all her hardships. Wait a moment – are they Dragons? It wouldn't
surprise me at all if they were. Are you a Dragon?"

"It is time that I left," she said, getting up to reach for her
coat.

I don't know why I left it at that, but part of me sensed that I should. Mrs. Nguyen asked me to take her home, and I agreed that she and My-An and Chau should join us after dinner that night to hear what Kevin had to say. On the way, I asked her if she and her family had settled in this town because of Mrs. Chatsle.

"She was a very brave lady, like your brother's mother-in-law, and we did come here to help her. After her death, we had to lure Kevin Occley back to the house, using notes that suggested he'd be reward-ed with news of the Chatsles' involvement in his sister's murder. He fell for it, and took the part-time job of night watchman. Then we helped him find the diaries. When you moved in, we wanted you to translate them too for Mr. McNiall, who has power and is a good man. We had to pray that you would think of My-An to translate them for you, and you did. Vietnamese find that such happy coincidences mean good fortune for all concerned. It is karma. It was meant to be. Coincidences bring together parts of the theme or composition that make up our lives this time around, our story, if you will. We knew of Mrs. Chatsle's efforts to find her son, and how Mr. Occley had helped her, and why he too wanted to find her son. Mrs. Chatsle wanted him to know the story, so that is why I also translate for him without his knowing it, and have My-An leave him the notes. I did not want him to know who was helping him. It is better karma that way – more honorable. Kevin Occley is a good man, I think." I nodded in agree-ment. "We know good men. That is fortunate. Take assurance from this, Mrs. Bremer. You are on the good side."

Mrs. Nguyen looked very weary, so I let her go. She replied that she was tired, but relieved that she didn't have to deceive me any longer. My-An, especially, would be relieved.

"I will need to rest before tonight," she said, as she bowed and left me to go into the little shop, where Chau and My-An anxious-ly were awaiting her. The slat on the upstairs window was raised slightly too, so great grandma also must be in on this.

Rob was home when I arrived back. He greeted me with,

"Who do you think just called to say they were flying in tonight from Seattle?" I put my woolen gloves on the coffee table, and hoped that it was Gary. I suddenly wanted all my family around me, where I hoped they'd be safe.

"Gary?" I ventured, hopefully.

"Yeah", Rob nodded. I was so relieved, I could have cried. "And guess who else?" I gave him a blank look.

"He's bringing a girlfriend?"

"Nope"

"Well, who then?"

"John and Rhian."

"You're kidding!" I couldn't believe my ears. It was too coincidental for words. My half brother, John, who had been Andy Chatsle's closest childhood friend, was arriving tonight of all nights.

"He apologized for the short notice, but they had flown over from Britain to attend a conference in Seattle. They had a hectic schedule, so they thought that they wouldn't be able to come here, but they could phone us at least, and hopefully see Gary, but it turned out that they have free days today and tomorrow, as some speakers have been delayed in arriving, so they decided to fly on over and take us out to dinner tonight, then fly back tomorrow morning. They've contacted Gary, and he said that he'd come home with them. Gary will be able to stay with us through the weekend. Isn't that great? John and Ria have booked into a motel. They didn't want to put us to any bother. I ask you, tonight of all nights! What are we going to do? Shall I cancel Kevin and Mike?"

"When are John, Ria and Gary arriving?"

"Six o'clock. They are renting a car at the airport, and Gary can return it when he flies out on Monday."

"Perfect. They'll be here for dinner. We'll have an indoor barbecue. It's freezing out, and it's blowing up a storm. I think there's snow on the way. It will be cosy eating in tonight. We don't have to stand on ceremony."

"I don't know, Sal. How often does your brother visit?"

"He'll prefer to be casual, and so will Ria. Are the girls with them?"

"No. The university semesters in the UK are not over for Christmas yet. What shall we do about Kev and Mike?"

"Let them come. By the way, all the Nguyen ladies will be here too. I don't know if great grandma will come, but My-An, her mother and grandmother will be coming."

"What! Why?"

"It's a long story, and one I'll have to fill you in on as we get ready. Brad will be coming over tonight, won't he?"

"Yep, he said he'd be here for dinner. Sean and Tali are in for the evening too, as you requested."

"Do they know that Gary, John and Ria are coming?'

"Yep, I've told them already."

"Oh Rob, it's great that John will be here. There may be mysteries in Andy's life on which he can shed some light."

"Yeah. What a coincidence!"

"Do you know that coincidences bring good fortune?"

"Oh, by the way, Sal, did you watch T.V. today?"

"No, why?"

"Claire Caventry is involved in another scandal. One of her young aides in DC is being sought in connection with the brutal murder of another young aide, a young woman. Claire's aide is, of course, a young man. Well it looks like Claire was having a fling with this guy, but he was seeing this other woman, the murder victim, and they think that she threatened to tell Claire of their affair, and the guy killed her, brutally. She was a pretty young blonde girl from the Dakotas. It is a horrible mess! Claire is denying any knowledge of it all, and denying any relationship, other than a professional one, with this guy, but this reporter from Seattle has managed to get some really damning evidence of secret meetings and trysts between Claire and this fellow. Oh it's bad, and this could see the end of Claire's checkered career in politics, and she was being groomed as a possible presidential candidate too."

"Serves her right," I replied. "Poor Ken. I wonder how he is dealing with this. Will he stick by her this time?"

"You know, I bet he does," Rob shook his head sadly. "I don't think Ken will ever desert Claire. They're bound together in some sick sort of way."

I went off to shower, smiling at the perplexed look on Rob's adorable face. So convinced was I that all would be well, that I decided to ignore a sudden icy, cold draft that came from under the door to the attic, and a sudden ominous deepening of the shadows in the recess that led to the attic steps.

I stood out on the ridge and summoned all Nature to my aid. I felt those waves, those swing beats of different paths of consciousness, that keep us all going after…well, one path of consciousness ends, race across the Cosmos to the House on Kalalua.

CHAPTER FIFTEEN

Kev met Kelly for an early dinner at Nally's Crab Shack. Over a delicious meal of clam chowder, salmon, long grain rice, and Caesar's Salad, accompanied by a Fumé Blanc, Kev told Kelly about his meeting at the Chatsle House that night. He told her all about the weird goings on there, and about the threat he had received. He had not told Kelly about the threatening note before, which was just as well, as she went ballistic about it. The restaurant was crowded, and her outburst attracted quite a lot of attention. This is just what Kev wanted. He leaned over and whispered in Kelly's ear.

"Do not react to what I'm going to say, just keep that angry look on your face, and when I'm done, grab your coat and storm out of here. Get in your truck and head over to my place. Get Tin Pan and go to your place and get your animals, then go over to Huckleberry, to Cliff's Garage. Manny Mack lives in the house behind the garage. Phil Mingus and Father Petrie will be with Manny. I want you to stay with them. They will fill you in on all this. Now don't argue, but please, just go, and go quickly, but cautiously."

"But Kev, for God's sake, you're making me nervous!" Kelly had the good sense to whisper, while still looking as if she were angry with him.

"Just go."

She gave him one last look of appeal, and then she played her part to perfection, and stormed out of the restaurant. Kev demanded the bill. Everyone was watching him, uncertain whether he deserved their sympathy or not. He was relieved to note that no one left. Kelly might make a clean getaway.

Kelly's world definitely was taking a turn for the worse. She got in her truck and slammed the door, but not before she gave the cabin and the bed of the truck a quick once over to make sure that she was alone, and that nothing had been disturbed in any way. As she drove through the steady rain to her house, she wanted out of this whole set-up. She liked thrillers, but she'd never thought that she have to live one in real life. She drove into the garage and lowered the door. She had left a light burning in the kitchen and living room, and all looked well. The dogs got up to greet her, and they looked sleepy, so no one had been around there at least. She got the three dogs into the SUV, not the truck. Kelly needed the privacy offered by the SUV's darkened windows, so that no observer would notice that she had her animals with her. It might alert them to the fact that she knew she was in danger, and the SUV also would provide more protection for the animals than the open bed of the truck. The dogs had presented no problem, as they loved an outing, and they were wide awake now, tongues lolling happily, tails wagging in anticipation of the ride. The three cats did not give her any trouble either; now that was surprising and not a little alarming. Kelly raised the garage door and backed out the SUV. She lowered the garage door, peering into the dark night around her as she did so. No sign of anything out of the ordinary. She drove to her clinic. If she were being followed, then it would seem that she had to check up on her patients. She drove the SUV into the garage there and lowered the door. The lights were off in the boarding kennels, the surgery, office and waiting area, but the lights were still on in the back apartment where the three student assistants lived. Kelly rented the apartment out to local veterinary students, so that her animals wouldn't be alone at night. There was always someone there to check on their welfare and keep an eye on the premises. The door to the apartment opened, blinding Kelly with a bright light. The noise of the television had been a quiet background hum of laughs and chatter with the door closed; now it filled the waiting room. She quickly pushed Connor back into the apartment and closed the door. The other two students, who were lounging on the couch watching television, looked back at her in surprise.

"Connor, may I borrow your truck? I can't tell you why I need it, but I'll leave you my SUV. You have darkened windows on your truck right?" Connor nodded, a puzzled look on his face. "Listen, my animals are in the SUV, get them in here with you, and whatever you do stay awake tonight, and keep a watchful eye on everything. Keep the lights off in the clinic when you get my guys in, so no one outside can see you do it."

"What the Hell, Kel?" Connor stammered. "What is going on?"

"Not now, right. Just do as I say, and don't let anyone in."

"What if there's an emergency?" asked Stu. Kelly thought for a few seconds.

"Call in Dr. Simmonds, okay?" They nodded. "Then, one of you go to help him, and two of you stay in the apartment with my guys with the door closed." She gave each of them a quick kiss on their concerned and puzzled faces. They got her three dogs and the cats into the apartment, hurrying them through the darkened clinic. That accomplished, Kelly slipped out the back to where Connor's truck was parked. She borrowed Sandy's parka and pulled the hood up over her head before she raced out into the rain.

Kelly kept checking the road behind her as she drove over to Kev's apartment. She parked in front of a nearby launderette;

slipped by the late night customers doing their washing, and came out the back exit, which was near the stairs to Kev's apartment. She ran up the steps, fumbling for the key Kev had given her, but when she stood in front of his door, it was slightly ajar. Kelly froze. Fear clutched at her chest. She gently pushed the door open, and whispered Tin Pan's name. She knew that she should on no account go into the room. She could tell from the small space she could see, that everything had been pulled about. She was torn. She loved old Tin Pan. What if he was lying in there, alive, but urgently in need of help? She jumped out her skin, as something furry rubbed against her leg. Oh, the relief to see Tin Pan there, looking up at her! She pulled the door closed and locked it, plucked up Tin Pan, ran down the steps, back through the launderette and out into the truck. She glanced into the bed of the truck to make sure it was empty, before she tossed poor old Tin Pan into the cabin and jumped in herself. The truck screamed off into the night, heading in the opposite direction to the road to Huckleberry. Two figures in dark suits were running for all they were worth to the parking lot in front of the apartment building, in a vain attempt to catch a glimpse of the vehicle she was driving, and in what direction she was heading. Kelly had foiled them. A slight figure, standing in the shadow of an alleyway, stubbed out his cigarette and smiled. Removing his hands from his parka pockets, Kev slipped into his truck and headed off for the Chatsle House.

CHAPTER SIXTEEN

Kelly drove at a reasonable speed so as not to attract undue attention, but few people knew of this back track to Huckleberry, and even those who did know of it, seldom used it. The windshield wipers were working a mile a minute, but the rain was too heavy, and Kelly had to peer out through rivulets of cascading water at the narrow winding road that ran between the towering rocky crags on one side and the deep and treacherous banks of the lake on the other. The rain pounded on the truck roof, and old Tin Pan huddled in the passenger seat, his eyes as large as could be, his ears flattened against his head. Kelly glanced over at him, and gave him a quick fondle before she had to use two hands to negotiate the bumpy track ahead.

Huckleberry could not be called a town, not even a village. It had only a garage, a coffee shop and small grocery store, and a few small two room shacks scattered here and there on either side of the sandy, now muddy, track, locals called a street. Kelly struggled over the ruts and pulled up at a two-room shack just behind the garage. She sat there for a moment, holding Tin Pan and listening to the rain hammering down on poor Connor's much abused truck. The fact that the single light, from what appeared to be a paraffin lamp in the window, had been turned off as she'd stopped out front, gave her pause for thought. As she peered out of the rain-drenched windows, the door to the shack opened a crack, and a tall, lanky figure emerged. He beckoned for her to come on in. Kelly took a deep breath, and hugging Tin Pan close to her, she got out of the truck, locked it, and clambered over the mud ruts.

"Hey there! C'mon in," the man whispered. Kelly, against her better judgement, followed the lanky stranger into the shack. It was warm inside, and it smelled of recently fried eggs and bacon. Someone had pulled the ragged old drapes across the window and re-lit the paraffin lamp. Kelly, soaked to the skin, and clutching a wet, bedraggled cat close to her chest, looked around her at the peeling walls and leaky ceiling. Three men stood in the cramped room with her. The tall, lanky fellow with graying red hair and long red nose introduced himself.

"Hey, I'm Manny Mack," he said, holding out his rough, callused hand. One of the other men, the short, dark, kind looking one, came and relieved Kelly of Tin Pan. He murmured endearments to the cat as he placed him on a soft towel and gently rubbed his fur. Tin Pan seemed quite at ease, as if he knew these guys well. He even purred.

"I'm Father Petrie," the short dark man said, smiling up at Kelly. "And this surly looking tough guy is Phil Mingus. We're all friends of Kev's."

"What the Hell is going on?" said Kelly, who struggled to keep her calm, but was on the verge of hysteria.

"Are your animals safe?" Father Petrie continued, in a soothing priest-like tone. Kelly glared at him.

"They had better be. Now please will you fill me in on all this?" The three men just looked at her. "Yes, they are safe. They are at the clinic with my students. No one knows they are there. I took precautions." The men relaxed some.

"Won't you take off that wet parka and wrap yourself in this blanket. It is quite clean, I assure you." Father Petrie smiled at her, and held out a Pendleton blanket. Kelly did as she was told, and settled in a lumpy old chair by the small gas fire. "We have a great deal to tell you tonight," Father Petrie continued. "Some of it will be hard to take in. Some of it will be just beyond belief, but don't worry, Kelly, you are on the side of good, and while we are talking here, Kev and his friends up at the Chatsle House will be preparing for their battle; one Kev has been waging for some time now."

Kelly looked up in alarm as the door to the back room opened and a tall black man stood there, two mugs of steaming coffee in his large hands. He handed Kelly a mug. She took it readily in her blue-cold hands, and nursed it, feeling the comfort it offered seep into her tense body, rigid with cold and fear.

"Hey there, Kelly, nice to meet you at last, and hey there Tin Pan, ol' buddy, how's things?" Tin Pan mewed and purred as the man bent to fondle the cat's ears. Suddenly, looking into the man's jet black eyes, kind eyes, wise eyes, brave eyes, eyes that had scanned the expanses of time, Kelly felt as if she were being lulled into a sense of well-being and calm. Her body began to relax, despite all her silent, yet inwardly screaming protestations that she needed to have her wits about her.

"Kelly, " said Father Petrie, a broad smile on his fine-featured, thin, dark, ascetic face - a smile also reflected in the depths of his golden brown eyes. "I'd like you to meet a hero of these parts. You may or may not have heard of him: Kelly, meet Seb Stan Gretavia."

Kelly stared up at Seb. "But you're supposed to be missing in action." She paused as she did the mental arithmetic. "You've been missing for almost twenty and some years now."

"I went MIA sometime after February 8, 1971 – twenty three years ago. Kev, Andy and I were twenty-eight years old, and the other youngsters on our special mission were in their early twenties: like Manny's brother, Colm, and Tony Arviso, also from these parts. Some were even younger, still in their teens," said Seb sadly, but with a touch of anger.

"Gee, I was all of nineteen, and still an undergrad in Vancouver then." To think that these guys had been putting their lives on the line in the jungles of Vietnam, while she'd been carefree and relatively safe in one of the World's less paranoid countries.

"Canada's a good country," Phil Mingus said, nodding his head in agreement with his own humble opinion. The others refrained from making a comment. All countries have their deep, dark secrets. Seb sat on the floor in front of the small gas fire and hugged his bony knees to his chest.

"Do you mind if I do a bit of story-telling here, Kelly? I need you to understand all of this." Kelly settled into the lumpy chair and pulled the blanket around her. Tin Pan jumped up onto her lap, and she lifted the blanket so that he could snuggle under it too. He purred, and with only his head showing, he settled down, his eyes closing in contented bliss, while Seb began his tale:

"Kev and I first arrived in Viet Nam in 1965. Kev was a raw recruit, but I had had to survive in that jungle as a child. I had fought against the very best General Giap had thrown at the French at Dien Bien Phu in 1954, and even before that, I had traveled with my parents and fought in battles in the jungles and mountains throughout Viet Nam.

Kev, like all the other young Americans, didn't have a clue how to survive. I taught Kev all I knew, but I never told him about my past there. He just attributed my expertise to being good ol' Seb, who could dance his way through life, and jump all the hurdles it threw at him. I dragged Kev through that tour of duty, and when we returned to the States, Kev and I decided that we needed to be better prepared for the next time we had to go, so we signed up for Delta Forces, where we learned to become elite killing machines.

The training was tough, but there was a lot of playing with our minds too. I could see it work on Kev, but whatever psycho-magic they weaved to control my mind had no effect. I was, shall we say, kinda immune. After we'd completed our training with Delta Forces - special ops forces - we returned to Viet Nam.

My father had fought in the French Indochinese War in the late forties and early fifties. He was with the French Foreign Legion out of North Africa. My mother was his woman – a camp follower, if you like, but those gals were brave and loyal to their men. My mother had worked in the bordellos of Marseilles ever since she'd been a child. She'd met my father there and followed him back to North Africa. When he was sent to Viet Nam, she went too. These women fought alongside their men, and worked as spies in the towns and villages. They had a good rapport with locals, but that didn't save them, and they died alongside their men too. France did not honor that bravery until recently. French women soldiers, doctors, nurses, all got medals, but not these women, who also fought bravely and tended the sick and injured. They stayed to the bitter end, and were in the last desperate battle at Dien Bien Phu in 1954. I was a young boy then, and I acted as a runner. I could sneak through Giap's encirclement with messages, and also with whatever supplies I could get when the planes dropped them, but usually these ended up in the possession of the enemy. On the very last day, when the injured and the dead were piled up in our last dug out, the ammunition, medicines, food and water had run out, I made one last bid to break out to get help, but I was shot to pieces. My parents had been killed; my father several days before; my mother that day.

It was many days before I regained consciousness. I was pretty beat up. Every single body part had been torn with shrapnel. I remember opening my eyes to a bright white light, and gentle moans and coughs, the rattle of enamel dishes, tubes floating in the air, until I could see they were coming from plastic bags and bottles. I could smell disinfectant, rubbing alcohol, iodine – and all around was clean and white. I sniffed and sniffed the air. There was the faint smell of canvas dust, grit and that red dusty soil, but where the hell were all the smells of that hell hole of a dugout: the smell of earth, piles of human waste, blood - fresh and old and putrid – gangrene, septic, pus-filled gaping wounds, gaping bodies and mangled brains and flesh, cordite, phosphorous, smoke, burning tar, petroleum – where the hell were those?

A face loomed up into my field of view – a black woman, who was speaking French. Her voice took some time to come down from the heavens, where I thought she'd come from to get me. She told me that she was my Aunt Albertine from America. She'd grown up with my mother in Marseilles. She told me that she would look after me now, and that we'd live with a lovely lady who also had grown up with them in Marseilles. A beautiful white woman appeared by her side. She had black hair, like the Vietnamese, but she had silver-green eyes and freckles and a kind smile, a beautiful smile. 'Hi," she said. 'I'm Nika D'Emeraude. We want to take you home with us'.

They came to see me lots of times over the weeks. They brought gifts and food. I got to love them so much that I thought I'd landed in clover. Mrs. D'Emeraude told me that her name was Cici Chatsle now that she was an American. I liked the man too, Mr. Chatsle. He was a great guy. They'd all been going on about their son Andy. I was going to grow up with him. We'd be like brothers. I was kinda excited about that – a brother. I'd been an only child, and I had kinda wanted to have a brother or sister. One day, just before I was to be discharged, they all arrived with a thin young boy in tow. His hair was so blond, but it was his eyes that blasted me out of all the silly notions I'd had that we'd be brothers. He had the coldest blue eyes I ever did see; at least they sure were cold as death when he looked at me.

We returned to the States, and I was taken in by two of the kindest folks you could hope for: Stan and Anthea Gretavia, and

Aunt Albertine visited me often and so did Mrs. Chatsle, but Andy never came, and I never went up to the house to play with him. Andy had drawn the line quite emphatically on having anything to do with me. So there you have it, Kelly. I went to school and made friends with Kev, Phil and Manny here, but Kev and I were the closest.

I watched Kev's back in 'Nam. I knew the jungles so well and was a crack shot, so that I always carried out recon, sniper, maneuvers. I wasn't able to be with Kev's group all the time, but I tried to be. Kev trusted my reports, trusted also that I had their welfare at heart, his and his men, and I did. Kev and I, as old hands, didn't give a darn for winning battles, just for getting as many of us as possible through alive and well, and that was no easy feat, given all the dumb plans of I Corps and military command. Then up turns Andy Chatsle, fresh out of CIA in DC. I thought Kev would die from shock on seeing Andy right there within strangling reach. I was real nervous for them both, but more so for Kev, because he'd get in trouble big time if he did anything to Andy. Andy came with all the rank and prestige that the wealthy and powerful can give their young, but in the jungle everything kinda evens out, or even reverses, shall we say.

The guys we relied on the most were the Huey crews. Hell, those guys who flew the Hueys, the helicopters, they were real heroes. Man, they risked life and limb for us time after time. I thank the Lord for those guys. Why just when you'd thought you'd had it, whirr, whirr, whirr, and there they'd be hovering up over the ridge, gunfire all around, mortar shells exploding around them, bombs falling, and there they'd damn well be – salvation. God, I loved those guys. They'd balance those big ol' birds over flaming, gaping Hades itself, until they'd made sure we were all aboard, alive, torn up or dead, it didn't matter, they'd risk life and limb to save us all. They were our guardian angels delivering us from the jaws of Hell."

Seb had to pause here to regain control of his emotions. Manny and Phil blew their noses. Even Father Petrie bowed his head. Seb continued:

"Andy had come on a special mission. The whole operation was not kosher. We were to penetrate across the Laotian border, where American troops had no right being. The object was to find the secret routes the Viet Cong and Northern troops took to safe bases in Laos. The enemy would attack us, and then would return across the border into Laos to hide, re-arm, seek sanctuary. It was our goal to pinpoint their trails and hideouts for the fly boys to swoop in and destroy. Naturally, we'd do some destroying too.

Colm Mack and I were advanced recon. We'd been out on the trails for weeks. We'd seen the enemy marching along these trails by the hundreds, carrying heavy weapons, ammo, supplies, you name it, they carried it. Their women were amazing. They'd carry parts, Bren guns, huge bags of food, and there these delicate ladies were, tripping through the undergrowth, dancing over poisonous snakes, thrashing their way through dense grasses and vines. They'd be covered in leeches, bugs of all sorts, bitten relentlessly by bomber sized mosquitoes, and yet they made it. You had to admire their determination to re-form their own country in their own way, free from any foreign domination. Old Colm and I shook our heads. We had to hand it to those Nationalist guerillas. The rigid communists were not so easy to admire. They were like robotic parrots screeching the party creed, which their people didn't really need, just as they didn't need our old creed either. They just wanted a fair life, a chance to make something of themselves as an independent nation.

Well one day, Colm and I came across some sort of gathering in a clearing in the jungle on the mountain track that led over the border into Laos. There were Northern soldiers there and Viet Cong. The Viet Cong were led by a handsome son of a gun. Colm and I were hidden up in the trees, watching it all, when we heard a jeep roaring and sputtering up over the ridge. The jeep came into view, and we couldn't believe our eyes, for in the jeep were four white men, old men, with grey hair. One was short and thin, with glasses, another, tall and fat, a cigar clamped in his teeth, the third and fourth fellas took our breath away, for standing there with the enemy were none other than Curt Caventry and Biff Chatsle. We tried to get closer to overhear what they were saying. Colm was gritting his teeth in anger. We could hear that they were speaking in English, but not what was being said. There was a shaking of hands, slaps on the shoulder, laughter. Then the big fat guy goes to the jeep, rummages in one of the boxes they had there, and comes back carrying a new kind of automatic rifle with grenade launcher and all. The small skinny fella had a foreign accent – Russian, German, wasn't sure what it was. Biff stood there silently watching. The Viet Cong guy did too – the handsome one. I was watching them through binoculars, and I caught them looking at each other a few times, as if they were in cahoots about something. They looked worried, the kinda look you have when you are undercover. There are signs we are taught to look out for, behavior that cannot be hidden, no matter how good and convincing guys may be, but folks not trained in this don't pick up on it. Colm didn't, cos he was ready to blast Curt and Biff away, but I had the strongest vibes that Biff and this Viet Cong guy were not what they seemed to be.

We'd seen strange things while in the jungle. We'd seen black guys and white guys fighting with the enemy. I knew that Algerians and Moroccans had visited the Northern communists, both giving and gaining information ready for their own battles for liberation, just as the Vietnamese Freedom fighters had gone to North Africa to train in guerrilla warfare. The former colonies were united in their fight to regain independence, regain their former cultures, languages and beliefs – regain their former identities.

The Americans and Russians and Chinese used them to gain victory for their notions, but they were unnecessary interferences the people fighting for their identity had to put up with, and had to pay for with their blood and lives. They were the crosses these poor smaller nations bent on freedom had to bear. I tell you, the Capitalists and Communists have been a rotten burden the rest of the world has had to endure, and they both are well past their sell-by date. These smaller nations may well be the way to enlightenment and some better notions that benefit all, but there is a lot of evil rubbish left over from empire that we have yet to pitch out before that can happen.

We could see that deals had been made, but what they were about we didn't know. Biff and friends got back into the jeep and left, going back into Laos.

'That damned gun was bitchin' well better than anythin' we got,' snarled Colm.

'That's the way,' I replied. 'All the fighting I done, the enemy was better armed than we were, and with American arms. We got what the lowest bidder offered the damn government. A lady I once knew always said that 'Capitalists don't have nations. They have customers.' That lady was Mrs. C., but I couldn't tell Colm that right there and then. Now just where did she figure in all this?

I had the devil's own job to try and convince Colm not to tell the others what we'd seen. He'd gone along with it finally. I told him that we might blow some real important undercover work of Biff's, but I could not be sure that Colm wouldn't spill the beans when he saw Kev back at camp, and he'd tell his best pal, Tony Arviso, too – boys from back home, who knew Biff and Curt Caventry only too well, and had no love for their kind, especially Kev, who had that ol' axe to grind against the Chatsles. I told Colm that things could get pretty explosive between Kev and Andy, and we couldn't risk that, surrounded as we were by the enemy. He'd have to keep it all to himself until we were back in Da Nang.

We returned to camp. Andy looked from one to the other of us, and asked what Colm and I were doing back. What had happened that was so important that we had to return to camp? We should be out there watching the enemy trails. I asked to talk to him alone, but Colm wouldn't go for it. Andy became suspicious, and so did Kev. They wanted to know why I needed to talk to Andy alone, and why Colm looked so doggone furious. Kev told the youngsters, with Andy, to go and get some chow. It's funny how guys from the same town pick up on something that relates to them, cos Tony Arviso refused to leave us too. I told Colm to stand guard, and to take Tony with him. Oh Colm argued back, but I stood my ground, and he finally went off with Tony, who didn't look any too sure about this either.

Now I just had Kev to face, and he wasn't going anywhere. I could tell he would not let me talk alone with Andy. I took him aside and explained that I had uncovered something, but it was to do with I Corps stuff, and it was for Andy's ears only. I winked at him and said I'd let him in on it afterwards, when Andy had gone to sleep. Kev didn't like it, but he went along with it for now.

Andy paled up some when I told him what Colm and I had seen. After a long silence, when he was arguing with himself how much to tell me, or he was trying to find a lie that would work, Andy told me that his father was part of a CIA investigation of some bad elements in their ranks, some bad guys who were in cahoots with a Zurt Enterprises crowd. Biff had to work with these guys, be accepted by them, to find out just what they were up to. Andy told me that these bad old guys had fingers in lots of pies, and connections up the kazoo in every country, every government of the world. The good guys had a hard time ferreting them out. Andy had been sent as back up by the good guys at CIA to help his dad. Curt Caventry and several rotten politicians, powerful ones, were with this Zurt Enterprises. He told me that he'd need my help the next day to slip off into the jungle to meet up with his father at a certain location. He had the coordinates. His father would give him photos, plans, names, and Andy had to get them back to the good guys at CIA. This had been the goal of Andy's mission, not the attack on enemy supply lines into Laos. Kev and his boys were to find and destroy the supply lines and enemy hideouts, but Andy would sort of disappear into the jungle to meet his dad once that mission got underway. Andy told me to get Colm, and we'd do advanced recon for him the next day. It was the same route the boys would be taking, so we'd be doing recon for them too in a way. I wasn't convinced. I wanted to stay and protect the guys. Andy could look out for himself, as far as I was concerned, but Andy pointed out that what he and his father had uncovered was much more important down the line. He said that we had to expose this evil Zurt Enterprises. Exposing these armaments dealers, and their paid-for political stooges, could be a big step in ending all wars.

We returned to the men. I got Colm, and told Andy and Kev that Colm and I were going back out on advance recon. I expected them to follow the next day. I gave them bearings on the route I planned to follow. Kev wanted to talk to me, but I told him that he'd know it all later. It wasn't important right there and then. He was furious, but let it go.

'Friggin bloody marvelous, Seb,' Andy growled at me. I grabbed him and pulled him off into the trees. I told him that Colm had been there and lost his cool. What could I do then? Colm was a time bomb just waiting to explode and tell Kev and Tony all. Andy was mad with worry; he kept muttering that this could get his father killed if it got back. If those other guys of Zurt Enterprises found out we'd seen them with the enemy, it would be curtains for ol' Biff. This was what he was supposed to guard against. He lost his cool. 'I told you to take the trail to the east. What the hell were you doing there in any case?' I told him we'd been tracking back to find them, when we'd got side-tracked by what looked like some important guys heading to the northwest. Colm and I had followed them to see what was going on. Andy told me that it was going to be tricky. His father had to get away from the others without being seen. I asked Andy if Biff was going to bug out with us. He shook his head. 'Absolutely not. We can't rescue him, that's why this has to go without a hitch.' I can remember shaking my head at it all. How the hell would they meet up at a specific point in the jungle, when they would be surrounded by enemy troops? It was crazy and unrealistic. 'I must get that info Seb. I can't let Dad down. Please man, listen to me. It's got to work.' I asked Andy that if I managed to find Biff, could I get the info? I could be less obvious. I knew how to slip in and out of enemy camps unseen. Andy thought it over, and agreed that if I could do it, then I should, but to get back to him as soon as possible, and then we'd all bug out. We shook hands on it. Andy held onto mine. 'But Seb, I suggest you don't read what Dad gives you. Believe me, you won't want to know what this is all about. If we succeed in getting this info, it will be a small victory that never can be acknowledged. We can never let the people know there are such rotten elements in our government. These bastards will have to be eliminated quietly, off the public record, so to speak.'

I was glad to slip away into the familiar dangers of the jungle. They seemed tame by comparison. I thought to myself that these so called good guys, like Biff and Andy, could try to hide corruption in high places from the people, but I knew that somewhere, sometime down the road, a person would be found who would leak all this filth out to the folks who'd need to hear it, and could get the people to put an end to it. It all came down to the ordinary folks in the end.

The next day at dawn, I was approaching the reference point where Biff was supposed to be. Instead there were northern guerrilla units, who had dogged my footsteps since I'd left camp the night before. I was taken prisoner, and carted off into the jungles of Laos. There I met an interesting group, who were with that handsome Viet Cong guy, and I was, shall we say, enlightened?

As for Andy, Kev and the others, well they were ambushed. I can tell you that Kev fought until he dropped. Those great Huey guys saved his ass, and those of the other two youngsters with him. Colm and Tony were cut down by those damn guns Colm and I had seen the night before. Andy disappeared."

Manny Mack sobbed quietly. Phil patted his shoulder, while sniffing back his own tears. Father Petrie remained silent, gazing into the lights of the gas fire.

Kelly had followed Seb's sad story. She had questions she'd like to ask, such as what Seb had meant by his being enlightened. He was a calm spirit. How could this gentle soul with his down home ways have killed and avoided being killed in Vietnam? There must be another, not so Uncle Remus-like, side to him.

"I know about this Dragon Society?" Kelly said in a not altogether approving tone. Seb and the others shared a smile, and Seb shook his head, smiling broadly the while. What had she said that had been so amusing?

"How do you know about that?" Seb asked her.

"Kev read about it in those notes someone left him – notes from Mrs. Chatsle's diaries." Kelly noticed that while the others still smiled away, there had been a momentary flicker of concern in Seb's eyes. He noticed that she had caught this. They shared a long look: Kelly's eyes showing her intention of knowing more, and Seb's searching for a safe way out of this unexpected predicament in which he found himself.

"Mrs. Chatsle was a mighty brave and generous lady. She served in the French Resistance during the Second World War. She traveled back and forth to China with her husband in the closing years of that war. She could speak Chinese and Vietnamese. Her mother had been Vietnamese."

"I know this. Kev told me what was in the diaries that dated from her early childhood. She had an awful mother, who abandoned her to fight for Vietnamese independence from the French."

"Has Kev read her later diaries, when she went back to Vietnam to help them in their struggle for independence?"

"No, but you are avoiding the issue of the Dragon Society. Does it exist for real?"

"Yes; sort of."

"Have you considered that you are trying to control events?"

Seb nodded. "Yep, sure have. I suppose you think that we are taking matters into our own hands, and trying to control the people without their having a say in it? We don't though - least we try hard not to. We let the politicians put out their stuff for the public to hear, and we never interfere. We don't try to change how the people vote, or the results of their choices, but we try to keep tabs on the secret agendas the people don't know about, and we leak those, so that the people can know what is going on behind their backs. What they do then is up to them. We can make the right information reach the right people, or help the right people get into positions where they can begin to have doubts about what they are being asked to do. They get that old uncomfortable itch that things are not kosher. We give the people the truth, but sometimes they don't want it. We just have to wait, for the people, left to themselves, are pretty good at heart. They let Ford pardon Nixon. Sometimes the people just wannna move on. It's always the powers that be who force a witch hunt, and it is their paid lackeys who do the exposing. We never have a hand in that, and believe me, if the politicians force a witch hunt, it's because they feel safe enough to do so, and they can appear to be upholding our good old American values. God, they can be so sanctimonious – it just oozes out of 'em. If they back off, like they did with ol' Nixon, then you can be sure that unwanted fingers can be pointed at their involvement in the dirty work one way or another. We can only achieve little. We try to keep things honest and above board, but it gets harder and harder to find those good folks we can work through. Governments are powerful, and use more and more sophisticated stuff to watch us all the time. We can only use our wits. We may leave important stuff for good folks to happen across, but they are so scared these days, and with just cause. Look at the Kennedys, Martin Luther King. These are violent times, but that will change, a good person will come, who will care for the people, all the people, and not just the rich ones, I just know it, but we'll have some bad greedy rich guys to sort through first. Enlightenment is fast approaching, and the bad guys are trying to hold onto their old ways for as long as they can, but those old beliefs are on the way out, and true understanding, free from ruthless middle men, is on the way in."

"Why are you telling me all this? I have no intention of joining you, but I suppose Kev might." She gave this a moment's thought. "Or has he already?"

Seb laughed. "I am not going to recruit you, Kelly. Manny here, and Phil, they are not part of what I've been talking about." Manny and Phil nodded their heads in agreement, big smiles on their faces.

"And Father Petrie?" Kelly pressed. Father Petrie just smiled. Kelly waited, but she didn't get an answer to that one. "Was Mrs. Chatsle a Dragon? Was Andy? If Mrs. Chatsle is as good and brave as you say, then why does Kev think that the Chatsles are involved in Kitty's murder?"

"Because they are, but not in the way Kev thinks," Seb replied. Kelly suddenly realized that Kev did not know that Seb was back.

"Kev doesn't know you're back does he?" she asked, nervous at what this meant for Kev. Seb lowered his head and sighed.

"No, he doesn't, not yet. Don't worry, Kelly; we're on Kev's side, but he has a lot more trouble in store for him. He's gonna need you. I mean really need you. You better be sure you love him, and love him no questions asked. If not, then clear out now, while the going is good."

Kelly didn't say anything by way of response. She sunk back into her blanket, while she played with Tin Pan's ears and gazed into the red glow of the gas fire. The men exchanged worried glances. Seb took a sip of his coffee, and, like Kelly, lost himself in the hypnotic red light that flickered with hues of yellow and blue every now and again. Manny Mack and Phil Mingus, hands deep in the pockets of their jeans, their shoulders hunched, looked to Father Petrie for inspiration, but Kelly pre-empted him.

"Tell me all you know," she said, a worn out look on her face. "I love the guy; just help me to be prepared to help him."

"First of all, Kelly, Andy was not a Dragon."

"Just tell me before you begin if you are communists?"

"I've told you, Kelly, we don't follow any human dogma."

"Are you nature worshippers, environmentalists?"

They all laughed. "Not in any political or organized kinda way," replied Seb. "Why we don't really belong to anything. We're free spirits, you might say." Seb and Father Petrie shared a secret smile, missed by all the others, except Tin Pan, who purred and concurred. Kelly suddenly recalled how Tin Pan had seemed to know Seb, and yet Kev did not know Seb was alive.

"How does Tin Pan know you?"

Seb smiled that otherworldly sort of smile:

"Oh Tin Pan and I go way back"

"No! Stop these mind games," Kelly shouted, shaking her head as if to clear it. "It's not possible. Kev and I rescued Tin Pan some years ago. You were not around then."

"Have it your way." Seb offered no further explanation. He got up and went into the back room.

"Relax, Kelly, try to catch a few zzs." Father Petrie said. Manny and Phil heard something outside and turned off the lamp. They peered out into the stormy night.

"They're here," they said, turning to face Father Petrie, who stood up, his eyes closed, as if he were seeking help from a higher source. Tin Pan leapt out of the blanket, ready for action. Kelly was paralyzed by fear of the unknown dangers she might now have to face.

CHAPTER SEVENTEEN

I t was wonderful to be together again. I looked at my big strap-
ping sons as they greeted one another and their aunt and uncle. They towered over poor John. My brother was quite short in
stature, about 5'8". In coloring he resembled Rob and Sean, with
his dark brown hair and eyes. Neither John nor I looked like our
father. We each looked like our respective mothers. John had the
wide forehead and stocky build of the Kemps. Tali and I looked
like my mother, Ellyn, my father's second wife, with our fair coloring and smoky blue eyes and tall, long-legged build.

We exchanged family news over pre-dinner cocktails, and then
over dinner I filled all of them in on what Mrs. Nguyen had translated for me that day. We brought John and Ria up to date on
the whole affair, ghosts and all. John had not been able to add
much to the story. His mother had been a very close friend of Mrs.
Chatsle's, her only friend among the Lake Club Set, if truth be
told. Connie had been a very private person, and while she had
adored John, and been a very loving mother, she had not discussed

her personal life with him ever, and they never had discussed her friendship with Celeste Chatsle.

John had been only two years old when his mother and my father had divorced, but he had come to us every summer after he'd reached the age of eight, so we had shared much of our childhood summers together. John was six years older than I, and I'd sort of hero-worshipped him. I had been really smitten with his best friend, Andy Chatsle. All the girls loved Andy. My friends and I were way too young for him, but I could boast that he visited our house on the lake often with my brother. I had been the envy of all the girls.

"Andy and his mother made frequent trips to France throughout his childhood and adolescence," said John.

"Did Andy get on with his father?" I pressed.

"Seemed to. Andy teased him about being such a big shot, but Biff enjoyed that. He and Andy seemed quite close."

"Do you think that Andy murdered Kitty? I mean had he ever shown any interest in Kitty?"

John shook his head. "No, Andy did not murder Kitty Occley. Andy never mentioned Kitty to me. He was friendly to her when we were altogether at the marina, but not overly so. Wait a sec. There was that one time, I remember it now, it just popped into my head. We were at a party, and it was boring as heck. Claire Caventry was drunk and being awful to Ken, flirting about with everyone. She tried to get Andy to dance, but he wouldn't, and he said to me, after Claire had left us, that the only girl with any class and intelligence was Kit Occley. I'd looked at him somewhat skeptically, after all Kit was quite a flirt too, but in a more witty, fun way, obviously not being serious about it, and Andy had told me that Kit had hidden depths and was a grand girl. Look, Sal, I've kept a big secret all these years as far as Andy was concerned. Andy was gay."

We all gasped.

"What did I tell you?" said Rob with an air of self-vindication. "I wondered why he wore pink so much." We all had to laugh. The boys just hooted. Tali had a disapproving look on her face, but even she had to give way to a smirk.

"Andy told me he was gay when he visited me in Cambridge. That was the summer Kitty was murdered. I had no hint that he was gay, not at any time through the years of our friendship had I known or even guessed at it. He wasn't a womanizer, that was true, and with his looks he could have been. He'd turned up on my doorstep with a few gorgeous women over the years, but they had not turned into anything serious, and I'd thought that he just hadn't found the right girl yet. By the way, Andy phoned me from Paris the day Kitty was murdered, so he could not have done it. What would have been his motive, had he been home, in any case?"

"How did you take the news that he was gay, Uncle John?" asked Sean.

"I was surprised, but it didn't make a scrap of difference to me what his sexual preferences were."

"Quite right!" interjected Tali. "It shouldn't make any difference at all."

She gave the boys and Rob a pointed look, which they challenged, claiming that it wouldn't have made any difference to them either, so she needn't look at them like that. A lively argument ensued, and Ria and I left them to it, and cleared away the dishes. When we were alone in the kitchen, Ria said,

"My mother knew Dominique D'Emeraude, by reputation at least." I looked at her in stunned surprise. "My mother was part of the anti-Nazi resistance in Germany during the Second World War, and she worked with Rudy Von Silvren, to whom Mrs. Chatsle refers in her diaries. He was a close friend of my parents and grandparents over the years, until he died in 1974. Well my grandparents are gone now too. That generation of the two world wars is dying off. They are taking a lot of secrets with them. There are secrets in my family that my sister and I have not been let in on, but it is interesting that my mother named my younger sister, Dominique."

"I haven't brought it up yet, but your father is mentioned in Mrs. Chatsle's diary covering her work with the Maquis. She thought highly of him, and mentioned that he was madly in love with a German girl, who was working against the Nazis in Hamburg. I didn't bring it up out there with the others. I wanted to tell you first before mentioning it."

"Isn't all this coincidence amazing? I can hardly wait to tell my parents and Nikki. When Nikki asked Mum why she'd been named Dominique, and why she hadn't been given a Welsh name like I had, my mother favoring her Welsh roots over her German ones after the war, my mother had replied that Rudy had told her about the daring exploits of a very brave woman named Dominique D'Emeraude, and she'd thought she'd name her second daughter after her. She also had added, somewhat cryptically, that Gerd, whom I call uncle, as he and my mother grew up together, had been involved with this D'Emeraude woman while he'd been in Spain during the Spanish Civil War, but Mum wouldn't elucidate further on that. Uncle Gerd, as you know, runs a ski lodge in Aspen, and he made a wonderful love match with my Aunt Sheena, who is a Ute Indian, but before her, he'd fallen in a big way for this Dominique D'Emeraude, who apparently had saved him and his father from the evil machinations of the Fascists. Emil Franz, whom you said Mrs. Chatsle refers to in her diaries, as being part of the effort to rescue people from the clutches of the Nazis during the war, and bring them to the States, was also a very close friend of our family. His son, my mother and Uncle Gerd grew up together. Marc Franz, I also call 'uncle', and his wife, my Aunt Tsai, is Chinese. He met her during the war in China."

"My goodness, Ria, but it's a small world. These connections keep turning up. They make me feel as if we are playing roles in a script written for us well before we entered this life."

"Well, I can tell you that I was amazed to hear those names here tonight. John has told me all about the Chatsles, but he'd never known Mrs. Chatsle by any other name than Celeste, and then when you told us all about her diaries and that she had been named Dominique D'Emeraude, I nearly fell off my chair. I didn't say anything, because the story was fascinating and complicated enough, but isn't it a breathtaking coincidence that my family knows of her, and that my sister is named after her?"

"It's breathtaking alright, but what is even more so, is that you are here tonight at all. It is just too much of a coincidence."

"We hadn't planned to be here. If those speakers hadn't been late, we'd have met Gary for dinner in Seattle and left it at that. We wouldn't have had time to visit you, only to phone you."

"I know; it's too amazing for words, but all of it should mean good fortune in the outcome, I hope."

"Oh, you have that belief too, just like the Welsh," Ria smiled. I just stood there, a look of surprise on my face. The Welsh too? - I thought - and something like a spasm of reassurance passed through me.

Lights appeared on the driveway outside the kitchen window. Mike and Deb had arrived in time for dessert.

"Let's tell them all about this later," I said. "For now we have to bring Mike up to speed. He is fit to bust about Kevin Occley trespassing in the attic, and all this will just blow his mind."

CHAPTER EIGHTEEN

M ike and Deb were stunned to see John and Ria, and somewhat surprised to see all the kids with us too. Mike was a
little put out as he'd intended to rake poor old Kev over the coals.
He couldn't do this with all of us present. Deb was relieved, as she
confided to Ria and me in the kitchen,

"I mean, Kev didn't take anything, but it was trespassing on private property, and all that stuff up there in the attic is pretty valu-
able, but Kev had to take his chances where and when he could, I
suppose."

"He should have asked, Deb. Mike would have let him read the
diaries here. Heck, Mike would have been glad to have someone
who could read Vietnamese and Chinese, which Kev can."

"You're right. Why ever didn't Kev just ask? Who the hell is this
woman who gave him access to the attic? Mike is livid that, even
with security guards and all, strangers have been in the house and
going through god knows what."

"Rob is pretty angry too. He thinks that all these weird goings-
on have been perpetrated by whoever these other trespassers are,

which means that they are still around, and that gives Rob the shivers. They are in the house while we're lying asleep at night. They are here when one or other of us is here alone. It's pretty scary, and then there's the threatening note that Kev received. I tell you, Deb, Rob wants out. Oh, and before I forget, there will be some surprise guests tonight too."

Deb and Ria were most anxious to know who else was coming, other than Kevin Occley. They didn't have to wait long before a knock at the door announced the arrival of the Nguyen ladies: My-An, her mother and grandmother, but no great grandma. Kevin arrived shortly after I had settled everybody with cups of tea or coffee. Tali, Brad, Gary and Sean lay on cushions on the floor. Brad played with Bugsy, and Bubba sat near Ria, his tongue lolling happily as she gave in to his sad, hard-done-by look and fed him pieces of cookie.

Kevin greeted Mike warily, but Mike just waved it off, and said that they'd talk about it later. Kev could come to his office after work tomorrow. Here My-An spoke up and confessed to Mike that she too had trespassed in the house, and she had been the one who had enticed Kev to the attic each night, letting him in to get the diaries. She swore that she hadn't taken anything or damaged anything. Rob asked them if they had been responsible for all the other strange happenings, but here My-An and Kev had looked bewildered, and denied leaving lights on in the basement, leaving the door to the attic open, coming to the house at all since we had moved in, and they hadn't fooled with the Thunderbird either. My-An pointed out that they had made notes from what her grandmother remembered of her daily translations, and had left these for Kevin, so there had been no longer any need for them to trespass to get at the diaries, except that once, when they had removed them to protect them from the bad people. Mike and Deb jumped on that:

"When was that," they shouted in unision. My-An told us that it had been that awful night, when I had been scared out of my wits, when the Thunderbird had appeared to move, when Bubs had gone ballistic. "But how did you know they were here?" Mike pressed. Grandma Nguyen confessed to keeping an eye on the place. They had someone, one of their gardeners, who kept a watchful eye on us from the distance of the grounds at night. Rob glanced at me. Neither of us was pleased by this, but I suppose we should have been.

Kevin thanked My-An for her help in getting the diaries and for the notes, but he was completely at a loss as to why they would do this for him. They were in a lot of trouble. Mike could prosecute them all. Mike did not deny this, but just sat there, looking grim. I jumped in at this point and told them what Mrs. Nguyen had told me that morning about being entrusted with the safety of the diaries by Mrs. Chatsle herself. I also brought Mike and Deb and Kevin up to date on that morning's translation: the years 1937-1945. There followed a long silence.

"I think we should read on," Kev said in a very subdued tone. "I'm getting very bad vibes about what comes next, and if it's okay with you all, I think that we should press on."

I had brought the last diaries down from the attic. I reached for the years, 1946-1954, and with a trembling hand, I gave them to Kevin, and sitting with his back to the roaring fire, he began to translate. I looked out of the front window. The wind was gale force, and the rain came down in sheets. The tops of the tall evergreens were tossed about, and the rain pounded down on the flagstone terrace to run off in mini waterfalls down the wide stone steps.

Yunnan Province, China, March, 1945:
I stood on the craggy outcrop of rock that hid the entrance to our cave way up in the mountains, and gazed out over range after

range of mountain ridges and limestone cliffs, with endless miles of deep, forested ravines between. The valleys were hidden from view by the heavy rain clouds that had long since cleared the high peaks, leaving a pale rain-washed blue sky in their wake. The air was piercingly cold, fresh, invigorating, and it reminded me briefly of the French Alps, but there the resemblance ended. These mountains were endless, with deep ravines through which raging torrents ran, and there were no gentle alpine forests and wide green meadows – no, here the slopes were steep, covered in dense jungle forests with slippery outcrops and treacherously narrow, winding tracks. The air lower down was always misty, either cold and damp, or hot and stifling. Up at the altitude of our base camp, we had to dress in thick cumbersome quilted jackets, thick corduroy trousers tucked into our mountain boots. Our faces were burnt reddish brown by the sun and the wind. Andy's hair was bleached white blonde, but it seemed as if my black Asian hair had turned even darker, even straighter.

I sat down on the rocky outcrop and waited for Biff and his Chinese guides to return to the cave. I wouldn't be able to see them through the rain clouds below, but once they cleared the ridge, I would get a glimpse of them before the trail descended into the mists again, and then reappeared just below the entrance to the cave. They had gone ahead to reconnoiter. We were to cross the mountain ridges and descend into the jungles of Tonkin Province the next day. I was in a frenzy of excited anticipation, not just because I'd be back on Vietnamese soil, but also because I'd be part of their resistance forces, nationalist and communist, who were fighting the Japanese forces of occupation and their French colonial puppets.

I never had referred to my birthplace by the name imposed on it by the French, namely Annam, its people referred to as Annamites. My father and his friends called French Indochina, Viet Nam, Cambodia and Laos, and I insisted on doing the same, even though it had earned me the wrath of my French geography teachers, for whom Viet Nam was Cochin China in the south, Annam in the center, and Tonkin to the north. The French who worked closely with the OSS operators in China did not like my terminology either, so Biff begged me to relent in this case, because clarity of meaning was of the essence, so I yielded grudgingly.

We were to join the Viet Minh forces, but our local OSS operatives were in two minds about this. America had to help the Free French defeat the Japanese in the French colonies, but Roosevelt had made it clear that America also supported independence from former colonial rule. The Viet Minh leaders were, for the most part, communists. Their most charismatic leader was one, Ho Chi Minh, and yet, when he'd been interviewed by OSS operatives, he had shown a marked preference for American support in his country's struggle for independence from France. Some of our group were totally won over by him, but others thought he was too cunning for words, and wouldn't trust him an inch, but we didn't have much choice.

March 1945, the Japanese occupying forces put an end to French rule by abolishing the Vichy administration in Indochina and restoring Bao Dai as emperor, but as a Japanese puppet ruler.

Our airmen shot down over Japanese occupied territories would need help, and we badly needed intelligence about Japanese movements in the area. The Chinese and the Free French also had to acknowledge the need for such information, so we'd have to work with the Viet Minh, their communist inclinations not withstanding.

In the last few days of April, we followed Ho Chi Minh back to the rugged mountains of Pac Bo. There were about forty of us, and the trek through the dense jungle on the border between Tonkin and China was hard on us all. Andy had been allowed to come to China with us, because we had a house and amah arranged for our use in Kunming by the local OSS chief. Andy and our amah, Minh Li, a lady in her late forties, for Andy did not require a wet nurse, had accompanied us into the surrounding mountains of the border territory when we had done reconnaissance work there, and it had worked out rather well. Andy had been in good health and had enjoyed every minute of it. Minh Li also was extremely agile and physically fit for her age. She had graying black hair and very fine features, and she was tall for a Vietnamese. When we met her for the first time at the house in Kunming, my heart had lurched as my mind flashed back to that last glimpse I had of my mother running away from me through the market crowds on the Rue Catinat in Saigon. My mother's Vietnamese name had been Minh, but this lady reassured us that she had lived in Kunming all her life. Her parents had been Vietnamese, but her husband, now dead, had been a Chinese nationalist fighter. She detested the communists, and believed that they would ruin Viet Nam's chance for independence, for the Western powers would never let Indochina fall to communist control. She also did not like the wealthy and corrupt government of the Southern provinces, claiming that the wealthy classes would keep the peasants living in poverty and squalor, and that could not be allowed to go on either, so she believed in the nationalists, who wanted a free and united Viet Nam that would be also a democracy fair to all – a socialist state, but not one driven by communist dogma. I told her that her politics and mine were very similar. She smiled at this, but doubted that an American woman could hold such views.

It had been decided before we had met with Ho Chi MInh that I'd keep my French heritage a secret. Ho had been adamant that no French were allowed to join our mission to his resistance headquarters in Po Bac. I had to keep on reassuring our OSS leaders that I had no loyalties to France. I would not relay information to the French about the Viet Minh hideouts. I told them all about my father's work in helping nationalist rebels wanted by the colonial authorities in Indochina escape to France, and when back in France himself, he had continued to aid them.

Minh Li had commented many times on how my hair resembled the hair of Asian women, and my Vietnamese was too good, too fluent and idiomatic to have been learned only recently. I told her that my mother had been Vietnamese and my father, a Welsh sea captain, a renegade with no national ties, no political affiliations.

She'd given me a look of surprised skepticism.

"Welsh eh?" she'd said with a smirk. "They are a colonized people, who wish to be independent. They are people of the Fairy, the Magic Sword and … the Dragon, as are the Vietnamese. Our myths and legends are very similar."

I was stunned. I didn't know what to say. I decided to play dumb. Minh Li's eyes narrowed as she looked intently into mine.

"My father had a ring," I began. She tensed, and I was going to describe the ring my real French father wore, the one of the entwined dragons, but Biff entered the room, full of complaints about how unreasonable our Viet Minh contact was about what he wanted from us in return for his services. He wanted arms and information that we really did not want to give him.

"He wants enough armaments and supplies to get ready to fight the French when this Japanese war is over. I don't trust him one bit. The French are going to be livid, not to mention the Chinese nationalists. America is not going to arm a communist revolution for chrissake!"

I had to hide a quiet smile, for whether they knew it or not, the Americans were well on the way to providing the region with enough military ordinance to supply both the Indochinese communists and the Chinese communists, so that they could give the French and Chiang Kai-shek's nationalists a really hard and prolonged battle. It would just be a matter of time before the communists would take over all the military equipment we'd leave behind us when we left. They were that cunning, and the French that carelessly arrogant, and the Chinese nationalists and the Bao Dai regime in Viet Nam that corrupt, but what would the armaments dealers care? Zurt Enterprises would make out like bandits any which way.

Minh Li had slipped away when Biff had entered the room, but she'd given me a furtive glance before leaving to see to Andy.

I was to go to Pac Bo for two weeks only, but there was absolutely no way that we could take an infant. I was torn. I had not left Andy for such a long period since he'd been born, and there was no way that I was going to leave him alone with Minh Li. She was wonderful with him, and he adored her, but she reminded me too much of my mother, and I'd had dreams of chasing her through the crowds, as I'd chased my mother all those years ago, but in my dreams Minh Li was running away with Andy.

I was the team's linguist, and they would need me to eavesdrop on conversations amongst members of the Viet Minh. Ho had been able to speak English and French, and he'd wondered why a woman had been included as part of the team. He'd been told that Biff and I worked together, a wife and husband spy team, not generally allowed, but Donovan, head of OSS, had relented in our case, because of my special background. Ho knew that we could speak Chinese and Vietnamese, but he didn't know that I understood the other Indochinese languages and Russian. I think I had him covered in whatever language he could use to communicate secretly with his men.

It was decided that Andy and Minh Li would stay with a family of American missionaries in Kunming. The McCormacks were a warm and loving family, and I was reassured that they'd keep a watchful eye on my son and his amah in my absence.

The trek along dense jungle trails was arduous going, and so we had little chance to indulge in conversation. When we finally reached Ho Chi Minh's headquarters in Po Bac, we were exhausted and some of us were under the weather with dysentery and fevers. Biff was suffering from headaches and stomach cramps, so he spent the next few days in our bamboo hut, which was built on stilts. We led a Spartan existence. I loved being back in the jungle. It brought back memories of my early childhood, when my father, mother and I had traveled up the Mekong, and my father had helped me name all the wonderful creatures and plants we had seen. I had never forgotten the riotous array of colors, smells and sounds. My whole body reveled in being back in its natural element at long last. In all the years of my exile, I'd never felt so alive, so free and untamed.

The second evening we were at Pac Bo, I was alone, preparing some food by the small fire we'd lit in the deep recess of a cave to avoid the torrential rain falling outside. I'd adopted the same rough sort of rope sandals that the Viet Minh wore. Their forces were made up of a large number of women fighters as well as men. The women were expertly trained in guerrilla warfare, and they could carry heavy cans of petroleum and heavy pieces of machinery for miles over mountainous terrain and through jungles without difficulty. I had the opportunity for only brief glimpses of them as they came and went, and I wondered if my mother and my sister, Lien, were of their number. Lien had been finishing up her medical studies in Paris when I had left for the States, but she could have made it back here by now, and most probably with that handsome young nationalist, Khien. They could have made it back to Tonkin through Russia and China, especially if Rudy and Lev had helped them bypass war torn Europe.

I was lost in my reveries, when I sensed someone approaching. Ho Chi Minh squatted down beside me, and addressed me in French.

"Don't try to fool me, Dominique D'Emeraude. I knew your father way back. He helped me escape Saigon back in 1911, and I met up with him in 1923, at the Villa D'Emeraude, before I left France for Russia. You were a small child then, but your coloring was quite distinctive, with those silver green eyes and those freckles over your nose, and that silky black hair you inherited from your Vietnamese mother." I kept stirring the rice in the pot, not taking my eyes off it. Ho laughed. "I knew Rudy Von Silvren too. We were close friends while I was in Moscow for my, shall we say, re-education and indoctrination in communist dogma. Stalin felt, and still feels, that my nationalist ardor far exceeds my commitment to communism."

I looked up at him, and he was gazing over the dense cloud layer beneath us. It was as if we were of the sky, sitting on clouds like the gods, insubstantial, ethereal, no longer of the world below. He turned towards me, and he added with a sly smile,

"I have had many names, but then so have you. Isn't that so?" I still refused to answer him. He sighed, and continued. "You can squat on your haunches for hours like a native daughter, my child." He smiled to himself. "I can tell you that your mother is still alive, and as committed to our cause of uniting Viet Nam and throwing off the French yoke as ever. She has had to carry the burden of her French heritage with her through her life, but few dare to challenge her about it these days. Her loyalty to her Vietnamese people can never be in doubt. She is a wonderful doctor, and has skillfully and devotedly treated our guerrilla forces hiding in the south. Her husband was killed a few years ago. We lost a great national hero. He was a brave man and a good man, a compassionate man, except, of course, towards the French and the Japanese." I felt a stab of hatred for this man in my heart. I knew how my poor French father had suffered when she had left us for this oh so compassionate man. Ho watched me intently, and seemed to guess at my feelings.

"I am sorry my child, maybe you side with your father's people, and maybe you side with them too much. If you are here to spy on us, you will not leave here alive. Your life depends on a visitor I am expecting this evening. If what he says exonerates you as a French spy, then as the daughter of my old friend D'Emeraude you will be safe, but if it turns out that you are first a daughter of France, then your life will pay the forfeit of this little farce. You will not take out your revenge on your mother by threatening the safety of those who fight to free our country."

Ho stood up without effort after having squatted so long, and I did likewise, which brought yet another knowing smile to his thin lips. We looked at each other for a few seconds, and then he drifted back into the mist. I couldn't help but admire him. I had watched him closely as we'd traveled together. He was unflappable, patient, stoic, and he had a warm, witty wisdom. I had found myself liking him as a person, and the threats he had made had disturbed me, not just with fear for my life, but in some intangible way also. I felt as if I had been reprimanded by someone I had wanted to please, someone I had wanted to admire me and, if truth be told, by someone I sensed was very brave and good, but he'd become caught up in the meshes of unscrupulous, powerful people, people he hoped to manipulate to free his country, but people who, in the end, would compromise him in their hard and fast ideologies of subjugation. I believed that Ho really wanted to free his people, and dogma be damned.

The visitor who arrived that night came as no surprise. Rudy Von Silvren emerged from the surrounding jungle looking as fit as ever at the ripe old age of fifty-eight. He still had a hard, strong, lithe build, his neck powerful still, his black hair now silver, but still long and tied at the nape of his neck by a black cord. His face would never change, because it was a man-made one – a white pearlized sheen to his skin that was pulled tightly across the facial bones, his nose truncated, his mouth pulled down into a sneer, his eyes still a vibrant black. He'd lost his face in the First World War, but he'd found his calling in life – spymaster extraordinaire, Dragon master par excellence.

The Americans did not get to see him. They, Biff included, were asleep, their food surreptitiously drugged, and they were watched over discreetly by the Viet Minh. I was awakened quietly and led off down the mountain into a jungle clearing. The night was cool, but oppressively humid. It had stopped raining, but raindrops fell continuously from the jungle canopy overhead. There was complete darkness, for no moonlight, even if there had been no heavy cloud cover, could have penetrated the dense foliage. The darkness was far from silent. There was the usual unrelenting tropical din made by insects, night predators and God knows what other creatures of the night.

Our guides lit a small lantern, covered its top with a piece of rag and drifted back into the surrounding foliage, leaving Rudy, Lev Tashvin, my old Cossack mentor, who had taught me my spy trade in Paris before the war, Ho Chi Minh and me standing in a circle around the shielded lantern, our faces dimly lit from beneath.

Rudy, Lev and I greeted one other with bear hugs and fond smiles. Ho watched every look, every gesture.

"You are Nika D'Emeraude?"

"She is indeed," replied Rudy. "There is no one else like Nika here, no one near as difficult, opinionated and dangerous if pushed too far." This last was said in a tone of warning, but Ho wasn't the least perturbed. We were in his territory, surrounded by his people. "You don't have to worry. She isn't spying for the French. She worked with the Maquis and the French communists in Europe. We sent her to America to find out what plans the Americans have for after the war. She has no political affiliations."

"She is like you and Lev then?"

Rudy nodded. "And so were her father and mother, as you well know. If you hadn't been the one to win over the hearts of your people, and if you hadn't been so committed to their cause, you might have been one of us, but you are intended to lead, to play a part on the world stage, and you know that we can never do this."

Ho nodded. "I cannot work in the wings. I believe in my people's right to freedom, and I have always, like my father and grandfather before me, believed in a united Viet Nam. I would like my country to be a socialist democracy. I would favor a more moderate influence than Stalin's communism, but I do not think my own followers, those trained by Moscow, will allow me to adopt such moderation and flexibility. They are diehard Stalinists, but who knows, maybe over time, when we are in control of our own united country, they may be more malleable." Ho gave a wry laugh. "You warned me of Stalin's double dealings thirteen years ago, when Kirov was assassinated by Stalin's henchmen, and followers of Lenin were accused of the crime. My men watch me closely, and so do the nationalists among us, and it lessens my influence with them every time I kowtow to the Chinese nationalists and the French. The Americans are an unknown entity as yet. They are our hope against the French, but we cannot be sure how helpful they will be if France plays the communist expansion card, that is the ace up their sleeve. Americans will not let our country become a communist state under the control of Moscow. I do not want to be under the control of Stalin either, but as far as the Americans are concerned, I have muddied the waters for myself, and there is ample evidence, even though I tell them to the contrary, that I have worked hard for the communist party, both in France and throughout Indochina and France's other colonies. I don't know at this point how you can help me exonerate myself in the eyes of the West, or even whether I should bother. My people would flourish under capitalism, but only those who are already rich and corrupt would flourish, and the poor would still be exploited. I cannot go with capitalism, unless it is attached to a socialist welfare state that allows freedom for all individuals to flourish. I suppose that you Dragons will have to keep us honest, keep us on track."

Rudy placed a hand on Ho's slim shoulders. "I am not sure what we can do either, but we'll try. We have good people in place, people like Nika here. She'll keep you informed on how the Americans are thinking."

"The Americans will think along the lines their wealthy military suppliers and businessmen tell them to," I replied. "And I am in the best place possible to know how they are thinking. I am married to an undercover agent, who is keeping an eye on this wealthy cabal made up of oil magnates and bankers, who wield control over the military, intelligence services and media."

"You are in an important position, Nika, for if these corrupt men get their way, this poor country and its people will pay the price," said Rudy.

We took our leave of Rudy and Lev. They had to return to a Germany in ruins, but still fighting on; the Nazis retaining a death grip until the end. I followed Ho and his people back up to the camp. I thought that I would give anything to get away from all these machinations. I just wanted to raise my son, be with my son, play endlessly with him, watch him grow, teach him all about the beautiful natural world around us, as my father had taught me. I loved the Chatsle House. I wanted to romp on those lawns with Andy, take him sailing on the lakes, hiking into those heady evergreen forests, take him on motoring trips to Yellowstone Park, to the Oregon coast and let him explore the beauty of all the islands in Puget Sound – Oh God, I wanted to be free of all this, but I had nowhere to run and hide. They, Zurt Enterprises, would find me even if I took Andy and returned to the Villa D'Emeraude. I thought how wonderful it would be if Andy could know the freedoms I had known growing up as a wharf rat in Marseilles, and the wonderful summers I had spent, barefoot, burnt dark brown by the Mediterranean sun, that had shone off the waters of the swampy, reed-choked marshes of the Camargue. They'd find me, even if I tried to melt into the swampy reed marsh villages of the Mekong delta, or the jungle mountain hideouts of Laos and Cambodia. Their feelers extended everywhere.

In the next few weeks, the Viet Minh and our team provided weather reports, reports on Japanese troop movements and air reconnaissance schedules for the Americans, and we managed to rescue American pilots shot down over Tonkin, and return them to South China. I returned to Kunming after two weeks, but Biff and the others moved on with the Viet Minh to their new base in the mountain ranges far from major roads.

On my return to Kunming, I was interrogated by the local OSS and by the French, who had fled Viet Nam after the Japanese edict of March 9, and settled in southern China. I could tell them in perfect honesty that the Viet Minh had moved on from Pac Bo after I had left, and I had no idea where they were going. The French would have to wait until my husband returned to find out where the communists had their hideout now. The French were furious, just as Ho had hoped they'd be.

I was stunned on my return to find that Minh Li had gone. She hadn't told anyone where she was going, but had said that her very old mother was ill and needed her. I was bitterly disappointed to find her gone. I knew in my heart that she was a Dragon, and my mind tormented me with the obsessive belief that she was my mother.

Andy lay asleep in my lap as I sat by the long latticed window of the two-storey house, and looked out beyond the hustle and bustle of the military units in the street below to the far distant snow-capped mountains. I stroked his fine blond hair, and took satisfaction in the thought that my son had been seen by his grandmother, and he had loved her as I had done as an infant, and she had seemed to have loved him, but then with her, who knew what she had felt. I had derived a certain strange sort of satisfaction, consolation, but most probably fantasy, that she had chosen to come to Kunming to see us, to be my Dragon back up. If she was as important as Ho said, she could have chosen not to come; she could have sent someone else, but, no, she had come. I felt tears start and my heart contract with longing and the hope that she did love me and was proud of me at last. I could still delude myself with fanciful imaginings as far as my mother was concerned.

The people of the central and northern regions of Viet Nam had suffered horribly under the Japanese occupation. The rice the Vietnamese had grown had been sent to Japan. Bad weather made for a poor harvest, which resulted in a catastrophic famine. Hundreds of thousands died, certainly genocide on a par with the one taking place in Europe. The Japanese forces of occupation and the Vichy French did nothing to help out the starving millions.

This callousness to the suffering of the Vietnamese people of the central and northern provinces laid the groundwork for open rebellion against French rule and the Japanese. The Viet Minh were with their people, and the rural and mountain peoples gave them their full support. I had no doubts that, when the war in the Pacific ended, the Viet Minh popularity would make the Americans very nervous, and those of Zurt Enterprises would be rubbing their hands in greedy anticipation of riches to come.

CHAPTER NINETEEN

B iff stayed with the Viet Minh until the end of the war in August, 1945, and for some time after, but I returned home with Andy, and we had an idyllic time, just the two of us, until one day in early September, when I received a visit from the local ladies. Diana Wingo was a beautiful bitch, who helped her father-in-law run the shoe shop, while her husband, Wint, was away fighting in the Pacific. Dolly Caventry came from a wealthy family in Seattle, the Felspars. She had fallen in love with Curt Caventry, a train driver's son, and defied her family and married him. To give Curt credit, before the war, he had worked hard as a teller at the local bank, and had worked in his spare time at the diner to make enough money to show Dolly's family that he could make it without their help. Then there was Louise Birkly, who worked her hands to the bone, growing vegetables on her father's and father-in-law's dirt farms. The three Kemp sisters, Connie, Pam and Dilys, sold the Birklys' vegetables in their father's green grocer's shop. The Kemp sisters I liked. They were unpretentious and fun, but the insidious venom of the other three just flowed in a steady stream of seemingly harmless little innuendoes.

Diana Wingo was their fearless leader, who had poached on their men folk whenever she'd wanted to. She was beautiful; tall, long-legged, slender, with an incredibly lovely shade of red hair, deep and rich. She had long, laughing gray eyes and wide smile. She made no bones about having dated all of our husbands in high school, where she'd been Prom Queen, chief cheerleader, debating society president, and to top it off, even valedictorian. There was a lot of repressed anger and frustration in Diana Wingo. She could have gone far in life, left this 'hicksville' way behind her, but her parents were very poor, much too poor to send Diana to college. Her fashion sense and attractive looks had got her the job in Wingo's shoe shop, and she'd used this to her advantage, offering beauty treatments and fashion advice as a sideline. This had established her control over the other local women, except Dolly, who of course had come from high society in Seattle. Dolly, however, was a short, frumpy blonde, with large, frightened, pale watery blue eyes. She was in awe of Diana, who outclassed her in all but social background.

Biff had told me that Diana had made a serious play for him in high school, but he hadn't been interested. He wanted to travel, meet new and different types of women. Diana would have risen to the occasion, and been a splendid trophy wife, but not for Biff, apparently. She'd also tried to win the other wealthy guy in town, Craig McNiall, but he'd gone to university in Seattle, as Biff had, and he'd met a girl from a wealthy family there, Margaret Drysdale, and they'd settled in Seattle, and run McNiall's construction company from there.

Louise Birkly was Diana's partner in crime. She was nowhere near as fine and beautiful as Diana, but was a large boned blonde, with a longish face, hard, sulky blue eyes, lined mouth, mean and tight. Her hands were red and rough from farming, and her life was hard and demanding. The other women in town, who were on the fringes of this little coterie of so-called more socially acceptable ladies, were Patti Occley, Gloria Mack and Madge Mingus.

My housekeeper, Phyllis Flahertie, was my informant on all the town's goings on. Phyllis's husband had been the Chatsles' handyman for years, while Phyllis had looked after the house. They had a son, Brenden, fighting in Europe. He'd written home to say that he'd fallen for a German girl, and married her, and would be bringing her home now the war was over. Phyllis and Malachi had been fine with this. "She warn't no Nazi, and them Germans had it hard too," was Phyllis's comment. "She's got no family left, so we'll make it up to her." I had smiled to myself at how such ordinary people could reassure one as to the goodness in human hearts. I have to admit that I was not one to believe in the goodness or usefulness of human beings. I thought us, with our unraveled brains that had to learn everything afresh, a dreadful curse on all life.

Connie Kemp McDonnell was a beauty in her own right, one that could offer Diana Wingo serious competition. She and her sisters were slender blondes with large brown eyes, and whereas Pam and Dilys were still single and cute and fun, Connie was more serious.

These were women whose men had been off fighting a war, though some of the husbands had been stationed in some fun city stateside; either way, their men were free to fool around, and Diana Wingo was determined to match them at their game. Phyllis had told me that Diana made frequent trips to Seattle where, it was rumored, she was having an affair with some old, wealthy congressman, named Zebulon Zurt. He'd been to the house a few times to visit Biff, and he was involved with military arms acquisitions in DC. He met Diana at a party Biff gave just before America entered the war, back in late 1941. Biff left for DC shortly afterwards, to work for the OSS, during which time, he met me. The Caventrys, Curt and Dolly, the McNialls, Craig and Margaret, the Birklys,

Louise and Joe, had been at the party too, as well as Diana's husband, Wint Wingo, and another friend of that gang, Kerr Toddy.

"Those fellas met for talks all that weekend," Phyllis said. "Real hush, hush. The wives joined them in the evenings for cocktails and dinner. That Diana did look real glamorous mind you, real elegant and classy. She could work wonders with a sewing machine, and make an old second hand dress look real high class."

"The Kemps weren't asked?"

"Ah, no. They're too honest and above board for that lot." Then she slapped her hand over her mouth, making me laugh. "I'm real sorry Mrs. Chatsle. I didn't mean anything by that. It's just the Kemps stay out of all that local tomfoolery that those other guys get up to."

The reason for the ladies' visit to see me on that September day was, ostensibly, to ask for help in planning the welcome home festivities for the men when they returned from the war, and given that the wars in Europe and in the Pacific were over, this could be any day now.

The coming of peace seemed to be heralding in baby girls, for Dolly had Claire in June, 1945; Curt having made a quick trip Stateside in late September of 1944 to attend his father's funeral, and to get treatment for a spinal wound he received during the fighting in the Pacific. Biff returned home at that time too, after his briefing with the OSS in DC, and before Andy and I arrived in the States…and Patti Occley had a daughter, born nine months later, in June, 1945, and she'd named her Kitty.

"When will Biff get back?" Diana asked; a forced smile of not so innocent inquiry on her face. "He is doing some very important hush-hush work in China, isn't he?"

"Lord no!" I replied. "He is working with our intelligence services in China, but it's not hush-hush, you read about it every day in the newspapers. We are trying to help Chiang Kai-Shek's nationalists battle the communist rebels in the north."

"Those communists are so scary and evil," squeaked Dolly. "I bet our boys will have to fight them now. It just goes on and on. I hate those commies."

"Don't worry, Dolly, we've got clever, handsome devils like Biff keeping an eye on them for us. We'll be just fine," said Diana, giving me a sly smirk. I thought to myself that she had the right choice of words in any case; devils was an appropriate name for Biff's friends in their so-called 'Zurt Enterprises'." Congressman Zebulon Zurt figured big time in that evil, as one of the present day leaders of "Zurt Enterprises", following in the footsteps of a long line of ruthless devotees of the god Mammon.

Diana continued, "Biff is still out there fighting for us. You and Andy, at least, have a lovely lazy old time in his absence." She didn't know that Andy and I had been up in that harsh mountainous terrain with Biff, or that I had been fighting the Japanese in the jungles of Tonkin, as well as fighting the Germans in the French Alps and occupied cities of Europe well before that, or that I had taken part in that blood-soaked Civil War in Spain. I had been fighting for my life all my life, while she'd played Kiss and Tell, safe at home. Diana said with a sneer, "The French were a useless lot if you ask me. Wint wrote that most of the French supported the Nazis and were just as cruel. Old Ike had his work cut out for him dealing with that arrogant ass, De Gaulle."

The Kemp sisters were appalled by this, and Connie spoke up on my behalf.

"I don't think that living in an occupied country during war can be very easy. You don't know whom to trust, and every day must bring new dangers. I think that to form a resistance movement under such conditions must be hard, and to fight back brings dangers, not only to oneself, but to whole towns and villages, to many innocent people, by way of reprisals. I don't think we Americans have a right to judge."

"I'd fight tooth and claw," boasted Diana, giving me a challenging look. "Did you fight, Cici, if I may call you that?" I smiled and nodded, but changed the subject. I didn't have to explain anything to Diana Wingo.

"So what sort of celebrations are you planning?" I asked. Pam and Dilys launched into a list of parties, visits by local dignitaries and so on. When all these had been exhausted as topics of innocent conversation, Diana attempted to return to local gossip, but Connie got up and said that it was time they left. I had given them enough of my time, my coffee and pastries. Diana remained seated, and asked me if I had any wine. I stood and gave her a forced smile. Connie and her sisters laughed, and tried to usher out the other three, who looked most put out. On their way to the front door, Diana asked Connie if her divorce was finalized. Dilys, the shortest and feistiest of the sisters, immediately bristled with anger.

"Mind your own business, Diana. I hardly think it's appropriate to bring that up now."

"Oh, Dil, for goodness sake! I am concerned about Connie..."

"Sure you are!" retorted Dilys.

"And if you'll let me finish – I wanted Cici to feel like a part of our group – include her in more personal ways."

I smiled at Connie, "I don't need to know," I said. "I think I've gathered enough over the course of the afternoon. You have been quite open with me, Diana. You don't think much of the French. I have had a lovely irresponsible holiday instead of looking after Biff's concerns here, while you, Louise and Dolly have been working hard in your husbands' absence. You are all close friends, yet you think that Gloria Mack, Madge Mingus and Patti Occley are not socially acceptable, even though these ladies' husbands are fighting alongside yours, and these ladies are working their fingers to the bone to keep house and home together in their husbands' absence, just as you are."

Diana sneered at this. "Oh sure they are. I feel sorry for Tim Occley, that's all I've got to say. It won't be easy for him to come home to another mouth to feed, and one that isn't of his own making, if you get my drift." All the ladies tensed. The Kemp sisters avoided looking at me, while Dolly and Louise cast shifty eyes in my direction.

"I think that we should go," said Connie firmly, and she began to push her sisters down the wide terrace steps, and to pull Diana in their wake, cutting off Diana's protests at being manhandled with, "We'll call you later, when we've figured out where exactly you can help out." Connie shot me a friendly, understanding smile, which I returned.

That afternoon, after my guests had left, I sat out on the terrace alone. Andy was asleep in his crib in the downstairs master bedroom. I had left the wide windows open, so that I could hear him if he stirred, and reach in to bring him out to join me, but he'd slept on, as bees droned in and out, bypassing the cream colored linen drapes that stirred lazily in the soft warm air. I gazed up at the vivid blue sky above the tops of the evergreens, and breathed in the scent of pine, roses and honeysuckle. The air was caressingly warm, not stifling as it could be sometimes. I thought over Diana's innuendos and the local gossip Phyllis related to me every morning over breakfast. I knew that Patti Occley had given birth to a daughter, who wasn't her husband's, back in June. I thought to myself, as I soaked up the afternoon sun, that Connie and I could be very good friends, and hopefully our sons could be too.

Biff adored Andy, and he had been eager to become a father. It was I who had fallen out of love with Biff for his stupidity, for his connections to Zurt Enterprises, and his weakness in letting them use him to shield the infidelity of another of their number.

CHAPTER TWENTY

K ev had mumbled these last few sentences in disbelief. He'd gone pale ever since he'd read that Kitty had not been his father's child. We sat there, not quite sure what to say. Rob had looked at me, then at Mike. Deb had looked very upset, but no one had suggested that we stop reading, or that someone else should take over from Kev. Kev had paused only momentarily, when his throat had gone dry and his voice had cracked. He'd taken a sip of his drink before continuing to the end.

Kev just sat there on the floor in front of the fire, his head bent. I indicated to Sean, Brad, Tali and Gary that they should go upstairs and they did. Tali beckoned to My-An that she could join her, but My-An refused to budge. Tali shrugged and went on up to her room.

"Did any of you know this?" Kev asked in a whisper, not raising his head. We assured him that we hadn't. "Fletch must have known if those other rich guys did," Kev said, looking at Mike. Mike shook his head.

"Look Kev, if those rich guys at the lake knew something like this, it would have been all over, we'd all have known. It seems as if their mothers knew, but why hadn't they told their kids? C'mon Kev, don't you think that Claire Caventry, Celia Birkly and the Wingo girls would have teased poor Kit mercilessly? You bet that they'd have made her life miserable, but they didn't, so I'm guessing they didn't know."

"My pals didn't know either. I mean old Manny, Pete and Phil, because they'd have told me if they had known. Ma's friends, the guys' moms, Gloria Mack, Madge Mingus, must have known. They sure kept quiet about it all these years."

"Yeah, the community is too small for stuff like this not to have got around," said Mike.

"Did you know, John?" Kev asked. John shook his head.

"I bet Diana Wingo didn't know for sure," I interjected. "She was just casting her net. When we were kids, I certainly remember talk about her and Curt Caventry. Nowadays it's Claire Caventry we all talk about."

"Claire takes after her old man. They were close. He used to take Claire everywhere with him, sailing, tennis, golf, he was so proud of her, and yet he rarely took poor old Chuck anywhere with him. Chuck was closer to his mother, poor hard-done-by Dolly," said Mike.

"Was Chuck Caventry in Vietnam with you guys, Kev?" I asked.

"No, he stayed States-side. Only Fletch and Tank Birkly went to 'Nam with us poor kids," said Kev. "Ken Birkly was a naval doctor in Okinawa."

"It did sound as if all those women suspected Biff was the father of Patti's child, so why didn't it get to be general knowledge?" Deb asked

"I bet that when Curt Caventry and Wint Wingo got back, they cut off their wives' gossip at the pass. Biff was a powerful guy, loaded with contacts and money. He could have torpedoed those guys if he'd wanted to. Curt and Wint got a lot of business from Biff when they finished their training on the GI Bill. Biff had his money in Curt's bank, and I bet he helped Curt get rapid promotion to bank manager. Why Curt and Biff traveled to DC together often, and they entertained big business guys all the time. Wint was Biff's lawyer before he moved up to D.A., so Biff had him in his pocket too. It was beneficial for all those guys, who later got real rich, to pander to old Biff Chatsle, so you bet they'd stifle their wives' suspicions," said Mike. "As for the Kemp girls, well they wouldn't have gossiped. Fred Kemp, their brother, made old Collie's business a billion-dollar concern, but he did it without Biff's help. Fred was a clever guy in his own right, and he was an upstanding fellow. He and his father, old Collie, and Ross, Fred's brother, wouldn't have condoned any kind of gossip mongering in the family.

"Right," said John. "My mother was a closed book, and hated all kinds of gossip. My Uncle Fred was dead against it, as were my grandparents and Uncle Ross and Aunt Babs, and Aunt Dil and Aunt Pam."

"Dad wasn't a gossip either," I added, defending my side of the family. "Neither was my mom. If you wanted to know anything about the family you had to ask Aunt Hallie, but she moved to San Francisco after the war, and she'd been away in Labrador with the Red Cross during the war, so she didn't know anything about what went on here in those years."

We noticed that Kev was no longer following our speculations. He had begun to whisper, as if to himself:

"Curt Caventry and my old man were in the same theater of the war. They were on Iwo Jima in 1945. They both got Congressional medals. Much good that did my dad when he got home, but Caventry cashed in on his. Their outfit didn't get back until the war was over. Kit'd been about two or three months old when those boys got home. I remember I'd been a young 'un, about three years old, but I remember all the parades and flags and bands playing. My old man looked real sharp in his uniform, medals and all..." Kev struggled with his emotions. "I remember being so proud of him then. My old grandma had taken Kit for a few days after that. Guess that's when Ma had to do some fancy explaining. God, he must have been shocked to see little Kit in her arms…I can't remember…how he'd looked when he'd seen us…" Kev bent his head. Rob and Mike knelt beside him, their hands on his heaving shoulders, although Kev didn't make a sound. Tears were streaming down Deb's face and Ria's. They got up and went into the kitchen. The Nguyens sat there, as if in suspended animation. I asked Kev if I could get him anything. He just shook his head, but he controlled himself enough to continue.

"Ma was a real looker in those days, not unlike Kit. She and Dad had married out of high school in February, 1941. I was born June, 1942, but Dad had gone to the war by then. Heck, I was only three in 1945, but I remember Ma being so excited that Dad was coming home. She kitted out me and Kit in our finest, Kit being a baby of course, born the June before the fall Dad came back. I don't remember anything bad happening. Ma seemed real happy and all. It seems like she oughta have bin real scared. Dad hadn't bin home for two years, and here was Kit, a babe in arms. Mind you, the quarrels started, and Dad took to the bottle. Dad was good to Kit, but he always cried a lot and hugged us a lot… and then he just up and left one day. Next we heard was that he was dead of liver failure."

Kev just sat there, deep in thought.

"It doesn't make sense," I said. "Biff was covering for some guy in Zurt Enterprises, who must have had an affair with Patti. Curt Caventry fills the bill. He was home nine months before Kit was born. Claire, his legitimate daughter, was born about the same time to Dolly. We know Curt had to keep his affair a secret, because Zurt Enterprises wanted him to keep up his ties with an influential family in Seattle. Dolly's family, the Felspars, would fit in with that description."

"I remember my old man saying once that Curt and Patti had dated in high school. Maybe they'd met up, had a few drinks while reminiscing over old times and wham, they ended up in the sack, just for old times sake, nothing more," replied Mike. I glanced over at Kev. It must be hurting him to hear his mother talked about like this.

"I know kids don't remember moms being pregnant so much as they remember the sudden presence of a baby and being told this is your baby sister or brother, and hell, life changes from then on. I remember Mom waking me up and presenting me with a wrapped up bundle and saying, 'This is your own baby sister, Kev. What you wan to call her?' and I'd said Rover or Fido, or some such dog name, cos I'd wanted a dog, and Ma had laughed and said, 'How 'bout, Kit?' and that had been that. I remember that my grandma had been looking after me for a while, cos Ma had been away, working in one of the factories in L.A., and then, wham she was home, and had Kit with her."

Suddenly Bubba jumped up, his hackles raised, his fangs bared. He barked and growled menacingly as he struggled to gain traction on the wooden floor to make a mad dash up the stairs, but almost simultaneously a door banged up there and the lights went out. All four kids came tumbling down the stairs, Brad almost carrying Tali along with him. They looked petrified.

"Mom, God, Mom!" Sean screamed, his eyes wild with terror.

"What the hell?" shouted Rob, standing to take a shivering Tali into his arms.

"It's that darn attic, Dad. We were in my room playing with the computer. Tali was in her room…"

"Reading," she added, her eyes wide, her face pale.

"When the door to the attic crashed open with a blast of freezing wet wind, so cold we couldn't get our voices to scream. It seemed to strangle us, and Bubba was creating a racket. We got out to the stairs, and Brad noticed Tali standing as if in a daze in her room, and her door was closing, and she wasn't closing it," screamed Sean, still in a panic.

"I rammed the door back open," added Brad. "And I grabbed Tali and pushed her out and down the stairs after Sean and Gary. We all collided with Bubs on his way up, and Gary grabbed him by the collar and dragged him back down with us." Gary was still struggling with a furious Bubba. Bubs was growling and howling, but he was all a shiver too, from head to paw. Ria and Deb had come in from the kitchen to see what all the commotion was about, and to find out why the lights had gone out. Ria had retrieved a terrified Bugsy from under the sofa, where he'd gone to hide, and he was all atremble, his eyes popped out with terror. Ria held him close. Mrs. Nguyen moved cautiously to the foot of the stairs, and with a long bony finger, she pointed up into the darkness:

"There is someone up there," she said. My-An and Chau screamed and clung together. Kev, Rob and Mike pushed us all back into the living room away from the stairs.

"Who's there?" shouted Rob. A shrill laugh that sent shivers down our spines answered him. Bubba howled. Then the front door crashed open, and an old Vietnamese man stood there. He was dressed in what looked like old gardening clothes, a canvas hat on his grey hair. He was drenched and shivering. The Nguyen women screamed at him in Vietnamese. He looked terrified and pointed down the driveway.

"They are coming," he stammered in English. "The men in their big black vans are coming. Quickly close the doors and shutters." Then he stopped and looked in horror up the stairs. The shrill laugh had turned to a menacing, throaty one. Mike grabbed the old man and pulled him into the room, slamming the door shut behind him and bolting it. "You must secure the house," the old man kept screaming. "Forget about who is upstairs. He is not the one to worry about. Quickly close the shutters and lock all doors." Rob and the boys closed all the shutters, and checked that the back doors and door to the cellar were locked, but no one would go upstairs. Sean had noticed headlights down the drive before he'd locked the shutters, but the vans had stopped.

"There's a whole lot of deer out there, Mom, and they are blocking those guys from driving on up here."

"Who are those men out there?" Mike shouted at the poor old man, who stood there shivering and wet.

"Not good men," he replied.

"Not good men at all," drawled another voice, and a tall thin man dressed in a long grey raincoat, black polo neck sweater and jeans came slowly down the stairs. His hair was longish, below his ears, lank and a grey-blond in color. He had a full mustache and piercing amethyst-colored eyes. We all stood there, our mouths open in shock. He smiled at us, a slow knowing smile, that wreathed his long thin handsome face in deep lines and grooves, accented further by the flickering candle he held in his hands

"Well hello there, John, long time no see, and Kev, how are you?"

"Andy!" hollered Mike, at the same time that Tali recovered her senses and shouted,

"Alain!"

We all looked from her to Andy and back again in total shock.

"No, my dear one. I am not Alain Fournier, more's the pity. It was my face you saw in your dreams, because I was the one who disturbed your slumbers, and you saw me while still in that half sleeping state, but I'd gone when you awoke to find it was all a dream, actually optical illusions, done with mirrors and lenses and smoke."

Rob and the boys were furious, out of their minds that this creep may have harmed their sister in some way, and they launched themselves at Andy, but Mike and Kev blocked them. Andy had produced a gun from his raincoat pocket.

I gasped, and Ria and Deb screamed. The Nguyens huddled close together, the old man with them.

"I didn't touch your daughter, Rob Bremer. I am not interested in women, as I'm sure you know, what with 'pink shirts and all'. Oh yes, I have overheard all your conversations, and thank you, Tali for being my defender. You are not the first beautiful young lady to defend me; Kit preceded you in that." Here Andy looked over at Kev.

"Where the hell have you been all these years?" Kev asked in a voice, quiet, but loaded with deadly intent.

"I didn't kill Kit, Kev, and neither did my parents."

We all froze. Even Bubba, still held fast by Gary, had quieted down at last, resorting now and again to a low growl. Andy put a hand on John's shoulder.

John looked distressed, as if he didn't know whether to embrace Andy with relief that his old friend was alive, or whether to throttle him. They exchanged a long look, tempered by some strong emotion in Andy's case, confusion and sadness in John's.

"I think we should all sit down, and carry on reading my dear mother's diaries." Andy said, in a voice more serious now than sardonic.

"What about those guys out there?" screamed Brad.

"Oh, they won't bother us," Andy said, with an amused smile on his face. "I think that forces even beyond their control have taken a hand, and rest assured, those other forces are on your side." He sat down in the large leather chair by the fire, and elegantly crossed his long legs. "Are you going to translate Kev, or shall I, or maybe you'd like to translate for us Aunt Lien?" Andy looked over at Mrs. Nguyen. She looked daggers at Andy, while Chau and My-An huddled together, and waited with fearful eyes to see what Mrs. Nguyen would do.

"No, you translate," she snapped back, her black eyes as cold as flint.

Rob and Mike exchanged glances. I could tell what they had in mind. If Andy had to hold the diary to read it, then maybe they could rush him and overpower him, but Andy laughed, and looked as if he'd guessed at their intentions. He indicated that Tali should sit just in front of him, and he pointed the gun at her.

"No, I think that Kev should read on. If you want to know who murdered Kit, you had better read on," Andy said, smiling affably at Kev, whose face was haggard and white with anger. "You can all relax. I apologize for those ghoulish noises I made and the cold smoke. I assure you that the ghost that haunts this place is a much more sophisticated entity, bent on doing good, I think, but then with her one never can be sure. Let's do 1946. Auntie Lien will love that year, won't you, dear Aunt?" Mrs. Nguyen scowled at him, and then at the old Vietnamese man, who looked uncomfortable. Andy smiled. "You too, Khien. Now you take center stage, I think."

Kev was fed up with all these innuendos, and he snatched up the diary.

"Shut up, Chatsle, you sick bastard! You better not have had anything to do with Kit's death, or gun or no gun; I'm going to put an end to you once and for all. If you're a ghost or alive, it's not going to matter one bit." Kev clenched his jaw, kicked over a stool, righted it, sat down and began to read. Andy watched him with narrowed eyes, his mouth twisted into a sly, cruel smile. We all watched Andy. We couldn't believe our eyes. Here he was, alive, after all those years when his poor mother almost lost her mind looking for him, knowing in her heart that he was alive. Had he come back before she'd died? Oh God, no! He couldn't have killed her, could he?

CHAPTER TWENTY-ONE

Fontainebleau, Paris, 1946:

After Ho Chi Minh's Declaration of Independence on September 2nd, 1945, things started to go down hill fast, as far as hopes for a united, independent Viet Nam were concerned. The western allies were shoring up their defenses against the threat of communist expansion, and the Soviets were walking on eggs, not wanting to blow the chances communist parties had of getting into the governments of war torn Europe, and also not wanting to frighten the Americans into using nuclear weapons, which at this point, they and they alone, had the capability of so-doing.

Biff, Andy and I were in Paris for the Fontainebleau talks that July of 1946. Biff and his cronies were there for meetings of a more clandestine nature. They were going to provide the French with arms under the aegis of the American government, and, at the same time, their partners were at work in Tonkin province promising to arm the Viet Minh. The purpose of all this double-dealing was? – Well, war everlasting of course.

Andy would be three in the October of the year. He and I had lots of spare time to play in the wonderful parks and gardens of the city and take boat rides on the Seine. One morning, I left Andy with a caretaker provided by the Ritz, and I went shopping in the fabulous boutiques of the Rue de Rivoli. Paris had been relatively untouched by the war and the Nazi occupation. The other cities of Europe were still in ruins. I strolled across the Place Vendome in the brilliant mid-summer sunshine. The day was hot, but for some reason, the dark rainy November day came to mind, when I'd met my sister and Khien at the train station, and had taken them to my depressing little rooftop apartment, where the sheets on my bed still retained the scent of my lovemaking with that arrogant fool Alphonse Lambert. I'd been amused at this recollection, for how could two days have been so different: that far off one, and the glorious summer's day of the present? I eventually wandered off the main thoroughfare, and strolled down some of the back roads. Women shouted to one another from the windows above my head as they hung out their laundry to dry on lines that stretched across the narrow alleyways. I could have been stringing out Gilles's underwear to dry I thought as I sauntered along, a smile on my lips. Whatever had happened to Gilles Montfort? Had he survived the war? He'd been an active commander in the communist resistance just before I'd left to join the Maquis. Suddenly my reminiscences were interrupted by the shadow of a man blocking my path, and I looked up into the still handsome face of Khien.

We spent the rest of the afternoon in a small café, talking. Khien couldn't believe his eyes when he saw me stroll by the small bookshop in which he was looking for some book or other.

"You haven't changed much," he said.

"That's good to know. I'll be thirty in the autumn. You must be what now, twenty eight?"

He nodded. "Lien is twenty four. She finished her medical studies in June. We were both students during the German occupation of Paris. I finished my engineering degree in 1942, and I got a job in the Civil Engineering department. It was most useful. I knew where the Germans were planning to do road, rail and bridge repairs. At night, I worked with the communist resistance, and I helped blow up important military installations, troop convoys and such."

"Are you a communist then?" I asked. Khien shook his head.

"No, I didn't join the party. I am still a nationalist at heart. Lien worked in the resistance with me. She was very brave. You can be proud of her."

I didn't comment on that.

"Are you returning to Viet Nam?"

"We are waiting for the delegation to leave. We had tea with Ho Chi Minh yesterday. He is a very charismatic person. One can't help but like him. I am not a communist, but I do believe that Ho Chi Minh is the one to unite our country, and inspire the people to rise up against the French. Lien and I are hoping to travel back with him when he returns home, after these insulting talks are over."

"You may have to wait for Ho to leave. I have the feeling that he'll drag out his stay for a while, even after the delegation leaves."

"But why?"

"He'll be scared to go home with nothing, but it's also possible that he has other more strategic reasons for prolonging the trip."

"These talks have been degrading for him. I do not know why he'd want to prolong such an insult."

I changed the subject. I could tell by the way he looked at me that Khien was still attracted to me, but what about his feelings for Lien? He didn't know how to proceed, so I showed him how. Over the course of the hot summer's afternoon, I eased all his doubts away, and seduced him into making love to me in a small hotel in the heart of the artists' quarter in Montmartre. He must have harbored quite an infatuation for me over the last ten years, for his ardor was intense, and I found it difficult to restrain him, but he was indeed a beautiful young man, with a lean, lithe, athletic build, and the tensile strength of his people. He had a certain elegance and grace to his lovemaking that made the whole animal act a work of art. I had never known such artistry, such delicacy and romance before. He made me feel like a truly beautiful, desirable woman.

"You make love with the grace of a Vietnamese woman," he said, gazing down at me as I lay beneath him. Your hair, your body and your fragrance are Vietnamese."

As I was dressing to return to the Ritz, I could tell that he had begun to feel guilty.

"Dominique, I need you to realize that I have told Lien that I do not love her. There is no future for us as man and wife, but we shall always be friends and work together to free our people. I told her that I have loved you from the first time I saw you, but I did not think that we'd ever meet up again. I love Lien very much as a sister, a good friend. She is also a beautiful woman. I am filled with remorse for being so weak in giving into my lust like this. I don't know what you think of me: you cannot respect me."

"How can you respect me?" I replied. "I know my sister loves you, and yet I seduced you. I am also a married woman." Lien had lost that bookish look of hers then, since last we had met. Oh yes, I'd had revenge in mind – revenge for Lien's taking my mother's love from me, but during our love making, I'd realized that I'd fallen hopelessly in love with Khien.

"Are you only doing this to repay Lien for taking your place in your mother's heart?" he asked, as if he'd read my thoughts. I sat back down on the bed.

"I thought that I was," I replied. "But I think that I've fallen in love with you." He looked at me in silence, his eyes filled with tears, as did mine, and we fell into each other's arms.

It had gone midnight when I returned to the Ritz. Biff was asleep on the chair, and the caretaker had gone. I crept into the bedroom to check on Andy, and he was sleeping peacefully, but his face was puffy and red, as if he'd been crying. Biff had awakened, and he'd come up behind me, and taking my hand, he'd led me back into the sitting room.

"Where have you been?" he asked, more concerned than angry.

"I decided to go to the theater to see the production of Tartuffe that the Comedie Francaise is putting on." I showed him the program. "I'm sorry, Biff."

"Why didn't you come back, and we could have gone together?"

"I was outside the theater, and I just went in on impulse. It was such a lovely evening that I walked all over the city. It was lovely to roam around freely, without fear, without seeing swastikas all over the place. Oh Biff, I'd forgotten how much I love this city. I went into the theater to rest my aching feet, but also to enjoy French theater again. I am sorry. I know I should have called. Was Andy alright?"

"He was fine with that lady caretaker. They'd had fun, but when it got dark, and I returned without you, he began to worry about you. I think it was because you were out alone, and not with me, as is usually the case when we leave him with baby sitters at home."

"You didn't have to go out this evening?" I asked.

"Well if I had to, what would I have done? Who would have been here for Andy?"

"I thought that the Ritz would supply someone. They usually do. I told the lady this morning that she might have to arrange for another caretaker if I didn't get back by the time she had to leave, and she agreed she'd do that."

"Gees, Cici, I guess Paris has rekindled the carefree days of your youth. I'd never have thought you'd be so cavalier about Andy's safety. You've cross-examined every babysitter we've ever got for him."

"I am home," I replied. "I am among my own people, and it may have been a tad risky and negligent of me, but I trust them. I stayed in the Ritz many times as a child, and they always had someone to be with me when my father disappeared for a few days or so."

Biff let it go, and he said that he wanted to explore Paris with me. He wanted to see all my old haunts: where I'd lived as a student in the Sorbonne; where I'd lived with my lovers; where I'd lived when I'd returned from America to work with the communist resistance. He wanted to know every detail of my life before we'd met.

"We should go back to the Haute Savoie, Cici. We could hike those trails again with Andy in the back pack, just as we did when he was a baby." I'd indulged him in these romantic reflections, and even went so far as to respond with a modicum of lust to his lovemaking, but my thoughts were of Khien and when I'd be able to see him again.

Mrs. Nguyen, Chau, My-An and Khien had gone into the kitchen while Kev had translated. Andy had found such delicacy of feeling amusing. Ria had gone with them to make some more coffee and tea. All the time Kev had been translating, Rob had been peering through the shutters down the drive.

"Those black vans are still there," he said, looking at Andy. "Who the hell are those guys?"

"They are looking for me," Andy replied. They've been watching the house all these years, waiting for me to turn up. Don't worry, they know you guys are all innocent. They tried to throw Kev off the trail by threatening him, but they can't hurt us, Rob, believe me. The men keeping them in check out there will not let them hurt any of you, and if you had seen the news tonight, you would know that the days of those guys in those black vans are almost numbered."

"The deer have gone," said Brad. "I've never seen them behave like that before. They suddenly disappeared, and men have taken their place."

Andy just smiled. "Nice of them to help out like that, but I'd see it as just a strange fortuitous event if I were you, nothing more."

"What now?" Kev snapped impatiently. "I don't see that we're any closer to finding out who killed Kit, so why don't you just tell us – cut a long story short."

"Oh Kevin, don't you have an appreciation for fine theater?"

"No, not where the identity of my sister's killer is concerned. She died a brutal death, Andy, and I need to know who could have done that to Kit." Kev was beginning to lose his iron control, and understandably so.

"Andy," I broke my silence at last. "This is not 'theater', as you put it. It is torture, especially for Kev. I can't stand to see him suffer like this. He has had a terrible evening. I think that he's been through enough, so cut to the chase or get out of …" I stopped myself, as I realized that we were in his house.

"My house?" Andy asked, that same expression of amusement on his face. "I think that the house belongs to Mike now, but sorry Mike, I can't leave just yet." Andy waved the gun at us, just in case we had forgotten we were his hostages and that he was directing this tragic farce. "Read on, Kev, will you, there's a good fellow. Oh by the way, you people out there in the kitchen may want to stay out there until this year is over. It won't take long. Mother didn't record many of her nefarious doings from now on, and for good reason."

CHAPTER TWENTY-TWO

The thunder grumbled away and the lightening flashed as the trucks sped through the torrential downpour. Kelly had been ushered out of the shack into the cabin of one of the trucks waiting outside. There were about six vehicles altogether, as far as she could tell from one quick count. Nobody spoke. There was only the sound of the rain. She noticed that the trucks were full of men, silent men, wearing hooded parkas. She and Tin Pan were in the cab of the truck now being driven by Father Petrie. A man had got out to let them in, and he'd moved off into another truck, along with Seb, Manny and Phil. Father Petrie's face looked grim in the weak light of the headlights. He concentrated on keeping the truck on the track, a difficult task, as the mud threatened to have them sliding down the banks into the lake, the waters of which were deep and storm-tossed. Kelly was petrified.

"Who are these men?"

"Friends," Father Petrie replied curtly, but with a smile.

"They were carrying rifles. What exactly are we about to do?" Kelly was scared, and still not sure with what sort of outfit she'd got herself entangled.

"We're going to help Kev. You understand that what you are part of tonight very rarely happens," Father Petrie peered up at the sky briefly, the truck swerved, and he had to keep his attention fixed on the road ahead. "Sorry about that. You and Tin Pan okay?" Kelly nodded, but she clung onto the cat and the door handle.

"What do you mean?" she yelled back over the sound of the rain thumping on the cab roof and the constant slapping of the windschield wipers.

"I told you that our Dragon society was pretty ineffectual in changing the course of events. We can only operate through good guys, who aren't scared of taking on the big boys, but sometimes, like tonight, we need a little extra help."

"There isn't going to be any violent confrontation? How can you, a priest, take part in such an action? How can you, with church affiliations, be a Dragon?"

"I hope not. Violence is not what we have in mind. We're just making the odds more even for a change. I went to Viet Nam as a priest. There are good men who are priests, and they do not care for church politics and dissemination of the faith. They care for people, and helping them in this life. In fact they care for all life. The priesthood is just a cover. Dragons are everywhere, remember. The rich and powerful, who formed these religions, replaced the original socialist teachings of prophets like Jesus with political institutions to control the people, frightening them into obedience with threats of punishment in the afterlife, and rewards in the afterlife if they toed the line and committed horrors in the name of their church or faith. This is hell and gone, an apropos term, from what Jesus intended. Jesus and men and women like him down through the ages have advocated a more caring society, where rich and poor work together.

Communism has replaced organized religions with their own brutally oppressive creed. Religion is between a person and his faith in the force of creation. Politics should be a united, democratic effort, not competition between ideologies, not the creed of the gang over the good of the people."

Kelly sighed. "Tonight, Kev will know the truth, that's all that matters to me."

Father Petrie looked over at Kelly, and smiled quietly to himself.

They drove along the river to the base of the ridge that formed the back of the Chatsle estate. Here the men left Kelly and Tin Pan with Father Petrie, and climbed up the ridge, from which they descended into the forests that surrounded the house. Father Petrie reached back for his rifle.

"You stay here with Tin Pan, Kelly. You should be safe. I'll come for you when you can join Kev. Don't worry, he'll be alright." Smiling, Father Petrie left her, and made his way through the sodden undergrowth in the wake of the others. Kelly waited a few minutes, made sure Tin Pan was warm and secure in the cab, the window lowered enough to let air in, and then she set off through the woods, her way lit only by the intermittent flare of lightening. Tin Pan stood on his hind legs, his paws on the steering wheel, as he watched Kelly disappear into the darkness. His huge dark pupils glistened as with starlight.

CHAPTER TWENTY-THREE

Kev, barely holding himself in check, had continued reading. The Nguyens, Ria and the kids had come in from the kitchen. They couldn't stand the suspense out there, knowing what they had to hear might be hard on them, but it was better than waiting for it all to be over. We could see hooded men standing outside in the rain. They had rifles, and so no one thought of trying to escape. Other men seemed to be keeping the black vans way off, down the driveway.

⊶ ⊷

1946 – 1947:
I had many long days to myself, when I could wander through the forest and go over the ridge and down to the lake that formed the back boundary to the estate. I watched nature prepare for the onset of winter. The deciduous trees put on an amazing show of color, with their deep plum, russet red, brilliant orange-red and gold being offset to perfection by the deep shades of green and

blue-green of the evergreens. The smell of apples filled the air again, along with the smell of wood-burning fires: hickory, cedar, pine mixed with a hint of huckleberry and juniper.

Andy turned three at Halloween, and I was thirty. It seemed ridiculous to be in the throes of an almost adolescent passion at that age. I thought of Khien all the time. I wondered what he was doing, if he were still alive, for the situation in Indochina had worsened. There were battles between the Viet Minh and the French. The French Expedition Forces had driven the rebels into the swamps of the delta in the south. The country was being divided into two ideological halves, with a sort of no man's land in the center.

Ho Chi Minh's forces held the mountains of the north. They had resumed their guerilla lifestyle, after a brief quantum moment at the end of the war, when there had been the very real possibility of there being a true, democratically elected government that would be recognized by the rest of the world as the legitimate governing body of their country, but it was not to be. France wanted to retain control. I imagined that Khien had joined the Nationalists, and Lien too, and possibly my mother. It was a sad case of new, progressive ways being caught on the hooks of old colonial ways that refused to give way, and leaders who still thought power meant oppression and cruelty.

I had seen Khien every day that we had left in Paris. I was in love for the first time in my life. I felt so young and free. Fortunately, Biff had been preoccupied with 'business'. On our last afternoon together, I had felt so desolate that it should have been a rainy day, but nature was perverse, and it had been a beautiful day, the flowers a riot of color, white fluffy clouds drifting lazily against a vivid blue sky. The whole world was unconcerned with the desperate sorrow felt by a pair of lovers about to be separated for what could prove to be forever. I was saying goodbye to love, and to the man with whom I wanted to spend the whole of eternity. I hadn't abandoned Biff and Andy as my mother had abandoned my father and me for the great passion of her life. I had remembered Roza's warning that I would repeat my mother's sin, but, apart from committing adultery, I hadn't. I could not hurt Andy as my mother had hurt me. He shouldn't have to bear the burden of being abandoned as I had. I think that, as little children, we have a sense that we are as lovable as we're ever going to be, and if that doesn't win us protection, security and love, then what chance have we got as we press on through life? If my security and confidence had been shattered as a child, then what would that do to Andy, a boy? Boys need a secure and loving base from which to go out into that hard, competitive and dangerous world of men.

"I do not need to own you or your love," Khien had whispered as we'd made love for the last time. "I love you, and I always will."

"Will you marry Lien?"

"Of course not, but she is my trusted friend. She's knows that I can never love her that way, and she has accepted this. She has a very handsome young lover, a fellow medical student. He is from the south, and he is a fervent nationalist too, not a communist. He is a good person." Now that I felt love, I felt magnanimous to the world at large, and to Lien in particular. I was immensely happy and relieved to find that she was in love too, and not with Khien.

We stood in that dark dingy bedroom in that back alley hotel in Montmartre, and looked deep into each other's souls. We clung together at the curbside, and I sobbed until I thought my heart would break. Khien's eyes were brimming over with tears too. I felt as if we were a single entity that was being torn apart. I got into the waiting taxi, and, as it pulled away, I looked back at Khien through the rear window until the taxi had rounded the corner. My last glimpse was of him standing there, tall and straight, with the most sad and tragic expression on his handsome face. Roza claimed our lives were determined by our stars, and that mine had foretold that I'd run away with the love of my life and leave my child. Well, I had changed those stars.

Biff was away for most of the year. Events were heating up in China and Indochina. He was traveling back and forth between Washington and China, with side visits to Paris, Hanoi and Saigon, not as a representative of the American government, not even as an agent of the OSS, which became the Central Intelligence Agency in 1947, but in his undercover capacity with Zurt Enterprises.

I had surprised Biff by wanting to go to Viet Nam with him, but Biff was not the relaxed old boy he'd been of old, when we still had retained an aura of being semi-heroic. He was becoming more mired in deep dark machinations, and to give him credit, he wanted to protect Andy and me from his employers, so he wouldn't let us join him on his travels. I was still in the employment of the CIA, the officially sanctioned aspects of it at least, and I worked with those good people, who still believed that reliable intelligence, not contaminated by any other self-serving agenda, could prevent wars.

I never had any mail to speak of. Roza wrote seldom, and Kusco not at all. Dragons didn't communicate by mail. There was no way that Khien and I could have corresponded. Andy and I accompanied Biff to Washington DC on occasion, but I never expected to see Khien there.

I didn't see Khien again for almost eight years. In the intervening years, I just existed; my only delights were Andy and the close friendship I'd developed with Connie Kemp. Together, Connie and I managed to keep the gossiping ladies at bay. The Caventrys, Birklys and Wingos did very well after the war, and became very wealthy, due to their association with Biff and Zebulon Zurt. Under the influence of his mistress, Diana Wingo, Zebulon promoted the career of her lover, Curt Caventry, by leaps and bounds. Curt was now the banker of Zurt Enterprises, with financial ties worldwide. He wielded a lot of influence and power – a slap in the face to Dolly's family, who had thought him not good enough for her to marry.

In March of 1949, Biff was away in China, ostensibly to help Chiang Kai-shek's forces to evacuate the Chinese mainland for the island of Formosa. The communists, under their leader Mao Zedong, had won. China was now a formidable communist presence in that part of the world, and no doubt would aid the Viet Minh in their fight for independence. Truman's government was very nervous. There would be no American support for Viet Nam's fight for independence from the French if the Viet Minh were openly communist, and received aid from communist China next door. I couldn't help but wonder what tactic Ho Chi Minh would adopt. He'd want the aid of the Chinese, but to accept it could bring the Americans in on the French side of his country's battle for independence. As it was, America was supplying the French with modern weapons. Heaven forbid that should escalate into America supplying France with troops as well! Biff's clandestine employers no doubt had supplied both Mao and Chiang Kai-shek with weapons, and would make sure that the Viet Minh, as well as the French, would be adequately equipped to wage a nice long war. Where would Khien be in all this?

One blustery, bitingly cold day towards the end of the month, I had an unexpected visitor who had come to stay. Connie and I had been sitting by the roaring fire in the living room, sipping martinis, while the boys were upstairs in Andy's playroom, playing with their train sets in front of a cozy fire. Biff was due home the following week, and a big party was planned at the house for all the country club set. Connie and I were discussing what we'd wear, when there was a loud knock at the front door. People rarely came up to the house as Malachi usually stopped them at the gate, and phoned up from the caretaker's hut to see if I wanted to see them. That afternoon there had been no phone call from the gate, as he had taken Phyllis into town to see the doctor. She had not been feeling well for some time.

I peered out of the side window near the door, and there stood a young black woman. She was quite tall and of medium build. I opened the door, my curiosity peaked. She had a black hat that was trimmed with little white daisies, and she had on an old, rather worn, black coat.

"Madame Chatsle? Roza sent me from Marseilles." She spoke in French. She continued, "Kusco has died, and she is planning to move on. She wants to end her days in…" She glanced past me at Connie, and then gave me a questioning look. I shook my head slightly, indicating that Connie was not one of us, not a Dragon, and she needed to use caution when relating my past in France. Connie could speak French.

"Ah, so Roza is going back to her ancestral home," I supplied coolly, but my heart was struggling to beat as a suffocating wave of grief flooded my being. I had survived untold horrors and dangers without them, but knowing that Roza and Kusco were still this side of life had made me feel secure. I wanted to cry for Kusco, but I couldn't do so then. The woman looked at me askance. Obviously, she had not expected me to be so unaffected by her news, so unexcited by her arrival from so far away. Connie was watching us, a look of marked surprise on her face. I asked the woman to come on in and warm herself by the fire, while I escaped to the kitchen to get her some coffee. I opened the kitchen door to the dark blue gloom outside, and allowed myself to weep. The cold wet wind beat against my tear stained face, and I had to hug myself to stifle the deep and primal need to howl my sorrow into the buffeting gales.

When I had composed myself, I returned to the warmth of the living room, with coffee for the three of us. Our visitor had settled into the deep armchair, and she had switched to speaking English. She had been discussing her passport difficulties with Connie. She now smiled hesitantly at me over the rim of her coffee cup.

"She - Roza - said that you might find me a job here. I have an immigrant's visa and a work permit. I worked a little in New York when I first arrived. I have a sister there. My name is Albertine, Albertine Suchard."

"Your English is good. Where did you learn to speak such good English?" She told me that she had been taught English by Roza and the girls who had... She stopped short, no doubt thinking of something more appropriate to replace the truth. "The ladies who had frequented Roza's....beauty salon." I had to hide a smile. So Roza had sent me one of the girls who had worked in her brothel, and most probably had grown up there. Albertine looked at me and said, with some emphasis, that she had cooked and cleaned for Roza only. She had not been a ... beautician. Roza had taken her in when she'd been five years old. Her father had been killed in a brawl on the waterfront, leaving her an orphan, her mother having died already, and her mother had worked for Roza. She put special emphasis on the word "worked". I asked her her mother's name for I had been very fond of Roza's girls, and they had loved me and treated me well when I'd been a child. They'd had an assortment of children with them – their own and orphans they'd taken in. This woman must be near my age. We must have played together as children.

"Zulukha."

"Zulukha!" I exclaimed. "Why she was a lovely girl, and so kind to me when I was a child! She was from Tunisia, and she married a French-Moroccan soldier in the Foreign Legion, and went back to North Africa with him. I was eight or so at the time. She came to see us before she left, and she had a baby in her arms. That must have been you."

Albertine nodded. "My mother died of a fever in Morocco, where my father, Orlando Suchard, was stationed, and he was allowed to bring me back to Marseilles for Roza to look after, but he was killed in a fight on the dock before we ever got to the Villa D'Emeraude. I was five, but I managed to find the café, The Dirty Parrot, where we were supposed to be heading before my father was killed. Kusco took me to Roza. You were thirteen years old when I arrived. I used to watch you play with your cat, Violet, and your beautiful horse, Dreyfus. I'd watch you from behind the shed in the vegetable garden. You played with all of us little ones sometimes, and you read us stories. I used to love those stories about a magical kingdom called Viet Nam, with its fairy spirits and wonderful dragons..." Albertine stopped, and looked at us with an embarrassed smile on her round, pretty face.

"My goodness! I had forgotten that Zulukha had died in Africa, and that her child had come to us. How could I have forgotten? I'd been very fond of you. You look like dear Zulukha so much. You must be twenty two now," I said, doing some fast reckoning in my head. She nodded. I didn't prolong her suspense, and told her that of course she could live with us, and help Phyllis, who needed help around the house now that her health was not so good.

"I do not need to live here with you, unless you need me to. I have friends, who have just moved to the town, and I can lodge with them. They are named Stan and Anthea Gretavia. My sister in New York wrote to them to ask if I could live with them. They are a middle-aged couple. Stan has got work in the orchards. He is good with trees and growing things, and Anthea is an excellent seamstress. I would have helped her, but I wanted to see if you could use my services first."

"You said that you have a sister? Then Roza must have taken in the two of you."

"No. She is not my real sister, but another orphan raised by Roza. We call ourselves sisters. There were three of us Africans at Roza's. One "sister" is in New York, and my other "sister" fell in love with a soldier in the Foreign Legion. She followed him back to Africa, as my mother had followed my father. She has traveled all over with him, wherever the Legion is sent to fight. She is in Indochina with him now."

"Albertine, I do remember you and your two sisters. You three would watch me with those big dark eyes of yours. You were the most adorable little kids, the hardest working orphans Roza had, and the most cheerful. Roza used to say that just looking at your cheery faces would make her happy. Now, let me see, what were your sisters' names?"

"Salome and Ruby."

"That's right! My, how wonderful to see you again!"

She smiled and sipped her coffee. The three of us spent the rest of the afternoon talking about our lives. It was the beginning of a deep friendship and alliance for the three of us. We let Connie in on our colorful childhood in France, raised by the ladies of the night.

CHAPTER TWENTY-FOUR

"Stan and Anthea Gretavia! Why those are Seb's parents!" I exclaimed. "I didn't know that Seb had a connection to the Chatsles' maid."

"Neither did I," said Kev, shaking his head in disbelief. "Old Seb never mentioned it. In fact, he never mentioned the Chatsles at all. Not even you, Andy, and we were all of an age."

Andy smirked. "All of an age maybe, but I didn't go to school with you guys. I went to a private school back east. I was home only in the summertime when I was young, and not often then, as we traveled a lot."

"Seb and I grew up together. You'd have thought that he'd have mentioned Albertine at some point." Kev had a perplexed look on his face.

"No, you did not grow up together," said Andy with a sneer. "Think back to when you first met Seb. You met him for the first time in what must have been junior high."

"Nah. We were kids together. Seems like he'd been my pal ever since I could remember."

"No, Kev, think again. You and Seb met in junior high when you were ten or eleven or so, because Seb didn't move here until the autumn of 1954."

"How the hell do you know?" Kev snarled back. "If you were off in those fancy schools, how would you know?"

Rob and Mike were frowning, deep in thought.

"My Mom and I moved to San Diego when I was about ten or so, that would have been 1954," said John. "I don't remember Seb at all. I remember Albertine. I adored her. She was wonderful. She taught Andy and me to read."

"You guys were six years older than we were," said Mike. "Come to think of it, I can only remember Seb as an older teenager, not as a kid; whereas I do remember you, Manny and the Mingus boys as kids along with Fletch and the others – my older brother's friends. But old Seb was a character. It sure seemed as if he'd been around forever. Sal, you're the one with the great memory, do you remember Seb as a kid?"

I shook my head. "I remember Seb as a long, lanky, older teenager. He had the reputation of bringing good luck in his wake. Old Man Birkly's horses got sick one summer. They were dying, and the local vets couldn't figure out why. Seb had been off on one of his walkabouts, and he'd returned. Maisie Flahertie, Phyllis and Malachi's granddaughter, had sworn she'd seen him talking to the dying horses one evening she'd dropped off some laundry her Mom, Gretl, had done for the Birklys. She'd seen Seb lurking in the shadows of the stables, and muttering to the poor horses. The next day, Old Man Birkly and all the vets couldn't get over it. They'd gone out to shoot the horses, to put them out of their misery, and there the horses were, neighing and chomping down on their hay, looking fit and full of energy. Maisie told everyone what she had seen, and it came as no surprise to the older folks. Then there was the time my friend Donna Mack, Manny and Colm's little sister, had caught meningitis, and was not expected to live. She made a sudden recovery, and she told everyone that she was lying in her hospital bed at night, in terrible pain. The nurse had gone out to get some medicines. Seb stood in the doorway of the dark-ened room, a pale halo of light about him, and he blew her a kiss, and left some wild flowers on her bed stand, and she fell asleep, and when she awoke the next day, she felt wonderful, her headache and fever had gone. She thought that she'd dreamt it, but there by her bedside was a bunch of wild flowers. We kids grew up on these stories of Seb. That's why he was a legend around here, even before he'd turned up just in time to save Kev. That's why we've been ex-pecting him to turn up any day, even though he's been missing in action in Vietnam for more than twenty years now."

"We all know the stories about Old Seb," said Rob.

Andy scoffed at that. "Oh, Old Seb is special alright, but he didn't turn up here until 1954, and if you read on, Kev, you'll find out why."

Kev picked up the diary for 1948 -1954. Mrs. Chatsle hadn't recorded very much in these years. They had traveled a great deal. She made no mention of Khien. In 1950, we finally sat up and paid attention, for in the summer of that year, she finally mentioned Kitty Occley again. Her only mention of Kitty before this had been to say that Patti had a baby girl, supposedly Biff's, but really Curt's and Patti's, or so we surmised.

━═╬ ╬═━

Summer, 1950:
We spent our summer in the south of France, although Roza, Kusco and Dr. Fleury had gone, and I'd given the Villa D'Emeraude to the girls. They could do with it as they saw fit. Albertine and I went to Marseilles to sort out the paperwork, while Biff and Andy went to Antibes, where I joined them after I had settled my affairs. We

had a lovely lazy time, and sported golden tans. Andy's hair went platinum blond again, as it always did in the summer sun.

When we returned home, we spent our afternoons out on the lake, and I dressed Andy in his usual clothing, very short trousers, wide necked sailor tops, big old rope sandals like the little French boys wore, but Biff complained, and said that he should wear jeans and T shirts like the other American boys. He looked too girly in the clothes in which I dressed him. I hated it when Biff returned home after a long absence and decided to interfere in the way I was bringing up Andy. One day, he disrupted our morning class, telling Andy that I was working him too hard, and he needed to rough-house a bit more, and he scooped Andy out of the chair and carried him off on his big white horse, Trident, holding the boy in front of him as he raced the horse at top speed through the forest and over the ridge. Andy looked petrified, but he didn't cry, but he did cry that afternoon when Biff said that I was making him look too girly, and that I was changing Andy into a girl. It was a stupid thing to say in front of the child. A look of horror had passed across Andy's little face, and Biff and I had started quarreling. We hadn't notice that Andy had run off into the woods, and when we stopped arguing, and called for him, he didn't appear. Biff, Albertine and I combed the garden looking for him, but we didn't find him anywhere. We called our neighbors at the lake, the Caventrys and Wingos, and we all went out looking for him. Just when I'd been about to lose my mind with worry and desperation, Andy had walked back down the sandy lane, eyes red, face streaked with muddy tears, and he'd told us that he'd met a sweet little fairy princess with yellow hair like his, only it had been curly, and she'd told him that he didn't look like a girl, but like a strong handsome horse, like Old Man Birkly's palomino stallion. Andy was very proud of this, and informed his father that he was not a girl, and this princess had liked his clothes.

Albertine took Andy in for a bath, and I looked at Biff, who was deep in thought. A little fairy princess with curly yellow hair, now let me see, who could she have been? Why, none other than Andy's supposed little half-sister, Kitty Occley!

"How sweet," I said to Biff, a sly smile on my face. "You better make sure they know that people around here think that they are closely related. You better do it before they get much older, or Diana will scream incest, even though she knows it isn't so." I turned and walked into the house, leaving Biff to sort out the dilemma.

Poor Tim Occley had taken to drink. Patti raised the two children on her own, unless of course Biff helped her out without my knowing. I wouldn't have minded, but Curt should have been the one to do it. The two children were sweet little ones. Kevin was seven now and Kitty five. My how time just flew by! Well, it must have been hard for Tim to discover that his lovely young wife had not been exactly faithful in his absence, and he'd fought hard for his country and all, even getting the Congressional Medal of Honor. You may well have looked troubled, Biff Chatsle. It had been a rotten thing to let happen to a real hero like Tim Occley, but then what could Biff have done? Zurt held our lives, Andy's and mine, over Biff, to make him do as he was told, and there was no way that Biff could get out of his undercover assignment at this juncture. Biff also was a real hero, an unsung one, along with all our undercover agents.

Kev stopped reading, and took a sip of water. Andy had a strange expression on his face as he watched Kev.

"You mean to say that you didn't know I was known by certain folks to be your beloved half-sister's half brother?" Andy said, not in a mean way, but in more of a thoughtful, speculative way. Kev just looked at him, a weary, emotionally drained expression on his face. "How angry would you have been, Kev, if you had discovered this terrible secret?" Now Andy was taunting Kev.

"Just how angry were you, when you found out?" Kev replied quietly. "When did you find out, Andy? Was it that August day in 1964, when you arranged that date with Kit? Were you afraid of the scandal, or was it much more serious than that? Were you afraid that you'd have to share your father's fortune with Kit? You rich guys never like to share, do you?" Andy laughed, but kept looking at Kev as if he were trying to figure him out.

"Kit wasn't my sister, Kev, but I would have shared everything I owned with her, nevertheless." Finally, after looking at each other for several tense seconds, Andy told Kev to read on. There was nothing of further note until 1954.

March, 1954:
This has gone far enough! The fighting in Viet Nam between the French and the Viet Minh has escalated to the point where innocent lives are of no account. The Americans have given the French a horrible weapon called napalm, which incinerates everything for miles around in a raging inferno. The beautiful jungles with their fascinating and rich diversity of plant and animal life are destroyed, or are poisoned, the animals living on in terrible agony. What has this so called civilized man become? In America's rampant paranoia, President Eisenhower has considered using the atom bomb in tiny Viet Nam to eradicate the communist scourge. I ask you? Who in their right mind would thank him for so doing? If Ike did it to bluff, well it was worth a try, but if he meant it, then it may be a very strategic military and political thing to do, but he has lost sight of the cost and suffering to ordinary, innocent lives. Will these generals and presidents hold court in their bunkers

under the poisonous smoking crater that once was the world, and congratulate themselves on an ideological victory? Damn them all!

The men who fight to the death in those jungles are not just Frenchmen and Vietnamese, there are many Algerians, Moroccans, Senegalese, Koreans and others drafted to give their lives in the name of a country and a people not their own. The French Foreign Legion is there in force, and is in the thick of the fighting. The Viet Minh general, Vo Nguyen Giap, is waging an effective guerrilla war against these French forces, but to do so, the Viet Minh also have been ruthless, and have paid for every success and failure with an astronomical cost in their own lives. There is certainly outstanding courage in the individuals who fight, but for the generals and those politicians, military suppliers, businessmen, bankers, political strategists and leaders back home, watching from a safe distance, there is no glory or honor. I feel only disgust and abhorrence for them.

Albertine's sister, Salome, is with her French Algerian husband, who is fighting with the Foreign Legion in Viet Nam; so are all the wonderful women, the women of the fighting men, part camp followers, part nurses, part warriors – all brave, loyal women, who will not receive any kind of recognition for their bravery and sacrifice for their men. Many Frenchmen left their plantations and holdings in Viet Nam and fled to Hanoi, or even Paris, to save their business affairs, leaving their wives behind to protect and defend the homesteads, and this the brave women are doing.

Biff and I tried to console Albertine when she received letters from Salome describing all the horrible dangers she and the others faced every day, and yet Salome's letters were full of compassion and humor too. She worried about Albertine and Ruby. Were they safe and well, and well treated? Albertine and I clung together and wept. Biff stood by and watched, but not without remorse and commiseration. He was being torn apart by guilt, but he was in so deep, he could only protect us by carrying on.

Salome also wrote of her young son. He had accompanied her and her husband to Viet Nam in the late forties. Now that the fighting was becoming even more deadly, she was worried for his safety. Her husband's foreign legion battalion had been sent to the front lines, to a fortified position near the border with Laos, at a place called Dien Bien Phu. They were to try to prevent the Viet Minh fleeing to safety across the border, and to try to sabotage their supply lines, but, according to Biff, who should know, the Viet Minh had been digging in around the high hills overlooking Dien Bein Phu, and they had dug a system of tunnels under the French dug outs and bases. The Viet Minh also had carried out a tremendous feat in terms of man and woman power, by transporting huge pieces of artillery and other weapons on foot through the dense jungle and along the rough mountainous terrain to the hills around Dien Bien Phu. The French didn't stand a chance.

Biff told us this one dark, rainy day in March, just after Albertine had received the last letter she would get from Salome. Salome, her husband and young ten year-old son had arrived in Dien Bien Phu. Salome seemed to sense the impending disaster, for she asked Albertine to come and save her son, to take him back to America with her.

"I can't get you to Dien Bien Phu," said Biff, as the three of us stood in the gathering gloom, and the rain ran in rivulets down the large windowpanes. "The fighting has started, and it's bad. It's hell on earth, if truth be told. This battle should see the end of the French in Indochina, but we cannot let the communists fill the vacuum created by French withdrawal. There are many thousands of Vietnamese who have fought with the French against the Viet Minh. They are brave. God, are they brave, for terrible reprisals are taken on them if they are caught, and on their families. These Vietnamese, loyal to the French, fight 'with their hands tied behind their backs', and they are reviled by the French and the Viet

Minh. Their morale and confidence are being eroded, and they pay such a god-awful price.

Oh Lord, Cici, I don't know how to help them. I know we sell them arms to bolster them up, but it's not enough. I know Zurt Enterprises has armed both sides, but these poor people pay the cost with their lives. The French have been stupid, but so have we, and I feel that we are going to be even more stupid, but at this point, Cici, it's not just about selling arms, making a profit, it's about those poor people who believe in democracy and freedom to be their own people, to form their own nation again. Shouldn't we Americans of all people support them in this?"

"This is the result of treating war as a business, Biff."

Albertine had put on her hat and coat. When we finally noticed this, we reasoned with her that it was foolish to go out into the rain. We'd take her back to the Gretavias', but she wouldn't let us.

"I am tired of your arguments," she screamed. "My sister and her son are in danger. She has asked me to rescue the boy, and I am going to, no matter how dangerous or difficult it may be. The lives of the people I love are in danger, and I don't care a fig for all your fancy ideas. I am going to save them. Their lives are more important than anything. Keep your presidents, kings and politicians, I love my sister and nephew more than life itself, more than any of these stupid, stupid idiots!"The next day, Biff, Andy, Albertine and I were on a plane to Hanoi, courtesy of the strings Biff could pull. We ended up spending about two months there. We could not reach Dien Bien Phu, and the hopelessness of trying to save the poor people fighting there almost made us mad. The pilots, who could not fly in supplies, could not rescue the dead and dying, were beside themselves, all of them willing to make sacrificial runs, for any attempt to fly in there would be suicidal. The combat units could not get through. They were ambushed and killed. The Viet Minh had Dien Bien Phu truly isolated from all attempts at rescue.

The whole world watched and waited in agony. The men and women of all nationalities fought on bravely against overwhelming odds. They were heroes in every sense of the word. They faced death, fighting to their last breath, and that always demands our compassion and love. Those poor men and women, who would never see their families again, never see their homes; our hearts were with them all. Frenchmen had in some way regained a sort of honor, even if their goals had been delusional and arrogant.

Biff traveled back and forth from Hanoi to Beijing to Washington on legitimate business, and sometimes on business of a more illicit nature, while Albertine, Andy and I waited in our room in the Hotel Metropole in Hanoi. The old city still retained some of its colonial charm. The tree-lined boulevards were more pitted, and the bougainvillea ran riot.

One day, Albertine had gone to the Red Cross center to try to get some news from there, and Andy was attending one of the local French schools, so I decided to wander around on my own. I called in at the Governor's Mansion to pay my respects, and to garner whatever gems of information my American employers in the CIA might find interesting. I was taking my leave after an uneventful and unprofitable morning, when I noticed the governor talking to a group of Vietnamese soldiers in French uniform. I gave them no mind, and was about to walk out into the bright sunshine, when something made me stop to look back at them, and my heart skipped a beat, for standing among them was Khien. He was taller than most of them, and he looked so handsome in his uniform, but surely he had not gone over to the French? I moved behind a large potted palm and watched him. My mind was in torment. I wanted to run to him, to hold him in my arms again and feel his passionate kisses on my face, my neck, my body, but my brain was in a fever of curiosity as well as lust. Khien had been a fervent nationalist, who wanted the French out of his country, but he'd also despised the communists. He had said that he'd work with Ho Chi Minh's forces in a coalition effort to get rid of the French, but he'd oppose a communist run regime after they had gained independence. Had he decided that the communists were too strong since China had gone communist? Khien must have thought it the easier of two options to work with the non-communist nationalists, who had sided with the French, to oust the communists first. Then they could negotiate with the newly formed United Nations for independence. The Americans would help them, if there were no longer the threat of communist domination in Viet Nam. Was that what Khien had done? If so, I could see the sense in it.

They were taking their leave of the governor, and just as he was about to leave, Khien looked over in my direction. Our eyes met, and he froze. There was no way he could avoid being ushered out into a waiting taxi, but I managed to point at the Hotel Metropole, and he gave a barely perceptible nod that he understood. The taxi whisked him away from me. Just that brief glance had rejuvenated me, body and soul. He looked even more handsome, if that was possible. I hadn't seen him for eight years. He had filled out a little, but was still slender and athletic in build. His face had matured around the mouth and eyes. He was thirty-six years old now, and I was thirty-eight. I wondered if I looked old to him. I must have, and that may have accounted for some of the shock that had registered on his face on seeing me. I was still slim. I hadn't put on an ounce of weight. My hair was still jet black, but I too had more lines around the mouth, but not the eyes, not yet, thank goodness. I wondered if he were married, and if he had children, and my heart hurt to think that he had a new life, and that he most probably hadn't thought about me for years. Oh God, how I'd hate that, for I had thought of him all the time, and my one consolation had been that he had been thinking of me too. I had wanted to come to Hanoi to help Albertine, it was true, but all the time, at the back of my mind, I had hoped against hope that I'd see Khien again, and wonder of wonders, I had. What a miracle! I now believed in miracles with all my heart.

Fortune was on my side that night, for Albertine had called to say that she was going out to dine with some of the Algerian women still in Hanoi, and then she was going up country with them for a few days. They knew her sister well. I told her to be careful. Andy did his homework, and I watched the clock and waited for the desk to call up to tell me I had a visitor. I thought to myself that if Khien didn't come, then he was no longer interested in me. I writhed with longing and with doubt. Andy finished up, and told me he was too tired to play our usual game of chess, and he was going to bed. The climate wore him out. It was cloyingly humid, the air torpid, sapping the body and mind of energy. I gave him a goodnight kiss, and sat by the wireless listening to some inane polka music, while I gazed out of the window at people going to and fro on the street below, people going out to eat or to drink before curfew, when the streets had to be empty of all unofficial traffic and personnel. Then I saw him, striding along in some haste towards the hotel. I got up and took my key, locking the door to our room behind me and putting the "Do Not Disturb" notice on the door knob, so that Andy would not be frightened by a maid, and I hastened down to the lobby. The elevator doors opened just as Khien joined a line of people waiting to talk to the night receptionist. He saw me right away, and he came over to me, a smile on his lips. He was still in uniform, which was disappointing. I don't know why it was, but that was how I felt. It was so impersonal at that very significant of times I suppose. I took him up to my room, and I didn't care who saw us, but he had looked around a little nervously at those in the lobby before he'd got into the elevator. He was hesitant to enter the room too, and even more so when I told him that Andy was asleep in the bedroom, but I tip-toed to the bedroom door, and looked in on Andy, who was fast asleep, his mouth wide open. I took Khien into my bedroom, and I locked the door.

We made passionate love, our longing for each other, un-dimmed, unquenched. Khien had not married. He'd had wom-en, but he hadn't loved them. He reminded me that he'd told me he had loved me at first sight, and he'd loved me, and only me, since. He too had hoped beyond hope that we could somehow get together, and he didn't mind if he had to wait until Andy was of an age when Biff could no longer keep him from me. We parted just as the yellow and peach of dawn broke outside, and the cacophony of bird song, mixed with honking horns and the strident ringing of bicycle bells heralded the new day. It took an immense strength of will to let him go. I watched as his tall figure disappeared into the already hot citrus colored haze, redolent of traffic fumes, pungent human and animal odors emanating from the lake and waterways and the scent of jasmine, tamarind and lemon.

Khien had told me that he was still an ardent nationalist, but he was not with the French by choice. Ho Chi Minh had summoned him from the southern forces in the delta, and had asked him to join the Vietnamese fighting for the French, so that he could spy on them, and betray their plans to the Viet Minh through con-tacts in Hanoi. He was by no means the only spy within the French ranks. There were Viet Minh spies everywhere. I must admit it came as no surprise. I understood Khien spying for his country in his country. It was more honorable than spying for one's country in another country, but I was disappointed that he was doing this on behalf of the communists. Viet Nam may well end up like Korea, a nation and people divided. I'd asked Khien if he was a commu-nist, and much to my relief he'd answered that Ho Chi Minh still worked with loyal non-communist nationalists such as he, even if the other committed communists in the ranks of the Viet Minh were not happy about this. I was relieved, but my heart cried out a silent warning. Oh please be careful my love. You are in a pit of vipers, no matter which way you turn.

We met every night, and some afternoons: in my room, when Albertine was away, and in his room, on her return. I had told Albertine all about Khien.

Albertine was sorry for Biff. She admired Biff for putting up with the constant burden of guilt and fear to save us.

Khien and I made love for six glorious weeks, at the end of which, Biff returned. Biff and I had not made love for months. I was no longer able to pretend enough interest to even try to ease his load in life with a tender moment of passion.

When the operation to try to liberate Dien Bien Phu was set in motion, Biff moved heaven and earth to get us included on the mission. Khien had to stay in Hanoi, so that he could report to Ho Chi MInh on how the French were going to proceed after such a defeat. Ho needed spies to find out what the French and Americans planned for the peace negotiations that would take place in Geneva. Khien would be leaving for Geneva with the Vietnamese delegation before our return from the tragic waste of Dien Bien Phu.

The plan was to reach Dien Bien Phu through the jungles of Northern Laos. We left Andy with a trustworthy middle-aged couple, the Brewsters, who were American missionaries in Hanoi, and we set off into the trackless jungles in hopes of saving Salome, her husband and son.

We were under attack as we struggled day and night to hack our way through the dense vegetation. The Viet Minh had guerrilla forces throughout the region. We were eaten alive by mosquitoes as large as small birds. Some of the mission came down with dysentery, malaria and other strange sicknesses.

Albertine had never been in the jungle in her life, and yet her fierce determination to save Salome drove her on through all kinds of hazards and dangers. I followed in her wake. Biff struggled on too, despite suffering horribly from unrelenting dysentery. We were only forty miles away when Dien Bien Phu fell, May 7, 1954.

We rescued seventy-six stragglers who had made it out of the abattoir, and among them had been a little black boy named Achmed, Salome's son.

Achmed was in bad shape. The survivors told us that he had fought bravely alongside his parents, who had been killed when the Viet Minh overran their bunker. Achmed had fought like a maniac, and being small for his age and a fast runner, he had run the gauntlet many times trying to retrieve the supplies dropped from the air. The pilots had to avoid the anti-aircraft guns firing at them from the bunkers built deep into the densely forested hillsides, and so the supplies had to be dropped from higher altitudes. This meant that the landing sites were by no means accurate, and the defenders of Dien Bien Phu had to run into the jungle to retrieve the packages, thereby exposing themselves to enemy gunfire, and ambush. Achmed had made these runs, and had escaped by the skin of his teeth. When the Viet Minh overran the garrison, Achmed had hidden under some dense foliage with a machete, and he'd hacked at the legs of the enemy as they had run by, until, unable to locate him, they had strafed the jungle with machine gun fire. He had managed to run, but he was hampered by the thick underbrush, and so he was hit. He had serious concussion, deep lacerations all over his body and bullet fragments deeply imbedded in his legs, arms and back.

We arranged to have him airlifted out to Hanoi, where French surgeons worked on him for several days before they could tell us that he'd survive. Andy waited at the hospital with us. Andy had been intrigued to learn we were taking a boy back home with us, who would become like a brother to him. Andy had smiled. It was hard to know what he'd really thought. We had been so close when he'd been young, but since we'd been in Viet Nam, Andy had become closer to Biff.

Biff arranged all the paperwork. We could take Achmed back to the States with us. Albertine wanted to adopt him as her own, but shortly after our return, she was diagnosed with cancer, and given only a few months to live. It seemed as if life had taken a tragic turn. I had so enjoyed Albertine's company. She was someone who had kept me in touch with my childhood and Roza and Kusco and, in a way, my father. She had been a breath of France in my American existence. Stan and Anthea Gretavia readily offered to adopt the boy instead. Stan had wanted a son to help him out in his orchard business and the new greenhouse nursery business he'd managed to get going. They were a loving couple, and Achmed, although still coming to terms with the devastating changes in his young life, was a warm and caring young boy, who fitted in willingly and well. He was a happy little soul at heart, eager to please, eager to help and adapt. Stan and Anthea soon came to love him, and find his cheery nature and readiness to ease their load in life indispensable. They named him Achmed Stanley Gretavia, but to help the boy fit in more easily, and to maintain his ties to France, he got the name Sebastian, Seb.

Andy never did develop the close friendship with Seb for which I had hoped. Andy always managed to be off somewhere or other when Seb came over to visit, but he'd turn up just when Seb was leaving, and greet him with forced cheeriness and regret that he'd missed being with him yet again. Albertine and I would exchange knowing looks. We were cool with Andy each time he did this, but as Albertine said, you can't force friendships.

Connie and John had left to join Pam and Dilys in San Diego in 1954. All three Kemp girls were divorced, and Pam and Dil had two sons each, so the girls decided to raise their boys together. There were plenty of opportunities for work in San Diego, and they could all make a fresh start. Andy and I missed them terribly.

Andy was eleven years old when we returned from Viet Nam, and Biff thought that it would be a good idea for him to gain some measure of independence, while getting a first class education, so he sent Andy to a private school back east. I hated the idea.

I knew that Andy had distanced himself from me of late, and I didn't know if it was because of my fondness for Seb, or whether it was a normal distancing from one's mother a young boy goes through at adolescence. Andy had become much closer to Biff, and Biff had taken him off on fishing trips with the Wingos and the Birklys and Curt Caventry and his daughter, Claire. Curt and his son never were together. Chuck stayed with his mother. Claire was the apple of her father's eye, the son he openly claimed that he never had. Albertine, Biff and I felt sorry for Chuck. He seemed a nice enough lad. Andy felt sorry for Chuck too, and he absolutely detested Claire.

Curt and Diana Wingo had kept their secret affair going. Wint did not seem to know about it, but I think that Dolly did, possibly Chuck too, but Claire, if she did know, went out of her way to lavish her affection on Diana, and tried to emulate her in her dress, looks and mannerisms. Her own poor mother, Claire criticized constantly.

Albertine died in February, 1955. She'd been in constant pain for many months, and I had nursed her at home, refusing to leave her side. We'd talked over many things, but she kept returning to the subject of my feelings for Biff. She maintained that Biff was a good and a brave man. She knew that he loved me and Andy more than anything else in the world.

"Help him. He has such a difficult job to do," she said.

Later, when the pain had become too much to bear, Albertine had been under heavy sedation. Connie had returned from San Diego to be with us at the end. Albertine had been pleased to see her again. It had been a cold, rainy day in February when she died. Connie and I held her hands, and Stan and Anthea Gretavia were there, and Seb, because he insisted on being there, even though we tried to save him from further grief. Albertine had been asleep most the time, but she struggled through the morphine and pain, to look at Seb one last time.

"Fine boy," she whispered. Andy was not there. He'd insisted on starting at his new school in Philadelphia that January, half way through the school year, but they had taken him as he was so advanced in all subjects. "It's no matter," Albertine said, a smile on her face. "I know what Andy is feeling. When he is hurting, he prefers to be alone, and I know he loves me, and is suffering right now." I had my doubts.

Albertine's last words were to me, and she told me to trust in Biff: "Love him if you can. I know he is so good at heart." So saying, she died. Biff stood at the foot of her bed and sobbed his heart out. He went away the next day, and was gone for several weeks. Connie returned to San Diego, and I found myself alone with my grief.

CHAPTER TWENTY-FIVE

Kev put the diary down, and looked pointedly at Andy.
"No further along, Andy. What do you want me to do now? I am getting sick of this cat and mouse game of yours. Come clean, or that damned gun isn't going to save you."

"And risk the life of this lovely young girl, Kev?"

"Let the youngsters and the women go into the kitchen," said Rob. "We'll stay here and listen, but don't harm them."

"Not a chance! You all stay here to hear the end of this, but at this juncture, I think that I need to tell you my side of the story, and don't worry, I won't sugarcoat it in my favor. I am telling the truth as far as I know it."

Kev grunted at that. "Fine," he snarled. "Go ahead, why don't you!" Andy bowed his head in mock acquiescence.

"You will remember that my mother had been keeping an eye on all goings on in the CIA and in Zurt Enterprises for the Dragons. There were those she considered the good guys within the OSS, now the CIA. She took herself off to Washington in that lonely period immediately after Albertine's death to find out how much these guys had learned from my father. What they told her shocked her to her core. They had learned a lot about Zurt Enterprises's ways of operating, and their ties abroad, but nowhere near enough to make a strike at them. There were still sensitive connections that needed to be fully explored. Dad had done well in the early years. Zurt Enterprises seemed to have trusted him, and he'd been instrumental in bringing useful men into their fold, men like Curt Caventry and Wint Wingo, men Dad had given the choice to do as Craig McNiall had, and turn down Zurt's offer, but they hadn't. They were willing to take part in corrupt business practices to feather their own nests. Lately, however, after the outbreak of the war for independence from the French in Viet Nam, Zurt had given Dad less to do. They gave him unimportant work. It was as if they didn't trust him. There must have been a leak. The good guys at the CIA had kept this work strictly top secret, known only to the guys who had set up Dad.

On his return, my mother told my father that it was time she employed her particularly deadly talents to help him. Dad did not want my mother to get involved. These guys were dangerous, and they had told him already that his wife and son must remain at home during his trips, to keep Dad on track for them, and it worried him about how much they did know. Had his cover been blown?

How had Dad infiltrated Zurt Enterprises to begin with, you might wonder? He had infiltrated the corrupt organization before World War II. He had joined our military intelligence services after graduating from Harvard. Zebulon Zurt had been suspected of treasonous chicanery before the outbreak of war. He had very lucrative business ties to those wealthy people in Germany, who, afraid of the spread of communism, had supported Hitler and his Nazis. Many rich Americans, with financial ties to Germany, favored the Nazis, and saw them as the force to stop Stalin in his tracks. The Chatsles, as you know, were extremely wealthy, but their lumber industry wasn't doing too well. It was decided that Dad could arrange to meet and mix socially with this Zebulon guy, and get to know his cronies, maybe even convince them to cut him in on it all. This my father did by arranging an appointment with Zebulon to ask for his help in saving the Chatsles' lumber industry. Lumber would be a prized commodity with war looming on the horizon, so Zebulon saw his chance to recruit my father into the fold by giving him some kickbacks, some preference in getting government contracts, and thereby being able to blackmail Dad, or so he thought, should Dad ever decide to blow the whistle on the whole rotten deal. He didn't know that Dad was working within the intelligence services at the time.

"Now let me see, have I got this straight? Biff was in this damn Zurt thing before he met your mother?" Rob asked.

"Yes. My father met my mother just before America entered World War II, and fell hopelessly in love with her, but he couldn't get out of his undercover work, he was too deeply mired in its muck, and he was the only hope the good guys had of keeping track of these powerful and corrupt organizations that had infiltrated the military, media and intelligence services. There was no end to the danger they posed. My father did not want my mother to get involved with them. I think that he was wrong in this. My mother was a much more formidable spy than my father. She had worked with scumbags before the war, spying on them for the good guys, but realistically, there was no way she would have fitted in as an undercover spy within Zurt Enterprises. She'd most probably have killed the lot of them."

"And that would have been a bad thing?" Kev asked.

"The guys here would have been just the tip of the iceberg. There are so many more of them, and we needed these guys alive and operating to be able to sabotage and expose the many, many others. No – mother was a loose cannon.

Her employers at the CIA were not too happy with this love affair between one of their agents and one of the officers in the Vietnamese army that had remained loyal to the French. Mother did not inform the CIA that Khien was a nationalist, spying on the French for Ho Chi Minh, neither did she later reveal, when fighting broke out between the communist north and the American supported south, that Khien was a non-communist Viet Cong spy within Diem's corrupt and crazy regime.

After mother's visit to her employers at the CIA, she went to Saigon of her own accord. The French were out. Khien was there, involved in trying to set up a democratic government made up of all parties. The communists wanted all the power, and it was apparent that civil war would break out sooner or later between the communist backed north and the capitalist backed south.

Mother met up with Khien in Saigon in that spring of 1955. They managed to get away for a few weeks to a lovely resort, Dalat, up in the mountains. There they could forget all their troubles. My mother's diary for 1955 reads like a lurid romance novel."

Khien stood up in protest.

"You are wrong. It was not lurid, but beautiful. We were engaging in an adultcrous affair, yes, but we could not help it. There was so much more to our love than..."

"Sex?" Andy said, with a bored, uninterested drawl. Khien gave a curt nod, but was too overcome with emotion to take it any further, and he abruptly sat again, his head in his hands. Lien put a sympathetic hand on his shoulder, while giving Andy a disapproving glare.

"You would be surprised, Andy, how much wisdom can be conveyed in romance novels, when written by ordinary women. You learn a lot about a woman's life, and what is important to her. You men could learn the art of seduction, and the beauty of life thereby, and become aware of other, less brutal and ham-fisted ways of running this human world." Andy bowed his head for a moment. Was he acknowledging the truth of this? Then he raised his head, and seemed to shake off such notions.

"Lurid or not, that is why I'm giving you a quick synopsis. In any case, the result of all this passion was that, on her return to the States, my mother found herself pregnant. My father had returned home in the interim. It was time they laid their cards on the table so to speak, and confess all. Now Kev you might want to take up the story in the late spring of 1955."

Kev picked up the diary. He noticed that some pages had been written in red ink, and those were the entries for May 27, 1955. Cici and Biff had a quiet dinner together at the house. Both had a lot to say:

⟫⟨⟨ ⟩⟩⟨

Chatsle House: May 27, 1955:
I told Biff that I was pregnant with Khien's child. I told him all about our meetings in Paris and in Hanoi. I explained that Khien and I could not be together. I could not do to Andy what my mother had done to me, and Khien did not want me to torture myself for the rest of my life because of the heartbreak I might cause Andy if I left him for a lover. Biff had held his head in his hands the while, trying to control his emotions. He finally raised his head and looked at me, tears streaming down his face.

"There will never be a democratic government in Viet Nam, at least not in the near future. Zurt Enterprises have made sure of that. Their operatives within the communist held north have influenced Ho's men to take the communist hard line, and jettison the peace talks and plans for unification. They have convinced the leaders to go for all out war. I am afraid that corrupt parties in our own government are torpedoing plans for peaceful resolutions. We see Zurt influences, but it is hard to identify who is doing the actual coercing or bribing. Leaders, journalists and advisors are handed trumped up information that they believe to be true facts. The waters are so muddied that they don't know what is fact and what is fiction.

My only useful source of information was Zebulon, but he died from a heart attack while you were in Saigon. It surprised the hell out of me. I didn't think he had a heart, only a huge wallet. I don't know whether the rest are on to me, but I am effectively out of the loop. I don't know who these guys are working with now. I do know that you went to talk to my guys, and that you offered to help me. I was so thrilled, I could hardly wait for you to get home to show you how much I loved and admired you, not that I'd have let you help me. It would have been way too dangerous. A few days later, I was called back to DC, so that they could tell me you were having an affair with a high-ranking Vietnamese officer, who had supported the French, and now supported the non-communist nationalist party."

Biff gave me a questioning look. "Do you intend to keep on with the affair, or is it over? The child complicates matters I know, but I will accept it. We can say we adopted a Vietnamese half-caste baby. People here know that we have been over there helping out. You and I can travel throughout the pregnancy. Not even Andy need know. He is away until June, when school is out. You may not show until he returns to school in September. You'll only be three or four months along. You can hide it. You're thin and fit."

I could hardly believe my ears as Biff had gone on, working it all out. It was all neat and tidily planned, but it hadn't taken into account feelings, only face-saving practicalities. I felt the hysteria rising, bursting within me. I had given up Khien for Andy, but it hurt like hell. I didn't know how I'd go on without him. I began to panic. I got up from the table. I couldn't breathe. Tears flowed uncontrollably, and I began to sob, then to wail in anguish. Biff had risen, a look of terror on his face. He hadn't a clue how to handle me, and I couldn't help him. I was drowning in despair. He tried to hold me, but I hit him, and kept hitting him. I screamed and tossed about in his arms. He took a hell of a beating, but he held me until I fell at his feet in sheer physical and emotional exhaustion. Biff knelt beside me.

"Go to him, Cici. I can't see you suffer like this. I'll let you have Andy. I love the boy with every fiber of my being, as I love you, but I know that he loves you. You two are as close as a mother and child can be. He loves me too, but it isn't the same. He needs you. Just let him visit me sometimes, whenever he wants."

I shook my head in violent denial. "No! No! Biff I can't risk Andy's safety in Viet Nam. His life is back here. He'll hate me for taking him out of school, for destroying his hopes for a brilliant future. He hates Viet Nam. The climate isn't good for him. He'll never make friends there as he will here. I can't take him with me, and if truth be told, Biff, I can't take him from you. I thought you'd keep Andy as a way of holding onto me, but I can see now that you never have been that vindictive."

"Oh, yes I was, Cici. If you had tried to leave before this, I would have kept Andy from you."

"God, Biff, what sort of life do we lead?"

"I know it has been hard on you with everyone thinking that I'd cheated on you with Patti Occley, and that Kit is my daughter. I know how horrible Diana has been to you. Don't you think I've hated it? I've loved you ever since I laid eyes on you. You are the only woman for me, and I want to scream it from the rooftops. I want to tell everyone that I never could cheat on you. I adore you, Cici."

I felt as if I were in a dark twisting vortex of events spinning wildly around me. Everything went black.

CHAPTER TWENTY-SIX

Kev looked for more written pages, but there were none; the rest were blank. He glared up at Andy, and made to get up to hit him.

"There, there," laughed Andy. "Steady on, old chap. Just get the diary for 1956. Mother stopped writing for the rest of 1955. I guess it must have been too traumatic for her, and dangerous also to commit anything to paper. You know that Auntie Lien has been protecting the diaries, and returned them only when the Feds cleared out, but the bad guys, as Dad so euphemistically referred to them, have been watching the house all this time, waiting for me to turn up. They were quite correct in believing that the discriminating stuff must exist, and that we'd hidden it somewhere, somehow. When they saw your notes, Kev, and the Nguyens coming and going to the house, they knew something had been discovered. Someone had made it available. They didn't suspect that I had resurfaced.

My mother was killed, and right up to her death she persisted in her efforts to find me. Her sorrow at not so doing made it highly unlikely that I'd been found." Andy paused and seemed, for the first time, to lose his composure. He bent his head and struggled with his emotions. When he looked up at us again, he had become an altogether more ravaged soul. His sardonic, arrogant air of superiority had gone, to be replaced by what looked like genuine sadness, grief and something else, a physical and spiritual weariness. God knows how he had survived all this time. He must have lived on the edge; his life under constant threat. I looked over at Rob, Mike and Kev, did they see this too? It didn't look like it. Mike kept peering behind the blinds to look down the drive. Rob kept glancing at the boys, as if he sensed Andy was weakening, and they could rush him, and Kev was frantically perusing the diary for 1956.

The Nguyens clung together in terror. Andy glanced over at them.

"The bad guys don't know who you are, Auntie, although I bet they are scrambling to find out. Kev, let me continue if you can stand it.

I remember having a great summer traveling around Europe with my parents. I hadn't suspected a thing. Mom looked thinner to me, and I put it down to all the upset stomachs she had on our trip. I remember wondering why, because the food was fantastic. She panned out a little by the end of my vacation, and looked quite healthy by the time she and Dad took me back for the new school year. I had been amazed at how loving they were towards each other. They always had loved me, but for once they genuinely seemed to be enjoying each other's company. I had returned to school in the best of spirits."

Kev had not been listening, and who could blame him? We were all on tender hooks to find out who had been Kit's killer.

"Shut up!, Andy. I need to read this." Kev said absorbed in what he had found. Andy sat back and lifted the gun once more. I could sense Rob's frustration. Kev was about to begin, but Mike interrupted him.

"Look here, who are those guys out there? The guys in the vans I take it are these friggin Zurt Enterprises guys, but who are the others, the ones with those goddamn guns? Are they those Dragon guys?"

Andy smiled, "No, Mike, they are not. They are the good guys, the ones trying to keep this country honest. They are trying to keep it the country they thought they had been fighting for, given their all for. They need to know that their souls have not been compromised for some rotten evil. All fighting men, who killed and were killed, need to know that they haven't been duped by those preaching patriotism, God and country, while all the time really having an altogether more self-aggrandizing, evil agenda. To kill innocents is an awful thing. This you know when you face death. You know that you have no right to live, to expect any kind of reward in the afterlife, if there is such a thing, and as you cry out in pain and agony, it's the tortured faces of those you've killed you see before you, and it's your mother you cry out for, to bring your innocence back; the innocent child you were, when your mother loved you and protected you from evil, pain and horror." Andy looked at Kev, who had been watching him intently as he'd been talking to Mike. They both looked at each other, their sadness evident in their faces. These were men who had looked over the edge into the deep abyss of human suffering and evil. Andy nodded at the diary Kev held, and taking a sip of water, Kev started reading.

<hr/>

Saigon, February 1956:
Biff sat by my bedside. The rain ran down the window of my hospital room. Biff was absorbed in his reading, glasses on the end of his nose. Did I love him? Yes, I did, but not as I loved Khien. I thought over what he had revealed to me this past summer about the Patti Occley affair. I wish I had known all this sooner.

When he had returned to the States at the end of the summer of 1944, Biff had set up a meeting with Zebulon in a hotel in Seattle. Zebulon had wanted him to recruit local friends with influence to help grease future business dealings. Biff had approached Craig McNiall, but McNiall would have nothing to do with construction work for the military. He smelled a rat, and he did not trust or like Zebulon.

"Men like him are only out for themselves. They don't give a darn about our fighting boys," Craig had said, before he'd stormed out of Biff's office, slamming the door behind him. Biff had been proud of him. He had approached Craig, knowing he was an upright businessman, in the hope that he'd have an ally he could rely on within Zurt Enterprises, but Craig would have been too honest and upfront for such work. Still it had been worth a try. Biff was feeling vulnerable in his undercover work, and lonely."

We all looked at Mike, who had tears in his eyes, tears of pride at his old man's integrity. Kev continued:

"Zebulon said he'd been introduced to a promising young man by a lady friend of his, who came from Biff's town. 'You know her, Biff, Diana Wingo, a real classy girl. I met her at your party just before war broke out. She's become my er...well...mistress, and I do feel like one lucky son-of-a-gun. In any case, this fella is eager to get ahead. Father's a train driver, but this lad is keen on banking, getting in with the rich crowd. He lucked out and married into the Felspar Family in Seattle, big in electronics and chemicals, but downright snobbish folks. They don't cotton to me, and I don't cotton to them – stuck up rubbish. Anyway, they give this guy a hard time. He wants to show them he can get rich all by himself, without freeloading off them. In any case, Curt Caventry is his name, and I know he's another of your school chums, and he was at your house that night too, with that Felspar bitch he'd married.'" I'd cracked a wry grin at Biff's take-off of this vile Zebulon character.

It turned out that Curt was in Seattle, getting treatment for his back injury. His father had just died, and he'd been more determined than ever to free himself of his wife's family's money. Curt was a clever guy, good in math and economics, with an almost uncanny knack for banking and investing. Zebulon and Biff had met with him while he was in hospital.

To cut a long story short, Curt had agreed to work with them, if they would finance his way through university. They promised him a future filled with all kinds of promotions, prestige and wealth, and all he had to do was become Zurt Enterprises's banker when he'd completed all the necessary training, and ease the way for future transactions they might want to carry out in the Pacific Northwest.

Curt and Diana had fooled around in high school, and behind Wint's back after Diana and Wint had married, and even after Curt had married the wealthy Dolly - too wealthy to divorce. Diana wanted to be wealthy too, and she'd badgered Curt and Biff to get Wint into Zebulon's racket as well.

"Wint intends to go in for law, when he gets out of the navy," Diana had said, "He could be helpful to you, Biff, as an attorney." Biff hadn't wanted to involve his friends in this rotten business, but it had all got out of control after that damn party Zebulon had forced on Biff, insisting that he invite his local pals, who may have something to offer Zurt Enterprises. Biff had thought that not any of the guys he'd invited would have been influential or promising enough, but Zebulon had thought otherwise, especially in Diana's case, and she had done the rest, getting Curt and Wint involved. If Biff had objected in any way, it would have caused all kinds of alarms to go off in Zebulon's head. He barely trusted Biff as it was. Biff had shown too much integrity in other areas of his life, which he'd passed off to Zebulon as building up trust to further cover his real objectives for Zurt Enterprises down the road.

When Biff had been home in 1944, before Andy and I arrived that fall, Diana had approached him with another problem. She was pregnant with Curt's child. She was going to tell Wint's father and her parents that she had a job in Los Angeles with the USO. She could hide the pregnancy there, and decide what to do when the baby was born. She didn't want an abortion as it scared her. Wint might want more children after the war, and the abortion may prevent that, and the docs may tell Wint that she couldn't conceive because she had scar tissue from an abortion. This had happened to some girl she'd known. She couldn't risk that. Diana went on to tell Biff that Curt had a long-running friendship, innocent mind you, with Patti Occley, and they'd worked in the diner together. He'd said that Patti always needed money. Diana suggested that Biff could pay Patti to take the child when it was born, and have her pretend it was hers. She might agree if Biff paid her a good amount, and kept paying her to support the child.

Biff couldn't believe his ears. He asked her why she hadn't gone to Zebulon for help, but Diana said that was all over. Zebulon had found another, younger, woman, a wannabe starlet, and Diana was history. She'd looked a little drab of late, being in the early stages of pregnancy, and Zebulon had commented on it, and Diana had hinted that she was pregnant, and that he was the father. Zebulon had dropped her like a hot brick, offering no help. Biff asked her if she was sure that Curt was the father, and she said there was no doubt about it. She and Curt were madly in love, always had been, and she and Zebulon had taken strict precautions, whereas she and Curt had not.

Biff had refused, screaming at her that she was asking him to jeopardize his marriage to a woman he loved more than life. If people found out that he was giving money to Patti, then they'd assume that he was the father of the child. Diana pointed out that she and Curt could so easily trick Zebulon into doubting Biff's loyalty. If Zebulon had dumped Diana, he still liked her enough, and he was grateful to have a budding banker, Curt, and wannabe lawyer, Wint, as future Zurt Enterprises employees. Biff didn't go along with this. He went to Zebulon to expose Diana's ruse, but he couldn't get Diana in trouble by pointing out her infidelity to Zebulon. She would have been killed, and Curt too. He let Zebulon believe the child was his, Zebulon's, and he explained his own reluctance to help out lay in the fact that he loved his wife, and it would destroy his marriage. People would talk, because it would be very suspicious if he were paying money to Patti, when everyone knew she had a baby, and Tim hadn't been home for two years. It would be too obvious for words, and the gossip would get back to his new wife and she'd never tolerate what she thought was his unfaithfulness. Zebulon laughed, and told Biff that Diana's ruse was brilliant, and he must go along with it. Zebulon added the extra punch, that Biff's new wife and infant son could be removed from the picture altogether. Biff knew that this was no idle threat, and frightened to the core of his being, he agreed to this stupid plan.

Patti had been approached by Curt, and she'd agreed to go to Los Angeles with Diana to do USO work for nine months, if she could tell Tim about it in her letters, so that he wouldn't be upset seeing her with a child on his return.

She'd leave Kev with her mother. Curt agreed. He was rejoining his unit in any case, and Tim was in the same unit. He'd explain it all to him. What Curt did, however, was threaten Tim that his powerful connections would kill him, Patti and baby Kev, if they didn't do as they were told. Tim was a brave man, but he was a poor man, and if the war had taught him anything, it was that poor, ordinary guys always paid the price. It wouldn't matter what he claimed to be the truth, if Curt had powerful connections high up in the government; it would be their truth not his. How ironic, when Tim had a Congressional Medal for bravery above and beyond, had served his country with courage, honor and integrity!

Diana and Patti had returned home after the birth, Patti with Diana's and Curt's baby girl, named Kit, and Diana, just to rub in her revenge on Biff, who had spurned her advances in school, had let it slip to all her friends that she'd heard that Biff Chatsle was supporting Patti's child. Patti was just too blinded by the money, and the hold she thought she had over Curt and Diana that could lead to potential blackmail in the future, to do the right thing by Biff and her husband, Tim. Curt, however, disabused her of any attempts at blackmail by threatening her life and that of Tim's and Kev's, in no uncertain words. Thereafter, Tim and Patti lived in constant fear and guilt. It turned Tim to drink, and Patti to being lost in a fantasy world, in which she imagined Biff as her hero, and the delusion went so far as to Patti's believing that Biff actually did love her. He was so good and kind and all. Kit's later attachment to Andy, when they had been youngsters, only served to add to Patti's delusion of having something special with Biff.

I looked over at my falsely maligned husband, as he sat there reading. He had done so much good, but everyone thought he was a corrupt son of a gun, and let's face it, Biff had played that part well for public consumption.

There was a knock on the hospital room door. Biff and I were alert instantly. The door opened cautiously, and there stood my sister, Dr. Lien. She had taken a great risk in leaving her mountain hideout to come into Saigon. She was wanted as a Nationalist rebel. Biff thanked her profusely, but her eyes never left mine. Our lives had become so complicated. My emotions overflowed, and I started to cry, and she cried too. She told me that she was married, and that she had given birth in the jungle to two sons and a daughter. She looked older, haggard, thin, but then she lived a hard life hiding in jungle camps.

Biff left us. I asked after her welfare, her family and our mother. She assured me that all were fine. I thanked her for doing this for me. She made no comment. She just hung her head.

"Khien is very brave," she said at last. "He has always loved you, ever since he first laid eyes on you. I loved him for a long while, until I met my husband, with whom I am very much in love." She smiled shyly, and I returned her smile.

"I am so happy for you, but I worry about the dangerous life you lead."

"You forget that I have always led such a life. I was on the run with my parents from the moment I was born." Did I detect a flash of pride in her eyes?

She still had that over me, and it surprised me that it still hurt like hell. Now I was going to give up my daughter for the sake of my son. "We will look after her as well as we are able, until we can get her to our mother who lives in a safer hideout up on the border with China. She will take your child – her grandchild."

"I have met her I think," I said tentatively. "She posed as my son's amah in Kunming, early in 1945."

Lien nodded. "Yes, she was pleased to see her grandson, and now she will look after your daughter."

"Did she ever love me?" I had to ask, though I broke down in tears as I did so. Lien didn't answer right away. She took her time, but on reflection, I could tell that she was overcome by the moment also.

"She loved you very much, but she did not want to encourage you to find her, and lead such a dangerous life. I admit that, when we met in Paris I was a jealous younger sister, and I encouraged you to believe that our mother had loved me more than you, because I looked like a Vietnamese, and because I was the child of her lover, the man for whom she abandoned you, but she always loved you. She left you with your French father, because you would be safe. You didn't look Vietnamese enough to be accepted by the rebels. My father always knew that she had sacrificed much for him and their cause. He told me what a terrible thing she had to do in leaving you behind. It had broken her heart. Her cruelty to you before she left you was to make you hate her and forget her, but you never did, and this she discovered later, when she met you in Kunming. The way you had looked at her had revealed all the sorrow and yearning you had felt over the intervening years, and it broke her heart again, so much so, that she had to leave before you returned from your mission into Tonkin province. She said that there had been one moment when she would have told you her identity. She'd hinted at being a dragon, and you had responded, but your husband had come in, and the moment had been lost."

"Tell her I love her, and that is why I am giving her my daughter to bring up in place of me. I am told that my daughter, like you, looks Vietnamese. My son and I do not, and so I will stay with him, as I stayed, or rather was left, with my French father." Lien added that our mother had felt extreme gratitude and love for my father, and had left me with him out of her love for him, and his love for her and for me. She couldn't take me from him. It would have broken him completely. He had me to live for.

Biff held me close after Lien left, taking the baby girl I hadn't even seen away with her. Khien knew about his daughter, but in his vulnerable position as a spy, there was nothing he could to do to help out. Lien had been his idea, and I'd agreed, so long as she took the child to our mother.

Roza had been right after all. I had copied my mother's mistake, and if the rest of the fortune held true, then this girl would become a dragon in her time, and hate the mother who had given her up, who hadn't even set eyes upon her. Had I handed her my wretched life, always wondering why, always wondering if her mother loved her, was thinking about her at all?

CHAPTER TWENTY-SEVEN

There was a long silence, which Andy was the first to break: "It seems, Kev, that neither of us had Kit for a half-sister."

"She always will be my kid sister," Kev whispered throatily. "I grew up with her, and a fanciful little spirit she was. She was a fairy child, not of this world at all, and not in any way like those cold, horrible people, Diana Wingo and Curt Caventry. She was special, and she was meant to be ours, Ma's and mine. She brought light into our drab existence."

"She brought light into my life too, Kev," said Andy, genuine emotion in his voice, his eyes. "I loved her. She was, as you say, almost magical. We played in the most beautiful imaginary world, out there in the sunlit woods by the old backwater pond, that to us was an enchanted sea, and we were the prince and princess of the magical kingdom of Vetnum."

"It was never magical," sighed Mrs. Nguyen.

"Don't worry, Kev, you were always her knight in shining armor," Andy continued, not even giving his aunt a glance, but lowering his gun. No one made a move to take it from him. Tali stayed sitting at his feet. "I went to Harvard in 1960 to study political science and history. I knew of my father's and my mother's involvement with the CIA and Southeast Asia. I wanted to go into the same line of work. I wanted to serve humanity and my country.

I had told my parents, after I'd completed my doctorate in May 1967, that I wanted to work for the CIA, and could they wangle it for me? I remember the looks on their faces. They were devastated. They tried to get me to change my mind, reminding me of all the pitfalls and dangers, telling me that the present CIA was nowhere near as honorable as it had been in the good old days when it had been the OSS, though Mother had her doubts about its integrity even then. They told me how such work often compromised one's loyalties to the people, one's moral and ethical codes, one's very soul, but still I persisted.

My father knew that I was homosexual by this time, and he brought it up. 'Being gay blows your career in the CIA, right there,' he'd said, sitting down heavily, a look of exasperation on his face. I replied that I didn't think so. I could speak twelve languages fluently, including Vietnamese, Chinese, Japanese, Russian, Arabic and Farsi. I had intellectual tastes. I was a connoisseur of fine foods, wine, music, the theater, opera and art, thanks of course to Mother. I had traveled all over the world, and I was a handsome son of a gun, who didn't mind seducing women, as well as men. The CIA rarely managed to get their hands on such a gem. My parents had their doubts, but they conceded to my wishes.

My father arranged an interview for me. I felt confident, but what about my politics? I fabricated a more conservative attitude when questioned, whereas, of course, my natural inclinations were a little bit more liberal, more moderately socialist. I told them that, like my mother before me, I could infiltrate the leftist groups with ease, should that be required of me.

I went to work for the CIA in January, 1968. LBJ had been maneuvered away from his plans for social reform, and was being forced instead into stepping up military involvement in Viet Nam. No awards for guessing who was pushing the paranoia button in certain government, military and media circles, sensitive to such pressure. Yep, you got it – good old Zurt Enterprises.

It had been over twenty-five years since my father had been put behind the scenes to spy on these warmongers and mercenaries, and he had got nowhere of late. They had kind of humored Dad along after Zebulon had died. I, of course, was not supposed to know about my father's secret work, but he had told me.

My father and I had gone skiing in Chamonix during the Christmas of 1970. We had stopped to take in the breathtaking view from a high mountain slope. We could see way over the valley and lower alpine peaks. The sky was a deep unbroken blue, the sun warm on our perspiring red faces, the air brisk and fresh. My father reminded me yet again that I had been born in just such a place as this in the Haute Savoie. I knew their war stories well.

My father then told me that I had a sister somewhere in the depths of the jungles of Viet Nam, and that the wonderful amah I'd adored as a toddler had been none other than my grandmother. I was stunned beyond belief, but the point of this father-son opening of hearts and minds was that my father felt that Zurt Enterprises had tumbled to him, and that his life, and possibly mine and my mother's, were in danger.

My father had been ordered to attend a meeting being held in the mountainous terrain of the border country between Laos and Vietnam, to sell a new sort of grenade launcher to the North Vietnamese. The meeting was set for the coming new year, February 1971. Curt Caventry would be there. Curt seemed to be the man with a lot of influence in the organization these days. My father needed to tell his controllers in DC about this meeting, but he thought that Zurt Enterprises had penetrated the good guy set up. Many of the old guys my parents had worked with in the CIA were retired or dead. They were not sure of the loyalty of the new younger replacements. My father was convinced that someone had blown his cover. I told him that I'd look into it. There were still good guys in the CIA. I had colleagues I was sure I could trust. They had been trained by my mother, whose exploits were legendary. I asked him to introduce me to the men and women he reported to nowadays, as a replacement for him as undercover agent within Zurt Enterprises. My father adamantly refused to do this.

'It's a nest of vipers, Andy. God, look what it has done to my life, what it has done to my sense of integrity, my soul. I cannot let you become involved with these ghouls. You'll never know peace and security again. You'll have to watch your back constantly, and if you have people you love, you'll have to fear for their safety too.' He and I wouldn't have had much time to look into this when we returned to Washington in any case. My father's meeting with these Zurt Enterprises traitors was only a few weeks away.

My father flew home the next day, but I persuaded my mother to stay on in Paris with me for a few days. My father had given me a warning look as he'd boarded the airplane back to the States, but I'd waved, a wry grin of complicity on my face, that carried in it the reassurance that I would not tell Mother.

Mother already knew that something was up.

'You asked me to spend time with you in Paris, Andy. How gullible do you think I am?' she started in. 'You do not usually want me around.' She asked after my friend, the ballet dancer and choreographer, Franz Schuler-Dahl..."

Ria gasped, so Andy stopped in surprise. Ria looked steadily at Andy.

"How do you know Franz?" she asked in a horrified whisper.

"You first," Andy replied.

"He is my cousin – not a blood relative. Our mothers are very close friends. They went through the war together. They worked in the anti-Nazi resistance in Germany together. I adore him. He is a wonderful person."

"Yes he is. Well, well, what a small world! Franz and I have been lovers for some time, and we met when Mother took me to a ballet he'd choreographed and performed in back in 1962 in Paris. This was the time of the Cold War, and all kinds of crooked shenanigans were taking place, especially in Europe, but also in the States. Zurt Enterprises was not pleased with the Kennedys, as they were planning to raise taxes on the wealthy, and had started to question the need for military involvement in Asia and against Cuba. My parents had discussed this. They had expressed their fervent hopes that the Kennedys had wealth and power enough to protect themselves if they did this. I had overheard it all, but it had gone over my head. I was nineteen and in love. JFK's assassination brought it back into focus, and I was more determined than ever to work for Dad's good guys, with Dad, to destroy this corrupt Zurt organization that got rich off war, death, suffering and assassination.

I was with Franz in Paris that summer of 1964, when Kitty phoned me. She was in a panic. She'd…"

"Hold on there," Kev interrupted. "How the hell could Kitty call you in Paris? We didn't make international calls in my family. I don't remember seeing a foreign call on our phone bill."

"She called me on the Caventrys' phone."

We all sat bolt upright in surprise. The firelight danced across our frozen faces. Even Bubs and Bugsy raised their ears.

"In the summer of 1964, Chuck and Dolly Caventry had enough of being put down by Curt, Diana and Claire. Curt had threatened to leave all their money, their businesses and investments to Claire. He was cutting Chuck out of his will, and Wint Wingo was in the process of trying to prove Dolly mentally incompetent, so Curt could take over control of her personal fortune. Old man Felspar had hated Curt, and scared that Curt would do what in fact he was planning to do after his death, Felspar had taken precautions to protect Dolly's fortune when he died. He had died that summer of 1964. He'd left everything to Dolly, but he had named Craig

McNiall, his most trusted friend, as Dolly's financial advisor. Craig had to approve all expenditures. Curt had been about to put his plans into action the moment Felspar died. The papers had been drawn up to commit Dolly to an institution, and Chuck to penniless oblivion. Curt had attended the will reading in high spirits, and his anger at being cheated out of the Felspar millions had known no bounds. He had raged against Dolly, Chuck and Craig McNiall. He'd stormed out with the threat that he'd get back at them all, his dead father-in-law included. Craig McNiall straight away, as was his right in the will, vetoed all Curt's spending of Dolly's fortune, and very cleverly suggested Dolly support Curt and not leave him. Dolly's money was to go to Chuck if she died, or was committed to an institution. Craig felt that if Dolly stayed with Curt, she and Chuck might be safer. Thus advised, Dolly expressed her undying love for Curt, and surprise, surprise, her commitment papers went up in smoke, as Curt realized that he could still get Dolly's money through applying a bit of honey instead of vinegar. While still officially competent, Dolly might let Curt seduce her into changing her will in favor of him and Claire, so the situation returned to status quo, so to speak.

Dolly and Chuck had enjoyed their revenge, but this victory only had whetted their appetite for more. Dolly had learned of Curt's long time affair with Diana in a spiteful quarrel with Louise Birkly, who had let the cat out of the bag, but Dolly had not acted on it. It merely had proved what she had suspected, but had refused to fully realize for years. Louise had been too afraid to tell Diana what she had done, and was heartily relieved when Dolly told her that she didn't believe her for one second, and that she wouldn't honor this obvious lie by mentioning it to Curt and her dear friend, Diana. Dolly had told her beloved son, however. It had been at this juncture that old Chuck had revealed the ace up his sleeve. He had been watching his father's business associates come and go over the years, and he'd noticed that Curt had taken very special precautions with certain friends, that rotten old Zebulon Zurt for one, filing their papers in a secret cabinet hidden behind one of the wooden panels in the wall of his study. The key, Curt kept on a chain around his neck. The precautions that Curt had taken with this key had intrigued old Chuck. Why, Curt even kept it on while water skiing, and Chuck had watched Curt put the key in a zipped pocket in his swimming trunks when he went swimming. Chuck longed to get hold of that key. He had waited and waited for his chance. He told his mother this, when she told him about his father's affair with Diana. Now they both waited for the opportunity to find out what was in that filing cabinet.

Two days before Kit was murdered, Chuck's and Dolly's patience and perseverance were rewarded. Curt had an important meeting, and he had been about to file the papers in this secret file, when he'd received an urgent phone call. He'd taken the call, and his anger had been terrible to behold, but in his anger and frustration, he'd placed the key, which he had removed from the chain around his neck, on his desk. He'd been extremely upset, and had left the study to pace back and forth along the jetty out on the shores of the lake. Chuck had taken his chance and opened the file. He'd grabbed some papers, any old papers that came to hand, anything was better than nothing, and he'd re-locked the file, and placed the key back on the desk. Then he'd made off to his room to peruse his find – and what a find it proved to be!

Chuck had stumbled on the papers relating to Kit's birth, the legal documents that Curt had Patti sign, but amazingly he had been foolish enough to tell the whole story. What had made him commit it all to paper? Obviously he had loved Diana, and he hadn't wanted to let it go unrecorded that they had a child together, but giving into such a romantic indulgence had proved his downfall. Chuck could hardly contain his joy, could hardly believe his luck.

Dolly and Chuck put their heads together, and decided to tell Kit. Chuck was very fond of Kit. She had defended him when the others of the Lake crowd had teased him mercilessly; when his own sister, Claire, had made him the butt of all her nasty jokes, had undermined all his attempts to get girlfriends by ridiculing his flabby and clumsy physique, had taken his place in their father's affections and trust. Kit had such a clever and pithy wit, and she'd put Claire in her place on her own and Chuck's behalf many times. Chuck had adored her, so they invited a surprised Kit to an early afternoon tea.

Kit had been hurt and stunned to learn of all this duplicity surrounding her birth. She had loved you, Kev, and it had shaken her to her core to realize that you were not brother and sister; you were not related by blood in any way. Dolly said that Kit was a much better sister to Chuck, albeit half sister, than the sister she had given him. Chuck had hugged his mother, and wiped away her tears. He looked from Dolly to Kit and said that they looked more alike, with their softer, more feminine looks, large blue eyes, curly blonde hair, than Claire looked like Dolly. Claire looked like Diana. Kit had given Dolly a big hug.

When she was walking home, Kit thought it all over. She couldn't tell you Kev, and she was very angry with Patti, so she reached out to me. She went back to the Caventrys' and talked it over with Chuck and Dolly. They were worried about Dad's friendship with Curt, but I was an unknown entity in that regard, and this friendship Kit and I had shared may well prove a godsend, so they let Kit phone me in Paris. If Curt challenged the call on his bill, Chuck would say he had a friend in Paris. Curt would make him pay for it, but that was alright, seeing as Dolly would reimburse Chuck. Dolly actually admitted that she'd admired my mother for taking Diana to task on many occasions.

I told Kit, when she called, that my parents had told me the whole story. We both said that we were sad that we weren't brother and sister, but we'd acted like we had been over the years, so what the heck! We were still close, and we'd always hated Curt and

Claire Caventry and Diana Wingo. I told Kit that I'd taken great pleasure in the fact that we'd looked so alike, much more alike than you and Kit, Kev. She'd laughed, and told me to stop those jealous feelings I had about you. You were not her brother either, but you were her world, her hero. You'd always be her brother.

I warned Kit not to tackle anyone until I got home. I told her that she must go and see my mother. My father was away on business in DC, but mother was home. We hung up, but Kit had not gone straight away to see my mother. She bumped into Claire Caventry as she was leaving Dolly and Chuck. Now Kit and Claire loathed each other..."

"God did they ever," whispered Kev. "I teased Kit once that I fancied Claire, and I did sort of. She'd flirted with me a few times, and I'd kinda liked it. I told Kit this, and she hit me. She really let me have it but good. I laughed and fended her off, but she let rip, and wasn't going to be teased out of it, and that was before she knew...Holy shit, she was Claire's half sister!"

"In any case, Kit couldn't resist the temptation to stick it to Claire, and so she told her everything. Claire went ballistic when Kit told her. Oh, Kit hadn't stinted on any of the details. Kit told me later that, after ranting and raving at her for telling atrocious lies, Claire hit Kit with her tennis racket, but Chuck came running to Kit's aid, and held Claire by her arms, while she kicked at his feet and shins. Then Claire suddenly went deadly quiet. Chuck cautiously released his hold on her. She looked at the pair of them with eyes filled with hate. She picked up her tennis bag, and said that they would pay a terrible price for this, and off she went."

We looked from Kev to Andy, our mouths open and dry with suspense and anticipation for what would come next. Andy was deadly serious, as was Kev. They both stared at the floor for a few moments, breathing hard.

"Which of those psychos killed Kit?" Kev asked, raising his eyes to glower at Andy.

"Bear with me," Andy replied, a look of intense hatred in his eyes, but his hatred was not aimed at Kev. "When I got off the phone, I phoned John in Cambridge. I'd been meaning to, and so I got it out of the way while waiting for my flight home. I did not tell John I was going home. It would have been too complicated to explain in the time available, and as it turned out, I unintentionally gave myself an airtight alibi. Then I caught the first flight to DC, met briefly with my father at the airport, where we had arranged to meet in a hurried phone call before I left Paris, and then Dad arranged a private plane for me to fly home.

I got in the day Kit was killed. Kit had not been to see my mother. I waited and waited for Kit to show up at the house. I got fed up, and told Mother that I was going for a walk along the ridge and down into the woods, and that she should talk to Kit, keep her there until I got back. That was when you saw me, Kev, pink sweater and all."

Kev gave a huge sigh, and then he sobbed his heart out. We just sat there, helpless to be of comfort. What the poor man had gone through all those years ago, it had to hurt like hell. He'd just been vindicated in his belief that he'd seen Andy that day, as he'd testified.

Andy waited, and when Kev nodded for him to continue, he gave Tali the gun, explaining that it wasn't even loaded, and went over to place a hand on Kev's shoulder. They stayed like that for a few moments, Kev touching Andy's hand on his shoulder. Andy continued:

"Kit turned up finally by late afternoon. She told us about Claire's attack on her, and her threats. Kit also said that she was leaving that evening with the love of her life. She had told her mother that she was meeting a special man, but she hadn't told her about finding out about her real parents. Patti thought it had been me with whom Kit was leaving. She'd known of, and encouraged, our friendship over the years, but Kit never had told her that

I was homosexual. I begged Kit to tell me who this man was, but she would not. He had a miserable life, and she was his only confidante. I thought of Chuck, but Kit laughed, and pointed out that he was her half brother after all. I'd forgotten that. We wished her well, and warned her to cover her tracks as best she could. She told us to tell my father to talk to Patti."

"So you don't know who Kit was meeting that night? Oh God, how much more of this can I stand?" Kev was on the very edge of losing it.

"I have a good idea, Kev, …"

The suspense had been agonizing, and at last we were going to learn the truth, but Bubs shattered our wits by suddenly jumping up and rushing to the side kitchen door, barking his head off. There was a timid, yet frantic scratching at the kitchen door. This interruption produced a shock to our senses, which had been focused wholly and totally on what Andy would say next. We all looked at one another. Rob hung his head in exasperation, and angrily got up to answer the door. Andy took the gun from me. I had taken it from Tali as quickly as I possibly could. I don't trust those things. Andy warned Rob back from the door, and he crept up to peer out of the side window. We were all silent as the grave, our mouths dry with fear. We were not afraid of Andy any longer, or of the gun he held. He had exonerated himself in our eyes, and even Kev made no attempt to tackle Andy.

"There is a woman out there," Andy hissed back at us. "She is drenched and lying on the ground, tapping at the door. She looks terrified." He moved to the door and opened it a crack.

"Let me in. Oh please for pity's sake, let me in."

Andy opened the door, and quickly dragged her into the kitchen. Then he slammed the door and re-bolted it, taking one more glance through the window after he had done so. Kev pushed through us, crying,

"It's Kelly. Kel for God's sake what are you doing here?'

"Kev! Kev! Thank God you are alright!"

They clung together. Kelly was soaking wet, blue with cold, her teeth were chattering, her whole body shaking. She could barely control the shaking to speak. Ria went upstairs for blankets. She was the first to dare to venture up there since Andy had appeared in our midst. I could see Tali and Sean look at her as if she were mad to go up there, but she re-joined us, and was fine. I don't think Ria had given it a thought. She'd just thought of Kelly, and that she needed warming up. The rest of us were still frozen in a stupor of suspense and fear. Ria pushed Kev aside, and pulled at Kelly's sodden parka. Deb and I joined in, and I told the men to go back into the living room, which they did. We stripped Kelly, rubbed her arms, legs and feet. I held her to me and rubbed her back. The others wrapped her in the warm blankets, and Deb made her some tea with sugar in it, while John returned to the kitchen to hand Ria a glass of brandy. She made Kelly sip it until it was gone, and then we rubbed her hair and put her in one of Tali's spare track suits. We put woolen socks on her feet, while Tali blew dry Kelly's hair. Eventually the shaking ceased and the color began to return to Kelly's cheeks. She sobbed quietly to herself the whole time. Obviously she had been badly scared, but then she'd made it through whatever was going on outside. When dressed, and somewhat recovered, she asked to join Kev. We all returned to the living room, where the men stood around, pale anxious looks on their faces. Kev sat on the arm of the chair. He looked all wrung out, haggard. He leapt to his feet when he saw Kelly, and led her to the big armchair by the fire. Mike and Rob had built up the fire, so that a good blaze was going. Andy had put away the gun, and he and Brad had opened the shutters a crack to peer out into the stormy darkness. The rain was still coming down in sheets, and lightening tore across the sky. The wind howled relentlessly.

"Do you see anything?" Rob asked.

"Not a damn thing," Brad replied.

"Don't go out there," Kelly shouted, one arm clutching Kev, the other extended to Rob and Brad, a look of fear and urgency on her face.

"What is it, Kel?" Kev whispered into her hair. He held her close, and gently rocked her.

"Oh, Kev, I don't know...I..." she looked up at him, and then burst out crying. Ria handed Kev another brandy, and he made Kel sip it. She calmed down. She looked exhausted.

"Have you eaten, Kelly?" I asked. She shook her head. "Well try and nibble on this sandwich. You'll feel stronger once you have something in your stomach."

Mike looked over at Andy, a quizzical look on his face.

"Andy," he began. Andy looked over at him, sadness evident in his eyes, as if he knew what Mike was going to say. "You're going to think I'm nuts, but you are alive aren't you?"

"As alive as those guys out there."

Kelly whimpered, and we all looked back at Andy for an explanation.

"Did you and Kev ever see Fletch when you were over there?"

Andy laughed, "I take it you mean Viet Nam, not over there," Andy pointed up into the Hereafter?" Mike shook his head and looked away in embarrassment. Andy relented and apologized. Andy had not seen Fletch in Viet Nam, but Kev replied that Fletch had been killed before Andy had got to Viet Nam, but he'd seen Fletch in Da Nang, when he'd gone back for his second tour of duty.

"Fletch was in the administration office at Da Nang, but he'd been keen to get into the fighting. He felt that his family's influence had got him the cozy posting, and he felt guilty. He wanted to be an ordinary Joe. I told him not to be so stupid. Rich guys and poor guys were getting butchered everyday. They'd have given anything to have pulled a safer posting. I'd left and gone on a tour of duty up in the mountains, and when I returned I'd heard that

Fletch had got himself on a mission up into Co Ka Leuye, very mountainous terrain, covered with jungle. It was heavily infested with North Vietnamese troops, there to protect their trails into and out of Laos. The battles had been intense under difficult terrain and weather conditions, which often prevented air rescue of the wounded. Fletch had been seriously wounded by sniper fire in the beginning of March, 1969. They'd got him out, but he'd died of his wounds before reaching the hospital. His commander had written a glowing report of Fletch's bravery under fire. Fletch was a good old guy, Mike. The kids around the base loved him. He always gave them candy, sodas. He helped them with their animals, got their cuts and bruises seen to, helped the older girls too. He had a reputation for helping the prostitutes get medical care and food. They used to tease him, because he didn't have sex with them. They used to call him Papa Dime, because he always left dimes for the kids, the girls, wherever he went. It had become a game to find Papa Dime's coins when he left them to return to camp."

Mike, Rob and I exchanged smiles.

"He used to do that to us too, when we were kids," said Rob, blowing his nose, tears in his eyes. Mike was mopping away his tears too. Kev smiled sadly.

Kelly had calmed down. She sat up and looked around at us all.

"Why didn't you stay at Manny's?' Kev asked. Kelly gave him a long steady look. She then told us what had transpired at Manny's shack.

"Seb!" we all screamed as one. Kelly nodded, looking only at Kev. Kev was stunned, as were we all.

"Seb is alive and here?" Kev stammered. I'd noticed that neither the Nguyens nor Andy showed any surprise when Seb was mentioned, and Grandmother Nguyen stood up and approached Kev.

"We have been sheltering Seb since his return. We were the ones who rescued him when he went to save Mr. Chatsle, Biff, that long ago day. Khien had been present at the meeting between the

Northern Vietnamese, Mr. Caventry and Biff. He had returned to our hideout in the mountains to tell us that Biff had managed to tell him that Andy was out there somewhere, trying to watch his back." Khien got up and walked over to Kev.

"I asked Biff if Andy was with the secret illegal operation into Laos. Biff said that he was." Khien bowed his head at Andy, which Andy reciprocated. "I told Biff that we'd had them under surveillance all the time, and that we had orders to kill them all. Orders we had been given by Mr. Caventry. I warned Biff to be careful, and told him that I would try to save Andy. Biff had looked awful, pale, ill. I didn't know how else to ease his mind. I managed to slip back to my forces, to Lien, Chau and little Mai, who was then fourteen years old, but an effective fighter in our guerilla forces. Mai is, of course, my daughter and Dominique's, I mean Mrs. Chatsle's." Khien bowed his head again, this time to no one in particular. "Mrs. Chatsle had not seen our daughter since her birth, but Mr. Chatsle had visited us secretly every time he'd come to Viet Nam on business. The shady nature of his business meant that we could meet up in the jungles of Laos on occasion, and I'd made sure that he could have at least a glimpse of the girl as she'd grown up. He always managed to smuggle gifts to her through me. When I went back to meet with Lien's band of guerillas, whose presence was not known to the North Vietnamese, I told Mai that her Uncle Biff's son was in danger. She wanted to help him at once, not knowing that he was her half brother.

I had to return to the North Vietnamese unit to get my orders before returning to my undercover position as spy in the government of the South. Lien effected the rescue of both Seb and Andy."

"Yes, she did," said Andy. "Not that I appreciated it at the time. I was shot down when I rounded that corner, but I managed to crawl into the underbrush. I'd been hit in the chest. My lungs had been pierced, and I couldn't breathe. I passed out, and came to in a camp in the jungle. My chest was tightly bandaged, and I had an I.V. drip in my arm. I felt lousy, as weak as a kitten. I was in some pain, and I thought that I must be a prisoner of the North Vietnamese. I was, but not what I'd expected. In the chaos of the fighting, Aunt Lien's little unit had managed to smuggle me to their camp, hidden in the depths of the jungle between Laos and Viet Nam. My aunt, being an excellent doctor, nursed me back to health, and I got to meet my cousin, Chau. Unfortunately, my uncle and my aunt's sons had been killed some time ago. I had no idea that the young girl fighter with Chau was my sister. She was an amazing child, beautiful beyond compare, graceful, clever, a linguist, speaking English, French, Chinese and all the local dialects, and deadly. Mother would have been proud. Mai, of course, had no idea of our relationship either. I thought that Mai was Lien's daughter.

One day, we had a visitor in camp, an older woman, with gray hair, a beautiful face, tall and lithe figure. She looked down at me for some time as I lay there watching her, thinking that she resembled the nurse I had liked so much, when a toddler. Strange, I know, but her face had stayed in my mind, in my dreams.

'Your father is safe,' she said. I'd been going out of my mind with worry. I'd tried to break loose so many times, that my aunt had to have me tied down."

"He'd been very ill and delirious with his wounds," added Mrs. Nguyen. "He'd kept screaming for his father. I had to keep him sedated. One must not scream when one is in hiding in the jungle. We moved around silently. We very rarely spoke, and when we had to, we whispered."

"I asked this woman how she'd known my father was safe," continued Andy. "She said that he had returned to the States with 'that man of evil'. Unfortunately Khien had not been able to reach him to tell him that I was alive and relatively safe with them. My father had returned to the States full of worry about my safety, and he'd tried to return to Viet Nam, but Zurt Enterprises would not let him. Dad knew about the secret mission into Laos, and tried to get his good guys in the CIA to find out if it had gone well. He and my mother had lived in agony for several weeks, until finally they received the letter from my commanding officer that I was MIA, and that the men on the mission had been killed, except for Kev and two others, one of whom had since died. My father was on his way to DC to look into the matter, when he was killed in a car accident. My mother believed with all her heart that Khien had managed to rescue me, and that I was alive somewhere with her family. She, of course, made many visits to Viet Nam, both during the war and especially when it was over, with the Missing In Action group. She also had that tribunal look into whether Kev had been involved in any way with my disappearance. I am sorry about that Kev, but it would have been an excellent opportunity for you to have taken revenge on me for Kit's murder, and it was obvious to all that you had not been convinced that I had been in France, and of course I hadn't been. I had been out on the ridge. You had seen me that day, and you knew it. My mother must have been terrified, convinced that you had taken the opportunity to kill me in Viet Nam under battle conditions.

Aunt Lien looked after me for months. She told me all about the family, about my mother's childhood. She also told me about my mother and Khien and my sister, Mai, and it was then that I realized that the girl was the sister my father had told me about that Christmas skiing trip we'd taken to Chamonix. Lien also re-introduced me to my grandmother, Marie Claire, otherwise known as Minh Li.

Minh Li came to camp one day, just before I was due to be transported to a drop off place near an American base. I fully intended to get back to DC to resume my intelligence work, and hopefully, keep an eye on my father's work, but Grandma blasted those intentions.

'You can never go back,' she said. 'Your father has been murdered, killed in what appeared to be a car accident. You are in grave danger. They don't know of the association between your father and Khien. Khien attended a meeting with Zurt Enterprises and the more corrupt members of the South Vietnamese government and certain people in your CIA. One of their number betrayed your father. They know that you were working with your father. They still think that your parents are estranged, and that your mother does not know of your father's work with this Zurt Enterprises monster. The good element in the CIA have protected her well for Biff. Khien thinks that these good people will protect your mother still, but you will be killed as soon as you surface, and who will question your death? You are missing in action. You can just turn up dead'.

I'd begged her to let me try to save my mother and avenge my father, and that was when she told me about a group of people who might be able to help.

I was taken deep into Laos, and from there I traveled overland to their border with Burma. I had papers and a Canadian passport that claimed I was a Canadian freelance journalist. I was Jean Pierre Arendt from Montreal. My entry point into Burma already had been stamped in my passport, so I was cleared to leave there and go on to New Delhi, India. There I would be met by even more 'friends'. Imagine my great surprise and delight to find that these friends included my love, Franz Schuler-Dahl. We traveled on together, and he told me about this Dragon Society to which he belonged, as did my mother and my grandmother and all the people who had watched over me and helped me along my journey.

I returned to Paris with Franz, and assumed another identity, Carl Dumont, from Aix-en-Provence. I even had a professorship in the university there, where I taught political science. The years flew by. Then Franz returned from a recent ballet tour of the States, and told me that my mother was dead under strange circumstances. When he related the details to me, I knew that she had been murdered. Franz held me while I cried my heart out.

I felt such anger, the need for retribution on a grand scale, and Franz said 'All in Good Time'.

I could not actually contact my mother during the years of my exile. She was under constant surveillance. I did not know about Seb until recently. I had thought that he had been killed trying to meet up with my father that same day that our group had been attacked, and I had been wounded."

"We also managed to get to Seb as he'd made his way to rescue your father that day in the jungle," said Mrs. Nguyen. "We told him that we had matters in hand. He rebelled of course, tried to get away. We had to knock him unconscious. He was transported across the Laotian and Chinese borders to the high mountain ranges of Yunnan Province by Dragons, as his family was of our sect. He could not return home either. We told him that Mr Occley had survived, and that you were safe, Andy. We asked him to join us in our battle against Zurt Enterprises, and he could do that much more effectively out of the United States. He wanted to help Mr and Mrs. Chatsle, but he was shown a much better way to help them, even if it would take several years, and a great deal of traveling to reach enlightenment.

Seb has been all over the world. It has been revealed to him just how deeply entrenched Zurt Enterprises is in the governments and business and banking corporations in all countries. The only way to fight them is to try to ameliorate the effects of their evil doings by helping to inform the people of their rights, and of their might."

"Twenty-five years later, and here we both are," said Andy.

"Why didn't you let your mother know that you were alive?" I couldn't help asking. Andy looked at me.

"Sal, she knew. She just had to keep up the pretence of looking for me. That bedroom I heard you all wondering about, Tali's room, it was done out with a girl in mind – Mai – but the years slipped by, and although my mother knew that her family had escaped to

France, there was no safe way to contact them. She didn't want Zurt Enterprises looking into their backgrounds, because they were of interest to her. Khien had let mother know about us through an extremely deep undercover CIA agent, put in place, as were my father and mother, in the old OSS, well before war had broken out in Viet Nam. They had worked secretly for a Dr Emil Franz, who was a secret advisor to President Roosevelt, during WWII. You all know my father's deep cover back-up guy. He's from around here, Kerr Toddy, the engineer, who left in the early 1960's to work, supposedly, on a project in the Mekong Delta. Kerr has been of immeasurable help over the years. He returned States side after the fall of Saigon in 1975. He then traveled back and forth between the South of France and here on several engineering projects. He kept us in touch, and Zurt Enterprises never tumbled to him. Good old Kerr. He died of natural causes just before mother was killed. She bought his old blue Thunderbird. It would have broken his heart to think that his beloved car had killed her."

Needless to say, I was struck dumb by this revelation. I looked at Rob and the kids, and they were staring at me in disbelief. Mrs. Nguyen smiled at me.

"There are no coincidences," she said. "Only truths that relate to a problem that somehow or other manage to come together, and I believe that old car is going to provide us with some more."

Kev and Kelly had been very quiet through all this.

"Those men out there are strange," Kelly whispered. "They wear hooded jackets. I could not see their faces. They did not make a sound. I was supposed to stay in the truck with Tin Pan, but I had to know that Kev was safe. I let the men go on ahead, and then I left Tin Pan safe in the truck, and I made my own way down here, but as I crossed over the ridge, I saw those black vans with men with guns standing outside them in the pouring rain, and they were trying to drive off an enormous herd of deer. There were deer in the driveway, and through the trees and on the lawn. Then the deer moved off as Father Petrie and our men approached. Well I didn't see through all the rain what happened exactly, but suddenly the deer had disappeared and the men were there, holding the guys in the black vans at gun point. I couldn't rightly see, but, oh God, I...I...am not sure what was going on!

I was about to creep on down through the soaking undergrowth to the kitchen door, when this figure loomed up in front of me. I screamed, but the thunder and the wind and rain smothered the sound. He ignored me. He went on by as if I wasn't there. The lightening flashed as he'd stood in front of me, and I swear...Oh God, Kev! I don't know. He hadn't a face. The hood had the shape of a head, but it had been dark, no face, just darkness, and I don't mean that he was black or dark skinned. There had been no face. He'd made no sound. I was terrified. I ran for the house as fast as I could, but I fell, and all I could do was just lie there in the mud and rain. I had no energy to get up, for what must have been many minutes, an hour even. When I could move again, I was chilled to the bone and sodden. I just managed to make it to the door. I've never felt like that before. I'm telling you, Kev, it is strange out there. The sky, the air, the wind and rain, they're not normal, and neither are those men, the ones with whom Father Petrie, Manny, Phil and I came."

Andy broke the long silence that followed.

"Kev, the time has come to tell you who my parents and I figured killed Kit." Kev looked up at him as if in a dream. He didn't say a thing. Not any of us did. "I returned to France after Kit had left mother and me that day. Mother telephoned later the next day with the news that Kit had been brutally murdered out at our special place, the little backwater near Dub Mason's hut. I wanted to come home right away. I was grief stricken. I wanted to find out who had done it, and kill him in the most painful way imaginable, but my mother persuaded me to stay in Paris. She said that she had remembered to make a note in her diary, in the initials code she used to remind herself of things, that my father needed to see Patti."

"My God!" I exclaimed. I was right about those initials KB c A to tell B to c PB." Rob just cracked a smile at me. We all wanted Andy to continue.

Andy just shook his head. "Well, my father went to see Patti, and he told her about Kit finding out about her parentage, and the whole dirty rotten scam they had kept up all these years. Patti hadn't seen it as dirty, but as something special between them. She was more scared of losing this tie with my father, and about the cessation of my father's payments, now that it was out in the open, and Kit was dead. He promised that he'd still help her out. He told her that, if the story became public knowledge, then any one of them could be seen to have a reason to murder Kit, but he seriously doubted that Wint Wingo, the D.A., would want to expose his own wife's long lasting adulterous relationship with Curt Caventry.

My father was proved right, because Wint neatly had avoided all that by arresting you, Kev. You took the fall. Curt and Diana had got to Patti, and she was too terrified to think straight, that was why she let you take the fall. Curt had told her that they could get you off, but they didn't tell her how. Old Patti had trusted them as always. When you said that you had seen me on the ridge, well that was their way out. Diana was thrilled that they could put the blame on me, but my parents had been expecting this. They had thought ahead, and had made sure my trip home to talk to Kit had been well concealed and covered. There was no other suspect, and when you were exonerated by old Seb, the case went down as unsolved – very convenient all around, and then you went off to Viet Nam for years, and didn't return until the trail had grown cold.

My father and mother wanted to solve Kit's murder. We all felt that you and Kit, as well as your father, Kev, had paid the ultimate price for this stupid, cruel deception. My parents felt that, if Patti hadn't told you about Kit's birth, then it wasn't their place to do so. Patti was a lost cause. She was pathetically devoted to Curt and Diana. It had been the proudest moment in her life that, when they had been in dire straits, they had reached out to her for help. My father also suspected that Curt had frightened the life out of her when Kit had ended up dead, and Kev had been conveniently blamed for it. It had shown Patti that she had no way out.

My mother had used her astonishing female intuition to do some research of her own. Diana had not been looking very well of late, and two days before Kit had been killed, she had begged off a meeting of the Women's Charity Organization, saying she had to go for a medical check up in Seattle. This had been the same day that Chuck had taken the incriminating papers from his father's secret file, and he and Dolly had spoken with Kit. Mother still retained her talents as a spy. She went to the hospital in Seattle several days after you were arrested Kev. She and Diana had the same doctor, so it had been easy to get an appointment for a check-up. She arranged it so that she was the last patient the doctor saw that day. She left her handbag in his consultation room when she left. She went back for it and, as she'd hoped, the doctor was with his secretary, looking over the next day's schedule. She slipped into the empty consultation room through the door that opened into the main corridor, thus avoiding going through the waiting room, where the doctor and his secretary were. She found his file cabinet unlocked, and quickly rummaged through the files until she found Diana's file. She took it, and beat a hasty retreat. In her hotel room that night, she read the file, and found that Diana was terminally ill with cancer. There was a brief note that the doctor had called Curt Caventry after the diagnosis had been given to Mrs. Wingo that day. Mother surmised that it had been that call that had so upset Curt that he'd left his precious key unguarded, giving Chuck the chance he'd been waiting for all this time. Mother hadn't known what to do with this information. It hadn't added anything to the search for Kit's killer.

My parents knew that Kit had called me from the Caventrys, and they were rather keen to talk to Dolly and Chuck, but Chuck and Dolly refused to meet with them. Then several weeks later, my father was food shopping in Kemp's supermarket, when Rusty Kemp called him into his office. Imagine my father's surprise when he saw Chuck sitting there. Rusty left them alone, and Chuck told Dad that he and Dolly believed that Claire and Ken had killed Kit. My father asked for credible proof. Chuck told him that Claire had threatened him and Dolly after Kit had left that day, saying that her father would claim they had forged the papers to make it look as if he'd been unfaithful to Dolly, and thereby Dolly could sue for divorce and get her hands on his money. Claire had said she'd back up her father's accusations, and so would Ken Birkly and all her friends. They would all testify that Curt had loved Dolly faithfully. Dolly knew that Curt and Claire could pull off such a rotten trick. After this confrontation, their life returned to normal: a normal, loving family life for Dolly for public consumption, but a life of mental abuse in the privacy of their home. Unfortunately, Chuck had no tangible proof that Claire and Ken had been involved in Kit's death. My father asked why they had confided in him. He was one of Curt's business associates after all and close friend. Chuck had smiled, and replied that he was aware that Dad, Curt and Diana were involved in this cover-up, and that Dad had got Curt into this Zurt Enterprises thing that he'd had a chance to read about in his father's secret files, but he'd added, as a warning to my father, Curt had suspicions about Dad's real agenda. He had paid for a spy to infiltrate Dad's close friends at the CIA. He had not uncovered anything untoward yet, but Chuck felt that Dad should be alerted to the fact that he was being watched. Chuck added that he felt deep in his bones that my father was a good guy, a feeling that Craig McNiall had endorsed, and so had Kit, by wanting to call Andy. Chuck said that he was considered a foolish fellow, but he was willing to go out on a limb and trust in Dad. If

Dad was not an upright guy, and was in this thing up to his neck, well then, what else could Curt do to his son and wife that he already hadn't done? My father had thanked him for his trust in him, and said that Chuck and Dolly could rest assured that he wouldn't mention this meeting to Curt. He warned Chuck to be careful. Curt had become more and more ruthless. Chuck thanked him for the warning.

The years slipped by. My father was killed. Craig McNiall had entrusted Dolly's financial security to Kerr Toddy before he'd died, a condition that Dolly had agreed to in a secret meeting. She paid dearly for it. She was found dead in her bath tub, electrocuted by her hair dryer. Chuck inherited his mother's money, and Curt and Claire could not contest it. Kerr Toddy had continued Craig's protection of Chuck's rights, and his inheritance could not be touched. Chuck went to live in Seattle, entered the CIA as a good guy, married, and hopefully will live happily ever after.

Diana died a year after Kit. Curt and Claire had been bereft. Claire had done well in university. Ken Birkly was completing his medical education in San Francisco. They didn't marry until 1969, and then Ken went off to Okinawa and Viet Nam, where he served as a doctor at the base in Saigon until 1972. Since then, Ken has developed a lucrative practice in Seattle, and Claire has gone from strength to strength in Washington DC. She ran for Congressional candidate for our district and, as you all know, is now our State Senator. She always manages to serve on the Senate Military Armaments Appropriation Committee. Ken worked as a doctor at Bethesda for a while, but now he is back working in the hospital here in town. He and Claire fight. She cheats on him, and yet he stays with her. I only hope that he has a more lovable companion on the side."

"Why does Ken stay with Claire? What hold does she have over him, or that they have over each other?" asked Deb.

"Interesting question," replied Andy.

"So we'll never know who..." Kev began, with a deep heart-breaking sigh.

"Hey, dawn is breaking out there. It's still wild and strange, but those guys in black vans have gone. The other guys are still here," Brad said, peering out of the shutters. "Hold on, Father Petrie is out there," he shouted excitedly, "And he's coming up here with a tall black guy and Claire Caventry!" Brad stared back at us in alarm.

There was a loud hammering at the front door. Mike opened the door, and in came Claire Caventry, wrapped in a very stylish raincoat. She let the fur lined hood drop, and there she stood, the epitome of elegant, expensive taste; her platinum blonde hair glistening in the lamp light, an arrogant red-lipped sneer on her finely chiseled face – Diana Wingo reincarnated, except for the hair color.

"Got you at last, Chatsle." She gestured to Father Petrie and ... wonder of wonders – Seb - back from the dead, as we'd hoped all these years. Father Petrie held a gun on Andy, while Mike and Rob hugged Seb. Seb, however, while smiling and hugging back, kept his eyes on Kev. Kev was stunned. He got up slowly, and wended his way through the furniture, stepping over blankets and cushions, until finally they faced each other. It took a moment or two of just staring at each other in amazement, and then joyous relief, as the two old friends, reunited at last, after going through unbelievable horrors, clung to each other, tears streaming down their faces.

Claire Caventry cracked a smile.

"Good to see you boys back together again," she snapped. "Now then Chatsle, you are going to answer at last for your many sins, murder, desertion, deliberately putting your men in harm's way, and last, but not least...treason. You have earned the death penalty for every one of your heinous crimes." She looked around at all of us. "You all look somewhat dumbfounded. What tale has this master of tales been telling you? That he and his parents were the good guys within the corrupt old CIA? That they were finagled into working with an evil organization called Zurt Enterprises, with which my father and Wint Wingo were involved? How his parents were heroes of the resistance in World War II? So on and so on. Oh and incidently, Kev, you had seen this miserable bastard on the ridge the day Kit was murdered, and he killed her." Claire looked at Andy, "Didn't you, you evil son-of-a-bitch, and believe me that term is most appropriate as regards your mother. Go on, Seb, tell us what he did to you in Viet Nam."

Seb was busy trying to hold on to Kev, who was struggling to free himself to get at Andy, his face white with rage.

"Andy had betrayed us on that mission into Laos. We were surrounded by the North Vietnamese. They had us like fish in a barrel. Kev was lucky to escape with his life, and that other young soldier he rescued too. They were darn lucky. I was shot and taken prisoner. I spent the rest of the war in a prisoner-of-war camp way off in Siberia. Yep, that's where they shipped me. That's where I've been, until some visiting American big wigs negotiated for my release last year."

Claire Caventry kept nodding her head, a self-satisfied leer on her face.

"Phil Mingus and Manny Mack are eager to get their hands on you too, Chatsle. You got their brothers killed on that mission. Shame Seb and Colm happened to catch your old man at his double-dealing game on behalf of the enemy, and let's see, who was he betraying us with? Who was his contact with the North Vietnamese? Ah, yes, old Khien here, and the rest of Mrs. Chatsle's family. Old Cici had been a communist spy from way back, hadn't she, Andy, even before the Second World War, if memory serves me correctly? My, my, how she'd had us all fooled over the years! We've caught up with you all now though, and believe me, death is almost too good for you. Your mother cheated us, but you won't get away so lightly. Come on Chatsle, time to pay the piper."

Claire indicated to Seb and Father Petrie that they needed to take Andy away. We had followed all this in stunned amazement. We'd been on some wild ride that night. We hadn't noticed that another group of heavily armed men stood in the doorway. Claire had not noticed them either, and when she did, she stood there as if poleaxed.

"Hello, sister dear. What are you trying to pull here? I think you'll be interested to know that I have warrants for your arrest for the murder of Kitty Occley, back in 1964, and for the recent murder of Phyll Prentiss, whose body was found in marshland in Norfolk, Virginia the day before yesterday. You are also under arrest for corrupt dealings with armament dealers that involved treason against the United States of America, and willful harm to our forces fighting in foreign lands."

If we'd been shocked out of wits twice that evening already, this third one rendered all logical reasoning on our part impossible. Chuck Caventry stood there, warrants in his hands, a smile on his face. Claire had screamed and struggled as the men with Chuck had taken her away to a waiting van. We all looked at Chuck. Seb and Father Petrie hugged Andy, and they were laughing fit to bust, until they saw Kev's face. They sobered immediately.

"Sorry, Kev. We can never make it up to you, but we've waited and waited for this chance to give Claire Caventry her comeuppance. We have not been able to determine how many people were involved in Zurt Enterprises. We still can't, but there is no way they can use their influence to save Claire now. Curt has no remaining pull with those guys. He's too old, lived out his usefulness. Claire took his place in the organization, and was set to rise high in the government, as high as potential candidate for the presidency. We were helpless to stop her."

"When I escaped to Seattle and relative obscurity," said Chuck. "I did my best to destroy my father and Claire, and Zurt Enterprises. I had my mother's money, and I was going to use it to punish them for all that they had put her through. I made good connections through Kerr Toddy, and I joined the CIA. Kerr introduced me to the good guys. There were some left, but they were pretty hamstrung by never knowing who could be relied upon and who could not. They still can't, but we've had a small victory here tonight.

Claire has finally lost. On the point of realizing my father's ambitions for her, she has slipped up badly, all due to her violent jealousy and her stupid love affairs. She's fallen in a big way for this younger man, who had a promising career ahead of him in the State Department. He's handsome, talented, but foolish enough to have hitched his star to a rising presidential hopeful who is as psychotic as they come. He and Claire were hot and heavy, as they say, but a younger woman, who bore a strong resemblance to Kit, suddenly appeared on the scene. She was also a brilliant and beautiful young addition to the State Department, and Claire's boy could not resist a fling with her. Claire found out, followed the girl home and battered her to death, as she had done to Kit thirty years ago, and threw her body in the marsh. Now you may ask yourselves if Claire could manage that on her own, well, she didn't. She had help. The man whose help she had when she battered Kit and Phyll Prentiss to death was none other than her long-suffering, much abused husband, Ken Birkly."

We all gasped in horror. Andy took up the tale:

"I have been an undercover operative in the CIA in France all these years, under an assumed name. I didn't return to the States until two months ago, to be present at this long overdue showdown. I must leave again soon. We haven't got a hold on all the bad guys yet. Kerr Toddy has gone now, but luckily we have Chuck here as his replacement on the side of the good guys. Seb is an operative too, I can't reveal where. It is too sensitive."

"Goddamn it! What was all this fucking malarkey about tonight then with Claire?" Kev shouted. "I swear I can't take much more of this. I feel like punching the lights out of all of you so called friends."

I couldn't blame him. We all felt like that. Kelly tried to calm him down.

Chuck resumed the tale: "We had to get Claire here without her suspecting a thing. Father Petrie had phoned her in DC, and told her that you had surfaced at last, Andy. Seb, she knew about, because she'd been led to believe that a special prisoner exchange mission to Russia had discovered him and saved him, which of course they had, but we'd set that up with the aid of some Russian 'friends' shall we say. We made up all these lies about Andy to lure her to the greatest coup of her life – the capture of Andy Chatsle, and the chance to pay back Biff and Cici Chatsle, yet again, for their treachery against Zurt Enterprises and our father.

Claire hadn't a clue what I'd been doing with myself over the years, after she and my father had consigned me to oblivion. My chums at the CIA told her that Mrs. Chatsle had managed to get her Vietnamese family into the States, and that, even though they had fought against our boys, they had a man with them who had been undercover at some secret, illicit arms deals, and had information that would reveal the traitors who had been selling arms to our enemies. This had shocked Claire. She had to get her hands on him before he revealed who had been working against our American boys in Viet Nam. She must have been worried about what Mrs. Chatsle was planning now - seventy-eight years old, and still dangerous to Zurt Enterprises?"

"You bet," said Andy.

"So tonight, Claire arrived ready to catch Andy, and the Vietnamese man, namely Khien here, whom she considered an extreme threat, as he could prove that Zurt Enterprises and her father and, by association Claire herself, were traitors big time. Unfortunately for Claire, we got to Ken first. Claire, of course, was much too clever to provide anyone with clues as to her affair with this young man. Her secretaries, his and Claire's colleagues, may have speculated on the depth of their attachment, but Claire and the young man had been most discreet. We had no proof to suspect her of the Prentiss girl's murder, or Kit's for that matter. The young man, however, was questioned, and he was scared out of his wits, but he didn't own up to his relationship with Claire until this afternoon, when he was questioned by the expert journalist from Seattle, Mai Brent. She started in on him, with evidence she had managed to find of their hideaway trysts, and the fellow folded just like that, confessing all. Father Petrie maybe you would care to tell us Ken's tragic tale."

"I would not care to tell a soul what we have learned about Ken Birkly. It is a sordid, and, as you say, a tragic tale. Ken was a handsome lad when young: tall, dark, athletic figure, good at sports, at his studies, even an excellent surgeon, but the lad had a hard life. His parents, Louise and Joe Birkly, had gone up the social ladder after the Second World War. Joe had used the G.I. Bill to go through medical school, while Louise still worked away on the farm with Joe's father. When Ken was born, they were determined that he'd become a doctor, as his father had, and they encouraged his romance with Claire Caventry. Louise was besotted with Curt and Diana, and it was her greatest joy and reward in life when Claire and Ken started dating. Ken was thrilled too. I'd sure prefer if the young people left us at this juncture, Sal and Rob, if you don't mind."

Rob and I nodded at the kids, and they left the room and went into the kitchen. My-An joined them, and shut the door behind her. Father Petrie continued,

"Ken and Claire soon discovered that they shared sick fantasies. Claire liked to physically and mentally abuse Ken, and Ken liked to be abused." Father Petrie stopped to take a sip of water.

"It's okay, Father, I think I need to continue for you. It's not exactly stuff a priest should talk about," said Chuck. "When the lads, that is Manny, Phil and Father Petrie returned from 'Nam, they decide to help out Kev by keeping an eye on the Chatsles and the rest of the lake crowd. All of them were squeaky clean. Oh, there was the usual fooling around in the older age group, the Wingos, my father, but definitely not my mother, some of their other rich friends, but not the Chatsles, the Kemps or, oddly enough, the Birklys. Old Joe Birkly was a straight old bastard, and mean with it. Louise was too stupid and, if we want to be painfully honest, too plain and heavy to be likely to have an affair. When Kev, Ken and his crazy brother, Tank, returned from Vietnam, the boys watched Ken and Tank closely. Tank was an obvious mess and, like his old man, a mean son-of-a-gun, but he hadn't had anything to do with Kit way back in the old days at the lake, before Vietnam. Kit wouldn't have had any truck with the likes of Tank, but she had a soft spot in those days for the more intellectual, sophisticated Ken."

"You're kidding!" exclaimed Kev. "She never showed any interest in Ken that I remember. I don't even remember ever seeing them together."

Chuck sighed, "'Fraid so, Kev. Kit hated the way Claire treated Ken. She hated it when Claire flirted with you, Kev, because she knew how sick Claire was. Kit had come across Ken out by the backwater pond, where she'd also met Andy when they had been kids. Seems that was Kit's spot for finding and helping lame ducks, and I do mean the human variety. Sorry Andy." Andy gave a wry grin by way of response. "In any case, Ken hadn't had his shirt on, and he was trying to clean and dress deep whip marks across his chest and back. Kit had been appalled. She had helped him, and he'd told her about Claire's predilection for violent love-making. Now Ken had winning ways. He had that black hair and those brilliant turquoise eyes, and he could weave some romantic twaddle. In any case, Kit fell for it. It's surprising I know. Kit was clever, wary, not easy to fool, but she never could resist any critter in pain. To cut a long story short, they began a very romantic relationship. Ken was normal with Kit…"

"Goddamn, Chuck, are you sure? I'll kill the bastard if he so much as tried any of this sick nonsense with Kit." Kev was extremely distraught about all this, as were we all.

"I'm sure, Kev. Come on, Kit was your sister, you know she'd never do anything like that… like what Ken liked from Claire; you know, beatings and things. Why you may well ask, did Kit put up with his still seeing Claire? Well, Ken explained to her that his parents would beat the heck out of him, if he stopped going out with Claire. They wanted him to marry Claire Caventry, and they certainly would never let him marry Kit. Strange, isn't it? Now we all know that Kit was Curt and Diana's child, a Caventry too, but the Birklys didn't know that. In any case, to press on, Ken had got really angry with Claire flirting with Kev. He could take Claire flirting with the rich guys, but he could not stand for her to tease a working lad, especially Kev, because Kev was a class act. His class, like Kit's, came naturally. Ken decided he'd had enough, and he told Kit that they would run away that night and get married. Kit had been head-over-heels about it, and she had news for Ken too. She told him what she had learned that day from my mother and me about her birth. Kit also told him that Claire knew, and they'd had a fight. I had saved her from Claire's violent attack. Ken should have been very pleased. What a way to pay back Claire for all her two-timing! He was worried though, because Claire answered some of his desperate needs, and for this he believed he loved her. He knew he'd have to cheat on Kit to find sexual fulfillment. He and Claire, however, made an ideal match. He knew that it was highly unlikely that Claire would ever meet another man who met her sexual needs as he did. When he had reached this conclusion, Ken went straight to Claire and told her all about his intention to run away with Kit that night, that they'd been having a fling for some time, and that he knew about Kit being Curt and Diana's love child. Claire went crazy, as Ken hoped. After she'd spent her anger on him, much to his sick satisfaction, Ken suggested that he and Claire could have some fun getting back at Kit. He said that he'd meet with Kit as planned, but he'd take her to the backwater by Dub's cabin, where Claire could be waiting. Claire could get her revenge by seeing Kit jilted by Ken. Ken would tell Kit how much he and Claire loved each other. They could really rub it in. They could make fun of her for ever thinking that Ken would fall for her, a diner waitress's and a drunk's daughter; for that is what she was, no matter who her real parents were. In no way did Kit resemble the beautiful and glamorous Diana, but it was a just reward of sorts that Claire was like Diana, the mother she should have had. Claire loved the whole idea. She made violent love to Ken, dominated him, punished him - what they called love.

Ken met Kit. He got her to Dub's backwater pond where Claire was waiting. Ken and Claire had let Kit have it, but only by jeering at her. Kit had been stony faced. She hadn't cried. She replied that she was glad Patti and Tim had taken her. If she had been raised by her real parents, Curt and Diana, she would have been as sick and perverted as Claire. This had infuriated Claire. She attacked Kit with a metal rod she'd hidden behind her back. Kit went down. She struggled, but Claire beat her and beat her. Ken could only watch. The sick bastard was mesmerized by the blood and violence to Kit's beautiful face." Chuck stopped. He'd gone too far. He paled, and had to sit down, tears coursing down his face. We had looked at Kev. Chuck held up his hand by way of apology. Kev was white-faced. Kelly held him.

"God, Chuck, how the hell do you know all this," said Rob, wiping away his own tears. We were all torn apart at having to relive poor Kit's death this way.

Chuck didn't answer Rob. He continued.

"They cleaned themselves up, destroyed all incriminating evidence, and, as you remember in their testimonies, they went onto Rusty Kemp's house, saying that they'd arrived late as they'd stopped to…'well you know, smooch a little'."

"How do you know all this, Chuck?" I asked, feeling sick to my stomach. Kev was in torment, his head in his heads. Kelly was trying to console him.

"Claire has not bothered with Ken for some time, but of course they had Kit's murder to hold over each other's heads all these years. Well, Ken suspected that Claire was about to cut him loose. He was afraid that, now she was thinking of running for President, and she was so well connected in Zurt Enterprises, she'd have him killed. He had become an embarrassment to her of late. He'd taken to drink and drugs, had visited dubious sex parlors, and had lost his good looks, and could no longer function responsibly as a surgeon. Her cronies at Zurt Enterprises had succeeded in covering up all of Ken's indiscretions, but they wanted her to get rid of him. Claire had told him this the night they killed Phyll Prentiss. Ken could tell that Claire was in her psycho state when she'd turned up that night. She'd told him that if he helped her one last time, she'd never leave him, and she'd save him from Zurt Enterprises. Ken had not believed her, so unbeknownst to Claire, he'd hidden a tape recorder under his shirt, and he'd taped the whole gruesome thing.

Yesterday, I received a phone call from Ken. He'd been approached by the reporter, Mai Brent, about Claire's relationship with her young aide. He found out from her that I worked for the CIA in Seattle. He'd been amazed, yet somewhat relieved. He knew I detested my sister, and he hoped he'd find a sympathetic ear if he told me all about his life with Claire. He asked me to go over to his and Claire's home in DC in my official capacity, and to bring men with me. It was not my official turf, but DC sent me along with their men. We got there, and found Ken had shot himself in the head. He'd put the tape on a five-page letter he'd written explaining it all: Kit's murder and Phyll Prentiss's.

Some time before all this, I had learned from Kerr Toddy, before he died, where Andy and Seb were, and even though they were in deep cover, hiding from the Zurt Enterprises element within the CIA, they returned States side to help avenge Kit's and Mr. and Mrs. Chatsle's deaths, and since Ken's confession, to set up Claire, and to help ease you into the truth, Kev."

"We could not just turn up after all these years, when we've been undercover to save our lives, and tell you, Kev, that I hadn't killed your sister," said Andy. "You might not have believed me, so we got the Nguyens to lay a secret trail for you to follow. When you bought the place, Mike, and then had Sal and Rob and family move in, we decided you should know the truth too. Your father had protected Dolly and Chuck. You should know this, unless you already did, of course...?" Mike shook his head. He hadn't known a thing about it. "When you had Sal translate the diaries, it was most fortuitous that she asked My An to help, but Aunt Lien and Khien neatly had put My An in your way, Sal, so to speak. I was wrong to play ghost, but I wanted to keep an eye on the diaries, and how you were thinking about what was in them. I got carried away with my ghostly larks, and I apologize, especially to Tali. I share her love for Alain Fournier's book, Le Grand Meulnes."

"Andy," I said. "Do you know who killed your mother?"

Andy hung his head, "No, but someone did kill her. It was not an accident. The car did not push her down the slope of its own accord."

I sat back in my chair and looked over at Rob. He smiled at me. I had been right about the dear old Bluebird after all.

Mike approached Andy, a somewhat embarrassed look on his face.

"Andy, I've bought the house, but if you want it back, I understand, and it is yours..."

"No, Mike. I must remain undercover. Those guys we stopped tonight are still not sure that I am back. They don't know what is going on. They are Zurt Enterprises's men in the CIA, and they work with Claire. They were watching the house, and they had told her that something important was going on here tonight. Claire had been set up by Seb and Father Petrie to believe that I was back from the dead, and she told the Zurt Enterprises' thugs out there that they were going to apprehend a traitor to their rotten cause here tonight, someone who could threaten the work of their Zurt bosses. Our guys stopped them, with some help, which I won't go into. You'd never believe it in any case."

Father Petrie took up the story. "Then Claire arrived, and they wanted to accompany her to the house, but our guys reassured them that they'd take Senator Caventry to the house and arrest the traitor. They hinted that they belonged to Special Forces, which they had in their youth in Viet Nam, but let's say they were retired with honor a long time ago. Claire was going to protest that she wanted her own men with her, but they said that she needed to be accompanied by them, as they had a suspect in the murder of Phyll Prentiss, and were holding him up at the house until she arrived. This flummoxed her, but she was somewhat relieved to have someone else to take the fall for her crime, and curious to know who it could be. Without further argument, Claire strode on up to the house, and that's when she burst in and was overjoyed to see Andy. Now she'd gain the glory within her rotten organization for finally catching their archenemy. Our guys slipped away to keep an eye on her men, and Chuck's men turned up and arrested Claire's goons, and now have arrested Claire. They have evidence carefully collected over the years to put them all away. Zurt Enterprises are going to have to maintain a low profile for a while."

Brad must have been peering out of the kitchen window, for he came into the room, the other kids in tow.

"Chuck, the men in the black vans have gone, and most of the other guys have disappeared into the trees, but there seems to be a problem out there. I can't see too clearly what is going on. There is a woman talking to Manny Mack and Phil Mingus and Claire Caventry. I can't make out who she is, as she's all covered up." Brad had moved to the big front window, and drawn back the shutters. "Oh my God! I can see now, the woman has a gun and she's holding them at gunpoint, it looks like. One of them is undoing Claire's handcuffs."

We all ran to the window. Chuck, Father Petrie and Kev went out on the terrace. The woman turned and screamed at them to keep out of it, and that's when we recognized her. It was Patti Occley.

"Mom, what the hell..?" Kev yelled back.

"Stay out of it, Kev. I'm going to help Claire. I'm loyal to my friends. Curt and Diana were good to me. Curt worked with me at the diner when he was a poor lad, and he worked so hard to get where he got, and he didn't forget his old pal, Patti, when he made it big time. He and Diana made me feel special, important. They set me up with Biff, and we had something real special. He didn't love that awful old French hag of his. She kept us apart, but Biff loved me. Kit and Andy would have lived the life we couldn't. They loved each other too."

"Mom, listen to me. Kit and Andy were not lovers." Patti shook her head in vehement denial. It was obvious she had lost her hold on sanity. "Mom, I know what you did for Curt and Diana. You took their daughter and raised her as your own. That was pay back enough. You don't owe the Caventrys a thing. They paid you money over the years, but they ruined our lives too. Claire and Ken killed our Kit. They killed her. Do you hear me? You owe them only vengeance, not loyalty. We must get justice for what they did to Kit, to us."

Patti started to laugh. "I am protecting their child," she screamed hysterically. "Claire is their child. Look at her. She is so like Diana. Curt could not let their love child out of his sight. He had me change their baby for Dolly's in the hospital. The girls were born a day or so apart. Curt and I had flown up from L.A. with the baby, his and Diana's, Claire here. Dolly had jaundice, and had to stay in hospital for a few days. Curt and I crept in at night and changed Kit with Claire. Dolly raised Curt's and Diana's daughter, and I raised Dolly's, and I sought revenge for Curt and Diana and Biff and me, and I killed that godawful woman. I killed her with that car there." Patti pointed up the slope at the Thunderbird.

Claire fell to the ground sobbing, no doubt with heartfelt relief that she had been her beloved Diana's daughter after all, and not Dolly's, whom she had despised. Chuck muttered to himself in amazement,

"No wonder Mom and Kit looked so much alike."

Suddenly, I noticed that the Thunderbird was moving, approaching the slope, and Patti was standing in front of the old sycamore down the slope. The car picked up speed, and it ploughed relentlessly over the edge right down into Patti. Patti screamed. She hadn't seen it coming. The car pinned her to the tree. We couldn't believe our eyes. Kev and Father Petrie ran to her, but Father Petrie looked up at us and shook his head. Claire was screaming that the Chatsle Woman had done it. It seemed as if Claire had lost her mind too, but we followed her terrified gaze, and standing on the crest of the slope was an old lady, tall, a look of defiance on her still incredibly beautiful face, despite her extreme age, and at the side of the old lady, sat a big ginger cat.

"Mother!" screamed Mrs. Nguyen. She, Chau and My-An ran to the woman, whose silver white hair blew about her in the wet gusts of dawn. So this was Minh Li, Dominique D'Emeraude's mother. We were speechless. We couldn't take it in. Kelly slowly approached and picked up the cat and held it to her. Tali was in tears, and I held her close.

Chuck's men refastened Claire's handcuffs, and placed her in their van. She was still sobbing. Kev kissed Patti's cheek. Father Petrie knelt and prayed. Poor Kev, what a horrible night it had been for him. He turned and walked slowly back up the slope. Kelly approached him, the cat in her arms.

"Tin Pan, what you doing here?" Kev said, as if in a daze. He absentmindedly fondled the cat's ears, and Kelly laid her head on Kev's shoulder.

Chuck approached the Nguyen ladies and Khien, who had joined them. Minh Li held herself erect. Her eyes showed her pain. She looked at once devastated, broken, and yet also defiant, vindicated.

"That Occley woman killed my…" She fought to control her overwhelming sadness. "My beautiful and wonderful daughter…" and here she crumbled. She fell to the ground, sobbing. My-An, Lien, Chau and Khien also bent down to hold her, sobbing themselves. It was a tragic sight. My own heart felt as if it were breaking. So this was the culmination of that small child's, Dominique D'Emeraude's, incredible life. Kev held Kelly and Tin Pan from him, and slowly approached the sad little group. He had tears in his eyes. He bent down and held Minh Li's hands. She looked up at him.

"Thank you," he said. "How can I ever thank you for giving me back my life and my sanity? I am so sorry for what my mother did. She was obviously very ill, and acting under an incredible delusion that Biff Chatsle loved her."

"I had to kill her," said Minh Li through her tears. I had been with my daughter that day. I had gone into the kitchen. Dominique was getting the bags from the car. We had such fun together. I looked out of the window, and Dominique had gone down the slope to get a paper bag that had blown away. She had difficulty catching it. I didn't notice your mother get into the car, but I saw Dominique look up in dismay, and the car was moving towards her down the slope. The woman, your mother, was laughing. She had released the brake and had helped the car along the crest. She didn't know I was there. She must have arrived after I had gone into the house. The car hit my beloved daughter with a sickening thud, and I passed out. When I regained consciousness, I checked to see if my daughter was alive. She was not. I kissed her and fled. I did not know who the woman was who killed her. I walked all the way home. I don't know how I did it. I was distraught, grief stricken, angry. Lien was shocked to see me, and in such a state. She said that we must keep quiet. We could not get involved yet.

Tonight, I was keeping watch all this time from the wood. I saw this woman creep up through the underbrush. I saw the men arrest that evil daughter of an evil man, and then I saw this woman, who had killed my child, try to rescue the Caventry woman. Evil helps evil. I could not let her get away. I had to avenge my child. I had to make it up to her, show her I always had been her mother." She broke down into heart-rending sobs.

We all turned our attention to Chuck. What was he going to do? He approached Minh Li and the Nguyens:

"I think that you will receive an honorable citation for helping to stop a crime, to stop a person interfering with the arrest of a psychotic killer and traitor to the United States of America." Chuck looked over at Kev. "Sorry, Kev, but that's what Patti was doing after all." Kev just shrugged. He looked totally defeated. "And," added Chuck, "Kit was my full-blood sister. You and Andy have done your best to avenge her death, and bring the killers to justice, and I have seen it through to completion. We all loved Kit. She was our sister." Kev seemed stunned, but had to nod his head in acknowledgement of Chuck's rightful position as Kit's brother. Andy lowered his head and nodded too.

"Patti won't have to face life in an institution for the criminally insane, Kev," Kelly said. "She'd have had to face a trial for the murder of Mrs. Chatsle." Kev nodded, but she had been his mother, and as the good son he was, he still had not wanted his mother to die, and to die this way, but then she had died instantly. She hadn't suffered.

Chuck took his leave of us. His men had collected Patti's body, and were taking it to the police morgue. Father Petrie, Manny Mack and Phil Mingus moved off through the trees with their men. When they had gone, Andy and Seb emerged from the house. It was still somewhat dark, although the white line of a new day had widened along the horizon. The sky was still stormy, but it had stopped raining. Rain dripped off the trees, off the patio and the roof. The wind was less ferocious, but still freezing cold and moisture laden. The air was heavy with the scent of wet underbrush and evergreens.

"We have to go back into hiding, Kev. If ever you want to reach us, Chuck can get news to us. I don't suppose you want to join us in our work?" Seb asked. Kev shook his head. "Guess you've had enough of all this kind of thing. Don't blame you for going for a bit of the 'ol normal life. Enjoy what comes your way, Kev. You've done enough suffering to last a life time."

Kev and Seb embraced, and they seemed reluctant to say goodbye. Andy watched them. He had taken his leave of the rest of us. When Kev was free, they looked at each other. Andy extended his hand. Kev looked at it. We all waited, afraid to move. Kev stepped up to Andy and embraced him. Andy returned the embrace.

"I have hated you all my life," Kev said. "I do apologize for that. There has been too much hatred. I came to respect your mother, and now I can respect her son."

"I am the one to apologize, Kev. My parents and I let you take the rap for Kit's murder. We didn't know how to exonerate you. We didn't know who had killed Kit. We knew that it couldn't have been you, but we had no idea who the man was that Kit was going to elope with that night, so we couldn't help you out. My mother and father were distraught, and tried desperately to find clues, any clues as to who Kit's lover had been, but all to no avail. They were sure of one thing, and that was that Zurt Enterprises must have been involved in some way. No, Kev, we can never make it up to you, but if you need me, I'll come running, I promise." Kev slapped Andy on the back, but made no comment. He didn't need to.

Andy and Seb left, melting into the darkness. Kev left with Kelly and Tin Pan. They had to go to Huckleberry to collect Connor's pick up. The Nguyens left too, in a beat up old truck Khien and Minh Li had used to drive up to the house in haste that night. John and Ria had been up all night, and yet they had to leave for the airport to fly back to Seattle. We hugged and promised to get together for a longer and less exciting visit.

"You have tales to tell me when we next get together," I said to Ria. "I want to hear all about your mother's work in the anti-Nazi underground during the war, and her connection and your's to Andy's lover."

"Oh Lord, Sal! That is quite a story, let me tell you. I can't get it straight in my head. Nikki and I have tried to get Mum to write it all down. There's our grandparents' story, and the Welsh connection-believe me, Sal – it's a whole other experience, another level of existence."

"I want you to try and tell me, Ria, and bring Nikki along too. I want to cross-examine you Welsh witches," I laughed. Ria got into the car and waved goodbye through the rain spattered window. Gary took them off to the airport. He was staying for the rest of the weekend, for which I was glad. Brad decided to stay with us too, rather than return to his apartment in town.

Deb, Mike, Rob, Tali, Brad, Sean and I stood on the steps. Brad was fondling old Bubs' ears. Bubs had quite an evening, yet he had a happy look on his face, his tongue lolling out of the side of his mouth. Tali had a forlorn look on her face, as she cuddled Bugsy in her arms.

"What are you going to do with the place?" Rob asked Mike. Mike shook his head.

"I don't know, Rob, I just don't know."

"I am never going to live here," Deb said emphatically. Mike looked at me, expectantly.

"No," said Rob. "We are only here until our house is finished, and I am not sure that we'll stay until then. After tonight, I'm ready to go to a motel."

"No. We'll stay until our house is ready, Mike. You can show the house, and we'll leave if you get an interested buyer before our house is finished."

"Hey look over there," said Mike, a little alarmed. "There's one of those guys over there, just standing at the edge of the forest." We looked over at the strange figure. He was hooded, we couldn't see his face. He waved, and then disappeared into the darkness of the trees, but some shining objects lay on the ground where he'd stood. Brad ran over to retrieve them.

"Please be careful," I yelled after him.

"It's alright," Brad yelled back. "They are only dimes." Mike, Rob and I just froze.

It's over for me. I can go on my afterlife adventures now. The deer are back, grazing contentedly on the lawn. Kev has found closure. Kev and Kelly can have a good life together. He'll never forgive himself for not being there for Kit, but she's safe and happy now...Tin Pan, the battered alley cat, Kev and Kelly rescued, can cuddle contentedly in their love and care for the rest of his time on this particular adventure of his - that sprang out of another's adventure that brutally was cut short. Andy had to have one last trick up his sleeve, and he'd set up that dime thing at the end, as a sort of gift of sorts to Mike, Rob and Sal, though I don't share his notion of this as an appropriate parting gesture at all.

We are surrounded by that strange entity called consciousness. There are continual streams, quantum streams, if you will, of consciousness, and we all, all things, slip in and out of different ones all the time. Life is but another quantum moment, and there are so many different dimensions to explore. Such adventures are never-ending. They spread way into infinity, for you cannot have something without nothing and vice versa. My stream-of-being shared a path with these wonderful beings, human and non-human on this adventure. All of us, all entities of being, share cosmic adventures and identities over the infinity of existence.

⊷⊷ ⊶⊶

One last postscript from beyond, before I go off into another cosmic consciousness:

Mike had a buyer for the house. He called Rob and Sal into his office one Sunday afternoon just after New Year's Day. He wanted them to see who would take over the house and the estate that Sal still dearly loved and worried about.

Sal had her Christmas in the house, and it had looked beautiful in the snow, and the rooms had blazed with Christmas candles. A huge Christmas tree had been set up in the foyer, and a big log fire lit in the hearth. All the rooms had been warm and cozy. The dark presence in the attic had gone. The light stayed off, when turned off in the cellar. There were evergreen garlands up the stairs and on the doors, and the kitchen was lively as Sal, Tali and Deb prepared their favorite Christmas dishes. All Sal's youngsters were home. Bubba and Bugsy were overfed and contented. The Nguyen family came to Christmas dinner, along with Kev, Kelly, Tin Pan and Father Petrie, Manny Mack and Phil Mingus.

The deer grazing on the bales of hay put out for them on the snow covered lawn that Christmas night, looked up at all the fun and games going on inside the brightly lit house. As the deer grazed on, and the evening progressed, the laughter gave way to the sound of carol singing around the baby grand piano. The old house deserved such happiness, and its happiness will be ensured from now on.

325

Sal and Rob sat in Mike's office that fifth day of the New Year, 1995. They stood when they heard voices in the hallway outside Mike's office – voices speaking Vietnamese. They looked at Mike, surprise evident on their faces. Mike, smiling, raised his hand to stop their questions. The door opened, and in walked a beautiful woman, possibly in her late thirties, stylish. She was accompanied by Minh Li. The younger woman made the introductions. She said that her name was Mai Brent. She was a journalist from Seattle and Brent was her married name. She wanted to take up residence in her mother's home with her family and her grandmother, whom they already knew.

"Minh Li you know," she said, "But she is also called Marie Claire Aspinall D'Emeraude." They also bought the Thunderbird. Their first night in the house was a happy one, as were the days and nights that followed.

⊷ ⊶

Every evening, in the last light of day, Khien stands alone by the sycamore tree. I can't feel regret or heartache now, but I can feel love. There is love for all in this state I am in. I make sure that Khien always will have some sign of our love in this adventure we had shared, and in which he continues: – a sweet breath of night-scented air; a stirring in the trees; eye contact with some wild creature when he looks up; a flower fallen by the roots of the old sycamore, something tangible for him to hold on to.

Khien stands there by the tree every evening. He is bathed in the golden rays of a setting sun. Sometimes Mai stands there with him. She forgave me. She never actually hated me. My mother, Lien, Khien and Biff saw to that. We finally met, and I told her that I was so very proud of her. She has love and understanding in her heart – well done mother, well done Lien and oh so well done, Khien, my love, and well done Biff, who has begun another adventure, in which I hope he finds complete happiness and his just reward, for he sacrificed a great deal for us, and I do mean all of us, not only in America, but throughout this difficult world, where good and evil battle constantly. I loved him. He was my security, my life. Khien was my special love, almost a fantasy, not an everyday, routine love, as Biff was. One thing changed by chance. Mai wanted to play an active role in combating evil. She was more like a whistle-blower than a behind the scenes Dragon, so she no longer is a Dragon, and as I told Roza, my son did become a Dragon. I can feel the stars laugh - Roza laugh.

I am fulfilled. My soul is at rest. My mother has brought my daughter home to the wonderful old Chatsle House, the House on Kalalua. Now off I go on my next adventures. There is a poem by that wonderful spirit, Emily Dickinson, which says something of leaving life in this existence is not an end. The adventure continues in infinite episodes.

The thunderbird, Bluebird, stood on the slope and faced the driveway. It was a brilliantly starry night, and as a lone cougar slunk off over the ridge, the starlight twinkled in the old car's headlights like a wink.

ACKNOWLEDGEMENTS

This story is a work of fiction, and its fictional characters are not based on any persons living or dead. Any similarities in names to those of persons living or dead, or existing enterprises or places, are purely coincidental. Real life historical personages and events are involved only in a fictional context with the characters of the story. As far as I know, there is no organization of any sort named Zurt Enterprises and no Red Dragon Society, such as referred to in my work of fiction.

I was inspired to write this novel by the true story of a house and its inhabitants told to me by my mother-in-law and sister-in-law. Naturally I made up my own characters and story, but the real life story did act as a stimulus for my imagination. The Chatsle House and Villa D'Emeraude of my story are works of fiction.

I want to thank my family, human and non-human, for their support; my mother-in-law; my sister-in-law and brother–in-law and their family and animals; my dear friends Linda and Daniel Ardrey, Lydia Fabbroni and Pam Quinlan, my parents, my husband, who is a constant source of technical and editing help, and my daughters, son-in-law and grandsons who keep me up to date, and who are a constant source of enlightenment and sound advice. Many thanks also to all at Create Space and Amazon Kindle.

Any shortcomings and errors are mine and mine alone.

Davies McGinnis

ABOUT THE AUTHOR

Davies McGinnis received her doctorate in animal behavior at the University of Cambridge, England. She was a postdoctoral fellow at Stanford University, a visiting professor at the University of Massachesetts Harbor Campus, and a research associate at Harvard University and The Kennedy School of Government. She is a native of Wales, and now resides in New Mexico with her husband.

OTHER TITLES BY DAVIES MCGINNIS
Five Cats of Hamburg
Bougainvillea Exile

SUGGESTED READINGS

- Fall, Bernard B, 1994, <u>Street Without Joy</u>, Stackpole Books.
- Jackson, Julian, 2003, <u>France: The Dark Years: 1940-1944</u>, Oxford University Press.
- Kamm, Henry, 1996, <u>Dragon Ascending: Vietnam and The Vietnamese</u>, Arcade Publishing, New York.
- Karnow, Stanley, 1984, <u>Vietnam: A History</u>, Penguin Books.
- Truong Nhu Tang (with David Chanoff and Doan Van Toai), 1986, <u>Viet Cong Memoir: An Inside Account of the Vietnam War and its Aftermath</u>, Vintage Books, a division of Random House, New York.

CPSIA information can be obtained
at www.ICGtesting.com
Printed in the USA
FSOW01n1020260118
43831FS

9 781532 822148